CONTENTS

Chapter 1	2
Chapter 2	14
Chapter 3	20
Chapter 4	31
Chapter 5	40
Chapter 6	45
Chapter 7	60
Chapter 8	70
Chapter 9	73
Chapter 10	80
Chapter 11	87
Chapter 12	95
Chapter 13	106
Chapter 14	121
Chapter 15	130
Chapter 16	137
Chapter 17	141
Chapter 18	148
Chapter 19	157
Chapter 20	161
Chapter 21	169

Chapter 22	175
Chapter 23	187
Chapter 24	196
Chapter 25	200
Chapter 26	206
Chapter 27	209
Chapter 28	216
Chapter 29	238
Chapter 30	243
Chapter 31	247
Chapter 32	252
Chapter 33	259
Chapter 34	266
Chapter 35	271
Chapter 36	276
Chapter 37	282
Chapter 38	290
Chapter 39	294
Chapter 40	302
Chapter 41	306
Chapter 42	311
Chapter 43	319
Chapter 44	323
Chapter 45	328
Chapter 46	334
Chapter 47	339
Chapter 48	345
Chapter 49	359

Chapter 50	363
Chapter 51	365
Chapter 52	371
Chapter 53	374

The Slippery Path

By
Jon H Davies

CHAPTER 1
(1970's)

The hooded Thug lurked in the shadows of the heavily graffitied entrance to the YMCA. Ranch-type cafeteria doors that had seen better days were bolted and padlocked for the day, but that didn't matter to him: subsidised pie and chips were not on his menu. The Thug hungered for cash, and lifeless eyes were glued to the activities ongoing in the Jewellers across the street.

The sole proprietor, Michael Moore, a rotund man, balding on top, with ruby-red cheeks and a Mexican-style moustache, was hovering, hand on hip, limply holding the reinforced glass door ajar. Surely a big enough hint to the indecisive, elderly customer that he was eager to shut up shop for the day and rush home.

Sid 'The Bowls' Williams had been humming and harring for the past 45 minutes or so: should he choose the gold cufflinks with a solitary diamond inset or the gilt-edged, studded with mother of pearl? Which pair would best complement his choice of a heavy gold bracelet, gleaming like a polished sun in its decorative box, and awaiting payment on Mr Moore's granite-topped counter?

Sid needed to look dapper next week at the club's annual presentation dinner: it was to be his last as club skip, and he wanted to go out with a bang. For well over thirty years, he'd been directing proceedings on the green, and time had caught up with him. Tactfully, he'd been cajoled into handing over the reins to a younger man, and Charlie Morris was that man; the committee had already decided.

'Hell,' pondered Sid, still smarting and lost in his thoughts.

'Charlie Morris was barely out of nappies — a mere fifty-eight.'

The Jeweller, normally a very patient man, was becoming agitated: he was desperate to get away. The blind date had been arranged: three o'clock in the snug of The Rose and Crown, and after? Well — who knows…

He wanted to freshen up a bit before he met him. You know, a spray of cologne here
and a spray there. Hell, he couldn't wait — butterflies like a teenager, and testicles
that were already tingling with anticipation.

The tone of voice was tinged with frustration.

"Listen, Sid, why don't you go home, think about it, and come back first thing tomorrow morning? I'm pulling the shutter down as soon as you leave…"

His hand strayed from the hip, gesturing flamboyantly towards the glass display unit.

"…I promise the cufflinks and the bracelet will be on that counter waiting for you."

For the umpteenth time, he checked the gold-plated pocket watch dangling from the waistcoat of his Prince of Wales checked suit, simultaneously chewing at the nail on his index finger as he mumbled.

"You can take all day to make your mind up."

Sighing, his eyes drifted back to the other side of the street and he nodded — muttering to himself.

"Yes, I thought so — there is somebody there."

Nudging his head forward and squinting in an attempt to make out the faceless silhouette of the person in the darkness, the Jeweller's innocence instantly typecast him.

'A lost soul in need of shelter.'

Someone Mr Moore would normally help and reach out to — a couple of quid to buy a meal. But not this afternoon, oh no, no, no, needs must, and an array of his sexual needs sprang to the forefront of his thoughts...

The Thug was clicking: something he always did when his patience was frazzled, but like most foibles, he was unaware. He was indeed a lost soul, but not the type Michael Moore envisaged. And not the type to whom Michael Moore would offer charity; especially if he knew what horrifying atrocities this lost soul would inflict on him over the next couple of minutes.

He'd nicked the getaway car about an hour ago and tucked it away in the allocated bays behind the YMCA. That back lane led onto the main Heads of the Valleys road so he could be out of Neath long before the coppers got their act together.

He pulled on the reefer, gasping as the heat hit the back of his throat. His eyes were

on Sid.

"Come on, you old bastard, do one, or by fuck you'll have it as well as Mr Red

Cheeks."

The clicking increased, but fondling the coldness of the length of steel, out of sight to busybodies, in a specially adapted pocket inside his Parka, reassured him, and he smirked.

"Mr Red Cheeks will be biting on this beauty in the not-too-distant if he don't hand over the takings to me pronto..."

The voice was raised

"...Now sod off home!"

There was movement: the customer was backing out of the door, and with a shake of the hand, the Jeweller was helping him on his way.

Instant increase in the Thug's heart rate — there would be no turning back from here. He spat the roach at the puddle, hissing as it hit the dampness, and stepped into the rain. Crossing the street, he kept his head bowed towards the tarmac and, as an afterthought, yanked at the roll neck of his sweater, pulling it over his mouth and nose. The Thug's concern was unnecessary: the old timer had drawn level and shuffled on without even giving him a passing glance. An anxious breath filled his lungs as he tugged the fur-lined hood closer to his eyes and exhaled as he pushed the door into the brightness of the shop.

Mr Moore was in the process of locking the till and had his back to him. He closed his eyes, shook his head, and grimaced in frustration when he heard the telltale chimes.

'Bloody hell! Who on earth is this at quarter past two on my half-day?'

His voice was high-pitched and shrill. His accent — Swansea Valley.

"We're closed, sorry. I'm afraid you'll have to come back in the morning. We open at 9 o'clock sharp."

The chilling response would remain with the man forever.

"Empty the till, you fat bastard, and put the fucking lot into one of those posh plastic bags with your name plastered all over it."

Mr Moore lost control of both bodily functions when he spun around to face eyes that were devoid of expression and deeply set beneath bushy brows. The Thug, merely the width of the counter away, was brandishing a shortened crowbar with a sharpened point, repeatedly smacking it into the palm of his left hand.

Trembling hands were raised to his mouth, and the Jeweller started to cry.

"Don't hurt me, you can have it all. I beg you — please don't hurt me."

The disdain in the retort was irrefutable.

"You people make me sick..." Nodding towards the till. "...Come on — empty it!"

The lifeless eyes veered to check out the street, and there was an urgency in the raised command.

"...And get a bloody move on!"

The panic alarm, wired directly to the control room at Neath Police Station, was tucked away under the granite, but Mr Moore had his back to it; his hand shaking as he fingered notes from the clipped compartments. Business had been unusually good that morning: why hadn't he popped into Nat West Bank earlier like he always did on a half-day? He knew why — his mind had been distracted — focused on other things...

The stench from what he had off-loaded into his Y fronts filtered through to his nostrils, and he gagged. The man was ashamed. So ashamed and so angry with himself that he made a rash decision: one he would regret for the rest of his life. A decision that would leave him so disabled he would never walk again.

He stuffed the notes back into the till, locked it, and spun around. Blinking away the tears, he stared into the robber's eyes; threw the key to the far end of the shop, reached under the counter, and flicked the switch. He grinned in defiance as deafening bells rang within the shop, and a piercing alarm sounded out from the box above the entrance, shattering the stillness of the dismal afternoon.

That grin was to be his last. Never again would a smile stretch those ruddy-coloured cheeks and put a sparkle into eyes that always appeared to shine with devilment. The bar of unforgiving cold steel put paid to that when it smashed into his nose, splintering cartilage and reducing the organ to a spongy blob.

The terrifying sight of that lump of iron flashing towards his face was the last thing

he saw before losing his balance, twisting, and slumping unconscious across the till. His final but unintentional act of defiance: the sheer mass of his body prevented the attacker's access to the proceeds.

A spine-tingling scream spewed from within the Thug, and the crowbar was raised high before crashing down against Mr Moore's skull: the sickening clunk and crunching of bone clearly audible above the ringing of the bells. Dragging phlegm from the depths of his guts, he spat it at the blood oozing from the wound.

"Should have just given me your poxy cash — you pathetic arsehole."

Pausing beneath the flashing alarm box, he checked both directions, and apart from the slow-moving and preoccupied, aged bowler, the street was empty.
There was no time to waste: sirens were wailing close by, but that wasn't a concern. The Thug had planned it well: only a few strides across the street, nip down an alleyway, and he was out of sight.
The first police car screeched to a halt as the Thug was sliding into the stolen vehicle. He turned the key in the ignition and as the finely tuned six-cylinder engine roared into life, a sneer distorted his face.
"Why do silly tossers leave their cars unlocked with the keys tucked behind the sun visor?"
The sneer turned to a laugh when he stamped on the accelerator.
"Yes! Shit-hot motor this — fast as fuck."
At the junction with the main road, it turned right, away from the action, and into the general direction of where he needed to go. Catching a glimpse of the solid 18-carat gold bracelet and the two pairs of cufflinks nestled together where they'd landed on the passenger seat brought a thin smile to his face.
"Better than sod-all, I suppose."
The Ford Capri sped towards the busy artery that cut through the Valleys and connected Wales' second-largest city to its border with England. But the Thug wasn't going that way — not just yet. His intention was to head west. Still in need of some readies, plan B would have to come into play.

*

Taff Robbo was in his back garden when the alarm started wailing, and he tutted when the police sirens followed suit. Shaking his head in frustration, the six-and-a-half-foot former military man cursed.
"How many times a day does the peace and quiet have to be ravaged by bloody bells blasting out? It wouldn't be so bad if something was really happening."

The pickaxe, like a plastic toy in his grasp, rose high above strong shoulders before slamming into the clay and breaking it into manageable chunks ready for shovelling into the wheelbarrow.

Stripped to the waist, Robbo's torso is ripped: a mass of well-honed muscles, and as he stoops to pick up the shovel, sopping wet, ebony-coloured hair straggles over his brow — covering his eyes. A muddy hand brushes the locks away: leaving finger streaks like war paint across his forehead and cheeks. Catching sight of himself in the mirrored shed window stimulates a smile, and a momentary sparkle lights up soulful and saddened eyes.

He chats with himself again.

"What do you look like, Mr Roberts, eh?"

He laughed out loud, and those saddened eyes shifted towards the heavens.

"Not very fetching, is it, my darling? But hey, no doubt you've seen them so many times before."

His thoughts wandered — back to the jungles of Borneo. Every day, he had streaks of camouflage cream zig-zagging across his face, breaking up the contours of his skin. Life or death in those times. If the bandits spotted him, it was curtains for everyone. Robbo had been the sniper — a crack shot. One of a band of four brothers inching their way along well-trodden paths through the dense undergrowth on the bad side of the Sarawak border, painstakingly mapping the terrain for others to follow in their footsteps.

Ex SAS, Mr Gareth Bryan Roberts was struggling to cope with the mundane world outside of the Regiment, and he was digging a hole in the pissing-down rain: constructing a pond. He didn't need a pond, he didn't even want a bloody pond: it was something to do — keep him out of the boozer for a few extra hours…

"Some sounds, that's what's needed. A bit of Deep Purple to drown out the racket of those bloody bells."

Stepping into the shed, the widower's tormented eyes scan the

meticulously arranged shelves for his cassette recorder, and deep in thought, he frowns — asking himself the question.
"Where the hell is it, Robbo?"
His hand slaps against his forehead as it comes back to him.
"Shit — it's in the bloody car."
Patting the pockets of his DPM fatigues, he feels for the keys to his beloved Ford Capri, and the hand hits the forehead again.
"Bloody hell — they must still be behind the flippin' sun visor…"

*

The rain hadn't abated: if anything, it was worse. A constant deluge of fresh water gushing from the heavens splattered against the windscreen of Taff Robbo's Ford Capri as it hurtled west. It was the attractive, much-gossiped-about local celebrity's pride and joy: a 3-litre V6 head-turner with a mega sound system. But on this occasion, it wasn't Robbo at the wheel — it was a delinquent thug. A sadistic, vicious, evil specimen of a human being with only one thought in his pea-sized brain, and that thought was for himself. Nothing else mattered — it was always all about him.
"You tight bastard!"
He screamed at the dashboard.
"You could have filled it up for me!"
The fuel gauge was in the red zone, and he didn't have any cash. He knew that as he turned onto the busy service station. But who the hell needs cash? Paying never even entered his thoughts.
Tugging at the roll neck on his sweater, he pulled up by a pump close to a display of petrol cans and raised the hood on his Parka. Choosing a can, he brimmed it, and did the same with the Capri.
The Thug was starving. He hadn't eaten since his release early that morning, and he had a yearning for bacon. A luxury in Borstal: one reserved for those that conformed, and sniggering, he gave a wry laugh.
"Wonder why me and Barry were never invited to sit with

those fucking crawlers at that table of arse lickers."
Loaded with a bacon, lettuce, and tomato sarnie; a packet of cheese and onion, a pork pie, and a bottle of cola, he kept his head low as he strode back to the Capri. Wheel spinning away from the forecourt, he scowled as the futile, animated actions of the attendant were trapped in the rearview mirror.
"Shit — if she's clocked the reg number, I haven't got much time."
The Thug needed to get to Carmarthen before the shop closed. Find the Jewellers that Barry had told him about; park up, and watch it for a while. You know, get a feel for the place.
"Barry reckons the woman who owns it uses the same type of till as that fat fucker in Neath. Why did he have to go and collapse on top of the bloody thing? Selfish bastard! I could be nearly home by now with a roll of banknotes stuffed in my arse pocket…"
He screamed at the windscreen, spittle spewing over the steering wheel. His eyes wild — deranged.
"Instead of fannying around in a pissing-down, bastard hurricane."
The Thug knew the shop was somewhere at the top of town, but he didn't know the exact whereabouts, and the encroaching darkness would make spotting it even more difficult.
He screamed again.
"Bastard rain — piss off!"
Head-banging to rock music blaring from the upgraded speakers, wide eyes scanned both sides of the one-way street: frantically seeking out the premises.
"This must be the street — it's got to be — it's just like Barry had described. Shit, it's getting late!"
He flicked the switch for the headlights, and as the telltale signs of anxiety gripped him, he floored the accelerator, pushing the vehicle to its limits. Working at the double, the wipers struggled to clear the downpour, and only a small section of the road was visible at intermittent intervals

following each stroke of the blades. Condensation had masked the windows, and increasing the demister to maximum had little effect; he leant in closer to the screen.

"Where the hell is the bloody Jewelle…"

Thud! Bang! Something had hit the toughened glass, bounced onto the roof, and disappeared.

"Argh — what the fucking hell was that?"

His heart is racing, he can't see out of the fastback's rear screen, and terrified eyes dart to the driver's wing mirror: they make out a body lying prone in the roadway, and flashes of yellow illuminate the car.

He screams out in fear and frustration.

"No, no, no — it's a Zebra crossing — I've ploughed into somebody!"

Heartlessness sets in.

"Fuck 'em — it's their fault! Crazy bastards! What the hell are they doing out in the pissing down rain anyway?"

The Thug doesn't stop. Time to dump the car and get rid of the evidence. That's another thing Barry always preached: never leave a trace.

He speeds out of town, searching for the perfect spot, and he finds it. Waste ground, out of sight of the road, and only overlooked by a solitary house.

"Not far from the train station too — that's a bonus."

Keeping the engine running, he ransacks the car. A couple of cushions and a blanket from the back seat; together with a metal flask and a cassette recorder. That reminds him, and he ejects the tape from the car sound system — Deep Purple's 'Machine Head.'

"Awesome."

In the passenger's footwell is a large UK road atlas, and he grabs it.

"This'll do nicely."

The glove compartment is locked.

"Mmmm, hello, hello, hello," he laughs sarcastically. "What have we got in here, then?"

The laugh turns into a vicious scowl, distorting his face as he screams into the darkness.

"Fucking coppers — I hate you all — you bastards!"

He rummages for the key and finds it in a matter of seconds: it's on the fob in the ignition. The Thug tuts and shakes his head.

"What's the point of that, Mr Ford Capri man, eh? You don't lock something and keep the key right next to it, do you? You dozy pillock. Mr Ford Capri man needs his arse spanked."

The subsequent find shoots a shiver through his torso.

"Oh shit — maybe I won't be giving a slap to Mr Ford Capri man — not if he's the owner of these two beauties. I'll stay well clear of him. And what's this key? I've never seen one like this before. What a weird shape..."

He tosses it and it bounces off the roof lining, catching it in the palm of his hand.

"...Bloody hell — it's solid."

Stowing those items together with the gold merchandise in the large pocket of his Parka, he grabs some cassette tapes that had been masked by the road atlas and restarts the car.

"Time to get rid of any clues."

He laughs and mimics Barry's Scouse accent.

"Burn the fuckin' lot, and leave nottn' for the Bizzies to get their stinkin' 'ands on."

Robbo's pride and joy is doused with petrol, and remembering the items from the glove compartment, the Thug's hand delves back into the pocket and retrieves one. He glares with contempt at the infamous SAS cap badge mounted onto the plated silver casing of a flip-top petrol lighter and smirks as he runs his thumb over the serrated striker wheel. Sparking the fuel, he's dazzled by the flame and he pauses to take in the aroma.

"Never thought your precious lighter would be used to burn your precious fucking motor, did you, Mr SAS man?"

That brief energy source lit up a young face already heavily lined, hardened, weathered, and evil. A face full of contempt and sorely lacking any form of compassion. The innocent human being he had ploughed into and left dying on the rain-sodden roadway was nowhere in his thoughts, and neither was poor Mr Michael Moore: they had deserved their plight.

The heat from the tip of blue, orange, and yellow tickled the heavily fingered edge of page number 23 in the road atlas, and the face smiled as it consumed Pembrokeshire. Before it had devoured the road bridge across the Bristol Channel, he tossed it, together with the petrol can, onto the driver's seat and laughed as flames engulfed Robbo's Black Ford Capri. Stepping back from the intense heat that was tightening the skin on his cheeks, he smirked, and you could hear the sheer loathing in his voice.

"SAS, eh? Well, you're fuck-all without a gun and a grenade. I could take you any day — no problem. Bring it on, Mr SAS man." Forming a sack out of the blanket and stowing the other stuff, he flung it over his shoulder, and like Dick Whittington, strides away towards the railway station. A shiver pulses through him when the blast shatters the stillness of the brief lull in the storm, and he turns to witness flames spitting debris into the darkness. A beacon of light, and a calling out to the nine, nine, niners that serve us.

He tugs the Parka's fur-edged hood closer to his face and slinks into the shadows of the hedgerow.

"Those bastard coppers won't be long."

CHAPTER 2

The attractive Mrs Edith Jones finds herself a young, grieving widow. The once vibrant, effervescent life and soul of any gathering is now lonely, deeply saddened, reclusive, and angry. The reason? Her husband's warmth, laughter, support, and adoration have been ruthlessly stolen away from her by a monster in charge of a lethal weapon.

Bernard Jones had lived on this planet for a mere 44 years before his promising life was cut short. The well-liked and respected Head of Road Safety and Highway Development had been renowned as a meticulous stickler for precision, planning, and caution. So wasn't it ironic that he fell foul of a hit-and-run driver while innocently crossing the high street?

Even more ironic was that he had planned and sanctioned that pedestrian crossing upon which he met his demise.

Edith's third and most challenging instance of irony to have to endure was a material fact: it was Bernie's burning desire to celebrate his love for her that had placed him on that crossing at that precise time of the afternoon. Tucked away in the inside pocket of his raincoat was a gift-wrapped presentation box showcasing a sterling silver set of necklace, earrings, and bracelet. It was to be their 25th wedding anniversary the very next day.

The last person to see Bernard Jones alive was a close family friend: Cllr. Fiona Phillips — the sole owner and proprietor of 'Sparkles, Gifts, and Jewels'. She gave a tearful account to PC Anthony O'Sullivan at the scene; the emergency light rotating on top of the ambulance casting an intermittent blue glow across the faces of the witness and the officer while its two highly trained operatives fought to save Bernard's life. That was a pointless exercise: Bernard was already dead. The flinching of the prone body as the rain battered its skin was nothing more than post-mortem reflex twitching.

Cllr. Phillips reached for a tissue and dabbed at her eyes; her voice quiet, broken and shaky.

"I'd finished engraving the back of the bracelet at about 3 o'clock. They were Bernard's own words and had been scribbled on the back of his calling card..."

She shied away from the tragic ongoings.

"...Do you know, officer, I've known him and Edith all these years and I hadn't realised: he must have been a closet romantic."

The County Councillor read from the piece of card, her eyes pooling once more: "'Edith – My Eternal Silver Lining.' Beautiful words and very apt considering their occasion — don't you think so, officer?"

PC O'Sullivan said nothing. He gave an empathic, weak smile and nodded. What more could he do? Sometimes you just have to listen.

"I'd left a brief message for him with June Scott: his secretary at his office, and when Bernard came rushing into the shop it was dark. Torrential rain was bouncing off the pavement, but he wouldn't wait.

'What was the point, Fi?' He'd explained — out of breath from rushing through the downpour. 'I'm already drenched.'

To be fair to him, there wasn't a car in sight when he stepped out of the shop and onto the crossing."

Phillips turned back to the scene and pointed her wedding finger towards the corpse; her hand was trembling, and the solitaire diamond engagement ring glistened in the brightness of the street lamp.

"Bernard was within the safe confines of the crossing when I heard the loud, screaming engine noise, and I could see him quickening his stride..."

She shook her head, and a faint, knowing smile broke out as her eyes relived the moment.

"...But he had no chance, poor man: it came at him like a bat from the bowels of hell. I clearly saw it: an eerie, black shape. Bernard stopped abruptly; turned to face it, and he sort of stooped. You know, bent his knees and held out both arms with the palms upturned..."

She swallowed repeatedly but failed to fight back the tears that were freely rolling down her cheeks. Her voice squeaking with the emotion.

"...as if he could hold the car at bay. But of course, he couldn't, could he, officer? Then there was the terrible scream..."

Her lips were quivering, and the ringed hand moved to caress her chin, pausing for a moment to gather herself.

"...The scream was quickly followed by the thud — a sickening thud. For as long as I live, I will never forget that sound. But what was most horrifying and disturbing was the failure of the driver to stop: the car didn't even slow down. I rushed out to try and get the number, but all I could see were its red lights: disappearing into the gloom — the bat had flown..."

PC O'Sullivan later relayed the Councillor's sequence of events, together with those of another eyewitness, a Mrs Alison Davies, to Detective Chief Inspector Richard Lewis at Police Headquarters.

O'Sullivan had earlier sheltered with Mrs Davies under a large Dior umbrella and,
intoxicated by the fragrance of her Chanel perfume, he had jotted down the attractive
young mother's words in his pocket notebook.

"That poor man had no chance."

She had solemnly spoken, her shoulder-length blonde hair curling with the dampness of the early evening.

"I was coming out of the post office when the car literally flew past me. The driver must have been..."

Her left hand brushed the Constable's arm.

"...excuse my language, Officer — a bloody maniac. That desperate man was already in the middle of the crossing. Even I could see that, so the driver must have seen him. The next thing I saw was it crashing into him, striking him like a bowling ball, but the pin didn't stay down. It flipped up onto the roof of the car and tumbled to the road in front of me. It was awful and the maniac didn't even stop..."

The sentiment in her voice broke through, and a tear escaped; angrily, she flicked it from her cheek.

"...I'm kicking myself because it happened so fast, and I was unable to catch the registration number."

Detective Constable Bill John, the scenes of crime officer, shook his head as he returned to the Detective Chief Inspector's office from the scene of the fire. His facial expression was grave — defeated.

"Nothing, Boss — burnt down to the chassis. It's a Ford Capri, and we've managed to get the engine number. P.N.C. comes back as stolen today from Neath. Kate Morgan's on the phone to them as we speak, and one more thing. Only one house overlooks the waste ground, a Mrs ..."

The S.O.C.O. glanced at his clipboard.

"...Angela Pritchard. She was upstairs in the bathroom when she heard the blast and opened the window straight away, but she could see nothing — just the flames."

At the post-mortem, acclaimed home office pathologist Sir James Rees-Bartlett determined that death would most definitely have been instantaneous, as virtually every major bone in his body had been shattered. A break in one of the first three ribs had punctured the main aorta, causing major haemorrhage, while breaks in the middle ribs had punctured both lungs, causing them to collapse.

Typical of Bernard Jones's ethos.

'If you are going to do something, then do it properly.'

*

Edith Jones will never forget the anguished, ashen look ingrained on the face of Police Constable Anthony O'Sullivan when she opened the door to him on that eventful, life-changing day.

That day, which began so happily. That day, like any other day, when Edith got on with what she wanted to do when she wanted to do it. That day that had started especially exciting though, as unbeknown to Bernard, she was planning a surprise party to celebrate their milestone anniversary. All their family and close friends were aware; each one as guilty as the other for the white lies that had passed their lips to protect Edith's plan.

It was early evening on that day and she was putting the final touches to the preparations when she was startled by the chimes of the doorbell.

'Who could that be?'

Her mind was working overtime.

"The flowers, it must be Tom, on his way home."

Believing the caller to be a long-standing family friend, Tom Hughes from the florists in the market, the slim mother of two rushed to answer, pulling at her apron ties and stuffing it in a random drawer on route. He'll be laden with an abundance of fuchsia pink chrysanthemums: St Mark and the Apostles had been beautifully adorned with the same majestic blooms on their wedding day. A quick appearance-checking glance in a full-length mirror, hand through her hair, and with a radiant smile, she flicked on the outside light and opened the door.

"Oh!"

That was her first word to Anthony O'Sullivan. The shock of seeing the young, uniformed police officer standing there on her threshold and not Tom Hughes was obvious.

He failed to clear the dryness from his throat; his eyes drifting away from her gaze as
he spoke.

"I'm so sorry if I startled you. I'm PC O'Sullivan from Carmarthen Police Station. Are you Mrs Edith Jones?"

The welcoming smile that seconds earlier had lit up her face was rapidly replaced with the same grey and anguished look painfully exhibited by the officer. Something was wrong: she could sense his discomfort.

She pleaded, tears already spilling and rolling down her cheeks. "Is it my husband? Is it Bernard?"

"I'm so sorry, Mrs Jones. Is there anybody here with you?"

CHAPTER 3

The engine in the maroon-coloured Austin 1800 was rattling like a string of rusty tin cans being dragged in the wake of a wedding car, and the Thug was clicking. Clicking and tapping on the steering wheel. Lifeless eyes darted to the dashboard clock for the eighth time in as many minutes, and his right foot stamped down hard on the accelerator, holding the revs in frustration.
"I won't be long, boyo. Keep the motor ticking over, boyo. That's what he said. Shitting hell, Barry, that was yonks ago. What the hell are you doing?"
Barry George Murphy was easy on the eye. The type of fella that all eyes turned to when he sauntered into a room, and he knew it. You've seen the ones: tall and athletic, jet black, tight curly hair, chocolate brown eyes that undressed every woman he met, gleaming white teeth, and muscles on top of muscles. He also had an infectious charm, a cocky swagger, and the gift of the gab. And it hadn't taken him long to talk the knickers off Jim the dealer's missus.
He was giving her one while she was bent over the twin tub. One of her eyes squashed up against the motif of a bulbous tomato ketchup dispenser, and the other fixed on the door to the reinforced metal shed at the bottom of the garden: where her man was sorting out wraps of high-end cocaine. She was biting at her bottom lip — curtailing the screams and moans

that she wanted to let rip.
The accent was strong — pure Scouse.
"Faster, Barry, 'arder — oh my God — fuck me — fuck me 'ard."
Deep down, she wanted Jim to catch them at it: he deserved it the way he'd been treating her lately. It wasn't her fault he couldn't get it up anymore, was it? That was all down to the big H, so why use her as a punch bag every bleedin' day? Her arms were black and blue, and this morning had been the last straw. He'd really hurt her, so this bit of action with Mr Dreamboat was a welcome bonus. But, realistically, of course she couldn't let Jim catch them at it. She needed the heroin as much as he did, and didn't Jim always make sure she had her fair share of that brown beauty?"
The grunts are louder; the strokes are faster, and the thrusts are deeper. Murphy is on the verge of ecstasy, and the grip on the cheeks of her arse tightens. Squeezing and forcing them apart: exposing and stretching everything that is turning him on. His muscles have tensed; his breathing has shallowed, and the orgasm is battling its way to explosion. The once-had, never-forgotten feeling that releases a multitude of pent-up anxieties is imminent, and at that precise point — she forced him out of her.
The fear in her voice is palpable.
"Jim's comin' — 'e'll fuckin' kill me if 'e catches us!"
The aggression in the recently released jailbird's tone is chilling, and his accent is just as strong.
"Fuck Jim, I was fuckin' comin'! I've been banged up for nine soddin' months…"
Demented eyes bore into the terrified young woman as he grabs at peroxided locks and yanks her face towards his erection.
"'Ere — suck on this, you bitch: come on — finish me off!"
Rusted hinges creak as the kitchen door edges open, and Jim, his eyes down, methodically counting the wraps in the palm of his hand, ambles in.
"Och, Barry, I've chucked in a few extra for keepin' ma name

ou…"

The bottle of strong lager smashing over the Scot's head spares him the humbling sight of his semi-naked missus on her knees with her mouth full of prime meat: totally oblivious, Jim had collapsed unconscious to the floor beside her.

Raising what was left of the bottle to his lips, Murphy slurped at the residue before shifting the piece of jagged glass to his fingertips. Locking eyes with those of the silently pleading woman, he held it out directly above the drug dealer's head. A sadistic grin, together with a slow shake of the head, was his response to her appeal for mercy, and, as if in slow motion, he released the feeble grip on the dart-like chunk of glass. Gathering momentum, it spiralled towards Jim's neck and with a sickening thwack, it pierced the exposed skin, spurting blood over his woman's right breast.

Flashing his teeth, the grin widened to a victorious smile, and with a wink of the eye, Murphy flicked back the curls that had momentarily slipped towards the bridge of his nose.

"Right then, blondie — where were we?"

*

The rattling and the clicking had ceased; they were on the move, and the motor was cruising along the busy Park Road towards the City's Cathedral.

The Thug's tone of voice was irate and aggressive.

"What the hell took you so long, Barry? Two fucking minutes you said you'd be."

Barry didn't answer him — he didn't need to: the extended look of disdain spoke volumes. You know the one — like when you realise you've just stepped in dog shit.

He turned his face away, wound down the window, and took in the air; a deep sniff filled the nostrils and he held the breath before slowly releasing it back to the street. He could smell the Dingle. Hear the many accents drifting on the breeze: Irish, Welsh, Scottish, and his — good old Scouse.

He was home and back where he belonged: back where he was

the Daddy. Back on his patch of turf after all those months of being stuck behind bars, and he was going to collect what was his. Those that owed knew he would be coming for them, and by now, following his set-to with Sid, the jungle drums will have started banging out their beat. The message loud and clear — Barry Murphy is back in town, and it's business as usual.

The Thug was clicking again, and from the corner of his eye, a bemused Barry studied the wiry teenager with the noticeable high forehead and close-cropped hair, topped with a quiff.

'What the hell is this sheep shagger on? The weirdo is clicking like a grasshopper on speed. Another hour or so and he can piss off back to the valleys. One more job, a little debt recovery visit, and then cheery-bye. Nice seeing you again, boyo — now sod off home to Tom Jones and fucking choirs.'

He nodded towards the street, arguing with himself.

'Alright, he has helped me out, hasn't he? Nicked this crock of shite and picked me up from the wooden gates, but didn't I, Barry George Murphy, help him out? You bet your life I did! Pointed him in the right direction and warned him which screws would turn a blind eye if someone needed a good kicking. Let him in on the ones who could get him some weed — even class A if he had the readies. And, somehow or other, he just happened to get his fair share of class A. So, how did he pay for that, you might ask? He didn't have no cash. Gossip on the landing was that he was partial to a bit of hairy-arsed attention and didn't mind slinking into the shadows and bending over every now and again. Even screws have nonces amongst them, don't they? And those fucking skin-tinglers would slink to any depths to satisfy their sordid cravings. Toddling off home to their wives and kids after the dirty deed was done. All pious and upstanding; denying their depravity until the next sick urge kicked in and another desperate adolescent would be enticed.'

Seeing the gnarled, furrowing of the swarthy skin above the Thug's bushy brows, and the spooky eyes staring intensely at

the road ahead reminded him that this lunatic could flip at any second. Barry was confident that he could easily take him out but well aware that he needed to be on high alert to any sudden manic acts of aggression, and at least try to pacify him for the time being. Once he'd passed his date of usefulness, he didn't give a shit what he did.
The Thug's eyes narrowed, the scowling intensified, and the clicking increased in volume.
'What the hell is he clicking for?'
Flashing his teeth, Barry leant towards the dash.
"Fancy a bit of 'appy dust, boyo? You know, a little somethin' to give us a buzz?"
He opened his fist, and Jim the dealer's wraps of cocaine fell to the black vinyl.
The Thug's eyes widened.
"Fuck me, Barry, there's…"
He painstakingly tried to count them out loud, his eyes wide, his head nodding with
every number — he gave up after six…
"…more than seven, and I thought you were skint! You told me you were fucking skint!"
Grimacing, Barry turned away, pursed his lips, and expelled some of the built-up aggression.
'Who the hell does this arse-wipe think he is? Questioning me — Barry George Murphy. Respect! That's what he needs to show. Needs to know his fucking place.'
Letting more pent-up air escape, he reminds himself to cool down.
'Not long now, Barry. One more job, mate. Just one more job.'
He unfolds one of the wraps and bends his head to meet it. A finger firms his left nostril while the right hoovers up the white powder, and instantly his head springs back — his eyes smarting.
"Whoosh — good shit, Jimmy-boy — good fuckin' shit!"
The sun, low in the sky, masks the approach of the marked police patrol car, and it's on them before they can do anything

about it. Fortunately for the two former cellmates, that was a good thing: any sudden manoeuvre or movement in the vehicle would have attracted the attention of the double-manned crew. As it was, they didn't even notice it, and why would they? They were enjoying the crisp, sunny morning, and life was good. The shift had been quiet, and they'd had a few laughs. Always plenty of them to be had: the characters they dealt with on a daily basis in 'The Pool' made sure of that. And, why would they have been aware of a vehicle reported stolen during the night from South West Wales? That was way too many miles away. Their brief from the shift sergeant was about the Scallies coming over from Birkenhead to nick the silver and lead from the many churches dotted in and around the City. They'd just checked in with Father O'Connell at St. Patrick's and had a brew with a little snifter. But, if they had spotted Barry George Murphy in that car, it would have turned their peaceful shift upside down: all hell would have broken out.

His type cannot get any higher on the police radar: to them, he is scum. An evil, self-centred oxygen thief who should have been shoved in a sack at birth and dumped in the Mersey... He had crossed the thin blue line when he attacked and seriously injured one of their own, and all because the officer had the audacity to chase and force off the road a stolen car that was being driven out of control.

The hearing at the Crown Court Room in Liverpool's St. George's Hall was a joke. Murphy's legal team conned the judge by quoting excerpts from the defence barrister's 'Bible of Quotes', by Freeda Criminal, and the result? An eighteen-month custodial sentence — guaranteed to be back out on the streets in nine. And the police officer? Well, let's just say that the deep facial wound caused by the slashing of the blade is slowly healing, but the mental scarring? That injury to the mind? The one that isn't visible? Tragically — that is with her for the rest of her life.

The Scouser spun around to see the tail end of the patrol car disappearing.

"Fuckin' 'ell, boyo, that was a close shave: luckily the bizzies didn't spot me — I'd be dragged straight back to the big 'ouse if they 'ad."

He started laughing, his eyes widening, pursing his lips as he placed his hand over his heart.

"An' all before me dear ol' mam gets the chance to smother me with kisses and take a lovin' peek at the apple of 'er eye."

His laughter increased: the cocaine was doing its job, and he was already unwrapping another line of the mind-distorting powder.

The Thug was not amused — pissed off at being Murphy's lackey. As far as he was concerned, his debt to him had been settled, and it was time to head off home. Back to Pembroke Dock where he was the Daddy; back to where he was the controller of the easily led. He eyed the small parcels of coke.

'I'll snort one of those wraps; blag another couple for the drive home, and Amen, that would be that.'

Murphy pointed ahead to a hip-roofed, red-brick building; set back from the road, and with several motors parked in front of the picture windows. A metal name sign indicating it to be 'The Brick and Mortar' was swinging freely in the breeze from a black ornate bracket bolted high above the entrance.

"Pull into that boozer, boyo — this gear's gonna blow you away."

Considering the early hour, the pub was rammed, and the Thug tucked the 1800 into a spot well away from the prying eyes of the regulars perched on stools at high tables.

The hit was what he needed — he was knackered: he'd nicked the car and driven through the night to get to the prison before daylight.

Unwrapping the glossy paper, he sucked on his finger, dipped it into the powder, and rubbed it into his gums. The remnants were hoovered up, and he sat back to await the buzz. The hit was instant, and the tingling in his limbs signalled the return of a much-needed energy boost. The drive home was going to

be a doddle.
Barry was on his third wrap and laughing hysterically.
"Come on then, boyo, one last favour to me. Only a few more miles down the road, and I can collect the debt. Someone owes me big time, and because I'm so fuckin' kind-hearted, I'll give you some of the dosh. Make it worth your while — if you know wot I mean."
The Thug was past caring: the stimulant had done its job, and it wasn't just the motor that was speeding into Everton — both young men were flying. Laughing, singing, and shouting out to identically dressed young girls with identical hairstyles who were parading the pavements like peacocks.

*

The two tower blocks looming in the distance looked ominous as they rose from the mass of terraced houses that surrounded them, and Murphy pointed a finger, the nail chewed to the quick.
"That's where we're 'edin', boyo, and we'll go in the back way; keep our arrival low-key — if you get me drift..."
He gave a laugh — heavy with sarcasm.
"...I doubt they'd be puttin' the bloody flags up if they knew we woz comin' anyway..."
He faced the Thug and grinned.
"Not long now, matey, and you can 'ed off 'ome to Wales."
They pulled onto some rough ground, and floors upon floors of balconies looked down on them. Makeshift washing lines, strewn across their widths, were littered with towelling nappies and kiddies' clothes. Not a soul in sight — but eyes were everywhere...
Reaching for another wrap, Murphy craned his neck to scan the upper floors before pointing the same digit at a large evergreen.
"Stop 'ere — under this tree, and keep the engine tickin' over: things could turn nasty and we might need a quick getaway."
The car skidded to a halt, and the thug twisted his head to face him; his face screwed up with rage.

"Hey, I'm coming with you, Barry. No way am I hanging around like a fucking puppet waiting for you again."

Drug-laden eyes pierced into those of the driver — processing that response. It took a while before a grin crossed the handsome face, and Murphy cracked up laughing.

"Come on then — maybe you'll be 'andy in your own little way, and anyway, I might need some extra muscle — puff out your chest and walk on fuckin' tip-toes…"

Murphy's cackling continued as he strode towards the flats; blissfully unaware of the incessant clicking coming from the youth lagging behind him. Little did he know — he would never hear the Thug clicking again.

He passed a community refuse facility on his right-hand side, and was only a few steps away from making a right turn onto the parking area in front of the high rises when a tall, gangly man of West Indian origin stepped out from the shadows to confront him.

Edwin Clarence Baptiste — known locally as John — was not alone, and every member of the despot's gang was carrying a baseball bat; they fanned out. Heavy footsteps behind him told Murphy he had even more company, and a quick glance over his shoulder confirmed what he already knew: he was in for a bloody good kicking. Surrounded, there was nowhere for him to run, but no way would he beg: he was too proud, too bloody stubborn, and the amount of powder he'd shoved up his nose was controlling his rationality. He was wired — feared no man, and ready for the battle.

"Nice of you to arrange a welcome 'ome party for mc, John."

That was the arrogant youngster's opening line, and before he voiced the second, he had placed his right hand over his heart — his speech slurred but confident.

"Very kind of you, and I'm so overwhelmed by your thoughtfulness."

The West Indian folded his arms and grinned, exposing teeth so heavily stained from toking dope that they were the same coffee colour as his skin. The gravelly voice told a similar story.

"You haven't changed, Barry, still as cocky as ever. But time has caught up with you, brother, and it just so 'appens that lucky ol' me is going to be the man to have first dibs at the chance of taking advantage of your bad piece of judgement. Word is out on the street: Jim's paying big to get some satisfaction, and make no bones about it, you were way out of order. Now you're going to pay the heavy price."

The cocaine had added to Barry's swagger, and he laughed as he brought the same hand to his face, caressing the stubble on his chin as he eyeballed Baptiste's entourage.

"Well, I'm not impressed with this little reception committee, and I mean LITTLE. Bloody hell, where is she, John? The only person missing is Snow fuckin' White…"

No one else laughed, but like a pack of hyenas, the hostile faces moved in for the kill.

"I tell you wot, John, you pay me wot you owe me — wot you promised me for keepin' me gob shut all these months, and I'll walk away from this little joke of a gang of yours."

He splayed both arms in front of him and winked.

"I'll even forget that you turned against me."

The West Indian was laughing and shaking his head as he spoke, causing the dreads to tumble across a face that had a scar running the full length of its left cheek. A deep Barbadian twang drawled from his lips.

"I've got to give it to you, Barry, you've got some bloody cheek, man. You don't get it, do you, brother: you're in no position to barter, and I've got a lot riding on this."

He outstretched long, spindly arms to his gang.

"Unlimited gear for me and my boys for the foreseeable. My debt to you wiped clean, and oh, I nearly forgot. Jim's little blonde bombshell. Mine whenever I want her."

Fingers soiled by nicotine cupped his manhood.

"Once she's experienced this mother inside her, well, she ain't going to remember your couple of inches is sh.."

Barry kicked out — his right size 12 snapping two of the fingers, and the lunge with his left fist smacked against the West Indian's nose: splattering it between his cheeks.

That was the young Scouser's final act of violence: his short and wayward life ended there and then. He was struck twice in quick succession from behind and collapsed on top of Baptiste. The other wooden staves that pummelled his body were struck in vain. Barry George Murphy had died when the first blow connected: it had shattered his skull and pierced the cerebrum. The Thug had been watching from a distance and had witnessed the thick-set male with the spider web tattoo on the back of his neck, the one they were calling Beef, strike the fatal blow. He shrugged his shoulders and backed towards the car.

"Sod-all to do with me — I'm outta here."

Sat in the driver's seat, he had one eye on the deranged mob sprinting towards him and the other in the rearview mirror as he reversed at pace across the rough ground. And that's when he spotted Barry Murphy's black-coloured hold-all on the back seat.

"Fuck him — I'll have that, and his fucking wraps."

CHAPTER 4

Edith Jones' life, as she had grown accustomed to, had unravelled beyond all recognition.

Her twin daughters, Molly and April, were married and lived nearby. They visited frequently, but sadly those visits were not enough to fend away the tentacles of depression that now gripped her.

Dropping off to sleep alone and waking up alone. Forcing herself to go out of the house in an attempt to find solace, then the inevitable dread that overcame her as she opened the door back to emptiness.

The blackness that had engulfed her gradually lightened following the Winter Solstice, and by the time the daffodils were nodding their heads in the early Spring breeze, she was more comfortable in braving daily walks into town and mingling with the crowds; witnessing laughter and happiness without becoming distraught became a regular occurrence. Yes, the grieving process was evolving.

On one unusually warm and sunny day for the time of year, Edith sat reading on a
wooden slatted bench; recently refreshed with cornflower blue. She'd taken a fondness to this particular bench as it was shaded by a large, mature oak and donated to the park several years ago by a grieving widow in memory of her loving husband, Alan.

The brass plaque riveted to the back support indicated that Alan and Annie had spent many an afternoon together at that spot, enjoying literary delights. It profoundly read: 'Conversation is not essential to intimacy.'

Edith had smiled and wept when she first read it: the happy memories of her previous life flooding her mind with examples. How true were those six words...

So engrossed was she in the riveting thriller that she was startled, yet again, by PC O'Sullivan. His approach to her along the meandering gravel path had gone unnoticed, but on this occasion, he wasn't the bearer of such horrific news.

"Hello Mrs Jones — a good book is it?"

She gasped and raised her head to try and focus on the police officer, but her vision was affected by the brightness of the silver-coloured badge on his helmet, glistening in the sunlight. She shielded her eyes with the novel.

Gone was the heavy, dark-blue jacket: a light blue cotton shirt with the sleeves rolled up to just below the elbow sufficed, and the silver numbers on his epaulettes, also mirroring the sunshine, identified him as Police Constable number 989. A black clip-on tie, dark blue trousers, black leather belt, and the same colour Dr Martens' boots completed the uniform.

His melodious voice was as energising as the day.

"Whoops, startled you again..." he sang, "...sorry, Mrs Jones, and how are you keeping?"

Removing his helmet set free a mass of tight, curly, ginger hair tapering to closely cropped at the back and sides. The curls flopped over his forehead, and he pushed them back with his hand. They shimmered with sweat and enhanced the freckles dotted across his nose.

Edith hadn't seen the officer since the coroner's inquest, and sad recollections came flooding back. She forced a smile that didn't go unnoticed to the trained eyes of Anthony O'Sullivan, but the mental pain and suffering were still visibly etched on that grief-stricken face for any eyes to see.

"Oh, it's okay, Tony. My fault for being so focused on this

fiction..."
She fibbed, and it wasn't convincing.
"...I'm fine, thanks."
Tony O'Sullivan picked up on it, smiled, and decided that a bit of cheering up was what the doctor ordered.
"Do you mind if I join you under the shade of this fine specimen, Mrs Jones?"
He stooped under a branch, his hand dramatically flapping in front of his face.
"...My skin doesn't take too kindly to these hot rays, and unfortunately, I don't go a film star shade of chestnut brown: more akin to an angry hue of pink."
The humour sparked a chuckle, and she edged over, revealing more of the cornflower blue for him to sit alongside her. Surprisingly, she could feel the weight of anxiety starting to lift, and the shallow, rapid breaths from her upper lungs that she'd become used to seemed to be slowing to a more gentle breathing pattern.
Edith had begun to relax.
An angry, authoritative voice crackled from the officer's radio.
"Carrots — where the bloody hell are you, boy?"
PC O'Sullivan shot up and his head collided with the branch.
"Ouch," was the cry: his hand instinctively rubbing his crown while simultaneously twisting his head in all directions — like a meerkat on sentry duty — desperately trying to ascertain if the owner of the voice was in sight and watching.
The curls fell over his eyes and while blowing into one part of the walkie-talkie, he held the other above his head as he paced around in front of Edith. Once clear of the overhanging branches and confident that the supervisor wasn't spying on him, he spoke into the transmitter.
"Sorry, Sarge — I got a bit waylaid. Be back in ten minutes."
The angry voice persisted.
"Well, don't be any bloody longer — we're choking here. Dying of bloody thirst!"
"Yes, Sarge — will do, Sarge."

Ambling back into the shade, he sighed as he sat down.

"Sorry about the bad language, Mrs Jones: the Sergeant wants a cup of tea, and we've run out of milk. I was on my way to the Spar."

A warm smile had brought a sparkle to her eyes.

"I presume that Carrots is your nickname, Tony?"

With his complexion getting redder by the second, the officer grimaced and pushed back the curls.

"Comes with this ginger hair, I'm afraid, Mrs Jones. Not very original though, is it?"

The smile widened, and a warmth melted her heart.

"Well, don't you be so embarrassed. I think your hair is beautiful. There are definitely lots of jealous men around who would love to have hair like yours. One little query, though, Tony…"

She cupped her chin with the palm of her hand as she spoke — deep in thought.

"…Why do you have two walkie-talkies? And why were you holding that one above your head when you were speaking to the Sergeant?"

It was PC O'Sullivan's turn to smile.

"Well, funny you should say that — sometimes I look like a blooming contortionist in a travelling circus."

He laughed, and that made Edith chuckle again.

'Oh, how good it felt to laugh — how good it felt to feel normal.'

"One is a receiver, which is this one. Look, you can see that it has a little aerial, and I was holding it high above my head, trying to get a good signal: they are so temperamental. It depends on where you position yourself for you to receive and transmit. And that is why the Sergeant's voice sounded all crackly until I moved away from this beautiful oak. This one is the transmitter: you speak into it, and it sends the message…"

He paused for a brief moment; his eyes narrowing.

"…Umm, at least, I think that's how it works. Sometimes I have to stand on something to be able to speak and receive. Hell of a job when you're struggling with some drunk in the roadway."

They both laughed out loud. PC O'Sullivan was reminiscing, shaking his head in exasperation.

"I'll quickly tell you something that happened to me just the other weekend of nights, Mrs Jones. I think it'll bring a smile to your face — do you have the time to spare?"

"Yes, yes..." was the excitable response, "... I have all the time in the world. Carry on, Tony. Please do — I'm intrigued."

She marked the page and placed the novel back into her bag: she could read that anytime. This true story is sure to be even more exciting.

"Well, as I said, I was working nights and driving through the town centre when I heard him, and I thought, 'Oh no, no, no, why me? Not tonight — give me a break'

I knew who he was, you see. A local character — an Irishman called Shamus..."

He was laughing as he stood up.

"...Shamus the drunk, and he was urinating against the display window of Woolworths while belting out 'Sweet Molly Malone.' I stopped the Panda car, wound down the window, and shouted over to him. Well, Mrs Jones, he told me in no uncertain terms to go forth and multiply!"

Mrs Jones's hand shot up to cover her mouth, not knowing whether or not to appear shocked: attempting to but failing to stifle the laugh. Oh, how good she was starting to feel.

"Shamus is our most regular Friday or Saturday night visitor to the cells. Sometimes on both nights. This Irish navvy with hands the size of shovels works like a Trojan all week but drinks just as hard all weekend. I'd managed to get the rear door open and to get Shamus perched on the edge of the seat, but his legs were still outside, and so was his head — it was a stalemate. A crowd of jeerers were milling around, egging on Shamus, and I couldn't get any reception with the radio to call for some help. At this point — I'm shattered.

Shamus is a beast of a man: a gentle giant, and well-loved throughout the town centre public houses, and likewise in most other local communities. He's a charmer with a soft Irish

lilt, but alcohol is his demon, and he can very quickly become a bloody nuisance.
The struggle with him had taken its toll, and I needed a breather. I stepped back from Shamus, resting one hand on the roof of the panda and the other on the top of the door. Our eyes met, and Shamus smiled knowingly..."
The officer mimicked a strong Irish accent.
"....'You're fecked, aren't you?'
Mrs Jones laughed again — her eyes wide and sparkling.
"A hiccup and a thunderous belch dispatching an overpowering whiff of whiskey and pork scratchings hit me full-on in the face with the force of a hurricane."
The hand moved to hide her eyes — her fingers spreading so she could peep through them.
"Urgh — what a revolting man!"
Anthony O'Sullivan chuckled and continued with the Irish twang. He loved telling these stories, and was pleased that his bit of cheering-up therapy was working.
"Ociffer, here's you all on yr tod and here's me wit you; wit everyone else in t whole world watching us. Now t' be sure, wouldn't it be better for us both if you just let me go on my merry way into that there hostelry for a wee shot of Irish. T' b'Jesus, why don't you come wit me, and I'll get you a shot of T' Virgin Mary's favourite nectar as well.'
My eyes looked down towards his huge, size fourteen work boots, wondering how I was going to gather them up from the road and squeeze them between the panda's rear and front passenger seats. And, at the same time, get him to bow his head and shoulders so that they would pass through the gap."
Tony O'Sullivan couldn't contain his laughter anymore and started to guffaw, which set Mrs Jones off again. He was wiping the tears from his eyes, trying to stop the laughter by taking deep breaths and fanning his face with his hand.
"This is the best bit, Mrs Jones — this is the best bit."
The policeman's voice was squeaking as he tried his best not to laugh anymore.

"It was then that I saw the Irish man's penis poking out from the crotch of his jeans."

Mrs Jones pushed out her other hand towards the officer — giggling like a teenager.

"Oh no, Tony — oh no…" her eyes widened, "…what happened then?"

"Well, the darker shade of denim from the knee down to his size fourteens told its own story: they were sodden, but Shamus was oblivious. I coughed, nodded towards his groin, and spoke in a very authoritative voice.

'Put that thing away, Shamus. It's a very dangerous weapon…"

Mrs Jones gasped, then giggled — both hands covering her eyes — the fingers parting as soon as PC O'Sullivan carried on.

"…His bloodshot and glazed eyes managed to get it in focus: 'Oh feckin hell — it's escaped again, and I can see that it's been trying to launder me Wranglers.'

The Irish man's eyes drifted away from the jeans and fixed on my neck; he pointed a finger the size of a Walls finest pork sausage.

'T' be sure, that's a very smart tie that yr wearing ociffer: I used t' have one exactly t' same colour as that, so I did. In fact, that tie could be the very same tie that I used t' have…'

Shamus gulped, hiccuped, and struggled to swallow before continuing.

'…I last wore it t' Paddy T' teeth O'Connor's wake, but I drank so much Guinness that the button popped off me trousers, and I had to use me tie t' hold t'em up. I must have passed out, but when I woke up me head was resting on Paddy's emerald green velvet waistcoat. B'Jesus t'was a fine waistcoat, so it was. At first, I didn't know where I was. I was so warm and comfortable, but then I saw Paddy's huge teeth smiling down at me. I shot up wit a jolt, and me trousers fell t' me boots. My tie had been thieved! And t' be sure, Paddy t' teeth was wearing one the exact same colour as mine when they lowered him into t' ground.'

Shamus finished with several signs of the cross in front of his chest and was mumbling.

'Sweet Mary, mother of Jesus — sweet Mary, mother of Jesus.'

Thinking of a ploy to get him back to the Police Station, I unclipped my tie and held it out to him.

'Listen, Shamus, if you get into the panda car, you can have this tie. It will be my present to you — that I promise.'

He looked up at me as if I was ridiculously stupid.

'Oh b'Jesus, that's a fine gesture, ociffer, but t' be sure, your tie wouldn't be long enough for me!"

Edith was sobbing with laughter, picturing the scene as clearly as if it were before her at that very moment. Her face had softened, and she looked and felt ten years younger. A new lease of life was oozing through the pores of her skin, rejuvenating her whole being. It had softened her body language, released the tension that had been gripping her muscles like an engineer's vice, and enabled a warmth of relaxation to flow through her veins. Edith was alive again, and she was ready for a new challenge.

The officer ducked to pick up his helmet.

"Well, Mrs Jones, I've interrupted your peace and quiet for long enough now..."

He pointed at the paperback poking out of her bag.

"...And I'm sure you're keen to discover WhoDunnit..."

He chuckled again, sweeping his curls back with his hand before refitting the headwear.

"...And the Sergeant wants his tea, so I must be off. Crime won't solve itself, you know."

The warmth in her face and the beaming smile spoke volumes.

"It's been a pleasure chatting with you, Tony. You are the tonic that I needed to brighten me up, and I don't think I've laughed so much since Ber..."

She paused, swallowing in an attempt to compose herself.

"...well, for a long time now — thank you. I don't suppose that you're looking for lodgings, are you?"

She winked.

"I serve a mean bacon and eggs, you know."

He was slowly shaking his head as he replied.

"It's very tempting, Mrs Jones — all I get is muesli! My Alice thinks I need to shed a few pounds."

He was grimacing as he pushed out and patted his stomach.

"All paid for, mind you. Joking aside, they are looking for more landladies at Police Headquarters. There's a new batch of Police Cadets starting in early September, and they all need lodgings. You could easily take on a couple in your house, and you'd still have a spare bedroom. Have a think about it, and if you want, I'll have a word in the right ears..."

His right index finger pointed and wagged.

"...Only if I can pop in at breakfast time, though, when I'm on an early shift..."

He winked and grinned, smacking his lips together.

"...I love bacon butties, but don't you let on to my Alice."

The Sergeant's voice boomed from the radio.

"Carrots — for crying out loud. I could have gone to the parlour, milked Daisy the cow, and churned out some bloody butter by now. Where the hell are you?"

The officer tutted, gave a flick of the head, rolled his eyes, and grinned.

"Sorry, Mrs Jones, but duty calls. Have a think about the lodgers and let me know."

Edith Jones followed the officer's animated strides until he was out of her sight. Laughing as she listened to him shouting into the transmitter while holding the receiver up and over his head, out to the side, then down towards the path.

Deep in thought, she wiped the tears away and reached for the thriller.

"What a lovely young man. Two police cadets, hmm — now that sounds very interesting."

CHAPTER 5

(Several months later)

Lloyd didn't see the first blow coming, but hell, he certainly felt it. The open palm slapping against his left ear had jarred his skull, causing the brain to jig in its protective gel from one side of the cranium to the other.

The drenched-in-sweat teenager had done a quick recce of the house and, convinced the occupants to be safely tucked up in bed, had edged into the darkness. Subconsciously holding his breath, he'd checked out the stairs before inching the door closed and slowly turning the key. There was no giveaway click, and fingering droplets of sweat away from his brow, he released a controlled sigh of relief.

His stealth had been wasted: the strong arms in waiting grabbed him from the shadows, thrust him into the living room, and delivered that stinging blow.

Head spinning, the youngster floundered in the darkness, already aware from the telltale whiff of stale Old Spice that the assailant was his father.

He spun around in time to catch a glimpse of the second blow coming and instinctively ducked, but still dazed, he was too slow, and the open palm connected with his right ear, knocking his skull in the other direction. His father cursed as the metal expandable strap on his wristwatch snapped and spiralled into the fire grate.

Lloyd slumped to his knees, instinctively throwing his arms up and around his ears. He hadn't cried out, but tears rolled down his cheeks until they found his open mouth before dripping into the deep pile of the Axminster. They were silent tears. Yes, tears of pain, but mainly tears of humiliation and profound regret.

"Not so bloody tough now, are you? You selfish little shit. Where the hell have you been? What the hell have you been doing, Lloyd?"

The boy didn't speak — better not to. His father had never hit him so ferociously before; Lloyd had crossed into unknown territory.

"Look at you — you're dripping with sweat. It's nearly two in the morning, and you've been gone since bloody breakfast. Your mother is frantic with worry."

Lloyd could hear her crying: sobbing with hurt, worry, anger, and relief...

"We know all about your results, Lloyd: bloody shite! Your mother has phoned everyone she could think of, trying to find out where you are, and nobody knew. But they all knew about your pathetic results. Why the hell couldn't you have just come home and told us yourself? Or at least telephoned to let us know that you were safe. Are we that unapproachable? You reek of bloody booze, fags, and ..."

He sniffed the air like Sherlock's dog.

"...oh my God, Lloyd, whacky-backy! You don't need that crazy stuff, boy: bloody hell, fresh air makes you whacky enough. A selfish, egotistical waste of space, that's what you've become, and don't even think about going back to school: you can get a bloody job. Mark my words, son, I'll see you down the bloody pits first!"

His dad's voice hadn't been raised, but the tone was chilling and the words were succinct and clear. Lloyd was under no illusion as to where his future lay.

The father stooped to pick up his watch and cursed as he realised the expense of the repair. No more words were necessary at that unearthly hour, and leaving his second-born on his knees, he struggled to curb the tears as he glanced behind him. Six years between his two lads, but hell, they were as different as garlic and grapes. With a deep sigh, he climbed the stairs to the marital bed. It destroyed him that he had to be so harsh, but wasn't this son a chip off the old block? The father knew better than anyone that without a vice-like grip now, this son would be forever lost to the wrong side of good.

The teenager could hear them talking; his mother was desperate to come downstairs, and he, knowing how easily he could manipulate her, was hoping that would be the case. But his father was hurting, and he was lashing out in despair; the same tone of voice was used again and for the last time.

"Don't you go down those stairs, Vera. It's your fault he's turned out this way. He's bloody ruined! Now, one of us has got work in the morning, and the morning's going to come too bloody quickly."

Darkness smothered the light that had briefly stolen onto the landing, and with his ears ringing and smarting, Lloyd eventually rose and dragged himself onto the sofa. He had never entirely understood what it meant to box someone's ears — he knew now.

The boy ached all over, and his head was pounding: the after-effects of the cannabis, the booze, the run home, and the couple of slaps from his dad. He didn't want to move, but he had to; it had reached bursting point.

Getting in there just in time, he reached over to turn on the hot water tap while the urine splattered into the toilet bowl. He was itching down below. God only knows what he'd picked up earlier, and he needed to bathe. He needed to cleanse away a disturbing memory.

Condensation had masked the mirror above the sink, and as his fingers wiped it away, sad, sunken eyes peered back at him. They were welling with tears. Lloyd shook his head in anger, swilled the tear tracks from his cheeks, and stared back at the misty reflection. A devilish smirk gradually distorted the face as he vividly recalled the events of that previous day.

*

(16 hours earlier)
Hoots and cheers of joy echoed within the confines of the covered reception area preceding the main entrance to Pembroke Grammar School. Lots of celebratory back-slapping, handshakes, and excited squeals. Plans already in the making: what subjects to take at A-level, talk of sixth form, prestigious universities, colleges, scholarships, and degrees.

It was 'O' level results day, and they had gathered there early. Some were excited and some were nervous — the majority both. The pupils' grades had been displayed on the glass panels either side of the main door: their attainments following five years of hard labour, and the happy melee had viewed them. But, those same sad and sunken eyes that were behind the condensation on the mirror were still staring, disbelieving at his results.

They weren't spectacular, they weren't even promising — they were, as his father had quite eloquently termed it — shite! Took seven and failed seven. Not even a bloody D. All Es — E for examination-failure extraordinaire.

With legs like lead balloons, Lloyd was rooted to the spot, and his senses were dysfunctional apart from sight: the one sense he could quite happily be without at that humbling moment in time. Pete, one of the few remaining friends clinging on to the possibility that the 'old Lloyd' might return, tried consoling him, but his motivating words were muffled and incomprehensible: a million miles away.

He and a close few had watched their friend's decline, but talking to him had been a waste of effort: Lloyd knew better — recently he always did. He had become blinkered and unwilling to accept what everyone else could see, that the new influence in his life was dragging him down to the gutter.

So alone he stood, staring like a zombie at his pathetic results. A complete and utter failure of his own making, but in Lloyd's world, when the shit hit the fan, his immediate go-to defence was to apportion blame. It was always somebody else's fault. The missing senses had returned, and his heart beat like a rock breaker, but the clammy skin, the lightheadedness, and the nausea had been short-lived: swiftly replaced by an immature façade, and the pretence kicked in.

"Sod the exams — I'll resit them and do better at Christmas. I'm outta here — congratulations — see ya around."

He shoved his way through the throng of joyous celebration, and with shoulders
slumped and hands thrust deep into pockets, he slouched away from the revellers. Pete's cries of "Lloyd, Lloyd," falling on deaf ears.

"Fuck 'em — Fuck 'em all — who gives a flying fuck anyway?"

CHAPTER 6

The magnet that was The Dock Estate drew the adolescent like a mere shard of scrap metal and, like a honeybee to nectar, he scurried through the familiar labyrinth of alleyways.

Lloyd heard him before setting eyes on him: a stream of expletives, clearly audible above the barking of the obligatory mongrels and the continuous drone from the traffic on the busy road that abutted the humdrum-painted rectangles with lichen-covered roofs.

He'd not stepped inside his home before and, never knowing what to expect when he met up with him, Lloyd nervously chuckled. On turning out of the back lane, he was greeted by the sight of him, kneeling as if in prayer and flattening the daisies that poked through the cracked paving stones leading to the paint-starved door. His face was up close to the letterbox, wedged open with both hands while peering through and shouting obscenities. No doubt directed at his mother, Rose Price, and going by the gist of his demands, she was refusing to let him into the house. His mood was on the cusp of boiling over.

Sensing the approach of his latest young impressionable, his eyes veered from the letterbox and locked onto him. A heavy-lidded, dark stare probed deep into the visitor, searching and questioning. Lloyd gulped — his nervousness justified. Perhaps he should backtrack and flee like the trapped butterflies which were darting around and tapping at the lining of his gut, doing their damndest to break free.

For Mikey Price was a thug and a bully. A young man only days short of eighteen years, who had already endured two long stretches in a detention centre. A borstal sat amidst the hills on the Welsh Marches, renowned for strict discipline, bleak conditions, and tough warders. A grim and unforgiving cauldron of iniquity, founded with the aim of correcting and assisting young wrongdoers. Helping them to conform and succeed in their future lives.

This young wrongdoer was not one of their most prized examples of successful rehabilitation. He had strutted back to his little pond on both occasions with not a solitary bone in his evil skeleton showing the slightest sign of reform, and full of contempt for any concept of authority.

Borstal had succeeded in providing an education, yes, but not the desired one preached by the tough warders. Oh no, what Price had devoured was other criminal skills coming directly from the mouths of his captive peers, boasting of their sordid exploits and modus operandi while attempting to elevate their status in that very shallow end of the gene pool.

Not short and not tall, perhaps five-eight in platform boots and a quiff: the quiff more enhanced by an unusually high and steely forehead which rose from bushy brows. Mikey was dark-skinned, Romany-looking, and gossip suggested his father to be a gipsy. A bare-knuckle prizefighter who had fought to the death the champion of Irish Tinkers in one of the old Sunderland Seaplane hangars in the Dockyard. The venue was a secret. The battle was a secret, and the audience was tight-lipped and privileged. No advertising was necessary, and no tickets were necessary; they just knew and they gambled.

Folklore depicts that droves of travellers from far and beyond descended upon the former military town and wreaked havoc on one wet and windy weekend. Their caravans monopolised the car parks and spilled over onto grass verges bordering busy highways. The pubs were drunk dry, the off-licences emptied, and the supermarkets ransacked. Local police couldn't cope, and neither could the summoned reinforcements.

On the Sunday morning following the bloody contest, that same gipsy prizefighter was spotted slinking away from Rose Price's parents' house and witnessed limping through the alleyways — never to be seen again. Talk is that he met his demise shortly after, brawling in Cardiff's notorious Tiger Bay. Mikey was a bastard in more ways than the definition, and he had to be tough to survive. No doubt the early years of abuse at the hands of older bullies, constantly being the target of scorn and ridicule, were the catalyst of his viciousness. The ingredients of self-preservation, mixed together with a wicked DNA from the Romany prizefighter, and inherent genes gifted by a mother spawned from a family rich in violent antecedents, have released onto society a truly evil specimen of a human being.

What Mikey lacked in height, he compensated for with speed, agility, and outright brutality. Anything that came to hand was a weapon, but his most lethal attribute was that high forehead. It was solid, and if he didn't overpower you with lightning-fast hand speed, the head-butt would. He was locally renowned, feared by many, but to the young Lloyd — Mikey Price was intoxicating.

The thin-lipped, lithe youth signalled his recognition with a raising of the brows, a slick backward toss of his head, and a thumbs-up. His speech was slurred.

"The old slag has locked me out."

He bent towards the letterbox and raised the flap.

"Open this bastard door or I swear to God I'll smash my way in."

Mikey was as high as a tower block and stinking of whisky and dope. The remnant of a joint behind his left ear and a partly consumed bottle of Jack Daniel's alongside the daisies told the story.

The tirade continued, the grating voice increasing in volume.

"For fuck's sake, woman, I'm busting for a piss — let me in."

They heard her before seeing her, the huskiness of forty-odd fags a day unmistakably clear as she struggled to clear the rattle at the back of her throat.

"Well, how the hell can I let you in when I'm not even in the fuckin' 'ouse meself? You dozy little shit!"

Both males spun around, and there she was. Larger than life, and shuffling towards them — thighs chaffing, and laden with a couple of plastic shopping bags; their straining handles protesting under the weight of the contents.

"I could hear you bellowin' from the fuckin' Co-op. Where's your key anyway? Lost the bastard, knowing you."

Rose pushed between them, the bags knocking the two boys out of the way, before setting them down on the pavers and resting both hands on her hips. Her breathing was heavy, and a hand strayed to her forehead, brushing away beads of perspiration.

"I needs two minutes — me asthma's playin' up; that fuckin' hill gets me every time."

Wheezing, she fumbles around in the trash littering her handbag and fishes out a pack of twenty: sticks one between her lips, bites onto the filter, and fires it up with a flip-top petrol lighter. Coughing and spluttering, she turned the key in the lock and with smoke billowing from her nostrils, kicked out at the rain-swollen timber. The door groaned before juddering on its hinges and crashing to a halt against mildew-plagued Anaglypta. Shuffling into the passageway, she nods at the shopping bags and barks out a command.

"Make yourself useful for once in your miserable life: bring those fuckers in and put them on the table. I needs a piss."

The loo was next to the front door, across the passageway from the kitchen, and Mikey tried pushing past her, already unzipping.

Grabbing hold of her son by the shoulder, she yanked him back.

"And you can wait your turn, you scumbag. Where have you been all night anyway? You treats me like a fuckin' skivvy. I told you to bring those bags in and put them on the table, didn't I? Now do it. I'm not puttin' up with your shit anymore. I've had a guts full!"

Embarrassed, Mikey shoots a furtive glance towards Lloyd.

"For fuck's sake, stop nagging, woman. What's up? Didn't lover boy pay you a visit last night?"

Raising her skirt and tugging at a snagged pair of black woollen tights, she snapped back at him.

"You leave Jimmy out of this. If he'd known you were going to be AWOL all bloody night, we would have had us a party. He probably didn't turn up because of you: you're a fuckin' psycho and after a sniff of the barmaid's apron, you just want to fight anything that looks at you the wrong way!"

Mikey, his patience wearing thin, started clicking, and for a second time in as many seconds, fearsome eyes found the adolescent. Rose was undermining his street cred, and the anger was churning in the pit of his stomach; any further mocking in front of this younger boy would result in an imminent eruption. Lloyd sensed the need to defuse the situation: he could see that Mikey had clenched his fists so tight that the knuckles on his swarthy skin had turned white. Cowering away from the menacing glare, he picked up the bags and headed for the kitchen.

The toilet door was ajar, and a gushing stream of urine was pelting like a hailstorm into the ceramic bowl. Rose's head appeared in the gap, and seeing it was Lloyd, the scowl turned to a smile.

"Ta, love — put them on the table."

Her face reddened and her voice strained as she continued.

"I'll be there nnnow"

She farted.

"Ahh, better out than in — I've had a pain in me guts all mornin'."

That sudden and overt expulsion of flatulence reduced the tension. Both lads burst out laughing, and the laughter amplified as she teetered out, hoisting up her underwear and trapping her skirt in the waistband of her knickers.

Rose was nearing sixteen when Mikey Price came into this world, but the saving grace was that her mother had given birth to her when she was barely fifteen.

"I'm only following the family tradition…" she would protest and add, "…at least the age gap between mother and child is increasing."

Until recently, she'd been a good looker and could scrub up well, but all those years of hard drinking and smoking had taken their toll. Yes, Rose was still only thirty-three, well thirty-four in a couple of weeks, but the heavily lined face, the puffiness of her skin and the thinning, greying hair portrayed a much older woman. Long gone was the slim, long-legged beauty with jet-black shiny hair, voluptuous breasts and a cute backside. Not overnight and not even over a few months, it just sort of happened, you know, crept up on her.

Alcohol, tobacco, laziness, and always the wrong type of food led to what she was now: bordering on obese, with decaying teeth, and unemployed. A regular visitor to the doctor's surgery, she flitted from one no-hoper to another, and so many of her friends and neighbours were precisely the same. They knew nothing different: there wasn't a fitting role model in their community with whom to compare. All they had were the dolly birds on the TV commercials with boobs and butt jobs, their faces made up like Hiawatha, and flashing ultra-white dental veneers. Rose's peers couldn't afford such luxuries, so they overdosed on booze and fags — settling for the war paint.

Rose emptied the contents of the shopping bags onto the kitchen worktop: three packets of twenty, four flagons of strong cider, two family packs of ready salted, and two of smoky bacon. Twisting open one of the bottles, she put it to her lips, knocked back her head, and took a long swig, gulping the warm, fermented apples. Using the back of her hand to wipe away drips from her chin, she placed it across her heart,

opened her mouth wide, and belched. It echoed within the confines of the tiny kitchen, and a rotten tang filled the air as Rose held out the bottle to Lloyd and grinned.
"Here y'are luv — 'ave a swig."
Overtly he laughed but inwardly Lloyd grimaced: he was shocked. The pungent odour of Rose's fetid breath had fused in his nostrils with the stink of stale grime which was ingrained in every exposed surface, and empty food packets littered the remainder. The ashtrays were overflowing, the bin was over spilling, and unwashed crockery was immersed in a diesel-like grunge. He'd never witnessed such laziness and squalor; reality whacked him with a sledgehammer. What had he done? What a complete and utter tosser. He'd had it on a plate, but no doubt he's thrown it all away. His recent criminal and wayward behaviour, culminating with those dire examination results, had probably made sure of that certainty.
He now knew that Mikey Price had very little. Yes, he dressed well, always the latest trends, and he had a seemingly never-ending supply of cash for booze, fags, and drugs. But he had no desire to work; that word evaded his vocabulary, so crime and a couple of quid every week from the dole office paid for those necessary items to con and seduce the easily impressed.
In comparison, Lloyd has hardworking, clean-living parents, good health, not hit with the ugly stick at birth, a grammar school education, and most importantly, he is loved, cherished, and has guidance. And what has he gone and done? Jeopardised everything — probably chucked it all on the scrap heap.
Craving the cider to help block out the self-pity, Lloyd took hold of the bottle only to feel bile rising to the back of his throat as he brought it to his lips. Traces of Rose's bright red lipstick, together with her saliva, were smeared around the neck, and mother and son were watching, so how could he wipe it clean without causing offence? Rose smiled, which exposed a few remaining teeth on the bottom row, and they were rotten, heavily stained, and coated in plaque. And, where

her bright red lipstick had become detached, there was an orange hue below. He shuddered, and immediately wanted to hand the bottle back, insisting that he didn't much care for cider, but he couldn't. Mikey knew differently: they had nicked a couple of flagons from the offi just a few weeks back and sunk them at a party…

His brain was in overdrive — would a ruse work? Should he point to the window behind them and shout out, 'Who the hell is that?' Then wipe away the offensive bodily secretion while they were distracted. No chance — that was way too risky, and anyway, time was getting on.

'I'll just have to wrap my gums around the neck of the bottle and savour the bitter-sweet taste of the apples mingled with the saltiness of Rose's slobber.'

"Let's party…" she shrieked — rescuing three glass tumblers from the murky depths and wiping them in her grubby blouse. "…I fancies a smoke and some cider punch; Mikey, you can be the barman."

She glanced over at a preoccupied Lloyd: gagging and wiping away drips of cider from his chin. A wet patch just below the neck on his T-shirt, the consequence of a failed attempt to pour booze down his throat without the slobber touching his lips…

"You're probably wondering, what the hell is cider punch? Aren't you — umm — what is your name anyway? Fuck it, I likes Bruce — from now on, you are Bruce — Brucie-boy."

Cackling, she put the tumblers onto the table, ripped open the three packets of crisps and stuffed some into her mouth, spraying Lloyd with fragments as she spoke.

"Get that spliff toked up, Mikey. You got some more weed, or do we need to go knocking on Lugsey's door? Hey, Brucie-boy, you got any dosh? We're not a fuckin' charity, are we, Mikey?"

Laughing sarcastically.

"Though we do help to empty the collection boxes every now and then… Change of plan — I'll sort the drinks."

The cackling increased as she overfilled the glasses with a cocktail of cider and Jack Daniel's, slurping from each of them and leaving smudges of the two coloured lipsticks.

Mikey took the spliff from behind his ear, put it to his lips, and patted his pockets, searching for a lighter. His mother reached over Lloyd, her breasts engulfing his head, and flicked open the petrol lighter.

Mikey leant in, offered the spliff to the flame, and sucked in the psychoactive fumes, relishing the instant hit that he always got.

Rose raised a glass while the other hand mixed together the two flavoured crisps.

"Cheers, Brucie-boy, and bottoms up. Enjoy your cider punch, and when you wakes up, you'll know exactly why we calls it cider punch."

Cackling again.

"Won't he, Mikey?"

Belching, she points a finger at Lloyd — struggling to swallow before speaking.

"I tell you what, Brucie, there's no need to wait until you wakes up: I'm gonna give you the heads-up right here and now."

Tapping her knuckles on his crown.

"This skull will feel like you've been knocked out flat with a fuckin' uppercut!"

Guffawing, she downed the lot and poured more of the mind-blowing concoction into her glass.

"Give us a toke, Mikey. I feels this party comin' on."

Lloyd took a swig, wincing as the potion bit the back of his throat but savoured the warmth as it slid to his stomach. He liked it and patted the pockets of his Levi's, checking for cash to offer to get some more. He knew that he'd brought a few quid with him that morning, anticipating that he and his friends would be going off and celebrating their exam results. It never crossed his mind that he'd end up here, drowning his sorrows with Mikey and Rose Price: drinking this cider punch and smoking dope. The illicit situation was already affecting his rationality, as contrary to minutes earlier he was now pleased to be in their company instead of stuck with his boring schoolmates. He belonged here, in this environment — this is what it was all about...

"Should I pop out to the off-licence and get some more booze and crisps, Mrs Price?"

Rose gave a rasping laugh, and tickled by the grammar school boy's use of vocabulary, she winked at her son.

"We're alright for a bit, Brucie, aren't we, Mikey? And once this lot's gone, I'll 'pop' out with you, because Mr Fisticuffs here..." ruffling her son's hair, "...got banned last week for kicking off in there. Didn't you, lovely boy?"

He swats her hand away.

"Hey, watch the quiff, and get some sounds on, Mother."

Taking a long drag before handing the joint to Rose, he clicks open a silver-coloured tobacco tin.

"I'm going to roll you a 'special fucker', Brucie-boy. This spliff will blow your brains out."

Rose winks at her son again.

"I tell you what, Brucie-boy, because I'm all heart, you give me your money and I'll stock up with extras while you and Mikey are enjoying yourselves. Maybe I'll get some more weed at the same time. You don't need to worry about 'popping' out. Just sit back, have a drink, have a smoke, and glide away to a happy place."

She pinched the roach end between thumb and pokey fingertips, sucked on it for an eternity, and watched as the spliff burned hot and bright. Taking the adolescent's money from the palm of his hand, she handed him the reefer, turned away, and grinned at Mikey as the cash was slipped into her handbag. Knocking back the whisky punch, she sashayed out of the room.

The sweet smell of the cannabis had overpowered the small kitchen, and while savouring the aroma, Lloyd eagerly sucked on the lipstick-coated roach end. Gasping as the hot smoke hit the back of his throat, he savoured the taste of the cannabis mingling with the alcohol before allowing the toxins to slowly escape through his nose.

'Smoke on the water' came blasting out from the room next door, and Deep Purple's opening riff stimulated Mikey's air guitar. He assumed the stance: left boot up on a pine chair and the other firmly on the grimy honeycomb-patterned Lino. His left elbow rested on his left knee, and his hand supported the neck of the imaginary instrument. Head-banging and singing the sound of his guitar, his fingers slid up and down the fretboard while his right hand elaborately strummed the strings by the sound hole.

"Dang, dang, daang, dang, dang, dang, daaang, dang, dang, daang, dang, daang".

Lloyd was flying. High above the highest of peaks, and the reefer had been toked to the roach. He'd knocked back the cider punch and was adding more when Rose came dancing into the kitchen. The off-white blouse had been discarded, and a stained, tight-fitting vest was straining over a micro-mini skirt, glued to her thighs. She raised both arms, and they swayed above her head, unleashing masses of black hair, billowing from her armpits.

Mikey dragged the pine chair closer to the small kitchen table, and needing more space to finish rolling the promised 'special fucker,' he used his arm to clear whatever was in its path. Licking two papers and sticking them together, he lined them with tobacco and sprinkled the chosen, freshly ground resin on top.

The papers were caressed into the shape of a fat cigarette, and a small piece of cardboard, torn from the Rizla packet, was moulded into a tube and pushed into one end of the spliff. The other was pinched and sealed — ready for the burn.

Mikey handed the 'special fucker' to Lloyd and laughed.

"You toke on that mother, Brucie-Boy, and you'll find yourself right up there with the Angels."

Rose had changed the music and was swaying provocatively in front of the grammar school boy. A toothless grin stretching her face as she removed the vest and thrust her colossal breasts towards his face, teasing him with the petrol-fuelled flame of the lighter. His head was spinning, and eyes like full moons were seeing objects in a completely different light: Rose was beautiful, and when those eyes managed to focus on the flame, he was mesmerised by its vibrant colours dancing inches from her breasts. Slowly, his hand reached out, aiming for her wrist — laughing hysterically when he grasped it on the third attempt and offered the joint to the rainbow blaze. Sucking on the piece of card until the fuel sparked into life, he relished the sweetness and craved the THC-laden smoke to flood his arteries: grinning as he felt his veins tingling with the sensation of the toxins speeding to his brain. Nodding to the beat, he sang along with the band — the smoke seeping from his mouth in tandem with the lyrics. Draining the contents of the glass tumbler, he took a couple of long tokes on the joint before slumping back in the chair: finally at one with the world, Lloyd wanted the feeling to last forever.

Lazy eyes, fighting to stay open, glanced over at Mikey and through a clouded haze saw that his friend had what looked like a tube of tin foil poking out from his mouth. Frantically, it chased after and sucked in smoke, spiralling from a folded piece of tin foil, held close to his face. Below the foil and in the other hand was a flame. The smoke ceased, the flame went out, and Mikey's chin flopped to his chest — the tube still dangling from his bottom lip. His eyes were wide open, and they stared at nothing, as the foil slipped from numb fingertips and floated to mingle with the other debris littering the honeycomb-patterned linoleum.

Musical instruments blasting inside Lloyd's head were as clear as a crisp winter's day as he turned to see a grinning Rose Price dancing towards him; a full glass of whisky punch in each hand. She slurped from both before resting them on her breasts and stooped in front of him. Laboriously, he reached out to grab a glass, and the vision of amber-coloured liquid overflowing and pooling in her cleavage was the last thing he would remember...

*

The boy's breathing was laboured; his mouth as arid as the Saharan sands, and his lips so dry that they had welded together. Generating moisture in the gums by clearing his throat and circulating saliva like a mouthwash, he was able to prise them open with his tongue; flinching as thin layers of skin separated and bled.

He had been comatose but was now semi-conscious and feeling hot, sweaty, and thirsty as hell. A stale, unwashed stench filtered through congested nostrils, and in an attempt to clear the blockage, he sniffed and choked.

'Phwoar, what the hell is that smell?'

While struggling to breathe solely through his mouth, something that was attached to him moved and murmured. The pang of fear that gripped him sent his heart racing, thudding against his rib cage, and the boy, too scared to open his eyes, hoped that he was dreaming. He wasn't — it moved again — releasing an even stronger, rank whiff. Somebody or something was lying in front of him, and they were locked together like spoons. His arm was around its unclothed waist, and he was cupping a flabby breast: the nipple trapped between his middle fingers where they met at the palm.

His eyelids sprung open, but it was too dark in the room to see, so he lay there, frozen rigid: too frightened to take another breath.

Where was he? Who was she? More importantly — what had they done?

Lloyd's drug-fuddled memory kicked into gear, and the realisation whacked him full on.

'No, oh no — please God — NO!'

Naked and busting for a piss, he had no choice but to move. Gently releasing the nipple, he eased his arm from between the folds of clammy flesh, wrestled himself free from her mass, shifted onto his back and paused to listen to her breathing: she was fast asleep. He rolled out of bed and tip-toed, arms outstretched, towards a faint shaft of light sneaking under the bedroom door. Rose murmured again, and he froze in midstride.

'Don't you wake up — please don't wake up.'

He slowly, robotically, turned his head in time to see her shimmy across like a beached whale onto the recently vacated warm patch.

Shuddering with disbelief and flinching as he licked the saltiness of the blood from his lips, Lloyd monitored the mammal as he slowly turned the handle.

'Please don't creak — please don't creak.'

The bathroom was in front of him, across the landing; the door was ajar, and the light was on. He checked his wristwatch, and it brutally told him that it was half past midnight.

'Shit, shit, shit.'

He was definitely in the deepest of shit. By the time he ran the five or six miles home, it would be nearing 2 a.m. Anxiety attacked him with the pace of a tsunami as the stored-away memory of his dire examination results battled through the hangover, and both hands shot to his forehead. Fingers gripped the hair that had strayed over his eyes, and he forced it back to the crown, punishing himself by digging the tips into his skull.

"What the hell is wrong with me?"

Shame and dread had overwhelmed him; his thoughts dominated by what his parents must be going through and the inevitable rollocking that awaited him.

The stillness of the night was broken by the sounds of deep breathing coming from the bedroom alongside the bathroom, suggesting that Mikey was in there, and going by the racket, well and truly outers. The boy pushed the door into the room and directly in front of him, minus a seat, was the toilet pan. Sticking up from the securing holes were bent brass fixings and a quick glance to its left located the broken seat: stashed behind a wire-meshed bin crammed with tissues and used sanitary towels.

Pointing it in the right direction, he sighed as urine drained from a fully stretched bladder and splattered into the limescale-stained bowl. It was while he was aiming the hot torrent at a dubious-looking furry deposit, left high and dry above the waterline, that he spotted it and froze.

"Oh my god — I've been bleeding — it's plastered in blood — what the hell has happened?"

Panicking, he wiped at it with trembling fingers, interfering with the flow, which caused the urine to miss the bowl and spray the contents of the wire-meshed bin. Stooping to scrutinise his manhood, he realised that it wasn't blood, and his heart sank to an all-time low as he shook his head in disbelief.

"No, no, no — it can't be."

Lloyd had seen and tasted it earlier — orange and red lipstick...

CHAPTER 7

(The Christening)
Several weeks later.
"Phyllis Doris," proclaimed the King.
He punched the air triumphantly and crowed as if announcing the dawn of a brand-new day. Puffing out his chest, he clenched his fists as tightly as a bare-knuckle boxer's and swaggered around the stuffy, dingy portakabin like a randy cockerel showing off to attract a brand-new mate. White blobs of spittle had gathered and dried in the corners of his mouth: a result of overexcitement and blabbing too much.
The other police cadets were falling about laughing, which fuelled the King's fervour, and the crowing increased, resonating within the confines of the temporary office. It was as if the largest of bass drums was being pummelled by the largest of beings, and the sound was confined and deafening.
Finding himself surrounded by a ring of wound-up adolescents, Lloyd slouched and fidgeted uncomfortably on a plastic-moulded office chair that had been somehow carried and tugged into the centre of the room.
'Who the hell was this Phyllis Doris anyway?'
He was riled and pissed off at the way he'd been treated. More significantly, he was gutted because, within two minutes of him being there, his carefully prepared plan had gone to rat shit. So much for keeping a low profile, blending into the

background, and being Mr Bloody Nobody. So much for not bringing any unwarranted attention to himself. Bloody hell, here he was, sitting in the middle of every single one of the new intake, and he was the absolute centre of their attention. His face and neck were on fire, burning the colour of a summer sunset, and he was gnawing at his bottom lip like a beaver with a toothache.

Why did he do that when he was wound up? God only knows, but he couldn't stop himself. And he was battling his inner self not to spring from the chair and punch the cockerel's bloody lights out. The Demon inside him was wrong, Lloyd was telling it.

'I can't. If I get done for scrapping on my first day as a police cadet, it will be curtains for me as far as my dad is concerned. Especially if I get chucked out. Bloody hell, it would be World War 3 if I'm sent home with a letter. Can you imagine it?'

Dear Mr Davies,

We are so sorry to have to inform you that you are in fact correct. Your son, Lloyd, is indeed a selfish, egotistical waste of space, and no way will he ever be a police officer.

We suggest banishment to the coal mines, as you threatened. Never to see the light of day again.

Kind regards,

A.N.Other Copper

No, he had to sit and take whatever shit was being chucked at him by this cadet they call the King and not retaliate. He wanted to prove to his father that he could do this, but most importantly, he had to prove it to himself. He had to rid himself of the label that had been pinned to his forehead like a winner's rosette on Derby Day. Not that he'd won anything, had he? His rosette was for being a selfish, egotistical waste of space.

It was his mother's fault that he was in this predicament. Now, I know what you're thinking, typical of Lloyd — blame somebody else. But it's true. She was the one who had come up with the name. And less than two minutes ago, he had to reveal to the King and the other cadets that he'd been saddled with a middle name more associated with the fairer sex. And why was that, you might ask? Because, and I know you are not going to believe this, there were two cadets with the name of Lloyd Davies. And the other? Well, he just didn't happen to have a middle one...

As long as Lloyd could recall, he had been embarrassed, ashamed even, to divulge the name to anyone. It didn't exist, but it did. And it had been the cause of many a schoolyard scrap since his first day as a five-year-old. Hell, man, he'd lost his incisors before the age of six, battling with a boy two years his senior.

He dreaded the daily reading out of the school register, closely followed by the inevitable piss-taking that he had to suffer. That old dragon, Miss Watkins, a frumpy, rotund woman with lank, dark hair straggling over her shoulders, would pause after receiving the whine of, "Present, Miss Watkins", from the lips of the always sickly Elaine Damon. She'd then peer at him distastefully over round, thick-rimmed, thick-lensed reading glasses perched on the edge of her nose and with a wry grin slowly read out his name in full; with an emphasis on his middle one. Why would she do that? She knew what would follow...

It didn't bother him that he'd lost his two front teeth, and he didn't give a toss that he sometimes lisped: that impediment was just complimentary to his excitable, nervous stutter and inability, no, downright laziness, to pronounce the letters T H at the start of a word. What bothered him most was his mother's idea to christen him Lloyd HILARY Davies.

"What the hell?"

No thought had gone into the unimaginable trauma that her younger son would endure by naming him after her sister and brother.

"Let's mash Hilda and Harry together, Trev."

Thank the Lord his dad didn't stamp his foot down and insist that they mash his sister and brother's names together — Faye and Danny...

So, within the first few minutes of the very first day of his new, straight life, his plan to remain incognito had been well and truly blown out of the water. His dodgy middle name, which for years he'd denied the existence, had been revealed to all and sundry, and to top it all, he'd been re-christened with another girl's name. Phyllis Doris!

'Who the hell is Phyllis Doris?'

"Do a runner," hissed the Demon. "You don't have to put up with this shit. Go on, leg it."

He couldn't — where would he go? Strength of character is what is required. Not to run away from the very first uncomfortable moment he faced. Running wasn't even an option: he had to succeed and prove the doubters wrong. He had to prove it to his father.

The Demon piped up again.

"And how the hell does Lloyd HILARY Davies think he can succeed? How can he, of all people, be a copper? You're a fucking crook! You're bent. A thieving druggie. You're the type of person these laughing policemen want to chase around, capture, and put behind bars. You and Mikey Price have done shit loads. Hell man, you were the fucking brains! Okay, you were never caught and on paper, you're squeaky clean. But you're not, are you? Mr fucking Police Cadet, ha ha, that's a joke. You're a criminal yet to be caught, and now your feeble plan has gone pear-shaped. Very soon, Lloyd, someone is going to start digging, and your association with Price will be unearthed. You should have gone down the pits and coughed your guts up in the dark, digging out coal in the dust and filth."

The onset of silence, broken only by the dragging of a plastic chair to within a hair's breadth of his knees, snapped Lloyd out of the trance. The King had straddled the seat, leaned towards his prey, and rested his arms on the backrest. The circle of boys and girls closed in — they weren't going to miss a thing.

Sweaty hands struggled to grip the tubular supports of the chair, and as Lloyd's senses heightened, the warning bells tolled.

'This isn't going to be pleasant, mate. So whatever happens, don't let go of this bloody chair, and don't do anything you'll regret and fret over for the rest of your life.'

The gnawing at the bottom lip increased, and he could taste the blood seeping from the bruising as his breathing suddenly shallowed. Deep down, he knew that this was all going to end in tears.

The King's face flushed a dark purply red, and beads of sweat dotted his forehead, stretching to the bridge of his nose. Brown, bordering on black eyes, stood out on stalks like a love-struck cartoon character spotting his beau for the very first time, and the spittle in the corners of his mouth had doubled in size, resembling two pieces of Wrigley's stored in readiness for a future chew.

A mischievous smile broke out as he reached over and placed two fingers under Lloyd's chin, raising his head until they had direct eye contact. And in a broad South West Wales accent, the King softly whispered.

"You don't know who the hell Phyllis Doris is, do you, Lloyd HILARY Davies?"

The over-emphasis on Hilary hit a nerve, and the Demon screamed inside the youngster's head.

"Nut him! He's taking the piss. Go on, you weakling, nut him!"

The King's jet-black, wavy hair glistened with sweat, and in the darkness of his eyes, Lloyd could clearly see Miss Watkins. She was back to haunt him, leering, laughing, and goading.

"Hilary, Hilary, Hilary."

The Demon was screeching inside his head.

"Nut him, nut him, nut him!"

Lloyd tightened his grip. Sweat was oozing between the fingers, and his knuckles, devoid of any blood, were now his last line of defence.

"Phyllis Doris is famous, you know."

The King's accent was exaggerated and camp, inciting more hoots of laughter from the others.

"For fuck's sake, Lloyd," nagged the Demon, "Are you a man or a worm? Look at them. They are all laughing at you. Do something about it — nut him!"

Lloyd flushed, and a river of sweat ran down his back as his heart hammered away at his chest — trying its best to break its way to freedom.

The King fanned Lloyd's face with his open palm, grinning and relishing the moment.

"Nervous are you, Phyllis Doris? Or is it — phew — extra hot in here?"

He leaned in closer and shrieked.

"Phyllis Doris is a woman!"

Putting both fists inside his shirt, he pushed them out at chest level towards Lloyd's face.

"A woman played by a man with massive bazookas."

The outburst of laughter clanged inside Lloyd's head, taunting and ridiculing him. In the King's dark pools, he could clearly see the old dragon doing the backstroke; her hands clapping like a performing seal's flippers above her head, and she was laughing and leering.

"Hilary, Hilary, Hilary."

The Demon changed tact and spoke softly. Just like his father had done during the early hours of that life-changing morning, and yet again, the words were succinct, clear, and chilling.

"For fuck's sake, son, put an end to this pantomime and nut the fucker!"

And he did — just like Mikey had taught him. His last line of defence was released from their vice-like grip, and his neck muscles, pumped up with blood, were tightened. He propelled his head forward with the ferocity of a black mamba, and the King didn't stand a chance. His only saving grace from permanent disfigurement was the slight backward motion he had already commenced, and that minuscule movement prior to impact nullified a stationary target. Fortunately, it lessened the consequence.

The King crumpled to the floor, and Lloyd, his self-control smashed to bits, pounced on top of him. They wrestled on the linoleum, arms flailing and blood gushing — the watchers screaming.

"King, King, King."

The door burst open, swung on its hinges, and crashed against the adjacent woodchip-papered wall. The stunned Training Sergeant, his feet trapped as if set in concrete, stood in the doorway, and his formidable bulk blacked out the bright autumn sunlight that had briefly crept in. The banging noise caused by the door's impact echoed around the room, and on its return, it slammed against the officer's left shoulder, bringing him back to his senses.

The bloody carnage that had greeted the ex-military police officer had brought back memories of wild fracas in the N.A.A.F.I. during foreign manoeuvres. But never before had he witnessed such a scene on home soil. Never before on his hallowed turf.

Police Sergeant Evan Peters, a giant of a man to those rookie cops, gulped, his eyes wide, struggling to process what was happening before them. He thought carefully in his native tongue before translating the Welsh into English, and the two sentences boomed methodically from his lips: a tremor noticeable in his voice.

"What the hell is going on in here, you bunch of miserable half-wits? I could hear you halfway down the road."

Immediately there was silence, and shocked, frightened faces stared back at him: including the two wrestlers who were still entangled — their faces and clothing plastered in blood.

A trembling hand pointed an index finger.

"You pair of hoodlums — pack it in!"

The finger motioned to the doorway, and his eyes glared as they focused on the others.

"And you lot — get outside and line up. How can you even think of becoming keepers of the Queen's peace if you behave in this way? You were acting like a frenzied mob at a bloody cock fight!"

A forlorn bunch with heads bowed to the floor, their eyes shying away from those of the sergeant's, squinted at the sudden brightness as they scuttled into the sunlight. The supervisor, still shaking his head in disbelief, was studying the two adversaries.

'Yes, both faces were bloodied, but only Robert King appeared to have a cut. Lloyd Davies had questionable reddening to the middle of his forehead, and the position of the wound suggested the cause to be a clashing together of heads.'

He shivered, his skin suddenly cold and dotted with goosebumps — his breathing shallow.

'I hope to God that injury was accidental.'

The gash to the bridge of his nose, the early signs of swelling, and the discolouration beneath both eyes were clear to see as the dishevelled Robert King tucked his shirt into his trousers and gingerly edged past the supervisor. He spoke with a slight lisp as he cheekily grinned and attempted a wink.

"Just a bit of fun, Sarge — no harm done. Getting to know each other — you know — bonding."

The ex-Welsh Guardsman sniffed his lungs full of air, and his eyes widened with rage. He bellowed his response, and the King was the first to feel the training sergeant's size twelve connect with their backside.

"You want to bond, do you, King? I'll give you bonding. Now, wipe that bloody dribble away from the corners of your gob and get in line."

Fidgeting with his trousers and head bowed, Lloyd followed, but his attempt to squeeze past the training sergeant was thwarted. The uniformed officer's arm shot out, blocked the escape route, and tugged the Cadet back into the gloom of the temporary office — slamming the door behind them to shelter from the mob's prying eyes.

They stood in silence, the supervisor's eyes never straying from the crown of the boy's head as he recalled the cadet-assessment days.

'This lad was promising: very bright and athletic. He flew through the tests and was more than capable, but what had been driving him? And why hadn't he mixed with any of his peers?'

He and the head of training, Chief Inspector Ann Lewis, had commented on that observation and discussed him at length. The background checks proved him to be of good stock and nothing was known criminally, but why was he such a loner?

Coming to the conclusion that he might be withdrawn because of nerves, maybe a tad shy, and possibly the trauma of the occasion getting to him, they had decided to give him the benefit of the doubt. Anxiousness overwhelmed the Sergeant, and he gulped.

'Could they have been wrong?'

He was still pondering what to do when he addressed the Cadet.

"Don't you have anything to say to me, boy? I've allowed you this time to reflect, and it's disappointing that you haven't come up with an explanation to account for your behaviour."

Lloyd raised his head, and his eyes met with those of the sergeant. The precious few seconds had been wisely used, but not to formulate an explanation for the violence: oh no, he'd been formulating words that might help salvage his immediate existence in the police force, and they rolled off the tip of his tongue.

"I'm very sorry, Sergeant, for my behaviour. I have let you and my parents down. I will apologise to the cadet and to all the others for getting them into trouble. Please give me a chance to prove myself. I promise I won't let you down again."

Evan Peters had been around the block too many times to be bamboozled by verbal diarrhoea, but the response did bring a momentary smile to his lips. Maybe it was the boy's quick thinking and guile that swayed the supervisor's thoughts.

'Give him a chance, Peters. Don't make a rash decision; do a bit of detective work and dig around. A discreet enquiry here and another one there. See what you can come up with. First off, you best speak with all the witnesses to the skirmish...'

He opened the door to the sunlight and, for the benefit of the watchers, he bellowed as was expected of a once-proud drill instructor.

"Join the other reprobates, Police Cadet Davies."

Leaning in close, his breath hot against the Cadet's ear, the training Sergeant whispered the last words that Lloyd wanted to hear.

"I'm watching you, boy."

CHAPTER 8

The picture postcard vista from the office window set it apart from the others dotted along the length of the spartan corridor in Police Headquarters. Yes, it had regulation carpet, regulation decor, and regulation furniture, but the sight of the River Towy meandering through the lowlands of Carmarthen was a stress buster, and the Training Sergeant was in dire need of such relieving therapy following the morning's antics.
He was troubled, burdened with anxiety, and worryingly, similar emotions had recently begun to invade his body more frequently. Absentmindedly, he was gazing at the indigenous swans, gliding with the tide on the slow-moving water towards the estuary, when a knock at the half-open door startled him, and bleary eyes picked out the visitor: the sole reason for this latest turmoil.
Forcing a smile, the Sergeant sat back in the chair and his left hand beckoned him to enter.
"Come on in, Lloyd, or should I say, Phyllis Doris?"
The attempt at humour failed to lighten the moment, and slouching awkwardly, the Cadet shuffled to the centre of the room — inadvertently blocking the Sergeant's view. Convinced that he was finished, he struggled to make eye contact and stood with rounded shoulders and his arms hanging limply by his sides. Why else would Sergeant Peters summon him if that wasn't the case? He'd seen him chatting with the others

earlier, and it didn't require the intelligence of Einstein to deduce from their furtive glances in his direction that he was the topic of the conversation. Rob King was the last cadet to be questioned, and the Sergeant had spent an age with him before it all seemed to die a natural death. Then suddenly, out of the blue, he got a message to immediately report to the Training Department. This was the moment of truth, the end of the line: he knew it.

The tired eyes studied the boy, and inwardly the Sergeant sighed; he had decided on a course of action, but would it come back and bite him on the bum? The lad was no doubt a stomach ulcer generator, yet there was something about him. Something that grabbed your eye, but was it enough to give him another chance?

He had kept the skirmish to himself, possibly putting his career on the line, but rightly or wrongly, that was what he had decided to do. He'd uncovered the bravado giving rise to the outcome and could understand the youngster snapping, but what he couldn't get his head around was the use of such extreme violence. Fortunately, there were no broken bones, and though at the time there appeared to be a lot of blood, the cut to Robert King's nose was superficial. At least, that's what the Sergeant had recorded on the incident report. He hadn't mentioned the head butt: as far as he was concerned, he couldn't recall that ever being said to him. He was under the impression that it was merely a clash of heads. Anyway, he'd done what he needed to do: used his discretion, and once this upcoming rollicking was over and done with, he'd file the report away. Hopefully, never to see the light of day again.

He raised his voice.

"Stand up straight, boy — that's it. Force your shoulders back and brace yourself. Arms rigid by your sides, stand tall and bloody hell, boy, look me in the eye!"

The Cadet had jumped to the commands — his back ramrod straight — his body quivering.

'This was it — he was a goner.'

The voice lowered in decibels.

"You have got everything going for you, Lloyd. You're a good looker, quick-thinking, athletic, and bright. The ideal template for me to hone into being a bloody good copper. That thick mass of blond hair stands you out in a crowd, and people's eyes are drawn to you. But you have to make sure that you are noticed for the right bloody reasons: not because you're a bloody hoodlum. Do you understand, boy? Say, 'Yes, Sergeant.'"

The Cadet gave the requested reply and, realising he wasn't going to be kicked out, he perked up and closed his eyes — forcing back the tears.

"Open those bloody eyes and listen to me, boy. I want your full attention. You have had your last chance. Your get-out-of-jail-free card has been gobbled up before you even reached The Old Kent Road, and there are no more cards where that came from. Do you understand? What do you say to me, boy?"

Lloyd repeatedly swallowed in an attempt to control his emotions, but his voice still quivered.

"Yes, Sergeant."

"Right — no more bloody shenanigans — from now on, you will be squeaky clean. You will go back to your new buddies and you will gel with them. Go out of your way to fit in and prove my faith in you to be warranted. Do you understand, boy?"

A deep sigh escaped.

"Yes, Sergeant, and thank you, Sergeant. I won't let you down."

CHAPTER 9

The Cadet Hut was a grey-coloured Portakabin sited on a grassed bank just off the private access road to the rear yard where all the police vehicles were either garaged or parked overnight.
Access was via a concrete step, and the interior was scantily furnished: black moulded plastic chairs, several Formica-topped tables, and a notice board screwed to the back wall. Every woodchip wall-papered surface was painted magnolia, and three small windows were the only source of natural light; having to battle entry through abused, damaged, and lob-sided Venetian blinds.
The only bright aspect was Gloria, and she took pride of place perched on one of the plastic chairs in the corner, to the left of the notice board. Her blond hair, always immaculate, was cropped close to her scalp, and she wore no clothes. Yes, she was completely naked apart from a beautiful, welcoming smile. At some time or another, all the cadets would eagerly press their lips up against that smile only to be filled with disappointment and later grumble that they had found her to be cold and unresponsive. Gloria was the first aid dummy, and her name originated several years ago following a snappy wisecrack made by a previous cadet, now a serving officer. He'd casually mentioned that Gloria reminded him of his ex-girlfriend: she too had been cold and unresponsive, but came

back to life when you massaged her chest...

Lloyd took a deep breath. He'd rehearsed his grovelling speech and had decided to blurt it out as soon as he stepped in through the door. He needn't have bothered: the others didn't give him a second glance. Two pieces of A4 had been tacked with red-coloured glass-headed pins to the cork veneer insert of the notice board, and the cadets were jostling to get a view: the papers listed their lodgings and roommates.

The other Lloyd Davies stood steadfast in the middle of the melee, and shoulders like a lumberjack hogged the prime position. His eyes were riveted to his name, hoping that by staring at it for long enough the information would change — it didn't.

He spun around and breached the cluster like a tank cutting through a thicket, and without altering his gaze grabbed a bursting-to-the-seams hold-all and strode towards the open door. The brusque tone of his voice highlighted his anger and disappointment.

"You're with me, Phyllis. Come on, I know the way."

Not another murmur passed his lips before stepping from the office, turning right and disappearing from view. That curt outburst hadn't gone unnoticed, and all remaining eyes turned and fixed on the violent one: the Cadet now known as Phyllis. What will be his reaction?

The boy shrugged his shoulders and opened out his arms; his wrists and hands outstretched.

"What the hell was that all about? What's his problem? I've never even spoken to the guy, apart from hello."

There was no response, nobody cared, and relieved eyes, thankful that they didn't have to share with the troubled one, were back scrutinising the notice board.

Needing confirmation, Phyllis pushed through to the front, and there it was, typed in black on white, fourth line down.

Lloyd DAVIES and Lloyd Hilary DAVIES — 38, Upper Water Street — Mrs Edith Jones.

'Shit — that's all he needed.'

He shook his head in frustration. Not a lot of thought had gone into that allocation, had it? Alphabetical order had obviously been employed, but come on, two persons with the same bloody name. And one of them has just made it quite clear how he felt about the future living arrangements.

Glassy eyes sought out a friendly face as he chewed on his thumbnail, but there wasn't one, and why would there be? Nobody wanted to know him, and who could blame them after the stunt he'd just pulled? Feeling a tap on the shoulder, he spun around, and it was a grinning Robert King; a dressing was covering the wound, and his hand was outstretched.

"You're still with us then?"

Phyllis gratefully shook it, instantly feeling the relief whizzing through his body; the pressure around his heart was no more, and a smile broke out, stretching the worry lines.

"Yep, Rob, looks like you're stuck with me for a bit longer…"

He opened his arms out to him.

"I'm sor…"

The King spoke over him.

"It's done and dusted, pal. Forget about it, and we'll start again."

He managed a wink, "Phyllis."

Nervous eyes had been fixed on the coming-together-again of the two adversaries, and everything appeared to be hunky-dory. The tension in the room was no more.

All Phyllis had to do now was win over his roommate.

*

He caught sight of him a fair way down the back lane leading towards the town centre and broke into a jog to make up some of the distance.

"Hey Lloyd, everything alright? You don't seem too pleased to be sharing with me. What's the problem?"

The cadet didn't turn around but spoke as he carried on striding away.

"I'm fine."

"Oh, okay. So you know where the lodgings are then, Lloyd? I

didn't even take note of the address or the couple's names?"
Carrying on walking, the larger of the cadets gave a knowing laugh.
"Well, that's because there's a huge difference between you and me. That's why I know exactly where we are going, and you haven't got a bloody clue. And, there is no couple, it's a Mrs Edith Jones."
Phyllis didn't bother to answer him — what was the point? He'd win him over soon enough, probably with pure charm and bullshit. That's it, that's the solution, baffle him with bullshit, and maybe a few shavings of blow on top of his muesli mightn't go amiss either. He started to laugh...
The larger boy stopped abruptly, turned, and dropped his bag at his feet. His face was bright red, his arms outstretched, and his eyes bulged with rage.
"I don't find it funny. Why did I have to draw the bloody short straw? I don't want to share with someone like you. Nobody did. That's it — I've said it."
Phyllis dropped his bag, copying the boy's stance, and they faced each other like a Western shoot-out.
"Hey, what do you mean, someone like me? What exactly is someone like me?"
Beads of sweat were breaking out on the larger boy's forehead.
"You're violent! I saw what you did to Rob King, and I shouldn't be sharing with you because you shouldn't even be here. You should have been kicked out. How the hell did you get away with it? You're different from me, and from the people that I'm used to being with, and, well, you make me feel uncomfortable."
Phyllis's anxiety was at bursting point, and once more he attacked the bruising on the inside of his bottom lip. Nibbling away at it and struggling to curtail the aggression that could erupt at any time if things didn't go right for him. This all started when he got involved with Mikey Price. The drugs, the alcohol, the violence, and the crime had turned him into a raving, bloody lunatic. Cannabis abuse can lead to paranoia

and anxiety: he'd read about it in the local library. It was a vicious circle. If he had a joint now, it would relax him, well, not even relax him, it would just make him feel better for a short while, but once the effects wore off, he would feel like shit again. Much worse than he had felt before the toxins had invaded his body. Still, he doubted Lloyd partook in a toke to take the edge off things. By the look of him, he was more of your ten pints and a few packets of pork scratchings type of lad. Maybe this is what he needed? Perhaps it would do him good to be around someone steadfast like Lloyd. Maybe it would sort out his fucked-up head and get him back onto the straight and narrow. Yes, he had to win Lloyd over and also charm Mrs Edith Jones: if he could get the pair of them onside, he was halfway to succeeding. He needed to fight the aggression, conjure up some inner strength, and dupe his soon-to-be roommate into believing that he cared. Acting was now normal to him. A draining daily occurrence of pretence, purporting to be somebody he wasn't. Who was the real Lloyd Hilary Davies anyway? Hell, it didn't matter now, did it? He was Phyllis, and maybe that was a good thing — a fresh name and a fresh start.

He picked up his bag, softened his voice, and edged closer.

"Lloyd, there are no excuses. I shouldn't have nutted Rob King; I was way out of order, and for that, I'm truly sorry. Rob and I have shaken hands, and the others seem okay about it. Perhaps you and I can move on as well? I want to be your friend, Lloyd. We're the same age, and we want the same outcome: to keep this job and do well. So what is the point in at least not trying, eh? What do you say?"

A wrought iron and slatted wooden bench had been bolted to the pavement close to The Falcon Hotel; Lloyd turned away, strolled the few steps to it, and sat down. Gazing up at the War Memorial on the island in the middle of the wide and busy one-way street, he blinked rapidly, managing to stop any tears from pooling, before turning to face his new roommate.

"I need this job — it's my dream job. All my life, that's all I've ever wanted — to be a policeman. You know, to help others and to catch the bad guys."

Phyllis gulped — taken aback by that information.

'Bloody hell, is he for real? Is that what the others want as well?'

"I come from a quiet, Welsh-speaking village not far from Cardigan, and I'm nervous about sharing with someone like you because you are nothing like me…"

He bowed his head to the pavement, then turned away towards the Picton Monument; struggling to curtail the emotion in his voice.

"…We are completely different and we have completely different wants out of life."

Phyllis sat down next to him, his hold-all, like Lloyd's, resting on the pavement between his legs. Directly opposite was a fish and chip restaurant, and it had bright red moulded plastic tables and chairs set close to a picture window. Probably for diners to watch the world go by while stuffing their faces with haddock and crispy chips. The tables were redundant, but the queue for the takeaway had spilt outside onto the street. Phyllis watched them for a while, hoping for some inspiration, and he got it.

"Lloyd, you don't know me. Hell, man, we've only just clapped eyes on each other, and yet you are surmising for some reason or another that I don't want the same as you do. How the hell do you know what I want? I don't even know what I want for myself in the future, so how could you possibly know? At this very moment, I want to be your friend and to take every day as it comes. See what happens."

He pointed over to the chippy.

"Those people waiting over there to be served are a good example: guaranteed they'll have different choices. What is that guy in the black duffle coat going to order, Lloyd? Is it cod and large chips? Steak and onion pie and mushy peas, or is he ordering for the family? Maybe Monday is a chippy day; a day that they all look forward to. Sitting down with a takeaway supper on their knees and watching Blue Peter on the telly. So come on, Lloyd, what's it going to be? What is that man's choice from the menu this evening?"

Lloyd was salivating.

"I don't know. How the hell am I supposed to know, Phyllis? I'm not a bloody clairvoyant, am I? If it were me, I'd have steak and kidney pie, two battered sausages, maybe a rissole, mushy peas, large chips, extra gravy, and two slices of bread and butter to mop it up — oh, and curry sauce, if they've got it."

'Bloody hell,' thought Phyllis, surreptitiously eyeing him up and down; mentally noting not to leave his plate unattended in Mrs Jones's house. Swallowing, he regained some composure before continuing.

"So, you don't know what he wants. Do you know what I would order? What would I want, Lloyd?"

The larger cadet sniffed, splaying his arms in front of him before answering.

"No, of course not, how could I? I just said, didn't I? I'm not a bloody clairvoyant: how could I possibly know what he wants or what you would want?"

Phyllis raised his arms to the sky.

"Precisely my point, Lloyd. You don't know what I would want. So how can you say that we have different wants? I'd probably want the same as you."

He paused to watch the ever-lengthening queue; licking his lips as he slipped a hand into the straps on his hold-all.

"Yes, Lloyd, my order would be exactly the same as yours."

Sniffing the air, he tapped his new friend on the thigh.

"What a bloody gorgeous smell, and I'm starving. Come on, mate, show me the way to our digs, and we'll see if this Mrs Edith Jones can rustle up something that tastes half as good as the smell coming from that fish and chip shop."

CHAPTER 10

Wanting everything to be just right for her new guests, Edith Jones was both excited and anxious; she couldn't suppress her emotions, though, and the warmth of her greeting, together with her bubbly personality, instantly settled any concerns that the two adolescents might have had. Sparkling eyes saying: 'Welcome, come on in and make yourselves at home,' filled the two boys with a feeling of belonging as they followed their landlady up to their room.
"I suppose you two are starving?..." pointing over to the bathroom, "...freshen up if you want — your towels are on the beds. Settle in and come downstairs when you're ready. I'll be dishing out in about 20 minutes. Sausages and mash, I hope you like that. Oh, and one other thing — it's going to be very confusing having two Lloyds in the same house. Do you have any middle names? A nickname, maybe?"

*

Their room was large enough, with a sash window that overlooked the back garden. Beneath the window was a small chest of drawers, and two single beds, separated by a cabinet, were up against the opposite wall; a small wardrobe was crammed into the corner at the foot of one of the beds, which faced you as the door opened into the room.
Perfect for what they needed. The house was spotless and warm — somewhere to get their heads down, wash, and eat.

Lloyd was drooling, his nose twitching.

"Come on, Phyllis, she's right, I am bloody starving: how the hell did she know that? I bet it's ready now, and if it tastes as good as it smells, then this place is bloody paradise."

"Before we go down, Lloyd, there's one thing bugging me and you've got to tell me — who the hell is Phyllis Doris?"

Lloyd fell back onto his bed laughing.

"Haven't you heard of Ryan and Ronnie? The Welsh double act with their own TV show? They're famous."

Phyllis shook his head: he didn't have a clue. Probably because he'd been too wrapped up in terrorising the locals and being a petty criminal with Mikey Price.

"They have a sketch where Ryan is in drag and he plays the mother of the house. Ronnie is Ryan's husband and they have a daughter called Phyllis Doris. She is always referred to as: 'that brazen hussy'."

Lloyd sees the look of horror on his roommate's face and starts laughing again.

"Rob King got it wrong though. He thought Phyllis Doris was played by a man in drag, but she's not. Phyllis Doris is played by an actual woman."

The inside of the Cadet's lips is taking another battering, and he shakes his head, determination etched on his face.

"Well, I promise you this, Lloyd. It's not going to last: Doris has already bitten the dust, so Phyllis will soon follow. I've been battling with Hilary all my life: the last thing I need now is another girl's name. You wait and see, Lloyd — mark my words. You just wait and see."

Lloyd didn't answer; he knew better. The nickname would probably stick forever.

*

Nearing the bottom of the stairs, Lloyd spotted a silhouette on the other side of the autumn leaf-patterned glass door, which opened into the kitchen. He stopped abruptly, causing his roommate to career into his backside and curse.

"What the f-ing hell have you stopped for?"

Lloyd turned to him, pointing and mouthing.

"Look, she's in there — doing something."

Phyllis copied the mouthing and whispered.

"Where the hell did you think she was going to be, Lloyd? She's cooking our bloody grub."

The larger boy flushed, unsure of what to do.

"Well, should we knock or just go straight in?"

Phyllis shrugged his shoulders, also unsure; his eyes now fixed on the silhouette.

"I don't know. Is there a bell or something?"

Lloyd raised his voice.

"A bell! Why would she have a bloody bell?"

"Shhhhhh!"

The forefinger shot up to Phyllis's lips, and the whispering increased in volume.

"I don't know. Perhaps we should just go straight in then."

With eyes set on the human shape, the adolescents eased down the remaining steps to the hall, and Phyllis started searching a console table which was between the autumn leaves and another door. Above it was an ornate brass, oval-shaped mirror.

On top of the table was a telephone, some ornaments, and a framed family photograph. Lloyd was watching and shaking his head.

"What the hell are you looking for?"

Phyllis looked up at him.

"I don't know, perhaps there's one of those little brass bells that you ring and shout out…"

He mimicked the voice of a posh aristocratic butler.

"… 'Dinner is served' — or maybe a sign saying, 'please knock before entering'."

Lloyd started to giggle, covering his mouth to stop the outburst of laughter. The same finger moved to Phyllis's lips, but the 'shhhhhh' turned into a guffaw and they huddled in the hallway next to the glass door, their faces reddening with the emotion.

'Ring, ring, ring.' The telephone was loud and shrill.

"Arghh", they screeched, jumping in shock.

The door on the other side of the console table opened, and into the hall appeared Mrs Jones.

"Arghh", they screeched again; stepping back towards the stairs. One eye on Mrs Jones and the other on the human shape that was still moving around in the kitchen.

Watching the two lads in the mirror, she was chuckling as she picked up the handset, and her tone of voice had an energy about it as she spoke.

"Hello Carmarthen 2149, Mrs Edith Jones speaking."

The sound of a gruff, male voice growled something which was inaudible to the cadets, and the sparkle in their landlady's eyes was gone. She swallowed, trying to rid the upset before speaking.

"Oh, hi Andy, how are you?"

Other inaudible words could be overheard from the male person, and a sadness that had rapidly overwhelmed Mrs Jones was noticeable as she replied.

"Yes, she's here, Andy. I'll get her for you now."

Needing to pause for a moment to compose herself, she clasped the handset to her chest before frowning and resting it on the console table. It was a forced smile that stretched the laughter lines around her eyes as she teased her two lodgers.

"Well, go on in, you pair. Don't be shy — she doesn't bite, you know."

Gliding past the statued cadets, a playful grin returned, and Mrs Jones opened the glass door, beckoning them to follow.

"Well, come on then, in you come."

She spoke to the shape in the kitchen.

"It's your Andy, sweetheart."

Sweetheart stood alongside an oval-shaped dining table which was covered with a cream, cotton cloth and set for two. She was their landlady's younger daughter by 33 minutes — Molly. Early twenties, long, dark, wavy hair, slim with curves in the right places and the most captivating dark brown eyes, which

twinkled as she smiled hello at her two obvious admirers.
Mrs Jones mouthed a warning.
"He doesn't seem best pleased that you are here, darling."
The twinkle had faded, and the smile was replaced with a determined scowl by the time Molly had closed the door behind her.
Mrs Jones clapped her hands together, forcing another smile.
"Well, don't just stand there, sit yourselves down. Would you prefer water or squash? Maybe a hot drink? You can tell me all your likes and dislikes later on, and I'll jot them down in my little red book. That way, we never—"
"Oh, grow up, Andrew, you know where I am, for goodness' sake. I'll see you later!"
The phone was slammed down, and a flushed Molly burst in from the hallway.
"Arghh, he is so annoying!"
Her body was trembling, and as she raised her hands to push back hair that had strayed over her eyes, the sleeves on her cardigan rose towards her elbows, exposing ugly green and yellow contusions to both wrists.
The cadets, mouths wide open, stared at each other, then towards Mrs Jones, who was also gaping. Flooded with tears, her eyes were fixed on the bruising. Molly realised, blushed, and instinctively placed her arms behind her back. Trying to think of something to say, she slightly tilted her eyes away from her mother's scrutiny before speaking.
"I'd better go, Mum: see to Andy before he dies of starvation."
The smile that she'd attempted to mask the unhappiness was unconvincing, and the captivating glint that had effortlessly enhanced her beauty earlier had been substituted. There was a drab sadness in its place, which darkened when she saw her mother's look of anguish.
A weak blow of a kiss towards the cadets, a brisk about-turn, and she was gone from their sight; Mrs Jones hot on her heels and closing the autumn leaves in her wake.
Muffled, agitated whispers filtered through to the two boys,

and prior to the slamming of the front door, they clearly heard Molly's raised and frustrated voice.
"And don't worry, Mum, I'll ring you later."

*

"Wow, those bruises were awful. Do you think her husband is beating her? That — you know…"
Lloyd was staring at the ceiling, the cogs in his brain whirring around.
"… that, what's his bloody name, Phyllis?"
He helped him out.
"Andy? Well, we presume Andy is her husband. No one actually confirmed that, did they? But you're probably right. The bruising was nasty. Did you see her, Lloyd? She hid her wrists when she realised that we were staring at them."
"Yeah, I clocked that. You'd think that she would have given some sort of explanation, you know, if it had happened accidentally. Mrs Jones saw them as well. Did you see the look on her face? I felt pity for her: she was about to cry. She had no idea that the bruises were there. That's why she looked over at us, checking to see if we had spotted them as well."
Phyllis was laughing, and Lloyd turned onto his side to face him, propping himself up on his elbow.
"What the hell is funny about that?"
"You! What explanation could she possibly give for it being accidental?"
Putting on a high-pitched, female voice.
"Oh, Andy and I were playing Chinese burns last night, and by accident, he got a bit rough."
Lloyd flushed again, feeling slightly out of his depth.
"Hell, I never thought about Chinese burns: how did that come into your head?"
Phyllis laughed again.
"I was joking, Lloyd. To me, it was more like a violent grab mark, don't you think so? Or a mark caused by friction, you know, like being tethered tightly and straining to break free."
Lloyd thought about it and his eyes widened.

"Hey, what if they're into kinky sex and Andy is still shackled in the bedroom, unable to get loose? Maybe that's why he phoned and was in such a bad mood. No wonder Molly was in a rush to go home: she'd probably forgotten all about him because she was too busy helping Mrs Jones. Do you think they're at it right now? I bet she's got a black leather whip: she was wearing black leather jeans. Did you notice those?"

Picturing the attractive young woman, Phyllis sighed, turned onto his back, and plumped up the pillow.

"Of course I bloody noticed, Lloyd. Mrs Jones also noticed that we noticed. She caught us, didn't she? Staring at her gorgeous daughter's fine posterior as she sashayed out of the room."

The larger of the two chuckled, flipped over, and put his hands behind his head. Seconds later, he rolled back onto his side and, following a clearing of the throat type of cough, asked the question.

"Umm, what's a posterior, Phyllis?"

The boy's thoughts didn't stray from the vivid image monopolising the darkness behind his eyes.

"An arse, Lloyd. Mrs Jones caught us staring at her daughter's fine arse."

CHAPTER 11

The din coming from the bed on the other side of the small table was keeping Phyllis awake. How the hell was he supposed to sleep through a racket like that? And how did his roommate manage to drop off so bloody quickly?

The boy struggled to fall asleep nowadays, and he'd had that issue for a while. Unsurprisingly, since he'd befriended the notorious Mikey Price. But surely this wayward behaviour must have been in him before Price's influences: maybe lying dormant and lurking with intent. Hell, you can't have a complete personality transplant overnight, can you?

Yes, he'd been attracted initially to what Mikey was all about, but hand on heart, he couldn't say that he liked him very much, and no way did he want to be similar to him. It was the buzz, that's what it was. The adventures and the laughs that they had. But at whose expense? There had always been a victim, and that fact had never occurred to him before.

He glanced over at Lloyd and smiled. Mrs Jones had already come up with a new name for him. She felt uncomfortable with Phyllis, so in order to differentiate between the two cadets, they'd agreed that she would refer to them as Lloyd and Big Lloyd.

Harmless, stoic Lloyd, AKA Big Lloyd, was flat on his back with his gob wide open and snoring for Wales. He was at one with the world; probably never done a wrong thing in his entire life.

Why couldn't he be the same as him? Instead of a highly strung bundle of fucked-up sinews. His colleague's stocky stature filled the bed, and his bulk reminded him of a mate from the past: Bill Brown — another of Mikey's young and easily impressed followers. The recollection of Bill brought a smile to his face and he recalled a well-planned, but complete and utter waste of effort.

*

(Several months ago)
It was dusk, and long shadows cast by mature conker trees in full leaf masked the presence of the two would-be burglars. In front of them was the boys' shower block, and not by chance had one of the windows been left unlatched. A window which, when fully open, provided an aperture large enough for a testosterone-fuelled teenager to scramble through. Especially one eager to gain a sneaky peek at the next day's Ordinary Level examination papers.
Now, the problem that Phyllis had envisaged was not the getting through the window but the getting up to it. The drop-down on the inside was simple enough: it was at waist height, but from the pathway it was well out of his reach, and that's where Bill Brown came into the equation. Bill was a fullback for The Swifts' youth soccer team, and he was squat with shoulders and thighs like an Olympic weightlifter. Well, maybe that's a little bit of an exaggeration. Let's say that he was bloody well-built, and not many strikers got past him; not with both legs intact anyway...
Hardly the sharpest tool in the shed, but the boy's choice of accomplice was robust, trustworthy, and he knew how to keep his bloody gob shut.
Both lads, dressed in black and wearing bobble hats pulled down to their eyebrows, were huddled together in the silence of the night, staring up at the task ahead of them.
Hell, it looked a long way up. Much higher than when he'd opened the window and checked it out that afternoon; perhaps

he should have bribed the centre-half instead...

The lads had already recce'd the building, and apart from the usual single night light illuminating the reception foyer, the rest of the Grammar School was in complete darkness. It should be straightforward enough: the place was empty...

The plan was to climb onto Bill's shoulders, pull the window to its fullest extent, and clamber through. Once on the inside, it was only a short jog to the Headmaster's office, and he could easily find his way there through the darkness. Hell, he could do it blindfolded. He'd been summoned there enough times, hadn't he? Felt the full force of Mr Whippy against the soft flesh of his backside on quite a few occasions; teeth grinding together while bent over and gripping the green leather-topped desk with both hands. On this occasion, though, he firmly believed the desktop would be blotted out by bundles of French, Geography, and English Language examination papers.

He'd spotted them there earlier and overheard the Head asking his secretary to organise them into piles relating to the subjects on test the next day.

Easy-peasy, pilfer one from each batch, take them home, and digest them at his leisure. Beats all that swotting crap.

His earlier concern was unwarranted, and the plan went like clockwork. He was into the block in no time at all and moving stealthily through vast corridors normally congested with youngsters, all chattering at once. It was weird, so quiet and so still.

He reached a junction where he had to turn left onto the main thoroughfare, which led towards the administration zone, and ultimately to the Headmaster's office. Thriving on exhilaration, excitement, and dicing with danger, he was floating along with that cocktail of highs pumping through his veins when suddenly extra lights illuminated the reception foyer, and his eyes instantly picked out the bulky silhouette of somebody behind the frosted glass. The shape was pushing the door open, and as it flicked on the lights to the main building,

THE SLIPPERY PATH

it stepped into the path of the rapidly advancing intruder. In danger of nearly overdosing on the adrenaline rush, the adolescent turned and sprinted back towards the junction. Racing against strip lights, flickering individually into life and illuminating sections of the thoroughfare in his wake, he managed to dive into the safety of darkness milliseconds before being trapped in their beam. He lay there motionless, his lungs gasping for air, and he listened.

There were no telltale sounds of heavy footsteps pacing in his direction and no inquisitive shouts. He hadn't been spotted, but who was it and, more importantly, where was that person and what were they doing in the building at that time of night? A shaft of light spilling out from the Headmaster's office answered the second question, and the sounds of movement inside, followed by the clanging of steel, confirmed the person was still in there. A matter of minutes later, a large-framed male with a definite slump in his shoulders appeared. The answer to the primary question: it was the Headmaster, and he strode from the office, out of the building, and disappeared from view. Total darkness had returned, and the slamming of a car door, followed by an engine firing into life, interrupted the silence. The breathing had calmed, and Phyllis watched the headlights pick out the steep driveway towards the exit.

"Bloody hell, that was way too close for comfort; he must have arrived when I was making my way through the corridors. Time to grab the papers and get out of here before somebody else turns up out of the blue."

Sprinting into the office, he felt for the tiny torch he'd brought with him, pointed it in the general direction of where the examination papers should be, and was instantly deflated. The desktop was virtually empty: apart from a telephone and a framed photo of some woman posing outside the gates of Buckingham Palace, he could see all of the green leather insert. 'Where the hell has the secretary stored them?'

Frantically scanning the office, the tiny beam picked out nothing of relevance until, in the corner, behind the door, it

uncovered the source of the steel clanging.
An extra-large Chubb and Sons safe…

*

The snoring was driving him nuts, and he wondered if Mrs Jones might still be up and sitting in the kitchen. He checked from the landing.
'Yes, there was a light on.'
She was relaxing on her comfy chair and gazing at the family photograph that he'd seen earlier. The gentle rattle with the fingers on the Autumn Leaves startled her, and as she looked up, he could see that her eyes were overflowing with tears. They were rolling towards her mouth, and she briskly swept them away with a sodden handkerchief as she spoke. Her voice croaky — her face reddening.
"Oh, hello, Lloyd, can't you get off to sleep? A strange bed, eh?"
The volume of the snoring carried in through the gap.
"Argh, no wonder you can't sleep…" she started chuckling, "…close that bloomin' door!"
Rising from the chair, she grabbed a tissue from a box on the sideboard and blew her nose.
"Right, I'm sure there are some of those foam earplugs in here somewhere…"
She paused to think; one hand resting on her hip while the other cupped her chin, and the chatting continued as she yanked open random drawers.
"Bernie, my late husband, gathered a hoard over the years. He was a planning officer for the County Council and often visited factories where there was loud machinery; he'd always grab a couple of packs from the box in reception. Aha, I remember now, it's in this bottom drawer.
Yes, here it is. Do you know, Lloyd?
She laughed.
"They never saw the light of day again once they ended up in this biscuit tin."
Yet another chuckle as she blew a kiss to the photograph and

handed a couple of packs to her new lodger.

"By the sound of the thunder coming from up above, I think you'll soon go through that stash. Well, you know where they are, love — help yourself."

Taking the earplugs, he smiled at her, thinking how lucky he and Big Lloyd were to have been housed with such a lovely lady.

"Is that your husband with you in the photograph, Mrs Jones? I noticed it on the table in the hall earlier on."

She sat opposite him, picked up the photograph, and stared at it; unable to stem the tears from flooding her eyes again.

"Yes, that's my dearest Bernie."

Enjoying this surprise company, and the boy's genuine interest in her family, she cheered up a bit, relaxed, and proudly introduced the subjects snapped in the photograph.

"Believe it or not, that's me."

She blushed, pushing a hand through her hair.

"To be fair, Lloyd, it was a few years ago. Oh my god, look at my dress! Do you know, I've still got it somewhere, and that reminds me."

She sighed and winked.

"I'd better organise a trip to the charity shop."

Giggling, she pointed to a young girl standing next to her: they were linking arms.

"This is my other daughter, April — the firstborn of the twins. You'll meet her soon enough. She's like a whirlwind, that one: can't keep still for more than two minutes. And of course, that is Molly."

He thought of the incident earlier but didn't think it right to mention it.

"It's a nice, happy photograph, Mrs Jones — I like it."

She returned the boy's smile and found herself relaxing.

"Thank you, Lloyd, I like it too, it's special. Unique really, because Bernie hadn't had the time to organise us, as he normally did, so it's haphazard and natural. The two girls and I are in fits of giggles because he is fussing around us and trying his best to influence Charlie, the photographer."

She points at the photograph again.

"And that's why he has that startled, 'rabbit caught in the headlights', look on his face. It was taken before he was ready, and he too had started to laugh. More in frustration, really. He'd be the first to admit that he was a fusspot, and he knew that we were giggling because of his fussing. Yet he couldn't stop himself. You can see his eyes shining with happiness: it took us all by surprise."

She wiped away a tear, and an even deeper sigh escaped.

"He had the most beautiful brown eyes: captivating and soulful. All-consuming, really, and when PC Anthony O'Sullivan came to the house on that dreadful day, well, my immediate thought was — I'm never going to be able to gaze into those oases of love ever again."

Her free hand was trembling, and the adolescent, who had never experienced such grief before, was fighting to hold back the tears as he moved his chair a little closer and took hold of it.

"What joy when out of the blue I received a phone call from Charlie, a close family friend. It was quite a while after Bernie had been taken from us, but he'd happened across this photograph while searching for something else, and he wanted to know if I wanted it? Did I want it? Of course, I wanted it. I wanted everything and anything that I could see, touch, and smell. Anything that kept Bernie's memory alive and gave me solace."

She raised her eyebrows, and a sheepish smile rounded her face as she relived the moment.

"I didn't say that to Charlie, though. He was being kind by asking me if I wanted the photograph: it was a lovely thought and gesture. I was so grateful that it hadn't been discarded. You see, Lloyd, it hadn't been included in the ones that we'd ordered because it was actually snapped off by mistake, and knowing Bernie, as he did, Charlie didn't think that he would appreciate one that..."

She chuckled again and spoke in a posh, regimented voice.

"'...hadn't been militarily co-ordinated.'

Luckily, Charlie had a soft spot for it too, and thankfully, he'd kept it all this time. It was tucked away among other photographs in his office."

The Cadet was smiling tenderly, trying to imagine what she must be going through. He could see the hurt in her face and hear the emotion entrenched in her voice. He thought of his mother: what if something similar ever happened to her? Brushing away a tear that had broken loose, he found himself speaking with an empathy he didn't realise he possessed.

"So now you can gaze into those brown eyes, blow him a kiss, and talk to him whenever you want."

She tried to make light of it.

"Yes, and he can't answer me back! You saw me doing that earlier, didn't you? Blowing a kiss towards the photograph. You're right, Lloyd. I talk to him every single day: it gives me so much comfort."

She laughed again.

"I even squabble with him."

The boy laughed with her. Noticing her eyes changing constantly from a twinkling, devilish sparkle to a sad and misty fog. And the tears that had been momentarily dammed by that delicate, glossy layer of mist escaped when she blinked. They meandered along laughter lines and followed the contours of her face to her lips. He reached for another tissue and passed it to her, holding onto her hand.

"Are you able to tell me what happened, Mrs Jones, or is it too painful?"

The grieving widow was at ease: somehow or other, this newcomer into her life had helped her to feel that way, and her glassy eyes saw a face that was innocent, kind, and caring. She saw eyes that indicated a genuine want to listen, and she, at long last, felt comfortable enough to open up. Months and months had passed since the sudden taking of the love of her life, and she had kept it all bottled up. Now she was ready, and it was a deeply emotional Mrs Jones who relived her most horrifying and life-changing nightmare.

CHAPTER 12

(The Search for the Killer of Bernard Jones)
A brief eyewitness description of Dai Insignificant would be: a bald, gangly man standing on stilts, with a pair of scaffolding poles hanging limply from his shoulders.
He was still young when the hair had started to thin on his crown, and not wishing to bear any resemblance to Friar Tuck without the habit, he decided to shave his head. What a transformation — his scalp was unblemished, and that feature, together with a Greek-shaped nose and his sheer size, depicted a strikingly handsome man.
Detective Sergeant David Charles Winters was a perfectionist; an immaculate human being with an overwhelming presence. No doubt about it, he was a head-turner. And when the Cadet met him that morning, there was no exception: it was a mature, male model that greeted him. A man surely kitted out by the best tailors of Savile Row, in a charcoal grey three-piece suit over a starched, white cotton shirt with a burnt red silk tie and matching pocket square.
As the right scaffolding pole stretched the depth of the leather-topped desk, offering a hand of welcome, the jacket's sleeve rose, revealing iridescent Mother of Pearl cufflinks shaped into miners' lamps. Mesmerised, the Cadet stared at the vibrant colours that shimmered beneath the artificial lights as his hand entwined with that of the Detective Sergeant.

A soft, South Yorkshire accent welcomed the visitor, and a flick of the wrist gestured to him to take a seat.

"They're intriguing, aren't they? A leaving present from my mates at the coal face."

The Cadet gave a subservient smile — he was in awe.

"Coal face, Sarge? You were a miner, were you?"

The Detective Sergeant chuckled as he sat straight-backed in a black leather reclining chair, reached into the desk's top drawer, and brought out a Calabash Porcelain Pipe.

"You don't mind if I smoke, do you, Lloyd? Or should I be calling you Phyllis, eh? Sergeant Peters filled me in on the origin of your new nickname when he told me that you were interested in looking into the case of Bernard Jones's tragic demise, and would I mind helping you with some of the background information?"

He shook his head and tutted.

"A complete mystery that — one of our most high-profile cold cases. The failure to make any headway wasn't for the lack of trying, though. I can assure you of that. The best of the best were summoned to Carmarthen in a bid to flush out his killer."

He held out the Calabash.

"This is my guilty pleasure: it prevents me from going absolutely bonkers."

He grinned, exposing a gold-veneered incisor, and winked as he removed a box of matches from the same drawer.

The Cadet was besotted: he wanted to be Detective Sergeant David Winters. He wanted to possess the charm, confidence, and charisma of this striking, inspiring man. Gaping, he watched him firm the tobacco in the bowl, strike a match, and suck as the flame ignited the fuel. The smoke billowed from the side of his mouth, instantly flooding the office with a sweet, aromatic bouquet, as he reclined and relaxed into the soft leather. Pushing a pair of designer spectacles from the tip of his nose to the bridge, he cursed.

"Bloody specs! I paid a small fortune for these, and every time I bend forward, they nearly slip off my hooter."

He chuckled and took another drag.

"My fault — the optician did warn me."

He winked again, once more flashing the gold incisor.

"But I liked the style, and my stubbornness set in: I chose not to listen to the man's advice, and now I can't take the blooming things back."

Laughter filled the office as he straightened the curve in his back.

"No doubt, young man, you've deduced that this chair is not your bog-standard Dyfed Powys Police issue office furniture. And you'd be damn right, it's my piece of luxury. My backside spends more time glued to this than at home on the bloody Chesterfield. What do you say, Lloyd, erm, Phyllis? Better to have a bit of comfort, eh?"

He took a long drag and held it, scrutinising his visitor.

'Good-looking boy, fit and athletic. Yes, he's going to break some young hearts.' He grinned, rubbing at his chin.

'A bit like me really.'

"So, you've been lumbered with Phyllis, eh?"

The Cadet glowered back at him.

"Oh, it won't last long, Sarge, they'll soon get fed up…"

The scaffolding pole shot out, palm up, cutting him off in mid-flow.

"Make no bones about it, young man. You are now Phyllis, end of! It will stay with you for the rest of your police career, and beyond. We are in Wales, boy, everyone's got a bloody nickname, and once some wise guy christens you, well, that's it. It will stick, excuse my French…"

He leaned in closer to the desk, mouthing the words.

"…Like shit to a bloody blanket. Take me as an example. You've probably guessed from my accent that I'm not Welsh: been here for hundreds of years, mind you. I felt like a change of scenery, a change of air, so I transferred pits, didn't I? From Doncaster to Llanelli. I couldn't even pronounce where I damn well lived — heck of a rugby team, though."

He winked, taking a long drag on the Calabash.

"I didn't get much fresh air either; the colliery was so busy I was married to the coal face. Anyway, I digress, as per usual. One of the boys on the shift, a David Williams from Llanerch, hell of a boy, pipe smoker, same as me, was being referred to as 'Gorgonzola'."

He smiled.

"Innocently, I mentioned this to the supervisor. I said to him, 'Hey Dai,' because every bugger here in Wales seems to be called Dai, 'Why are they calling him, Gorgonzola?' The supervisor laughed and said, 'Because David's great-grandfather had a wooden cart and used to push it around the streets of Llanelli selling cheeses from around the world.'

The Detective Sergeant, his eyes wide and grinning, open-armed gestured to the Cadet.

"It wasn't Dai on the coal face who sold cheese. It wasn't even his father who sold cheese. Neither was it his grandfather. It was his father's, father's, father who pushed the bloody cart around Llanelli peddling lumps of Gorgonzola!

I scratched my head, as you do when you're a bit confused. The supervisor clocked the look on my face, smiled, and helped me out.

'That's not unusual, David. All Welsh boys who are called David get their name shortened to Dai and they inherit the nicknames of their forefathers.'

He stood tall, which was bloody hard for him considering he was only about five foot and a fart — even on tip-toes. He puffed out his chest and the strong West Wales accent was even more emphasised.

'Most of us are proud to do so, you know.'

Slightly concerned because of my first name, and remember, I was still wet behind the ears back then, I stupidly blurted out — 'Well, if I get a nickname, I just hope that it's nothing insignificant…'

The man and the boy burst out laughing. The Cadet was loving it: no anxiety and no aggression. This is what it was all about. Could he bottle this moment and sip at the contents forever?

His eyes drifted to some sheets of A4 that were bound together with a star clip and sitting on top of the leather-topped desk. The Detective Sergeant didn't miss the eye deviation and reached over to them.

"I took the liberty of collating this information for you. Unfortunately, there's not much to go on: the special task force drew a blank. There was no description of the driver from eyewitnesses, no forensic evidence, and no information came from the public or police sources. Which was unusual considering the circumstances, and that a charitable organisation had offered a sizeable reward.

Are you aware that the killer stole the offending vehicle from Neath?"

The boy gave a nod of his head.

"Yes, Sarge, Mrs Jones told me last night."

"And, after causing the sudden death of her husband, it was discovered, burnt out, a couple of miles from the crime scene?"

He continued to nod.

"Okay, included in this little bundle is a copy of the original crime report detailing the theft of the car. The I.P. was ex-military — SAS no less."

He bit onto the pipe's stem, and the freed hand picked up a silver-plated letter opener from the blotting pad. Making a rapid sweeping movement close to his throat, he moved nearer to the Cadet and whispered.

"I wouldn't want to be in the thief's shoes when the police catch him and Mr Roberts gets his hands on the little shit — get my drift, Phyllis?"

Chuckling at the look of horror on the boy's face, he returned the knife.

"Yes, Mr Gareth Bryan Roberts, Taff Robbo to his mates, served in one of the elite squadrons, and lived off the land in the bloody jungle for three months at a time: Borneo of all places. According to Detective Sergeant Tony Beech, my counterpart in Neath, Robbo is a real gentleman, hard as nails, and has donated tons of his spare time to the local community by doing a lorry-load of stuff for charity. And this is how he gets repaid! Bloody typical, eh?"

The Detective Sergeant leant forward again, and pale blue eyes bored into the Police Cadet as he re-lit the Calabash; speaking through a cloud of smoke.

"Right then, young man, listen carefully to what I have to say. Some of the stuff listed on the crime report as being in the car when it was stolen would have gone up in flames. But, and this is a very important but, the scenes of crime officers didn't find any trace of any of the items made of metal. They found nothing: nada, zilch, nichts, diddly bloody squat. So what does that suggest to you, Phyllis, eh? Hell, you don't have to be Columbo to work out that the culprit took them with him, do you? Find Taff Robert's belongings, young man, and you will find the killer of Bernard Jones."

A wry smile stretched the face of Detective Sergeant David Winters when the rookie cop picked up the bundle of papers, said his thank-yous, and walked away.

He smiled, content that he'd humoured the boy — muttering to himself.

"Not a cat's chance in hell of progressing that enquiry any further: an incident room full of trained detectives drew a massive blank, but if it makes him happy — hell, what harm can he possibly come to?"

He frowned, recalling the look in the boy's eyes when asked about being lumbered with the nickname of Phyllis. There was something there and it had sent a little shiver up his spine, but he couldn't quite put his finger on what it was. Possibly a combination of determination, desire, and no fear.

He sat back in the recliner, relit the Calabash, took a long drag, and scratched an itch on the crown of his head with the stem.

"You never know, Mr Insignificant — you just never know — watch this bloody space."

*

The Cadet was gnawing away at the inside of his lip: he'd read the crime report numerous times, and something was niggling him. True enough, as Dai Insignificant had pointed out, the combustible items would all have been destroyed by the fire. That list included:

1. Two brown tweed cushions with a sporadic gold fleck and a matching blanket. (Recently purchased from British Home Stores.)
2. An A.A. road atlas of Great Britain.
3. The Who's Meaty, Beaty, Big and Bouncy. (cassette tape)
4. Deep Purple's Machine Head. (cassette tape)
5. David Bowie's Hunky Dory. (cassette tape)
6. A Sanyo cassette player.

Maybe the last item could have been placed in the non-combustible category because maybe some of its metal components might have survived the blaze? Anyway, it didn't matter: he'd checked the detailed S.O.C.O. report again in case he'd missed something, but there were no remnants of anything metal apart from objects associated with the vehicle. Also reported as being in Robbo's car when it was stolen were metal items that were sentimental to him and they were irreplaceable: gifts that had been presented to him at his retirement bash in Hereford.

1. A silver-plated tobacco tin with the SAS cap insignia emblazoned on the face of the lid. (A downward-pointing winged dagger above their motto — WHO DARES WINS.) More pertinent and crucial to its identification was the serial number engraved on the inside of the lid — 04680431 — it was unique to Robbo: his military registration number.

2. A silver-plated flip-top petrol lighter with the SAS cap insignia on the two faces and Robbo's number engraved on the underside.

3. A stainless steel pint-size thermos flask with the SAS cap insignia on the casting and Robbo's number engraved on the underside.

The boy closed his eyes, racking his brains. What was it that was niggling him, and how could he possibly know anything about this crime anyway? He'd never even heard of Bernard Jones until yesterday, and Taff Robbo this afternoon.

No wonder the task force had drawn a blank: there was nothing to go on — the torching of the car had seen to that. As Dai Insignificant had quite rightly pointed out: "Find Robbo's property and you will find the killer of Bernard Jones."

Despondency, fatigue, and the frustration of yet another probable failure in his life were setting in. His head had dropped into the palms of his hands and he was massaging the brow; pushing his fingers into the hairline and onto his scalp — questioning himself.

'Why did he even think that he could have helped Mrs Jones? He was just a wet-behind-the-ears kid who didn't know anyone from Neath or from Carmarthen. But if that was the case, then what the hell was niggling him?'

Nothing made any sense. Nothing that is until a familiar song crackled out from the tiny transistor radio, struggling to pick up the airwaves, and propped up against the window pane on top of the chest of drawers. Absentmindedly, he was nodding along to it and singing along to the opening riff: 'Dang, dang, daang. Dang, dang, dang, daaang. Dang, dang, daang. Dang, daang.'

That's when it hit him and his head shot out from the palms of his hands — clearly visualising the scene — Mikey Price playing air guitar on that examination results day. That's what had been niggling him. He'd seen Mikey with a silver-coloured tobacco tin, and from it he was choosing the makings to roll him, Brucie-Boy, a 'special fucker'.

'How could Mikey afford such an expensive-looking item? He couldn't — not unless he'd nicked it!'

He got up and paced around the tiny room, his breathing erratic, his mind awash with thoughts: working overtime trying to recall that day.

'Did that tobacco tin have an SAS cap badge on the lid?'

He hadn't noticed, but he wouldn't have been paying that much attention to its description, and anyway, those markings wouldn't have meant anything to him: he'd never heard of the SAS until this afternoon.

'And the song, 'Smoke on the Water' — that's by Deep Purple — it's on the album Machine Head. He's got a copy at home, and it's one of the cassette tapes recorded as being stolen from Robbo's car.'

The Cadet laughed out loud, shaking his head with frustration, when a familiar image popped up in the forefront of his mind. One that he feared would never be debited from his memory bank, and one that often haunts him, among other things, from that day, when he struggles with sleep during the witching hours... How did he not recall this spectacle earlier?

'Rose Price — her breasts, swaying inches away from his face, and the flame from a petrol lighter dancing right in front of his eyes.'

"Was it silver? Did it have any markings on it? Could it have been Robbo's?"

He didn't know — he couldn't remember. Hell, he wasn't paying that much attention to her flippin' lighter, was he? But it was definitely a flip-top petrol lighter.

And the song that was being played not long before he crashed out was, 'My Generation,' by The Who. He recalled singing along to it — because of the stuttering lyrics, it was one of his favourites. Is that a track from the album, Meaty, Beaty, Big and Bouncy? He didn't know, but that would be easy enough to find out. A visit to the record shop in town tomorrow will answer that question. And, guaranteed, it was Robbo's Sanyo cassette player that Rose was using to play the music on that day? Is it still in the living room in her house?

There was something bugging him: he couldn't remember Mikey having that silver tin prior to the day of the party. Having said that, he'd never watched him skin up before, so he could very well have been using it and he hadn't noticed. Or maybe he'd been keeping it out of sight, waiting for enough time to pass before using it?

There were too many unanswered questions — too many

coincidences — too many what-ifs.

Overheating, he sat down on the bed, shaking his head in disbelief at the possibility that his old partner in crime, Mikey Price, was the culprit that the police had been so desperate to trace.

Talking to himself.

"That's probably the reason why the detectives didn't receive any intelligence from informants. And why no members of the public had come forward to claim the reward. Mikey wouldn't have told anyone, and he lived thirty plus miles away from where Bernard Jones was killed. Factor in that Robbo's car was stolen from Neath, which is thirty plus miles in the opposite direction from Carmarthen, then it is understandable why a criminal from Pembroke Dock didn't pop up on the police radar as being a suspect.

Is it you, Mikey? Are you the killer of Bernard Jones?"

The heat from his body was becoming unbearable, and he darted from the bed, yanked down the sash window, and gulped in the fresh, night air, relishing the coolness. Mixed emotions were sweeping through him in waves: fear, disgust, contempt, and excitement.

Did the embryo of a law enforcer nurturing inside him want justice? Justice for Mrs Jones and her family. Justice for poor Bernard, and justice for Taff Robbo? Or, was it all for self-gratification and nothing to do with justice? Did he, Lloyd Hilary Davies, the criminal in a blue suit, want to be the hero? Reap the praise and recognition for being the only one able to solve the unsolvable and archived case.

Maybe it was a mixture of everything, but there were other driving motivations: his desire to help Mrs Jones for one. She is kind and caring. He'd felt an affectionate, maternalistic bond nurturing — something that until now he had only experienced with his mother. So yes, he did want to help her find the solace she desperately needed. And, the other major motivator was to prove to his father that he could succeed at something worthwhile. Would he finally be able to discard the label that weighed heavily on his mind? The label identifying him as being a selfish, egotistical waste of space.

What should he do? He couldn't divulge his suspicions to Dai Insignificant — not just yet: there were too many unanswered questions. He needed something concrete before he turned to him, and the only sure way to establish Mikey's involvement was to find out if the items that he saw in Rose's kitchen belonged to Robbo. He had to do the impossible and get invited back into Mikey's house. See for himself if the tobacco tin and petrol lighter did bear the SAS insignia. And if so, was Robbo's unique number engraved into the silver-coloured metal? Then and only then could he reveal his suspicions to Dai Insignificant. Because, until that moment, it was all purely speculation.

CHAPTER 13

(Saturday morning)

Mikey Price was a slave to his habit, and every day bar one, at roughly the same time, he was a visitor to the pharmacy: knocking back a green-coloured elixir under the watchful eye of the chemist, Mrs Catherine Eleanor Menzies. A substitute he craved, needed to help wean him off the evil and addictive drug that dictated every conscious second of his life — Heroin.

Brown, H, Smack, Scag, Horse, Beast — the labelling mattered not. It didn't detract from what it was — a Killer!

Swallowing the methadone under close supervision helped to take the edge off his craving for that day, but it too was addictive, and the addict couldn't be trusted to be prescribed more than the daily requirement. Historically, it was a proven fact: the temptation to sell some or consume it all in one hit was too overpowering, and once the effect had worn off, there was the inevitable return to the pharmacy: yelling and shouting at the lady in the white coat. Demanding more — threatening her until he was prescribed another fix. Cramp-like muscle spasms, bone pain, cold flushes, vomiting, diarrhoea, and sporadic itches were now a daily occurrence: well-documented side effects of the drug's misuse.

Solely on a Saturday morning did Mrs Menzies entrust Mikey Price with a single extra dose that he could take away with him: that amount barely sufficient to get him through to the end of the Lord's Holy Day. If he abused that arrangement, then it was his choice — there was no more available. Only the Lord would be open for business as usual: everywhere else was closed for the Sabbath.

The Cadet had positioned himself up on high ground, and was sitting on a picnic bench overlooking the Milford Haven waterway; a freezing blast battering him directly from the Irish Sea. The bench had a 360° panorama with the added bonus of overlooking the lower-lying thoroughfare, and he'd watched Price go into the pharmacy. Within minutes, he'd be dosed up and out again, the cravings at bay for the time being, but knowing Mikey as he did, the Cadet had bargained on him needing something else. A little extra boost to get him through the day.

He talked to himself, giving a running commentary on the addict's movements.

"There he is! He's out of the pharmacy and has turned his face away from the cold bite of the breeze. He's pulled the hood up around his ears and is shuffling along the road towards the front of the police station. Whoops, he's darted into the doorway of a terraced house — shit, he's looking right at me."

The Cadet instinctively turned away, but there was no need: Price couldn't see that far. Months and months of constant drug and alcohol abuse had wrecked his long vision. Price's eyes were now focused on himself, and his hand was deep inside his Parka.

"What the hell is he doing? Argh, thought so — he's prised out a bottle, and he's taking a swig. Flippin' hell, Mikey, that's what you call a swig. It's got to be whisky: you thrive on the stuff. Right, he's wiping his chin, and he's pulling the fur-lined hood closer to his face."

A wave of sadness washed over him: shocked by his friend's rapid decline in such a short span of time. Through gossip, the Cadet had become aware of Price's addiction and he recalled him sucking on the tin foil tube at the party on that life-changing day. At the time he didn't have a clue what his friend was doing — he knew now...

"What have you done to yourself, Mikey? You're skin and bones and desperate for the warmth of that coat: the heroin has hammered you. You're even struggling to press in the stud at your neck."

The sadness was short-lived: there was no time for sentiment — Price was on the move, and from the Cadet's vantage point, it was simple to monitor his movements. He was feeling a buzz — turned on that Mikey didn't have a clue that his every move was being monitored and his heart was beating at a much faster rate of knots than several minutes earlier. The adrenaline had kicked in, gripping him with excitement. Hopeful that the surveillance would lead to a positive identification of Robbo's property. But he didn't have to move, not just yet, not until Price had shuffled past the Police Station and come to a junction with a back lane which would be on his right. That was the first hazard. If Mikey ignored the lane, the Cadet could continue watching him from the bench, but if he chose to turn into the lane? Well, he'd have to move and move bloody quickly.

He was willing him to continue on the same route.

"Please don't turn, please don't turn, please don't turn."

He turned.

"Shit!"

The Cadet sprang from the bench and, still cursing, sprinted down the grassy bank: it would have been much simpler if Price had continued straight on to the junction with the main London Road. So much easier to follow him along that busy stretch: more cover. Loads of front doorways set back from the pavement to nip into, and numerous parked cars to duck behind.

The route that Mikey had chosen was parallel and headed in the general direction of his home, but there could be a problem. Within eye-shot of the junction was the rear entrance to a dealer's home address, and not any old dealer — Mikey's dealer.

*

The dealer was widely known as Lugsey, yet 23 years ago the Registrar of Births, Deaths, and Marriages had recorded the name Alfred Benjamin Jones in the official
register. Why then, might you ask, did everyone refer to him as Lugsey?
Well, if you were to meet Alfred Benjamin Jones for the very first time, say on a blind date and at a local focal point, for instance, in the shadows of the clock tower at St. John's Church, Lugsey wouldn't need to be holding and waving about that day's edition of The Sun newspaper. Neither would there be a necessity for him to be gripping a solitary red rose between his teeth, or to be wearing a pink-spotted sombrero.
No, if the man had been described to you with total honesty, it would be blatantly obvious as to whom you were meeting. The reason? The organs on each side of his head were a distinct size and shape. So much so, that a number of years ago, when his nickname came to be, the choice was a toss-up between Lugsey or Spock...
Like Mikey, he too was skin and bones but much taller. Several inches over six feet, with thin, straggly hair, cut in a mullet style, and plagued with a prominent conk that was similar to a rook's beak: stuck on as if added as an afterthought.
The Cadet got on alright with Lugsey, and in company with Mikey, had visited the house many times. Never once entering from the London Road though — always via the heavily graffitied reinforced door leading from that back lane.
His specialty was blow, speed, and prescription pills, but he could lay his hands on anything and everything as long as the purchaser was willing to pay upfront and wait.
Coke, tabs, and even H were on the menu. Most cold callers wanted Class B: a bit of smoke or some speed, but those who wanted the more potent stuff had to order and collect it when told. Strictly by appointment only — Lugsey didn't want Class A in the house for longer than necessary. Too many risks involved — way too heavy.
Somewhat ironic and a bit cheeky to be dealing within a stone's

throw of the local cop shop, but that close proximity hadn't impeded an illicit, successful, and lucrative business from thriving.

It was common knowledge that Lugsey had been busted several times, and many debated as to why the man hadn't been locked up. Was it pure luck that, apart from a few items of drug misuse such as paraphernalia, scales, lists of customers' initials, used bongs, etc., etc., no illegals had ever been found?

Word on the street following the outcome of most of the debates was that he was on the take, and that his name topped the list in the drug squad's paybooks. The gossip suggested that in return for the odd tit-bit of juicy intelligence, Lugsey would get a warning phone call: a tip-off to clear the decks and make anything illegal disappear.

In spite of the idle natter, those who needed that little extra something to get them through the day still bought from Lugsey: they had to have it — as simple as that...

*

The back lane was empty.

"Shit — he's gone in to score."

The Cadet had a problem. He couldn't keep an eye on the back and front doors at the same time, and he couldn't remain where he was: Lugsey had watchers. Eyes were everywhere, and once the jungle drums started beating, the youngster would be challenged, and the game would be over.

Using the girth of a telegraph pole as cover, he could see the graffitied reinforced steel door leading to Lugsey's backyard, and from past experience, knew that the dealer was at home, and gear was available: the curtains at the landing window were wide open, and a model replica of The Golden Hind was on display — Lugsey's 'tell-tale' — the store was open for business.

Guaranteed Mikey would continue along the rear lane once he'd bought at Lugsey's. It made sense for him to do that: less chance of him being spotted and tugged by Lilly Law. In order for his plan to work, the Cadet needed to bring about a chance meeting before Mikey got home, and he knew of the perfect spot.

*

Ripping open the brown paper bag, he squashed it into a ball, took aim, and lobbed it towards an overflowing waste bin. It missed and joined the other discarded items littering a grassed verge bordering the gravel path which led from Lugsey's gaff. In the other direction, and less than a ten-minute stroll away, was Rose's house.

The kiddies' park was deserted. Probably due to the Arctic breeze billowing up the natural wind tunnel, together with the state of the vandalised apparatus: only a solitary swing was usable, and the rusted bracket securing its chains to the crossbar screamed out for lubricant as the tired, moulded lump of plastic danced in the wind.

The Cadet unscrewed the cap from a bottle of Jack Daniel's and placed it onto the etched-out pieces of timber running between the end supports of a battered wrought-iron bench. He took a long swig and grimaced as it hit the back of his throat.

Not a personal choice of beverage, but he knew Mikey couldn't resist it, and the bottle was imperative: a big part of the adolescent's plan — 'act pissed, entice Mikey to drink with him, and, well, that's as far as he'd got! It would then be a case of suck it and see...'

The Dutch courage had started to kick in, and he winced again as more of the bitterness grated past his tonsils before he dangled the lure of the bottle between his legs and waited for his prey: Mikey shouldn't be long.

Unfortunately, the Cadet was last in the queue when they dished out patience at birth, and they probably ran out. Boredom set in faster than skin forming on a hot, milky coffee. He'd read all the misspelt carvings on the timber slats, and time was dragging. He checked his watch again.

"Come on, Mikey. What the hell are you doing? It doesn't take this long to score a bit of bloody blow, does it? You should have been here yonks ago."

Despondency was setting in, and he reached for the comfort of the Jack Daniel's.

"Maybe he's gone somewhere else or got wasted on heroin and crashed out on Lugsey's couch. That's more like it, and he'll probably be there all bloody day. What a waste of time and effort — flippin' crap plan!"

He stood up and as he bent his neck to put the bottle to his lips, he spotted Price in the distance.

"Bloody hell, there he is, and by the look of it, he's shifting along: the pace he's going, he must have popped a pill or snorted some powders. Shit, shit, shit, that's all I bloody need."

He knew Price was a handful: he'd seen him in action many times, but he'd been banking on it being a Mikey Price mellowed out on the calming effects of methadone. Not one who had swallowed some tabs or snorted a couple of wraps of speed on top of whatever it was he'd downed from that bottle earlier.

"He's going to be an absolute nightmare!"

Nerves set in — was he doing the right thing? His hand trembled as he left the cap where it was, sat down, and slumped further forward on the bench, staring at the concrete base with the bottle dangling between his legs.

The approaching footsteps on the gravel sounded like marbles being crunched together in the palm of your hand: louder and louder as they neared — the noise accentuated by the alcohol. His breathing quickened — this was it — their first meeting since he had done the unthinkable... No wonder his armpits felt like frogs could spawn in them...

The crunching stopped, and apart from the intermittent screeching of the swing, it was silent. The Cadet could feel Mikey's eyes boring into him, though the addict's vision would be blurred: impaired by what he'd shoved down his throat or snorted. He'd be struggling to focus, his head pushing forward like a tortoise. Squinting and trying to make out who it was sitting on HIS park bench. Who was this intruder to HIS patch? A fresher gust of wind dislodged the J.D. cap, blowing it to the

concrete base. Gathering momentum in the breeze, it crossed the grassed area towards Mikey, and the sight of it spinning towards him was too much of a challenge. Stepping onto the uneven ground like Bambi on ice, he tried his best to curb the cap's escape with the side of his boot but mistimed a stamp and trod on it. Cursing as he stooped to pick up the squashed cap, he lost his balance and staggered out of control into the metal stanchion of a climbing frame. That's when he spotted the bottle of Jack Daniel's.
His speech was slurred and slow.
"Oy — I've wrecked the stopper for your Jimmy D — squished it to fuck."
The Police Cadet's heart could not beat any faster or any harder: there was no way back from here. Gradually, he lifted his head and droopy, glazed eyes, squinting in the brightness of the early-autumn sunshine, were taken aback by the state of his one-time buddy. He hadn't seen Mikey for a while, and it was a heavily lined and gaunt face which returned the gaze.
The initial part of the plan was going like clockwork — too well — he was pissed: no acting required. His head was spinning, and it was close to a half-full bottle of Jack Daniel's that was laboriously raised to his mouth. Taking a long swig, he smacked his lips together in a theatrical, over-emphatic grimace; wiped the drips from his chin, held out the bottle, and genuinely slurred.
"Well, we'll just have to finish the fucker off then, won't we, Mikey?"
Price tilted his head to one side, recognising the voice, but from where? The Cadet could see him struggling to focus; those lifeless eyes not giving anything away, but he guessed that his friend's brain must be working overtime. Processing the information.
'How did he know this person?'
Finally, it clicked.
"Well, fuck me pink, it's Dixon of Dock Green. You've got a fucking nerve showing up here, you fuck. You got a death wish

or what?"

The nerves went — the heartbeat slowed — the challenge was on. The Cadet could do this — he was going to do this.

"You want some of this or what, Mikey?"

There was hatred and aggression in the addict's response.

"Fuck off, filth. I ain't drinking with no pig. You'd better get your arse off that bench and put some distance between us before I smash that Jimmy D over your fucking head!" The Cadet raised the bottle, goading him by taking another long swig; a trail of the amber-coloured fluid dribbling down to his neck.

"Please yourself, Mikey..." taking another mouthful, "...all the more for me. Didn't particularly want to share it with you anyway."

Mikey grunted, edging menacingly close, easily within striking distance. The Cadet was too pissed to be fazed — the Dutch courage had taken over — there was no fear. He knew Mikey was also pissed and probably too drugged up to fight. He backed himself to take him if he needed to, and held tightly in the grasp of his right hand was the ideal weapon... In the state he was in, he wouldn't have to think twice...

Still wary of any sudden outbreak of aggression, he shimmied forward on the bench and, as if readying himself to leave, teased Price by offering him the bottle.

"Looks like you've been on a bender, Mikey. Sure you don't fancy a bit more before I shoot off? It needs to be finished. I can't take an open bottle on the bus with me, can I?..." he sniggered, "...against the fucking law, ain't it? How's Rose, by the way?"

Grinning, he took another swig.

"Go on, Mikey, have a snifter..."

Shaking the bottle and holding it closer to the alcoholic, he baited him.

"...for old times' sake. You probably won't see me again, but hell, we had some laughs — didn't we?"

Price couldn't resist it: he grabbed the bottle, slumped towards

the bench, and the neck was kissing his lips before the denim covering his Y fronts made contact with the etchings. Deadpan, the Cadet stared straight ahead, but inside he was having a party: he'd got him. Through the corner of his left eye, he could see him gulping and the young cop's mind was working overtime: concocting the next step of the plan.
'Without Mikey becoming suspicious, how could he confirm what he suspected? Come on, you idiot — it's simple.'
"You got any smokes, Mikey? You know I ain't never got any fags, and I'm gagging for one. It's always the case in it..." laughing "...soon as I smell the alcohol, I gotta have a fag."
More laughter as Price joined him.
"That's the fucking truth, man, you're a tight fucker."
Price moved to put his right hand into the right thigh pocket of his Levis, but they were too tight, and his sitting position made it impossible. The Cadet clocked the bulge, the outline of a rectangle, the size and shape of a tobacco tin. There was an instant increase in his heart rate, and something living inside his stomach started jiggling about like half a dozen mackerel on a trace of feathers; all fighting to escape in different directions.
'It's got to be Robbo's.'
Mikey slumped back further, pushing out his legs until his boots scraped off the hard-standing and onto the grass. Then he raised his buttocks, straining to gain easier access to the pocket. He paused, turned his face up towards his friend, and from nowhere his mood changed to melancholy: his voice had softened.
"Why join the filth, man? You ain't no fucking copper. You've done loads of shit — worse than all of us put together."
The Cadet welcomed this sudden change, but he knew better than to relax: how long would melancholy last?
"But I was never captured, Mikey, was I? I'm squeaky clean, not even a little snifter of any wrongdoings. Fuck me, less than twelve months ago I was putting on a black smock with a white blouse and belting out 'All things bright n' beautiful' on

a Sunday morning. Fucking vicar couldn't understand why all the blood of Christ in the Vestry was as weak as piss. I'd necked half the fucker and topped up the bottles with holy water before we'd even started singing."

His forced laughter was prolonged: he was killing time. Striving to think of something convincing to appease Mikey. Something that would appeal to his mentality.

'Got it.'

"The honest truth is, Mikey, I had no choice. My old man went fucking mental when I fucked up my exams. His mate is the boss of the cop shop, and before I knew it, I was all dressed up in navy blue and wearing shiny boots. The good thing is, though, I won't be there for long, and whilst I am, I can suss out how they tick. Once I'm out, we can get up to something really hardcore, and you'll never, ever get nicked again."

It did the trick and Price started laughing hysterically.

"Can't believe you were a choir boy — all things bright and bloody beautiful — fucking priceless."

That was as long as melancholy lasted. This man had very little patience and no tolerance: his mood changed faster than traffic lights, and the inability to prise the tobacco tin from his pocket was driving him nuts. The laughter ceased, he started to click, and the tension was painful. It was infuriating for the Cadet that Price didn't possess the basic common sense to stand up. Mikey was wired, on the verge of snapping, and he did.

"Argh! For fuck's sake! Here, hold this bastard thing before I smash the fucker across your fucking cop face!"

He thrust the bottle into the Cadet's groin and left it where it landed. The contents oozing out and dampening his jeans in an area where it now looked like he'd pissed himself.

Mikey slumped further forward, the bench supporting merely his shoulder blades. His torso was like a bridge with his knees bent and his boots flattening a patch of buttercups. Muttering fucks, he finally managed to ease out the tin, and the bridge collapsed.

The pain caused by the hardness of the bottle meeting the soft skin of his manhood must have been excruciating. That, in conjunction with the fright caused by the deranged expression on Mikey's face, together with crazed, glaring eyes and flaring nostrils, would have been enough to unnerve most level-headed individuals. But at that precise moment, the Cadet felt nothing but elation. He'd clocked it, hadn't he? It, being the sole reason for his presence in this precarious situation, and its exposure had momentarily numbed the discomfort in his groin.

Slowly, it had slid into view, and his eyes had locked onto it like a sniper's sights. Mikey didn't have a clue. As far as he was concerned, the cop alongside him must have been doubled up in pain, his eyes sodden with tears, and totally out of focus. How much further from the truth could he have been?

Those eyes were wide in anticipation, recognition, and excitement. The Cadet had seen the silver-plated tobacco tin inch into view, and he had seen it momentarily resting on the concrete base. There was no necessity to give Mikey the slightest indication of his interest. Why risk stimulating thoughts inside Mikey's head? Thoughts that this trainee cop might suspect him to be the killer of his landlady's husband. So, in an overt act of exhibiting total disinterest, he had groaned and turned his head away to look in the other direction.

The Cadet had seen enough. Enough to make him want to dance naked around a campfire, punch the air in victory, and scream out, "Yes!"

The 'WHO DARES WINS', inscribed below a downward-pointing winged dagger, was mounted on the lid of the tobacco tin. All he had to do now was confirm that Taff Robbo's unique military number was engraved on the inside. Easier said than done, he thought, as the stabbing pain throbbed through to his groin.

Hearing a match striking close to his skin, he felt the brief warmth and smell of sulphur as it sparked into life. He also felt the stirrings of anxiety.

'Shit, he hasn't got the lighter. Where the hell is the lighter? Has Rose got it? Has he sold it? Lost it? Did he ever have it?'

Doubt and paranoia started to creep in.

'Maybe he didn't mow down Bernie Jones. Maybe it isn't even Robbo's tobacco tin.'

A familiar, pungent smell replaced that of sulphur, and Mikey tapped him on the arm.

"Here, you fucking pansy, have a toke on this beauty."

The Cadet slowly, dramatically, raised and turned his head towards him, groaning with every movement. The shape, back in Mikey's jeans, confirmed the whereabouts of the tin, but how was he going to get it out of there? The jeans were so tight-fitting they might as well have been sprayed on.

Mikey was grinning, comforted that he'd put this fucking copper well and truly in his place. A reminder to him that he, Mikey Price, was still running the show in these parts. Smugly, he offered the joint, the message in his body language clear.

'Here, share some of this weed, mate, but don't forget your place: I'm still the fucking daddy around here.'

"Cheers, Mikey, nice one."

His hand trembled as he put the cardboard tube to his lips. He hadn't bargained on this — it wasn't part of the plan. Was he about to savour the sweetness of the illicit cannabis? He couldn't refuse it, could he? That would undo all his hard work: whatever trust he'd managed to claw back would instantly be lost.

The smoke filled his mouth: he could taste it on his teeth, and forcing his tongue between his top lip and his incisors, he relished the flavour. But should he swallow it? Oh, how easy it would be to just swallow it and allow himself to float away on a cloud of tranquillity. He could find contentment and escape from his demons forever. An overpowering urge overwhelmed him: a desire to gaze from the mass of cotton wool and see nothing but blue. Pure and unadulterated blue, and he could cocoon himself in that infinite blue forever.

But he didn't. Mikey turned away, and the trainee cop allowed the disabling toxins to naturally escape; they hadn't passed further than his tonsils. He still had a job to do, no point in enduring all this trauma and not achieving an outcome. He needed to be focused, and he could only achieve that with a clear head: an intake of hash right now would render him absolutely bloody useless. But his head was already under the influence of Jack Daniel's, and the Demon's voice chirped up, taking advantage of a moment of weakness.

"You can do both, Phyllis-boy. Man up, don't waste this opportunity. One little toke won't do you any harm, and a couple more slugs of J.D. will get you well and truly back in Mikey's book of trust. Go on, matey, take a drag. You can still get the job done, and you can enjoy this bit of pot as well. Who's going to know?"

His right hand was trembling as he cosseted the joint between the index and middle fingers. Glazed eyes studied it, and he knew what he was going to do: he couldn't stop himself. The urge was way too powerful, and the demonic voices didn't help: they pestered away inside his head.

"Go on, Phyllis, you'll be fine, you've got enough on him already. You know it makes sense. Go on, boy, enjoy it."

Resistance was futile — the Demon was always going to be victorious.

He gently blew on the smouldering tip, and that little extra source of energy added more life to the flame. It was burning away the skins before he took a long and satisfying toke. No thoughts this time of discarding the toxic fumes harmlessly into the atmosphere. Oh no, there was only one destination for this mouthful of contentment, and that was deep inside him. The desire to fill his veins and head with endorphins was so intense that before he had expelled the residue, the reefer was back between his lips, and he was drawing on it once more.

He felt another tap on the arm.

"Hey, you greedy fucker — pass it here."

Mikey started laughing, totally relaxed — totally hoodwinked.

"Some fucking copper you are!"

The Police Cadet was gone. The marijuana had sped from his lungs, surged through his veins, and saturated his brain. A flood of dopamine created the pleasurable high he craved, and for no apparent reason, he too started laughing as he handed the reefer back to Mikey. Rescuing the bottle of Jack Daniel's from his bruised groin and putting the neck to his lips, he tilted his head and guzzled. The remnants of the THC, clinging to his tongue and teeth, mingled with the bittersweet liquid, and together they happily slipped along his gullet and into his gut. His eyes grew heavy as he swapped the bottle for the reefer, and caressing it with his lips, he fed off the proceeds. Nothing else mattered: solving Bernard Jones's case was far from his thoughts. His agenda had drastically changed: top of the juvenile's list was to consume as much cannabis and alcohol as he possibly could.

He had a new goal: to fly high like a Red Kite hovering on a therm of warmth — never having to come back down again. And, according to his nemesis, Mr Demon, this was by far the best, fastest, and easiest way to make his wish come true.

CHAPTER 14

The moment the stench hit the back of his throat, the Police Cadet knew where he was. The once-smelt, never-forgotten stink of stale filth had swamped his nostrils, and he shuddered as the memory of his previous visit returned; thankfully, he was alone this time — not nestled into the back of a rank and naked Rose.

But where in the house was he?

Ungluing the stickiness from his eyes, he struggled to see anything in the pitch black. His head was resting on a scabby cushion perched on the arm of a corduroy fabric armchair, and as he rescued it from an impossible angle, moonlight momentarily came to his aid. Escaping from low, dense cloud cover, it filtered through the threadbare curtains to cast a grainy aura, and he could make out a three-seater settee, merely an arm's length away. Stabbing pains shot into his neck, and as he circled his head to feel and hear the painful but satisfying sensation of nerve receptors crunching in defiance, a bewildering thought consumed him: 'Why the hell hadn't he crashed out on that bloody settee?'

He must be in the living room at the rear of the house — the room where Rose had been organising the sounds on that fateful visit, and Robbo's crime report flashed in front of him — is the Sanyo cassette player here? He bent over to search, and bile spewed from his stomach, entered the back of his throat, and rinsed his tonsils: the taste made him retch.

"Urgh, disgusting! What the hell had happened?"

The grim memory of how yesterday had panned out permeated through the pain that was clanging inside his temple, and he dropped his head into the palms of his hands, pushed his fingers through his hair, and massaged the back of his neck.

"What the hell have I done? A complete waste of effort, and I was so bloody close."

To feel sorry for himself was his initial reaction, closely followed by who could he blame? He closed his eyes, trying to alleviate the throbbing in his skull, and Mrs Jones appeared. She was sitting at the kitchen table, grief-stricken; her eyes swollen, red, and overrun with tears. How could he have let her down? And his parents, the disappointment in his father's voice and the desperation in his mother's, haunt him every single day. Biting at his lip, he forced the emotion away, and a doggedness returned. Sooner rather than later, he needed to pull himself together: there might not be much time. Maybe he'd already blown it, but maybe not... A brief smile crossed his lips.

"Look on the bright side, matey. You can take advantage of this situation and put it all down to your master plan. You knew it was a case of suck it and see once you'd got Mikey to drink with you. Well, that part worked, didn't it? And what happened next was a stroke of genius: look where you are. How else would you have gained enough trust to end up kipping in their front room?"

He chewed on his fingernails, trying to concentrate, but an overwhelming thirst had snared him, and he needed to drink before he could plan his next move.

Bleary eyes gradually accustomed to the grey conditions and he was about to creep to the kitchen when they picked out a similar cushion to the one he'd slept on. Together with a blanket, it was in the middle of the settee, and he recalled the list of property stolen from Robbo's car.

'Two brown tweed cushions with a sporadic gold fleck and a matching blanket — recently purchased from British Home Stores.'

The Cadet grabbed his pillow and held it out in front of him, erratically adjusting the focal length in an attempt to make out the colours, but it was too dark: the moonlight had been stolen back by the clouds — black and heavy with rain. He felt the fabric, and it was rougher to the touch than leather or that plastic leatherette stuff. Was it tweed? How the hell was he supposed to know — the boy wouldn't know tweed if it smacked him in the gob! Shaking his head in frustration, he knew that he needed a light source, but could he risk switching it on or might that alert Mikey and Rose?

Sitting in total darkness, he strained to listen for any movement, and the silence was soon broken by a heavy, drawn-out snore which came from the room directly above the kitchen: Mikey's bedroom. He grinned when a rasping fart accompanied by a wheeze followed from the other bedroom, and he thought of Rose, but the grin was short-lived. A very nasally, stuttering type of snore came into play, and it wasn't coming from upstairs. It was coming from the room next door — the kitchen.

"Shit! Someone else is in the house."

He closed his eyes, trying desperately to remember what had happened yesterday evening, but drew a complete blank.

"There's that snore again, who the hell is it, and do they know I'm in here?"

An uneasiness gripped his stomach.

"What will they do if they don't know, and then find out that a bloody copper is in the house with them?"

He can hear a heartbeat, pounding as if directly alongside him, and his eyes spring open — his brain on high alert.

'Shit, someone is in this room with me. They must have crashed out as well. Why can't I remember a bloody thing? And why is it so bloody dark?'

Swallowing hard and chewing at his lip, he pushed forward

to the edge of the armchair, trying to calm his breathing. He could hear the heartbeat again, much louder, frighteningly close. His head spun to face the sound, and his arm shot out in the same direction, feeling, searching in the darkness, but there was nothing. He was clammy, sweating profusely but cold, and the heartbeat was now booming like a drum, pulsating in his eardrums.

"Shit, shit, shit — it's me! It's me, you stupid idiot — calm down and get a bloody grip! What the bloody hell is wrong with you?"

Several deep breaths later, he eased himself from the armchair. There was something he needed to do: above anything else, he had to identify the snorer. Whoever it was might hurt him.

*

The door was ajar, and the gap wide enough to squeeze through without risking any giveaway-screeches from dodgy hinges. The kitchen light was on, the brightness spilled into the passage, and the snoring hadn't stopped, so whoever it was had crashed out regardless.

Wide eyes scanned the staircase to his left, searching into the darkness as far as his arc of vision would allow — his ears straining to pick out any warning noises. An almighty creaking noise came from Rose's room.

'Bloody hell, she's heard me and is coming to see what's going on.'

Holding his breath, he backed up and waited; there were no heavy footsteps, no inquisitive call-outs, and no further movement. A brief recall of her shimmying across the mattress like a beached whale flashed before his eyes, and he realised that she must have been changing her position in the bed. Shaking his head at the horror of the memory, he crept to the room where they'd partied all those weeks ago and stooped to peep around the door frame.

Panic over — the mystery snorer was Lugsey, and his backside was on a chair, with his upper body flopped across the table. Shit, he couldn't remember Lugsey being in the house, and come to think of it, he couldn't remember seeing Rose either. In fact, he still couldn't remember a bloody thing after getting off his face on that park bench. There's only one possible explanation as to how he is still here and in one piece: he must have filled their heads with the same bullshit he'd fed to Mikey. They think that he's only biding his time in the police before he jumps ship and teams up with them again.

Another thought crossed his mind: Lugsey wouldn't have turned up at the house empty-handed. Guaranteed they've done more gear. Shit — what other drugs had the trainee copper taken on board? What else had he rammed in his gob or snorted up his nose? He didn't have a clue, but going by the splitting headache and the overpowering thirst, it must have been something pretty heavy.

The feeling sorry for himself and an overwhelming desire to say sod it and get out of this dump filled his thoughts, but he couldn't. He wouldn't be able to cope with the failure of walking away from the challenge. He had to face it head-on, or Mr Demon would plague him for the rest of his life.

Back in the living room, he closes the door, flicks on the switch, and there is nothing — nothing because there is no bloody bulb!

"You tight, lazy bastards!"

The nearest other light fitting was in the passage, at the bottom of the stairs, but that was in clear view of Lugsey: way too risky... Sitting down to think, he remembers Rose using the toilet on the day he met her, and he whispers to himself.

"That room is right next to the front door, and it's in regular use. There's bound to be a bulb in there, and it's a safer option: it's not in Lugsey's line of sight."

Creeping back to the loo, he gently pushes the door towards the pan, but the hinges creak like a scene from a horror movie. He freezes, listening for any movement, his heart battering against his chest.

'Surely someone must have heard that bloody racket?'

They hadn't — apart from Lugsey blasting out stuttering

THE SLIPPERY PATH

snores like a grizzly with a walnut stuck up his nostril — the house was in complete silence. Looking up at the light fitting, he shook his head in disbelief.

'How do people live like this? Buy some bloody bulbs, you tight, idle shits.'

Apart from the bulb above Lugsey's head, the only other option on the ground floor was at the bottom of the stairs, but the initial concern still remained — it was in the drug dealer's direct line of sight.

The Cadet had no choice, and with every sinew screaming out under the pressure of his total body weight, he rose onto the tips of his toes and stretched to grip the holder. Struggling to keep his balance, he was straining to release the bulb from its bayonet fixing when Lugsey let out a loud gasp. You know the type, similar to somebody being starved of oxygen, then seconds before fainting, they're gifted some.

He freezes into a statue of a pirouetting ballerina with both eyes latched firmly onto Lugsey, who is now upright on the chair. He's less than two good strides away, and if he decides to turn his head in his direction, the game is over…

The index finger of the drug dealer's right hand is buried deep inside his left nostril, and it's excavating something that doesn't want to be displaced. Deciding on a change of tack, the finger is removed, pressed against the right nostril, and he blows out like a humpback whale. A snob of crusted, juicy body matter flies out and splatters against the tabletop. It's studied for what seems like forever before the dealer bends his head, flicks out his tongue like Jeremy Fisher, and flops back to his sleeping position.

Like air trapped in a radiator, a chest full of pent-up breath escapes as the Cadet relaxes, removes the bulb, and heads for the living room. The stuttering snores are no more, and the house is in complete silence as he eases the door into the frame, reaches up, and, forgetting that the switch is on, presses the bulb into the fitting. It illuminates in his hand, and he screams out in shock — drops it, and instinctively kicks out to cushion its fall to the carpet.

"Fuck, fuck, fuck! What else is going to go wrong? What the hell am I even doing here?"

He slumps back into the armchair, his head in his hands; maybe he should get out while he still can. Because let's face it, if he's caught snooping around in this house, it will be the end of him, and nobody else apart from the occupants know that he's here: his parents think he's staying over at a mate's house. What should he do? Breathing heavily, he pushes his fingers through his hair again, and it's while he's massaging the scalp that he picks out the shape of the bulb lying on the carpet. Curiosity takes over — is it still intact? He gives it a little shake, and there is no rattle — it seems okay. Maybe he should check out the blanket and cushions before he makes any rash decisions. No harm in doing that, is there? At least it'll determine his next move. Flicking off the switch, he fits the bulb and tries again.

"Yes!"

Light floods the room and his eyes veer towards the three items; they don't require any closer inspection. A matching set fitting the description recorded on the crime report — the gold fleck glinting in the sixty-watt shaft of light.

'They've got to be the ones from the Ford Capri — no way can their presence here in this house be a matter of coincidence, and the tobacco tin that was in Mikey's pocket must belong to Robbo.'

Forgetting the thirst, he searches for the Sanyo cassette recorder and finds it — sat on the carpet behind the settee, with a flex running to an electrical socket.

"Oh my God — that's got to be Robbo's."

Ejecting the tape, he sees that it's Deep Purple's 'Machine Head' and track number one on the flip side is 'Smoke on the Water'. The opening riff plays inside his head.

'Dang, dang daaang - dang, dang, dang, daaang- dang, dang, daang – dang, daang.'

He punches the air, jigging around the room. It's got to be the tape from Robbo's car, and that is the song that Mikey was air-guitarring to. The song to which Rose came dancing into the kitchen from this very room. The song that was being played on the radio in his bedroom at Mrs Jones's house when it had all clicked into place.

It's him! Mikey Price is the killer of Bernard Jones. The evil, murdering bastard mowed Bernie down and left him there to die. He knew he'd hit him, but he didn't stop to see if he could help him, did he? No, he left him alone on the wet tarmac in the pissing-down rain. Not a thought for anyone else, as long as Mikey Price was alright, everyone else could go to hell. Even having the cheek to search the car and rob what he could carry before torching it; craftily sending any trace of his involvement up in a cloud of smoke. And he thinks he's got away with it. He thinks there is nothing to link him to the crimes because if there was, Rose's front door would have been bashed open by now, and he would have been dragged kicking and screaming to the local cop shop. Well, you're wrong, Mikey Price — there is a link.

Nausea, guilt, and an overwhelming sense of shame suddenly grip him, and the boy questions himself, fighting with his conscience. Why did he have to get involved with such a shit-bag? Why did he abandon his true friends and go against his family's values? And why is he still doing it? Why is he here, in this dump of a house, mixing with the dregs of society and getting out of his skull on fuck knows what?

There is nobody else to blame: every action was his choice, his decision, and this latest instalment was all because he didn't have the strength of character to turn down the chance of a bit of weed. Yes, you could argue that he did it so he could solve the case. That he had to do it to make Mikey trust him again. Bull shit! Let's face it, he could have done what he needed to do without sucking on a reefer and necking most of a bottle of Jack Daniel's. He's intelligent enough to have conned Mikey Price when they were sat by the kids' play area, but he didn't. He chose to jeopardise everything to satisfy his own cravings and that's why he finds himself here in this precarious situation.

He flops into the armchair, his eyes glaring at the gold-flecked blanket: chastising himself.

"What the hell is wrong with you? Clear your head and get a bloody move on, there isn't much time left to do what's needed. You can feel sorry for yourself and scrap with Mr Demon later — when you're safely out of this house."

CHAPTER 15

Why would Mikey Price choose to dump the stolen car where he did? What was his connection to that location, and what the hell was he doing in Neath in the first place?
The Cadet didn't know any of the answers: he didn't know Price back then. But if Mikey had killed a man, surely he would have heard something on the grapevine. Pembroke Dock is a small town — everybody knows everybody, and this is seriously heavy stuff: yet not even a whisper. He couldn't have told anyone: that's the only possible explanation. He probably fed Rose a right yarn about Robbo's gear. Not that she'd have cared less about what he did, but Mikey is shrewd, and he wouldn't have wanted her to have something that serious over him. So heavy that it would have been too much of a bargaining chip: something Rose could feed off forever.
Mikey's a leech, so he probably stole everything he could carry from the car. If the tobacco tin does belong to Robbo, then the flip-top petrol lighter that Rose was using is also his, and the rest of the stuff, including the flask, has got to be here in this house as well.
The only way to move on is to search Mikey's room and see if Robbo's number is on the tobacco tin. But is it worth the risk of being caught? If Mikey suspected anything untoward, he would clear Robbo's gear from this house in an instant, and no one would see them or the Cadet again.

Right, let's think about this logically. Supposing the cushions, the blanket, and the cassette player are all from the Capri. How can Robbo prove that they were his? He can't, can he? All he can say is they are similar. Hell, British Home Stores would have sold thousands of the bloody things, and the same with the cassette player; how many millions of those models have Sanyo churned out? Bloody hell, the Cadet had a similar one of his own.

What was that word he'd read about in the Police Manual yesterday afternoon? Corroboration — that's it. If the police raid this house and find Taff Robbo's tobacco tin, then the prosecution can say that any recorded, unidentifiable items that are also found during the search can be assumed to belong to Robbo. It would be too much of a coincidence for them not to be his: they would corroborate the evidence against Mikey Price.

Chewing at his thumbnail, he flicked off the light, opened the door, and stepped into the passage. His mind was settled: he was going to sneak upstairs, find the cigarette case, check to see if it is Robbo's, and get out of this bloody house.

A couple of steps along the passage, and doubt returns. What reason can he give for being in Mikey's bedroom? He shivers — it doesn't bear thinking about. A wiser individual would seek advice before taking the next course of action. Shit, he's never used any wisdom before, but maybe now is the time. Maybe now is the time to grow up and use some common sense. Confide in Dai Insignificant and tell him what he's discovered so far. He'd know precisely what to do, wouldn't he? Hell, he's an experienced Detective Sergeant. That's it — that's the safest and wisest thing for him to do. He'll get out of this house, and on Monday morning, he'll go to Dai's office and tell him what he's discovered. Dai can sort it out.

He crept past the entrance to the kitchen — no change there: Lugsey was still out of it. The Cadet's eyes fixed onto the key sticking out from the mortice lock on the half-wood-panelled glass door. Yes, he's making the right decision — isn't he?

He can be out of that door in three seconds flat. Jog home, climb between freshly laundered sheets, and stay there until lunchtime. Why climb those stairs behind him and enter the lion's den? No need for it. Two paces, turn the key, and be gone. Forget about bloody Mikey Price — why put himself through all this trauma?

His hand was turning the key when the Demon piped up.

'So, Mr wanna-be-detective. You're going to go running to the Detective Sergeant like a scaredy-cat little boy, are you? Ask him what to do. You shit house! Get yourself up those bloody stairs and search for the evidence that you need. Not checking out the tobacco tin will haunt you forever. You want to know if it's Robbo's tobacco tin, don't you? Just go for it — you know it makes sense. You've done it before — many times, and you've always got away with it. Why would you be caught this time? Remember the caravan park — that job just a few months ago?

*

(Several months earlier)

Juvenile giggling echoed from the interior of the closed-for-the-night mini-market, followed by a small packet hurtling from the darkness via the wedged-open casement window. It hit Colin on the side of the head before landing on the grass at the feet of the edgy group. The burglar's hand had shot to his mouth, but it was too late to stem the cry of surprise from escaping into the darkness. Hissing sounds of "shhh" together with hissed profanities from the others disturbed the silence of the night. By the stars and the moonlight, they could make out a packet of Tampax lying on the grass.

"Argh!"

Another packet had been dispatched, this time catching Bill Brown on his shoulder, and landed alongside its predecessor.

More hissing sounds of "shhh" escaped from those lurking in the shadows, and further bouts of childish laughter came from the two boys trespassing in the camp store.

Phyllis's eyes darted all around him, nervously checking the occupied caravans for any sign of possible discovery.

"Pack it in, you lot — if we fuck this up, Mikey will go bloody ape shit!"

No lights came on in any of the caravans, and there were no signs of any movement. All very still, all very tranquil, but it should be. It was shortly after two in the morning: the clubhouse closed at eleven.

Children were snuggled into warm blankets with their dolls or favourite teddies. Some were sucking on dummies, while others gripped 'had to have' comforters, easing the innocents through the dark sleep hours.

Dads on their backs, mouths wide open and snoring — their guts full of beer and takeouts; gurgling away as their organs worked overtime to break up and digest what they'd recently crammed in.

Mothers slept peacefully, many in similar states as their hubbies. Others, who had gossiped most of the evening away, their eyes watching everything and missing nothing, dreamt of finer things.

They were all enjoying the family summer holiday by the sea, so why would they be alert to the clandestine goings-on just a few steps away from their home for seven nights? Why should they have heard the hissing sounds coming from the poisonous snakes at the rear of the park's convenience store?

Colin was rubbing the crown of his head, whispering fucks and bastards towards the open window, attracting more hissing from his accomplices. He picked up both packets and lobbed them back from where they had come; more by luck than judgement, the yelps from the blackness confirmed direct hits. Colin's gesture of a triumphant bent arm and a closed fist together with a yes towards Bill Brown was the catalyst for more nervous giggling. Phyllis hissed the rollicking.

"For fuck's sake, come on, boys. Let's have a bit of hush and get on with it. The sooner we get out of here, the better. Stick to the bloody plan."

Mikey had suggested the target, and Phyllis had come up with the plan. He'd visited the shop just before it closed for the day and released the casement stay so the window could easily be pulled open from the outside. A method he would go on to use again and again... Already in his young life, a modus operandi had formed.

The rattle of a diesel engine disturbed the moment, followed closely by headlights, illuminating the roadway alongside the shop. It scattered the youngsters, sending them diving into the darkness and cover of a small copse.

Tense whispering came from inside the shop.

"Who is it — what is it?"

The response was calming — organising.

"We can't see yet, but going by the engine noise, it's slowed right down, and it's behind us. Whoever is in it won't be able to see you if you creep underneath the window and pull it closed."

"O.k. I'll do it now."

The calming voice spoke again.

"Have you got what we want and made sure everything's how it was before you went in?"

The same voice replied.

"We're doing that now — Mike's searching for one of the boxes of Tampax..." More giggling.

"...It hit him on the head and rolled under a display."

"Good, the car's getting closer, but we still can't see it. It's going really slow."

The hiders in the undergrowth spotted the window closing seconds before it was captured by the full beam of the headlights. Nothing looked untoward; for all intents and purposes, everything was as it should be.

A shaft of light swept through the trees and undergrowth, searching but finding nothing. The boys were lying perfectly still with their faces shoved into the grass, breathing in the mustiness of the early morning dew. Their dark clothing blended into the background; all they had to do was hold their nerve. Any movement now would flaw their camouflage and give their presence away. The vehicle dawdled past them, and as soon as the darkness returned, they rescued their eyes from the dampness and focused on a small white van with a rotating floodlight mounted on the roof. Its shaft of light was scanning the grass bank leading up to some caravan pitches directly opposite the shop. It stopped parallel with the entrance, and the light swivelled to penetrate deep inside the building, illuminating the display shelves.

The back of the van rose as the handbrake was applied, but the engine remained ticking over, rattling in the darkness as the driver's door screeched open. A circle of light illuminated the road, spotlighting a pair of size ten work boots, and a tall, overweight man carrying a large flashlight came into view: limping towards the hiders.

Another instruction was whispered: "Keep your faces in the grass. If he clocks us, we'll do one. He's too fat to catch us, but it'll give Mike and By the chance to get out."

The beam of light was directed towards them, picking out the tall grasses, seeking and getting closer to the prone bodies with noses squashed into the soil — their breathing and hearts racing. Was the light going to expose them?

No. The beam changed direction, the noses came up for air, and their eyes watched the man struggling down some concrete steps towards the shop entrance.

Dors turned to Phyllis, and there was an urgency in the voice.

"Do you think he'll spot them? He must be security or something like that."

The response was whispered, hissing in the deathly silence of the night.

"I'm sure Mike and By will be well out of sight. I'll crawl towards the roadway until I can see him. Hopefully, once he's finished checking, he'll go back to the van and head further into the site."

Commando crawling through the undergrowth, he halted at the grass verge bordering the road. The driver had gone past the shop and was standing with his feet apart, hunched over, and facing a hedgerow. Phyllis crawled out of view, shot to his feet, and ran to his mates.

"He's a good way down and he's having a piss. It's safe enough to tap on the window and get the boys out?"
A more mature voice whispered from behind them.
"We're ahead of you, Lloydy-Boy."
Mike's face was grinning from the aperture.
"Come on then, children, we ain't got all day. By's keeping an eye on Torchy, so let's get outta here."
The bag of ill-gotten gains was passed through the window, and the two intruders squeezed out, pushing it closed behind them.
They waited silently in the shadows, watching and listening until the van drove away.
"What we got then, Mike? Did you get the smokes and the whisky for Mikey?"
The older boy gave a thumbs up.
"Don't you worry, Lloydy-Boy, we got plenty. Let's get back to the car and we can share it out. I bet it's nearly three, and I've got fucking work in the morning. You're a bad influence, you lot, leading me astray like this."
His cackle of laughter set them all off, and the hissing of "Shhh" returned, but the adrenaline-fuelled vipers were sky high, and their excitable whispers gradually increased in volume as they slithered through the shadows — back to their nest where Mikey Price was waiting in the stolen car.

CHAPTER 16

Chewing at a fingernail, and looking up at nothing but blackness, the Cadet lingered at the bottom of the stairs.
'How the hell am I going to spot the tobacco tin?'
A recall of its whereabouts on Mikey's person at the park bench battled its way through the hangover, and the gnawing on the nail shot up a level.
'If it's in that pocket, then the first thing I'm going to have to do is find the pair of jeans, and if he's still wearing them? Well, that'll be the end of it... I might as well get out of this hellhole and leave it all to Dai Insignificant.'
The hand moved to caress his chin, deep in thought.
'But, Mikey will definitely need a smoke as soon as he wakes, so he's bound to have a couple of spliffs skinned up and within easy reach — probably alongside the bed. I've got to look in his bedroom — simple as that — it's the only way to find out.'
Reluctantly, he stepped from the sanctuary of light, deeper into the unknown, and closer to Rose: to get to Mikey he had to pass her room. It would be on his immediate right, and feeling his way through the pitch-black, it was the erratic sound of her breathing that interrupted the eerie silence of the house — the door must be open...
A loud scraping noise screeched from the kitchen — startling him, and instinctively, he spun around; tripped over the top step, stumbled into the gap, and landed on Rose's carpet —

gagging as a vile stink hit him full in the face. His hand sprang to cover his mouth; finger and thumb pinching the nostrils as he swallowed repeatedly, battling to stem the vomit that had risen to the back of his throat.

'What the hell had she eaten?'

He shied away from the stench, kneeling where he'd landed, listening for sounds of movement: there weren't any, and the rapid breathing eased.

'It must have been Lugsey — pushing back on his chair or pushing against the table in his sleep...'

Rose hadn't stirred, and all seemed quiet across the landing at Mikey's, but that probing glance through the darkness had caught sight of a faint yellowish light spilling from his room: silhouetting a large rectangular shape looming from the carpet. The rapid breathing was back: that object wasn't there on his previous visit.

Nudging his head forward, his eyes widened — straining them to the limit in an attempt to make out the identity of the shape, but that slight movement of the neck had made no difference and an overwhelming feeling of dread consumed him: was it a warning? A sixth sense? Is this all going to go horribly wrong, and should he get out of the house while he can?

The Cadet was shaking his head as he got down onto his stomach — nothing had changed. The only way to make absolutely sure that the tobacco tin was Robbo's was to find it, and thinking it to be a safer option, he had decided to crawl across the carpet until he was past the bathroom: at least by that point, his night vision might have kicked in and his sight would be more accustomed to the dark.

The shape was a door — the door to Mikey's room, and it was propped up against the balustrade — resting on the handrail. Through the gap, the Cadet could see that an amber glow shining from a street lamp directly outside Mikey's bedroom window was the origin of the yellow light, and relaxing a little, he reached out to one of the wooden spindles and pulled himself to his feet.

He didn't relax for long — that glow now highlighted a disturbing bout of extreme violence: splintered wood, mangled hinges that were hanging limply by a couple of bent screws, and a dark, viscous fluid — dotted and congealing above the latch. The door had been ripped away from the frame.
The Cadet prodded at the fluid — sniffing at his finger.
'Bloody hell, that's blood! I'm sure that's blood! What the hell has happened here?'
He didn't want to enter the room, fighting with himself before coming to a compromise: he'd place his hands either side of the frame, rise onto the ball of his right foot, balance with his left leg stuck out behind him, stoop, and edge his head inside.
'Yes — that's what I'll do.'
He took a deep breath and listened: there were no sounds coming from within, and doubt began to creep in — was Mikey even in there? There was only one sure way to find out — he stepped towards the gap.
"Oh my God — he's dead!"
Gasping, he pushed away from the frame, his heel kicking against the door as he landed, and shell-shocked, he could only watch as it bounced against the handrail, slid towards the bathroom, and started to topple. Coming to his senses, he snatched at it, his hand slipping in the congealing fluid before managing to grip, inches before it crashed to the floor.
He stood there — bent over — breathing heavily — listening, and looking through the blackness towards Roses's domain. There were no accusing shouts — no sounds of movement from there, or the kitchen. Rose and Lugsey must be outers...
Sweat had seeped into his eyes, and rapidly blinking the moisture away, he focused onto the sanctuary of light below — an easy escape route from the nightmare he was caught up in. Should he just cut his losses and get out? Deny ever being upstairs?
He sighed as he repositioned the door — he couldn't. He couldn't just run away from what he'd seen in that room. He

had to find out what had happened to Mikey.

CHAPTER 17

The glow from the street lamp, filtering through filthy, once-white, net curtains, cast a greying tinge over the skin stretched across the addict's gaunt face. The skeletal frame was flat on its back in the centre of the room. Both eyes were wide open, staring at the ceiling, and had sunk deep into their sockets. There was no rising of the chest — no sound of breathing — no signs of any life. The body was wrapped up like a papoose, in a tattered, thin blanket — lying on a scabby-looking single mattress with its feet poking out — still wearing a pair of white-coloured trainers. There were no sheets and no bedstead.

The Cadet had never seen a dead body before. What should he do? What can he do? What the hell had happened to him? Was it something to do with the blood-splattered door? If that was the case, then why hadn't he heard the commotion? Was he in that much of a state that he'd slept through it all? Surely that couldn't be the case, and anyway, he'd heard Mikey snoring earlier, hadn't he?

The hand caressed the chin.

Unless it was Rose who had been snoring? Was he disoriented, confused as to which room the snores were coming from? He nodded his head in agreement with another possibility that slipped into the thought process: Mikey might have died of natural causes. Suffered a heart attack — maybe a stroke —

something like that?

'Hell, the amount of shit he's taken on board over his teenage years, that's hardly surprising.'

A sadness came over him as he stared through the gloom at the body of the young man who had been such an influence on his life. Mikey had died owning and achieving nothing worthwhile. Such a rapid decline in an individual who had once been strong and fearsome. A man revered by easily impressed adolescents such as himself — feared by many. Someone who would never take a backward step to avoid any confrontation, but look at his body now — a shadow of what it used to be — a body ravaged by heroin.

A gap in the dense cloud presented the full moon with an opportunity to ally with the street lamp, and the room was instantly flooded with more light. A glint from something metal caught the Cadet's eye: it shone alongside the mattress — close to Mikey's head.

'Wow — surely that's the tobacco tin.'

He shot a quick glance at the body — then back to the glint.

'I've got to check it out. It's just a case of picking up the tin, holding it against the window pane and seeing if Robbo's military number is engraved on the inside of the lid. If it is, I can put it back where it was, get out of this house, and tell Dai Insignificant a heavily censored version of what I've uncovered when I see him on Monday morning. As far as I'm concerned, Mikey was alive and sleeping when I left the house during the early hours. No need to mention anything about having to search upstairs.'

Getting down to his knees, he edged closer, stretched out a hand, and as his fingertips curled around the tin, Mikey shouted out.

"You thieving bastards!"

The young cop threw himself to the carpet; his heart battering against the rib cage, thudding into the well-trodden pile. His brain working overtime...

'Bloody hell — he's alive! How the hell is he alive? He can't be

alive: his eyes were wide open and sunk into his skull, and he wasn't breathing! Shit, what excuse can I give for crawling around on his floor in the middle of the night? He obviously thinks I'm trying to steal his tobacco tin...'
Mikey screamed out again.
"Argh, leave me alone — you thieving bastards — I never saw nothing."
The next voice was also masculine, but it wasn't Mikey and it wasn't Lugsey. It thundered from Rose's bedroom.
"Shut the fuck up, you lunatic, and go to fucking sleep. Shouting out like a fucking weirdo. What the fuck is wrong with you?"
The boy froze — his brain still struggling to process that Mikey wasn't dead.
'He's been alive the whole time that I was hovering over him — bloody reminiscing.'
Shaking his head in frustration, he badgered himself to concentrate.
'Get a bloody grip — forget about Mikey. No way was that Rose's voice, there's somebody else in the house! That voice was undoubtedly male, and the maker of those words sounds big, and he sounds bloody angry. And he must have been in bed with Rose when I was sat on her flippin' carpet.'
An almighty snore echoed within the confines of the bedroom, and the angry voice shouted out again.
"Turn onto your side, Mikey. Snoring like a fucking walrus and shouting out. How the fuck are we supposed to get some sleep? You selfish bastard!"
The Cadet raised his nose from the grime of the carpet — checking on Mickey. His arms were now free from the blanket, and his mouth was wide open — belting out another grating snore.
'He must have been comatose earlier, and now he's dreaming. Mikey's not a threat: the danger is coming from Rose's bedroom. She and that voice are squabbling, and their shenanigans are going to wake up Lugsey; that's the last thing

I need...

Shit — heavy footsteps — someone is walking about and going by the sound of those steps it must be a flippin' giant. Bloody hell — they're getting closer!'

He scanned the room — searching for somewhere to hide.

'There's a door at the foot of the mattress. It's probably a built-in cupboard or something similar. It's the only chance I've got.'

Grabbing the tin, he crawled over and lobbed it into the darkness. It was a wardrobe, and the interior was just big enough to squeeze into, kneel down, pull the Louvre-type door towards him, and leave it ajar. Twisting at the waist, his face was squashed against the thin wooden slats, and the only free space for his arms was outstretched above his head.

The footsteps entered. The unknown flicked the switch, and light from a shadeless bulb stole in through the gaps between the slats, illuminating the wardrobe. Beads of sweat, trickling down the Cadet's cheeks, were moistening his lips, while a torrent raged down the middle of his back, soaking the waistband of his underwear. His breathing was heavy, rapid, and pulsing in his eardrums.

'If I'm caught in here, I'm a goner! Urgh, what the hell is that smell?'

A distinct whiff of human excrement had flooded his nostrils, and while straining to bend his neck to see what he was kneeling on, he grimaced when he caught a glimpse of the tobacco tin — nestled amongst a pile of heavily skid-marked Y fronts...

'You dirty bastard, Mikey! Can't you even wipe your bloody arse?'

Why hadn't the Cadet taken the easy option? Why didn't he walk out of that front door when he had the chance? Simple — his mind wouldn't let him. He would torture himself for an age with what-ifs and maybes if he didn't confirm the tobacco tin to be Robbo's before reporting back to Dai Insignificant.

Total darkness engulfed him: the particles of light that had been sneaking through the slats were now blocked by the unknown's bulk. He had paused in front of the wardrobe, his breathing guttural and his chest rattling like a sixty-fags-a-day man suffering from acute bronchitis. And to top it all, he stank like a rabid skunk on heat.

Muttering to himself, he was searching for something, and when he squatted at the foot of the mattress, something had to give: there wasn't sufficient space, and the man's naked backside squelched against the wardrobe door, ramming it shut and shunting the Cadet into a space that wasn't there. The pain was excruciating as his body contorted in all directions and, struggling to stifle an almost certain giveaway scream, he drew blood as he bit into his bottom lip.

Totally oblivious, the man was shaking Mikey's legs.

"You're dreaming, Mikey, and you're snoring like a fucking pig. Roll onto your side and get back to sleep."

The addict's response was muffled, an incoherent load of gibberish, followed by instant deep breathing: he was on another planet.

The man was struggling to stand: he was wedged, and the rolls of fat pressing against and in between the flimsy slats of the Louvre door were buckling them to breaking point. Gripping the mattress, he wheezed as he spoke — tugging his mass free.

"What the fuck has he done with the smokes? The useless piece of shit."

He stood over the sleeper, nudging him with his foot — frustration rising in his voice.

"Where's your smokes, Mikey? We needs a fucking smoke."

There is no response, and the man, his self-control blitzed, kicks out at him in temper, misses, and loses his balance. His bulk careers towards the wardrobe door, and a heavily bandaged hand that he instinctively thrusts out smashes through the slats, missing the Cadet's face by a hair's breadth. The man screams out.

"Argh — not again! Look what you've made me do, you useless fuck. Where's the fucking smokes, Mikey? What have you done with the fucking smokes?"

The hand is yanked free from the slats, leaving segments of bandage trapped in the splintered timber. His blood has splattered against the hider's cheek — it's sliding towards his mouth, and the terrified boy can't move his hand to wipe it away. Panicking, he tilts his head, trying to rub his face against the sleeve of his jumper.
The man is cursing and sucking at the gaping wound to his wrist as he shuffles
around the perimeter of the mattress; frantically searching, his chest is crackling and
wheezing as he struggles to lift the quilted edge.
The Cadet eyes the tobacco tin — fear gnawing away at his gut — fighting the urge to lick away the blood which is tickling his top lip.
'Please don't look in here, bloody hell, why did I grab the tin? He's going to look in here next. I know he is — I've had it.'
His brain is thumping against his temple as he braces himself for the inevitable battering, and he comes up with a plan.
'As soon as he starts to pull open the door, I'll scream like a banshee and spring towards him. He'll cack his pants, fall backwards onto Mikey, and that'll give me the chance to run away.'
He remembers the tobacco tin.
'Shit! I'll have to grab that when I can move, and during the commotion I'll chuck it towards where I found it. At least then Mikey might not put two and two together.'
He could hear the man shuffling closer — hear his guttural breathing — smell the stench from his body.
'He's going to search in here any second!'
The light disappeared between the gaps in the slats, and the stink from the man's fetid breath fused with the whiff from the skid-marked Y-fronts as a podgy hand grasped the handle.
The boy braced himself.
It started to open.
'Oh my God, I'm dead...'
A familiar voice shouted out.

JON H. DAVIES

"Jimmy, I've found the smokes. They're under yr pillow, you dozy pillock."

CHAPTER 18

"Can you be absolutely, one hundred per cent certain that it was Taff Robbo's tobacco tin?"
The response was immediate.
"Yes, Sarge, definitely. I saw it and I saw Robbo's military registration number engraved on the inside of the lid — the tin can only be his."
Detective Sergeant Winters blew the smoke from the side of his mouth, removed the Calabash from his lips, and scratched his forehead with the stem. He couldn't believe it: all these years in the job, and he'd experienced nothing like this before.
His eyes fixed on those of the Cadet.
"Enlighten me, young man, what is Mr Roberts' military number?"
He blurted it out.
"04680431, Sarge — I've memorised it — I kept saying it over and over again. It was the best feeling ever when I opened the lid, and that number was staring back at me. I know this sounds weird, but it was as if it was smiling at me, you know, like a Genie from a lamp and I was its rescuer. I hated having to leave it there."
The Cadet half-smiled, blushed, and diverted his eyes.
'The Sergeant must think I'm bloody nuts...'
The pipe was back in Dai's mouth, and his eyes hadn't strayed from the boy's opposite. His mind, working overtime, was

processing that response.
'People like this boy don't come along very often, once, possibly twice in a generation, and they generally progress in one of two ways. They crash and burn, or they succeed in nigh on everything that they choose to do.
'Choose to' being the optimum words...'
"Looks like you've got a result then, young man..."
The Detective Sergeant stood up and his hand shot across the desk. A wide grin lit up his face.
"Well done, son, well done. Now, what to do with your hard work?"

*

It was 07:30 hrs on the Monday morning, and bargaining on Dai Insignificant being an early bird, the Cadet had gone in to see him first thing: prior to the hustle and bustle of the returning office staff following the weekend break. The two detectives working in the office a couple of doors up could be overheard, laughing and joking. Dai picked up the phone.
"Get in here, you two, and bring the file on Bernard Jones with you — you're going to love this.

*

"Gentlemen, take a seat."
He pointed the Calabash at Phyllis.
"This young man is Cadet Lloyd Davies and, like us, he has been saddled with a bizarre nickname. They call him Phyllis. I dare say he'll get used to it in time."
The Detective Sergeant paused for effect, tapped the residue from the pipe into an ash tray, and rested it on the edge.
"As we had to."
The Detectives were laughing as Dai introduced them.
"Phyllis, meet Bill and Clive Protheroe. Identical twins as you've no doubt noticed, except for..."
Dai glanced over at Bill.
"...you don't mind if I do the honours, do you, Bill?"
The detective shook his head and chuckled — he knew what was coming.

"You carry on, Dai."

"You can see how Bill's nose has a little dent in it. All to do with the use of forceps at birth. Stubborn little bugger wouldn't come out. Clive reckons he's a tight so-and-so and wouldn't leave his snuggly little home during the depths of winter because they'd have to put the bloody heating on! Anyway, back in the day, when he enlisted in the Royal Engineers, some wise guy pointed out that his nose resembled a little mushroom. What did they call him? Buttons! And Clive? Well — he's known as The Mule..."

Dai glared at the Cadet.

"...Don't even ask!"

Once the laughter subsided, the Detective Sergeant turned to the two brothers.

"You're probably wondering why I've called you in here so early on a Monday morning. Well, I wanted to include you in what young Phyllis is about to tell us. I know how hard you worked on the Bernard Jones case, and how deflated you were when the enquiry was scaled down. I believe, Gentleman, that we now have a prime suspect, and your input will be invaluable."

The Cadet recounted his adventure. Was he nervous? Of course, he was, who wouldn't be in that position, but he still had the presence of mind to omit any incriminating facts: no necessity for anyone else to be aware of his passion for a toke every once in a while, was there? And Mikey Price certainly wouldn't be telling anyone.

It didn't cross his mind though, that Dai Insignificant would be scrutinising his every word and watching his every body movement. And the Detective Sergeant didn't take long to suss out that the trainee cop was holding back. Hell, he'd been around too long not to. What impressed him, though, but at the same time concerned him, was the boy's strength of character and guile. Now, that could get the youngster into deep shit, unless he had someone looking out for him.

Dai was feeling a smattering of excitement in his belly: something that had been sorely missing for a long time. Maybe he, Detective Sergeant David Winters, was just the person to do that.

When the Cadet spoke about seeing Robbo's military number on the tobacco tin, Buttons raised his hand.

"Can I step in here, Dai, before Phyllis goes any further?"

He smiled at the Cadet, spotting the concerned look on his face.

"Nothing wrong, lad."

The smile quickly dissipated, and he swallowed, shaking his head and sighing as he handed the Detective Sergeant another undetected crime report.

"This is a bad one, Dai, and like our Bernard Jones case, South Wales Police haven't got a clue who did it. On the day that Robbo's Capri was nicked, this robbery happened."

The Detective Sergeant's face greyed as he read about the horrific attack on Michael Moore; his eyes peering over the top of the crime report as he spoke.

"Bloody hell, Phyllis, if the guy who did this turns out to be Mikey Price..."

He paused to gather himself, reaching for the Calabash and firming another hit of tobacco in the bowl.

"...you put yourself in extreme danger..."

He passed the crime report to the Cadet, lit the pipe, and expelled the smoke through the side of his mouth before continuing.

"...I doubt very much that you would be here now if that smelly slob had opened the door to that cupboard!"

*

The three detectives ticked off the items of stolen property that the Cadet had seen in Mikey's house, and a discussion ensued: words and phrases like warrant, real evidence, hearsay evidence, documentary evidence, burden of proof, agent provocateur, the inference to a court, and protection of the source formed the mind-blowing debate, and the Cadet didn't have a clue what they were going on about. He sat there in silence, his mind in turmoil, and Mr Demon was having a right go at him.

"That's it, matey, you've messed up big time. No one is going to believe this crock of shite. I'd keep your gob shut if I were you or you're finished!"

By the time the Detective Sergeant spoke to him, the Cadet's armpits were like an oasis in the Gobi desert.

"Right, Phyllis, initially we need to liaise with a Detective Inspector Pat Muldoon in Pembrokeshire. He'll be the officer coordinating the investigation, so he needs to be briefed on what we have to date…"

He pushed up his specs.

"…He'll require a synopsis of what you know to be true and you'll write that on an intelligence log…"

The deep swallow and the furrowing of the Cadet's forehead was a reminder to the Detective Sergeant.

"Don't you worry about that — I'll write it. We then fax him a copy together with the initial crime reports. The intelligence log is all that he'll need in order to swear out a search warrant for Rose Price's house."

He addressed Clive and Buttons, rubbing his hand across his forehead as he spoke.

"Buttons, can you get on the blower to Tony Beech in Neath? Appraise him and see if they have any forensic updates: prints, fibres, you know the crack. Can Michael Moore identify the sadistic bastard if we put him on a line-up? He gives a detailed enough description of his eyes — I'd put my house on it — Michael Moore sees that evil bastard's every time he closes his own…"

The Detective Sergeant gives a shiver and turns to the Cadet.

"Is it him? Are Price's eyes like that? Does he have a green-coloured Parka with a fur-lined hood?"

Phyllis nodded, slumping uncomfortably into the chair, struggling to compose himself. As soon as he read the description, he knew it was Mikey. The Parka, the bushy brows, the heavy-lidded stare that pierced into you; how many times had he been the recipient? Why the hell did he ever get involved with Mikey Price?

Dai spotted it and once more remembered just how young the boy was: he was in need of protection. This case was horrific, and the circumstances would give the most experienced of detectives bloody nightmares, let alone a kid fresh out of school.

"That's good enough for me, son. There is too much evidence pointing towards Mikey Price, so let's make sure we tick all the boxes and, excuse my French, padlock the fuckers. We are going to nail this sick bastard. Clive, check out his previous convictions and associates. Why would he be in Neath on that day? Why would he nick a car from that area and kill some innocent pedestrian with it in Carmarthen?"

Buttons raised his hand again.

"I've just had a thought, Sarge. It might be a long shot, but when Bernard Jones was mowed down, he had some silver jewellery in his pocket, and he'd just come out of 'Sparkles', you know, the jeweller's shop owned by that town councillor…"

He turned to his brother.

"…What's her bloody name, Clive?"

His hand rubbing his chin as he thought.

"Fiona Phillips, that's it, Councillor Phillips. Well, it might be a coincidence, but…"

Dai butted in.

"No such thing as coincidence, Buttons — you're spot on. The robbery had gone tits-up in Neath: was Price planning another? Something they can put to him on interview when we have the bastard banged up. Right, I would imagine they'll set up an eyeball on his home address sometime today as they'll need to confirm Mikey and Rose's whereabouts. It's paramount they are present when the search warrant is executed. You two have plenty to get on with."

He nodded towards Buttons.

"Just a thought, perhaps pay another visit to that Town Councillor and to the other witness — Mrs Davies — the young blonde. See if they can add any more to their initial statements, and keep me updated. I'll bell the Detective Chief Inspector

who was leading you lot on the initial enquiry — our beloved colleague, the wind-up merchant, Mr Richard Lewis. Brief him on the breakthrough. Perhaps a drop of his own medicine is in order, gentlemen. What do you think?"
A mischievous grin exposed the gold incisor as he winked.
"Something along the lines of: 'Bloody hell, Rich, all that experience at your disposal — weeks of enquiries — an unlimited budget and you still drew a blank. How come our Cadet cracked it all on his lonesome in a couple of hours and on a shoestring? Total outlay? A return bus ticket to Pembroke Dock and a bottle of Jack Daniel's.'"

*

The Cadet was quiet. His eyes had glazed over, and absentmindedly he was clenching his hands into fists.
Dai Insignificant had spotted the signs.
"Come on then, youngster, spit it out. What's on your mind?"
The boy briefly shied away from the detective's gaze, trying to compose himself.
"I'm worried about my parents, Sarge. Mikey's going to know that it's me, isn't he? He'll know that I'm the one who's grassed him up: it's not going to be hard for him to suss that out, is it?"
He wrings his hands together, fighting back the tears.
"Mikey knows where I live, but I'm hardly ever at home nowadays. What he did to that jeweller was brutal and sickening. I knew he was violent, but hell, Sarge, that was way off the scale. He's a raving nutcase, and his head will be full of revenge and hatred for me. And if he can't reach me, well, who's the next best thing? My dad's a fire officer and he brings the fire car home — parks it on the drive when he's on call."
Suddenly he felt cold, and he shivered, unable to prevent a lone tear from escaping. He shakes his head in annoyance, brushing it away.
"What if Mikey's sick mind decides to set fire to the house while they're asleep in bed? I can see him now, that evil scowl, those penetrating eyes — smirking and leering.
'Put that fucker out then, Mr Fire Chief: you fucking pig

producer!'"

The Detective Sergeant rose from the recliner, sat on the edge of his desk, rested a comforting hand on the Cadet's shoulder, and sighed.

'This lad could quite easily be my son. The child Susie and I never found the time to have.'

His voice is reassuring — the soft Yorkshire accent calming, oozing with confidence.

"I promise you, young man, everything will be fine. The officers who deal with this piece of shit will be switched on and fully briefed by Detective Inspector Pat Muldoon. He's no mug; I've known Pat for centuries. He lives and breathes the job, and he runs a tight, bloody ship. Yes, he'll pull out all the stops to put Price away, and he'll enjoy getting him off the streets. But your safety and that of your family will be top of his list of priorities. Your identity will be known, but only to him. I'll write the intelligence report, and your name won't be anywhere near it, but I'll have to divulge your details to Pat. In order for him to swear out the search warrant, the information has to be of a certain standard. When he's holding up the Bible in his right hand, he has to be confident enough to swear by Almighty God in front of the Magistrate that this information is spot on. On this particular occasion, Pat will be able to tell the Magistrate that the property we want to recover has recently been seen in the subject's house by a bloody trainee copper!"

The Detective Sergeant relaxed back in the recliner, pressed in a fresh dollop of tobacco, and lit the Calabash. The tobacco was glowing, and his mouth was full of the aromatic smoke when he continued.

"The importance of finding the tobacco tin, ideally, in this Mikey bloke's pocket is of supreme importance. If they find the petrol lighter as well, then we're quids in. And if they find the bloody flask..."

Dai took an elongated drag, speaking from the side of his mouth as the smoke spilt out with his words.

"...Well, we'll have a bloody full house, won't we?"
The sentences flowed, and the excitement in his voice was inspiring. The Detective Sergeant was once again at one with the world; a showman who had always led by example. He hadn't realised just how much he missed front-line policing: the crack, the excitement, the highs and the lows. But it had been taking a toll on his marriage. He and Susie were becoming strangers, and something had to give. This office job, normally dead man's shoes, came up, and he grabbed the opportunity before the coffin lid had been nailed down. Was he happy? He'd be lying if he said he was. Maybe he was content, you know, happy with his lot if you get my drift. He glanced at the boy sitting on the other side of the desk. Until the day this bloody youngster came along, and total mayhem was let loose. Turned his whole world upside down.
Dai Insignificant was alive again, the buzz was back, and he was loving it.
He clapped his hands together, got up, flicked on the kettle, tapped the debris from the Calabash into an ashtray, and exposed the gold veneer.
"Once they find that bloody tin, son, they can arrest Mikey and Rose Price on suspicion of murdering Bernard Jones."
The trainee cop shot up from his chair.
"B But I I don't think Rose had anything to do with it, Sarge: she only lives with him. It was all down to Mikey — he's brought the stolen goods to her house. Don't you —"
The right scaffolding pole with an upturned open palm shot across the desk, stopping him in mid-flow.
"It's a bargaining chip, boy, a mere bargaining chip — you never know, we might need to summon up a little bit of help from somewhere to get an admission of guilt..."

CHAPTER 19

Detective Inspector Patrick Liam Muldoon had seen it all, and what he didn't know about criminal investigations could be written on the raised edge of a freckle. But his philosophy of life was — you are never too old to learn — every day is a school day.
He could have retired 18 months ago, and he would have enjoyed a more than comfortable lifestyle, but what the hell, he loved the job: what else would he do?
He hadn't long replaced the handset following an enlightening conversation with Detective Sergeant David Winters, his friend and colleague at the Ivory Towers of Police Headquarters, and he was on sentry duty by the fax machine at Pembroke Dock Police Station. The sensitive documents clearly marked in red capital letters as 'Confidential' were imminent: a red rag to the inquisitive eyes of Cyril, the station constable, June, the telephonist, Rob, the handyman, and his wife, Audrey, the cleaner.
Striding back to his domain, the papers unread by any unauthorised eyes and secure in his grasp, he shouted out to his Detective Sergeant — Graham 'The Bull' Williams.
"Bull, grab Cadders and Tomo out of the canteen — meeting in my office..."
He checked his wristwatch — it was 0926.
"...twenty to ten, and check out the availability of a dog

handler. Oh, and get Cerys back from that bloody waste-of-time course she's on in Haverfordwest — we are going to need reinforcements ASAP!"

*

The phone was answered on the second ring: the voice cheery and welcoming.
"Good morning, Magistrates' Clerks' office, Amanda speaking, how can I help you?"
The male caller's tone was slow and assertive.
"Well, you can start by getting those pink, lace, knickers off."
The attractive brunette couldn't prevent the blush, and coy eyes darted around the bustling office, followed by a giggle.
"Pat, lower your voice, you'll get me sacked..."
Turning away from the melee, her hand partially covered her mouth as the cheery tone lowered to smooth and sultry: her eyes sparkling with devilment.
"By the way, lover-boy, I'm not wearing the pink, lace, knickers. They're still by the breakfast bar, I didn't have time to pick them up..."
He chuckled.
"Funny you should say that, Mrs Muldoon, we've just had a report of a flasher and I'm on my way over..."
The laughter ceased — it was business as usual.
"...On a serious note, love, is there a court sitting this morning? I need a search warrant."
"No, you sexy beast, and before you ask, the easiest magistrate to get hold of today is George Brown. Hang on a sec, I'll get you his number..."
Leaning back in her chair, they were eyes full of love that checked the list on the wall.
"Right Pat, it's 6934. Sounds like you're going to be late home tonight, darling. Don't forget — we've got pork chops."
The playful chuckle was back.
"Nothing will keep me away from your luscious chops, my sweetheart. I'll see you later — love you."
Pat Muldoon hadn't noticed the tall, stocky frame of Detective

Sergeant Graham Williams looming behind him in the doorway. The thick-necked officer pursed his lips, enhancing a couple of days' growth on his chin, and spoke in as high a pitched tone as his base vocal chords would stretch.
"Oh, I didn't know you cared, boss — I love you too."
He blew a kiss.
It was Muldoon's turn to blush.
"Ha ha, very funny. Sit down, Bull, we're going to pay one of our most cherished members of the parish a surprise visit. Any news on Cerys?"
The Detective Sergeant shook his head.
"You know what it's like nowadays, Pat. Bloody bureaucracy — she'll be at least a couple of hours."
"Shit — she would have been bloody handy: I've got a spot of surveillance in mind."
They were joined by the two Detective Constables, laughing about a joke some bright spark had acted out in the canteen.
"Morning, gents, take a seat, and close the door behind you."
The laughter ceased: something had happened and something big. The detectives sensed it and the adrenaline kicked in. This is why they got up in the mornings.
Scraping noises of chairs being dragged closer to the Detective Inspector's desk, eyebrows raised, forced smiles, nervous fidgeting, and inquisitive eyes darting back and forth all ceased when 'The Boss' tapped the star-clipped edges of A4 onto his desk. He could feel those eyes boring into him and a warmth gripped his insides. He was fortunate — this crew were as good as they came. Pat stood up and handed out the paper files minus the Cadet's intelligence report. No need for anyone else to be aware of that existence — not just yet anyway.
"Gentlemen, make yourselves familiar with these crime reports. I'm off upstairs to brief 'the old man'. I'll only be five minutes — ten tops".

*

35 minutes later, Muldoon was back in his office and feeling

like he'd been dragged through a clothes ringer. The Superintendent's probing questions had been answered — to a degree — well, let's just say he was abreast of what he needed to know and going by the heated debate on the merits of bringing back hanging, Bull, Tomo, and Cadders were up to speed with the atrocities of the crimes. But what was their involvement in serious crimes that had been committed in another division and even more unusually, in another police force? The atmosphere was buzzing.

Pat raised his arm, and there was silence.

"Gentlemen, we have a suspect. Surprisingly, bearing in mind the locations of the crimes, he is one of ours, and well known to us. What is not surprising, as you well know, is this individual's capability of inflicting such terror onto a fellow human being. The arsehole in question is..."

The fingers of both hands did a drum roll on the desk.

"...Mikey Price!"

Excitable chit-chat broke out, and Pat's hand was raised again.

"We don't have a great deal of time, and there is much to organise. This has to be done carefully, professionally, and..."

He cleared his throat, coughed, and spoke from the side of his mouth.

"... with the assistance of the Ways and Means Act of 1066..."

Laughter filled the small office.

You have no doubt sussed that there is a source, and it is vital for obvious reasons that this person is protected. Gentlemen, I have a plan, and I have every confidence that you will make it work. If all goes well, Mikey Price will not be sending us any Christmas cards this year..."

He sat back in the chair and grinned.

"... And hopefully, not for many years to come. This, my friends, is how we are going to do it..."

CHAPTER 20

"Standby, standby, standby — the target, Mikey Price, is out of the front door and oops, his mother is with him. Yes, Rose Price is standing in the doorway. She's not going anywhere, Sarge. She's wearing a pink dressing gown, pink fluffy slippers, and her hair is full of pink bloody curlers. They are arguing about something, and she's waved goodbye to him. Well, she flicked the V's and shouted, 'Fuck off!' Mikey has returned the same loving gesture and has taken a right towards the main drag."
The observing officer released the press-to-speak button, and the response from Bull was instant — frustration in his voice.
"What the fuck's he wearing, George?"
The observer flushed; cursing under his breath.
"Oh — sorry, Sarge. He's got on that green-coloured Parka coat that he always wears, and the hood is up. Blue jeans and white trainers."
"Cheers — let us know when he reaches the junction with the main road: we have an eyeball on that area and can take him from there."
"Will do, Sarge, and by the way, Rose has just slammed the door. She has remained in the house. I repeat, Rose has remained at home."
Temporary Detective Constable George Bradshaw felt the warmth of a slender hand on his bare shoulder, and long, unkempt hair tickled his back as Lucy Devonald whispered in

his right ear, her breath hot, the tip of her tongue catching the lobe.

"You want that cup of tea now, Georgie?"

Tingles shot down the spine of the wannabe detective, straight into his nether regions, and he struggled to keep his eyes on Mikey Price.

"Give us a sec, Lucy, and I'll be all yours."

She pressed her nipples into his back.

"I'll put the kettle on then. I'll have to pick up Jason from my mam's soon, but you can stay here if you want to, Georgie."

A long enough lecherous glance over the shoulder caught a fulfilling glimpse of the twenty-five-year-old's naked body disappearing into the kitchen: it also missed Mikey Price turning right into one of the maze of alleyways.

"Fuck, fuck, fuck — where's he gone? He could only have taken that first turning."

George chewed on his thumbnail.

"No way did Mikey have time to get to the next one and make a left."

He pressed the transmit button.

"He's turned right into the estate, Sarge. I repeat, he's turned right into the estate, and he's out of my view: general direction of the football pitch."

He stood up, tugging at his Y-fronts.

"Do you want me to follow him, Sarge?"

The response was firm.

"That's a no, no, George. I repeat — no, no. Stay in the O.P. and keep tabs on Rose as per Muldoon's plan. We need to know where they both are at all times."

"Yes, Sarge, understood, Sarge. Will do, Sarge."

George Bradshaw grinned as he placed the radio onto the arm of the chair...

"Still want that cuppa, Georgie?"

The Temporary Detective Constable swung around to see the young mother standing in the open doorway; her legs slightly apart, with one hand resting against the architrave and the

other on her hip. Sensually, she brushed her tongue across her top lip, and he felt the stirring in his groin again.
"What the hell do you think, Lucy?"

*

"I have eyes on the target, Bull, and he's staggering across the football field. This bloody wind is blowing him in all directions. I can't follow at the moment: it's too open, and he's too close, but he's on his way towards the town centre."
"No worries, Cadders. I'll drop Tomo off ahead of him."
"Noted — I can monitor him from here until you get into position. I'm covert enough."
Detective Constable Terrence William Caddering had recently received his Police Long Service and Good Conduct Medal: twenty-two years in the job. Having spurned the invitation to have it presented to him by the Chief Constable at a lavish ceremony with local dignitaries at H.Q., it remained unwrapped, on a worktop littered with unwashed crockery, in his rented bedsit: delivered as requested by Royal Mail a fortnight ago.
An opportunity to meet up and reminisce as the champagne flowed with all the other recipient officers and their spouses, many of whom he hadn't seen since basic training all those years ago, had passed him by. And his reason? It just hadn't felt right — not without his Emma. And she'd left him, hadn't she? Ran off three months ago with her boss at 'Secure Your Move', Estate Agents in Main Street, Pembroke.
A part-time job that she'd taken because she was bored.
"It's only a few hours a week and it'll get me out of the house, Terry, love..." she'd said. "...you know, while the kids are at school."
Apparently, she was seeing more of her boss than she did of him...
It was all his fault though, wasn't it? Always working, wasn't he?
"Married to the job," she'd said.
Tucked away inside a metal shelter, his hands resting on the

wooden spectator rail bordering the pitch, Cadders sighed as sad eyes surveyed Mikey Price shuffling in the wind across the damp turf.

"That greasy, bastard boss of hers had been seeing a lot more of my Emma than he should have been. And now, the sweet-talking, bull-shitting, arse-wipe is dossing in my fucking house! Shit, where's Price off to now?"

He fumbled in his pocket for the radio and pressed the transmit button.

The anxiety noticeable in his voice.

"Price has crossed the length of the pitch, Tomo, and he's cut through to a side street — can't think of the bloody name of it. He's out of my sight — general direction of the town centre ..."

There was no response.

"Shit, I can't see him now!"

The Detective Constable vaulted the rail and jogged across the turf; his breathing heavy as he shouted into the handset. His speech distorted by the howling wind.

"I'm making ground — have you got him, Tomo?"

Seconds seemed like hours passed until there was a response, and it was the Detective Sergeant.

"We're stuck in bloody traffic, Cadders. Some dozy idiot decided to do a three-point turn in front of us, and he's knocked over the soddin' keep-left bollard in the middle of the road. It's bloody bedlam here! Do you have eyes on Price?"

The Detective Constable shouted into the handset.

"I've lost him, Bull. He's bloody vanished!"

"Shit, what the hell are you saying, Cadders? You're breaking up!"

Bull didn't release the press-to-speak button, and Cadders couldn't transmit, but he could overhear Tomo screaming obscenities at the driver of the offending vehicle.

The supervisor's voice broke the silence.

"Repeat your last update, Cadders."

Picturing Tomo's irate outburst, Cadders was grinning as he opened his jacket to shield the radio.

"It's a total loss, Bull — I repeat — a total loss! Price last seen heading in the general direction of the town centre."

"No problem, Cadders. The road's clear now — the loss is close to the railway station so I'll drop Tomo off to cover that area and I'll cruise Law street and Water Street. He's got to come out somewhere in that vicinity. Good chance he's on his way to the chemists to get his hit of the green elixir."

"All received, Bull — I'll cross the track and check out the back lane to Lugsey's pad."

*

Mikey Price was shivering and had lost control of his few remaining teeth, which were tapping together faster than a Morse code typist. Desperate for any warmth he could muster, he was tugging at the fur lining of the hood when a gust of wind caught him sideways on, effortlessly finding its way up the ill-fitting Parka. It inflated like a helium balloon, and struggling to stay grounded, he wrapped his arms around himself, forcing out the cold that was biting into his bones. Fingers that ached tugged at the drawstring in the hem, but numbed by the freezing breeze, they failed to maintain a grip, and a gust snuck inside the garment again, ramming him against the handrail that bordered the playing field.

He'd lost more weight, and he knew it: the green-coloured Parka was hanging on him like a two-man tent, and the belt, necessary to prevent his jeans from gathering around his ankles, needed yet another extra hole. He couldn't eat, though the thought didn't enter his head anymore, and in any case, the smell of cooking made him puke. The big "H" was all that was on his mind: he desperately needed the drug — it was all he craved. But he didn't have any funds for a hit, and fingernails, chewed down to the skin, feverishly scratched at his cheeks.

"Where can I rob some cash?"

Rose had caught him rifling through her handbag earlier, and that had caused an almighty fucking row. She'd had the purse in the pocket of her dressing gown all the bastard time. Can you believe that? The bitch!

THE SLIPPERY PATH

"Get your arse out of my fuckin' house, you shit bag…"
She'd bellowed.
"… Go and get your script — look at the bloody state of you, Mikey. There's more meat on a sparrow's fuckin' knee cap!"
He couldn't be doing with all that shit.
"Fuck her — I'll get my own bastard money!"
His feet were squelching inside his trainers, and he cursed the decision to cut across a soaking wet football pitch in footwear that had a split in both soles. Sounding like a Sasquatch trudging through a bog, he was shuffling along a quiet street of semi-detached houses when he spotted her and upped the pace…

*

Maureen Morris was late: not an uncommon occurrence and a criticism that Maureen would be the first to raise her hand, give a nod of the head, and agree with. How many times had she badgered herself not to, but still insisted on making use of any spare minutes? Initially having tons of time, but instead of relaxing and enjoying the leisurely stroll to meet up with her friend, Gloria, she would squeeze in yet another unnecessary chore; end up rushing, and arrive at Gloria's red-faced and sweating like a sumo wrestler in a sauna.

Today was no exception, and she was arguing with herself as she slammed the front door, gave a reassuring tug on the handle, got as far as the gate, then returned and reached out to tug on the handle again…

Desperate to, but winning the battle not to make another security check, she forced herself over the uneven flagstones; her right hand gripping an empty pull-along shopping trolley. It was hovering in mid-air behind her while the other hand struggled to squeeze wooden toggles through the stiff hoops of an always-wanted, mulberry-coloured duffle coat: recently snapped up in the M& S Autumn sale. Maureen failed to stifle the curse when the shopping trolley collided with the hedge bordering number 9, and her handbag slipped from her shoulder to the pavement.

Mikey pounced!
Menacing eyes focused on the prize as he narrowed the distance to Maureen; his face grimacing with the pain caused by his ravaged body's overexertion. His chest was burning and his heart was straining as he raised his right hand to strike.
Totally oblivious to the impending attack, Maureen had managed to prise the toggles free from the wrong hoops, rearrange them correctly, lift the hood over her ears, yank up her handbag, and release the wheel from the capture of the woody fuchsia bush.
She sped away, leaving Mikey's pumped-up fist flailing harmlessly in her wake as his meatless frame crashed to the flagstones. A solitary tear escaped from lifeless eyes that watched helplessly as his prize made a right turn and disappeared from their view.
Mrs Sheila Thomas, on the opposite side of the road, at number 10, alerted by Maureen's curse of frustration, had witnessed the shocking near miss. A trembling hand gripped the receiver as the other dialled 999 and, stretching the telephone flex to its limit, strived to keep an eye on the failed attacker from her lounge window. Thankfully, her neighbour was out of sight, presumably safe, and the despicable young man was struggling to get to his feet.
"Good morning — emergency services — which service do you require?"
A shaken, high-pitched voice replied.
"The police, please…"

*

(Twenty-five minutes later)
"I've got him, Bull. He's just come out of Lugsey's back door, and the cheeky bastard is smoking a bloody joint."
The response was immediate.
"Couldn't have wished for anything better, Cadders. Tomo is back in the car with me — monitor Price into Water Street, and we'll give him a tug."
"Okay, Bull. Well, he's approaching the junction now, and it's a

left, left, left towards the Nick."

Bull squeezed in the press-to-speak, gave a thumbs up to Tomo, and a huge grin stretched the stubble as he spoke.

"That's precisely what the Doctor ordered, matey. We'll pull him directly in front of the foyer — we can grab that joint and drag the arsewipe straight into custody from there."

CHAPTER 21

(Simultaneously)
"A little bird has just told me all about your thrilling adventure over the weekend."
The wide-eyed look of horror on the Cadet's face was the giveaway, and Sergeant Peters raised his hand.
"Hey, don't you worry, Phyllis, it won't go any further than me. Detective Sergeant Winters had to let me know. It would have been unethical for him not to do so. After all, I am responsible for you."
The supervisor winked and looked to the heavens, clasping his hands together in prayer.
"Why me, God, why did you choose me to be a surrogate parent to this boy? What did I do to deserve such punishment?"
The laughter eased the tension.
Sergeant Peters was at his desk. A mound of beige-coloured cardboard files was stacked in a pile on a chair beside him, and assessment sheets were in front of him, screaming out to be completed. He pushed a sweaty hand through his hair and released a heavy sigh.
"Bloody paperwork — the worse aspect of the job! Everything nowadays has to be recorded and evidenced. Things are changing so fast — it wasn't like this back in the sixties. Bring them back, that's what I say."
He smiled as he placed a blank sheet of A4 over the assessment

he was updating... He was feeling quite pleased with himself that his decision to give the Cadet a chance had paid off.

"That was a remarkable piece of detective work, young man. I'm proud of you, well done. I'd like to believe it was all down to our little chat the other day."

His head shook from side to side, the smile altering to a grimace when there was no response from the miles-away Cadet.

"Erm, that's not quite the case, though, is it?"

He shrugged his shoulders.

"Well, maybe a little part of the pep talk might have hit the right nerve."

He chuckled.

"Who knows?"

He pushed himself out of the chair and offered his right hand across the table.

"It looks very much like you've single-handedly solved a serious crime. One that has been in the undetected column for a while, and Detective Sergeant Winters doubted it would ever have progressed to the big D column without your involvement. Mark my words, you'll get some form of recognition for this result. Bernard Jones was a close acquaintance of the Chief Constable, and he personally monitored that enquiry very closely. No doubt he'll be monitoring your future career from now on."

A strained smile appeared on the Cadet's lips, a gesture more associated with someone suffering from acute trapped wind.

'That's all he flippin' needed — the Chief Constable taking an interest in him. So much for keeping a low profile.'

He was laughing inside though as he made his way along the office-lined corridor, the final words from his boss fresh in his ears.

"You put yourself out over the weekend and, without any thoughts for your own safety, put yourself in grave danger. You worked diligently when you should have been enjoying your time off. So, young man, as a reward — take the rest of the day off."

*

"Hi Mrs Jones, it's only me."
As usual, her voice was energising.
"I'm in the conservatory, dear, doing the crossword, and I'm stuck — you're early?"
There was an inflection on early…
"Just popping up to the loo. I've got some exciting news to tell you. Be there in a tick."
"Can't wait, love — I'll put the kettle on. Oh, and I've been baking."
He kicked off his shoes and took the stairs two at a time. If she's been baking, then that means one thing — Eve's pudding. It was top of the list that she'd asked him and Lloyd to compile of their likes and dislikes.
It was when he was sitting on the bed putting on his slippers that he noticed that some of his money was missing from the top of the little chest of drawers. He'd left a five-pound note and some change there that morning, and now there were only a few 10p coins. He searched the drawers one by one, rummaging through his socks and pants but found nothing. He emptied his pockets, knowing full well the money wouldn't be there, and he was right. There was nothing.
Mrs Jones's cheerful voice broke the moment.
"Kettle's boiled, love, and the tea's in the pot. Come on, I want to hear your exciting news."
He spoke to himself, trying to make light of the missing money.
"It has to be Lloyd. He must have come back earlier and borrowed it for something at work. No doubt he'll tell me later on."
Patting his pockets for the third time, he negotiated the stairs…
Mrs Jones greeted him with a smile and a biro in her right hand, tapping it at a newspaper, spread open on the dining table.

"Before you enlighten me with your exciting news, Lloyd. This is the only clue that I can't do and it's so blooming annoying. Seven letters beginning with G and it's got an A as the third letter and an E next to the last one. The clue is: finally understood following a period of tuition."

His forehead furrowed as he thought for a second or two.

"Pass us the paper then, Mrs Jones. I can't do it without looking at it."

Mrs Jones studied the puzzle until the very last moment as she reluctantly pushed the newspaper towards him. She was aching to solve it and unwilling to give in — she wanted to solve it — not him.

He gave it a passing glance.

"Got it, that's simple, Mrs Jones. Now, let me tell you about my exciting news."

She splayed her arms in front of her and shrugged her shoulders.

"Excuse me, the answer then, please, or at least give me another clue. It's driving me mad."

He teased her.

"But my exciting news is much more important than crossword clues."

She folded her arms.

"No answer — no Eve's pudding. It's as simple as that."

She wagged a finger in front of his face.

"Ha ha — got you now, haven't I?"

He smiled, enjoying the banter.

"Okay then — it's got two syllables."

Questioning himself — chewing on a fingernail.

"At least I think there are two syllables: one very long, and a tiny one at the end. The first syllable rhymes with clasp, and the second one rhymes with bed."

She stared at him, perplexed, slowly shaking her head from side to side, and her lodger couldn't help but laugh: she snapped.

"Right, there's definitely no Eve's pudding for you. Big Lloyd

and I will enjoy it all."
He wiped the tears from his eyes, trying unsuccessfully to keep a straight face.
"Okay, okay — here's another clue. Imagine you're in a tug of war."
The look on her face was solemn, deep, deep in thought.
"Yeeesss — go on."
"And you've got a tight hold on the rope."
Her tone of voice teemed with frustration.
"Grip — gripped. That doesn't fit! That's got an i as the third letter, and that's nothing to do with understanding something. So, Lloyd, you are wrong!"
She unfolded her arms in triumph and stood up.
The laughter returned, and the boy was struggling to talk.
"Well, grip doesn't rhyme with clasp."
He wiped more tears away.
"Does it?"
"Glasp? That doesn't make sense. Glasp, glasped, grasped, grasp, grasped! It's grasped, isn't it? Of course, it is. To grasp something."
The arms are folded once more, high on her chest.
"How did YOU manage to get that, and so quickly?"
She grabbed the newspaper, sat back down, and inserted the missing letters — deep in thought.
"Hey, you cheated. Grasped is only one syllable — no wonder I couldn't do it."
Tears of laughter rolled down their cheeks.
The adolescent felt comfortable in her company, and his fondness for this vulnerable, deputising mother, with sadness etched into her face like words on a tombstone, was growing by the minute. A warmth gripped his insides. Hopefully, what he was about to tell her would ease her pain.
"Right, can I tell you my news now, and am I able to have some Eve's pudding?"
She put the newspaper down and placed the pen on top of it: the teasing wasn't over.

"Yes to question number one and in response to number two. Well, because you cheated, I'll have to seriously think about it." She winked and grinned, a mischievous glint back in her eye.
"Maybe I'll have to discuss the matter with Big Lloyd?"
The boy flopped across the table.
"Oh no — I've got no chance then — he'll eat it all."
The telephone started ringing and Mrs Jones looked up at the clock.
"Well, I wonder who that is?"
"Hello, Carmarthen 2149, Edith Jones speaking… Lloyd, which one? Oh yes, he's here, and who should I say is calling? Okay, Detective Sergeant Winters, I'll get him now."
She put her head around the door and whispered loudly.
"It's a Detective Sergeant Winters for you, Lloyd."
The Cadet jumped up — his heart racing.
'Detective Sergeant Winters? That's Dai Insignificant. Oh no — Mikey's blabbed about my past!'
He took the phone from Mrs Jones, his hand trembling.
"Hi S Sarge — i it's Phyllis."
"There's been a development, young man. All good and nothing to worry about; can you come in and see me now? Best we talk face to face — I'll have a brew on."

CHAPTER 22

The Detective Sergeant was at his desk. The Calabash was gripped between his teeth, a mug of coffee was creating yet another brown ring on the blotting pad, and he was busy writing on a sheet of A4.
The tap on the door disturbed his flow, and he looked up, pushing his specs back to where they should be.
"Argh, the young man of the moment, come in, Phyllis. Come in and have a seat. Do you want a coffee?"
The Cadet shook his head, easing himself onto the chair.
"Right then, boyo — brace yourself."
His heart sank.
"Oh no — w w what the hell's happened, Sarge?"
The Sergeant tapped the stem of the Calabash onto the desk.
"They've arrested Mikey Price."
The boy's eyes doubled in size, and his hand shot to his mouth, stuttering through his fingers.
"B b but I I thought they weren't going to do it until tomorrow?"
Dai sucked on the Calabash, his hand trembling. All these years in the job, and he still got excited. He took a swig of the coffee.
"It's good, Phyllis. In fact, it's better than good — it's gooder!"
The Detective Sergeant chuckled.
"I know that's not a word, but it should be, and what's even gooder is..."

He tapped a drumroll on the desktop.

"...You're completely out of the frame."

Dai took another gulp of coffee and a long pull on the pipe. The colour had drained from the Cadet's face.

" W What do you mean, ow out of the frame?"

"I'll explain all that later on, lad — watch my lips. HE ONLY HAD THE BLOODY TOBACCO TIN IN HIS POCKET!"

Dai shot up from his recliner and did a jig — pumping his arms in the air — shouting out. 'Hallelujah — hallelujah'.

The Cadet started laughing.

"Wow, wow, wow, w what happened, Sarge?"

A slight tap on the half-open door curtailed the Detective Sergeant's celebration, and the officer quickly composed himself when he saw Menna, the Chief Constable's secretary, poking her head around the door. The smartly dressed, attractive young woman's right index finger was up to her lips, and the other hand pointed up to the ceiling as she mouthed the words.

"He's got the H.M.I. in with him..."

She nodded her head — indicating to her left.

"... I've escaped, and I'm next door photoco—"

Her parting word was incomprehensible: the nodding of the head had caused her chin-length, bobbed hair to mask her mouth.

Dai tutted, sat down, and picked up the Calabash, sucking on it repeatedly until it sparked back to life.

"As soon as you left the office this morning, I telephoned Pat Muldoon. He's the Detective Inspector in Pembroke Dock, you know, the one I was telling you about. I briefed him and told him everything to do with the case."

Dai could see the concern etched on the youngster's face.

"No worries where Pat's concerned — he won't reveal your identity. He's a great bloke. I've watched his career develop, and we've been involved in a few hair-raising jobs together."

Dai tapped the Calabash against the side of his skull.

"Too many eye-popping stories from those good old days

stored away inside this old bonce of mine."

His eyes glazed over, and smoke was sifting from the corner of his mouth as he peered through the lenses at the Cadet, but he was looking straight through him. Finally, his lips broke into a smile.

"Fond memories — great days. Anyway, I digress. Pat and his team know this Mikey Price well, and going by what he was telling me, Pembrokeshire will be a lot safer place without the likes of him ruining the equilibrium. So, observations commenced this morning on the home address in the Dock Estate.

The smile widened on Dai's face.

"Fortunately, one of the team has a friendly 'auntie' living in one of the flats overlooking the Price's front door. According to Pat, the boy had been pissed up at the 'Parachute Cub', down at The British Legion a few weeks back, and he woke up the following morning between this 'auntie' and her bloody twin sister."

A huge grin had crossed Dai's face, and it broke into a chuckle — his eyes sparkling with devilment. In comparison, the Cadet's face was a picture of confusion — totally lost: his head, deep in thought, was tilted to one side as he spoke.

"I didn't know there was a Parachute Club in Pembroke Dock, Sarge. I would have loved to have learned how to parachute. I suppose the drug squad boy had been drinking because he was nervous? Maybe it was his maiden jump?"

Dai struggled to prevent a mouthful of coffee from spurting down his shirt and fought to stem the outburst of laughter. His hand was covering his mouth as he staggered out of the office towards the toilets. Leaving the Cadet dumbfounded: 'What the hell have I said?'

The specs were off, and Dai was wiping the tears from around his eyes when he sat back in the recliner, shaking his head and dabbing at drips of coffee dotted over his chin while he spoke.

"Phyllis, you're a bloody star boy. That's what you are — a bloody star."

The Cadet was shaking his head in bewilderment.

"S sorry, s sarge, b but I haven't got a clue what you're on about."

Dai reached for a tissue, cleaning his specs as he explained.

"Right, listen to me, sonny. The drug squad boy wasn't at the British Legion Club to learn how to parachute out of an RAF bomber: he'd been out on the beer with his rugby mates. They ended up there because every Wednesday night is a disco night, and it's known as 'The Parachute Club' — because you're..."

The Detective Sergeant put his specs down, stood up, clenched his fists, bent both his arms and thrust his pelvic region back and forth.

"...guaranteed a jump."

The Cadet's look of total confusion didn't alter, setting Dai off into more fits of laughter; he placed his right arm across his chest.

"Oh, oh, help me, God, please help me. I'm going to have a bloody heart attack."

Still laughing, he grabbed the tissue, wiped the remainder of the tears away, and sighed when he saw the look of complete bafflement written across the youngster's face. It brought it home to him as to how young and inexperienced the boy was. Much too young to be involved in such a sickening case and way too young to be involved with experienced, grown men. But without his youthfulness, these offences would still be gathering dust in the cold case file and with very little chance of progression.

He coughed to clear his throat, regained some composure, and having no desire at this particular moment in time to teach a lesson on the birds and the bees, badgered himself to try and be more aware of the adolescent's age.

"Right, where were we? O.P. that's it, yes, well, the boy in the O.P. hadn't even had time for a brew before Mikey was out of the house. Fortunately, Rose was at the front door tenderly waving him off with a few friendly fucks and bastards before going back inside, so she's safely housed and under control."

The Cadet's look of total confusion had gone away, and he was laughing: he could picture Rose in all her glory.

"Other members of the team were on standby, and they followed Mikey towards the town centre. He's spotted coming out of a dealer's house on The London Road — some guy called Lugsey?"

The Detective Sergeant had inflected the last four words, his arms splayed out in front of him, willing a response to the gesture. Nothing was forthcoming, and he slowly shook his head, his eyes locked onto those of the Cadet.

"Nah, you don't know him — do you? He's well known to the local police."

Phyllis could feel the nerves kicking in, trying to keep his face deadpan as he shook his head in denial. The least anyone knew about how well he knew Lugsey, the better.

The Detective Sergeant had clocked the slight hesitation in the Cadet's response: the minuscule eye deviation and the subtle reddening of his complexion — he knew the boy was lying. Why was the youngster being so selective with the truth? What was he hiding? Maybe he was protecting this Lugsey guy? Out of an adolescent sense of loyalty, maybe? Or maybe, as Dai already surmised, the Cadet knew a lot more than he was divulging. Better not press the matter any further. What was he going to gain by it? What did it matter if he knew the dealer but had moved on and didn't want to be associated with him? He decided to store his suspicions. Proving him to be a liar now could very well jeopardise the case against Price, and that's the last thing he wanted.

"Anyway, our Mikey Price wasn't in there for long, and guess what? He only comes out of the back of the house smoking a bloody joint! Can you believe that? The cheeky bastard! Apparently, this house backs onto the bloody cop shop — for Pete's sake!

Tomo and Bull, they're the two Detectives, wait until Price is out on the main road. In fact, he's directly in front of the bloody police station when they turn him over. Grab the joint from out of his gob and nick him for possession of cannabis. Mikey is kicking and screaming, shouting that he's got to go and get his script of methadone. Having a right, proper tantrum, he was. The violent bastard then puts the nut on Tomo — knocking him clean out! Luckily, a couple of uniforms come running to assist: they cuff Price, and drag him kicking and spitting into the cells."

Phyllis's mind was working overtime.

"So how am I out of the frame, Sarge?"

"Well, son, this is the bit of luck we needed. Once he's calmed down and they empty his pockets, they find some powders on him. Two or three wraps of probably speed. You heard of that — speed? It's slang for amphetamine?"

The Cadet frowned, shaking his head in denial, a sham look of confusion masking his face, which didn't fool the Detective Sergeant, but he played along.

"It's a stimulant, lad, supposed to give you more zest, you know, energy, especially when you're knackered. It's a Class B controlled drug, but it has to be sent away to the Forensic Science Laboratory for testing: you never know it might bounce back as cocaine. Now, that would be a result: cocaine is Class A. More time banged up. Keep that bloody vermin off our streets."

Dai relaxed into his chair, taking on board another hit of tobacco while pushing up the specs from the tip of his nose.

"Do you know something, Phyllis? That's why I joined the job. I saw all this drug abuse down the pits. Youngsters pocketing their pay packets on a Friday afternoon and then spending the weekend getting out of their skulls on whatever they can shove down their throats or up their noses. They're skint by Monday morning: knocking on the office door and begging the manager for a bloody sub."

Desperation and the desire to distance oneself from a situation can often lead to a course of action that is completely unnecessary. Those attempted deflections can very often have an adverse consequence and lead to more suspicion. The Cadet committed such a cardinal mistake by uttering the next couple of sentences.

"I don't know much about drugs, Sarge — what are wraps..."
He couldn't maintain eye contact.
"...I wouldn't know one if you shoved it in my hand."

Eager to hoodwink the Detective Sergeant, he felt that he had to lie. The last thing he needed was Dai getting his mates in Pembrokeshire to do a bit of digging and maybe expose the full extent of his criminal past.

Of course he knew what a wrap was, hell, Mikey was sniffing powders all the time. He remembered him having a couple of wraps of speed at a beach party during the early summer, and as per the norm, that had ended in disaster. Mikey hadn't slept for two nights, and the only thing keeping him going was the amphetamines. Lugsey had run out of gear, so Mikey had to buy from a couple of heavies — down for the party from Bristol. Unknown to Mikey and quite a few others, the gear had been cut with a white powdered laxative. It was a boiling hot day, and the party was heaving. Heavy metal sounds blaring out, and everyone was head-banging. Couples were disappearing into the dunes, and Mikey, off his face and dancing alone, was wearing a knee-length pair of white-coloured linen shorts. The large brown stain on his backside told its own story...

The more he thought that the boy was lying, the more sceptical the Detective Sergeant became: he was suspicious, but he couldn't be sure. The boy was trying to play a player in a dangerous game, and unknown to him, the stakes were as high as you could get. The case against Price could be a non-starter if the prime witness was proven to be a liar, but Dai knew if he kept his suspicions to himself, the case would progress naturally to the courts. Detective Inspector Muldoon's plan had worked. His team had carried it out to perfection, and because of their guile and hard work, the Cadet's information was no longer required. At this point in time, he was out of the prosecution equation: surplus to requirements.

Dai played along with the game — for the time being at least.

"Wraps are usually individual deals of powders. The suppliers weigh the drugs, then they wrap the powder in pieces of shiny paper. You know the type, like you'd get in a glossy magazine. That way none of the powder goes to waste because there's less chance of it being absorbed and it easily slides off. The paper is usually about two, maybe three inches square, and the dealer puts the powder in the centre before it's folded three or four times to create a sealed, safe, and dry compartment. In essence — it's wrapped up."

"Wow, that's clever, Sarge — you said he had the tobacco tin?"

That response to the Detective Sergeant's description of a wrap was too matter-of-fact, and it roused even more suspicion.

'He knows what a bloody wrap is. My bet is, he's trying to suss out what the police have uncovered, and has his name been mentioned in passing by Price? He knows a hell of a lot more about Price and his associates than he's letting on.'

Dai's emotions churned inside him: sadness, disappointment, but also admiration. Sadness and disappointment that this boy, someone he'd already become fond of, felt he couldn't trust him enough to say the truth. And admiration for the boy's cunning and bravery. But fear was another factor that was slowly coming into play. Had the police force inadvertently taken on a bloody bad one, and was there now a rogue cop amongst us?

Dai forced a smile. Was he being too cynical? He decided to push the bad thoughts to the back of his mind: he didn't want his suspicions, and to be fair, that's all they were, to spoil the moment. Give the boy the benefit of the doubt. If it wasn't for his input they'd have nothing.

"The finding of Robbo's tobacco tin in Mikey's possession is the icing on the cake. Those crafty detectives in Pembroke Dock don't pay much attention to it when Price empties his pockets. They open it, as would be the norm, to check out the contents for any illegals, and they clock Robbo's unique number on the inside of the lid, but they don't question what it is. Bull, the detective sergeant, feigns an interest in SAS memorabilia and matter-of-factly asks Mikey where he got it from?

Not suspecting anything untoward, Mikey quite happily replies that he bought it a couple of years ago from a street market in Tenby.

Hell, that's important, Phyllis."

The detective rubs his hands together, and the excitement is back. It's clear in the tone of his voice.

"How could Mikey buy it a couple of years ago? It was only nicked back in November. Now, do you want the cherry on top of the icing?"

The Cadet nodded, feeling more relaxed, and a smile broke the tension on his face.

"This part is very clever. Bull continues with his feigned interest in military memorabilia and asks Mikey if he bought any other SAS stuff from the street market or if he knows of anywhere else that sells similar items. Implying that he, Bull, would be interested in buying some for himself.

Mikey shook his head and went on to say that the only item he bought from the street market was the tobacco tin, and that he didn't know of the whereabouts of any other SAS memorabilia."

Phyllis was scratching his head, his face masked with confusion.

"I don't get it, Sarge. What difference does that make? How is that the cherry on top of the icing?"

"Well, young man, you told me that virtually all the items that were in that Capri before it was torched are now in Mikey's house."

"Yes, well, they were there a few days ago."

"Okay, our suspect Mikey Price has been arrested and he has an identifiable piece of property from that car: Robbo's tobacco tin. Is that correct?"

Nodding his head as he spoke.

"Yes, Sarge, but he's told the police that he bought it in a street market."

"Right, which is good for us because he's saying that happened a couple of years ago and we know that is impossible. He's also saying that he doesn't know the whereabouts of any other SAS memorabilia, and we know that there's a good chance that Rose has the petrol lighter on her person. She is in the house and being monitored by the drug squad as we speak. If she decides to leave in the meantime, she'll be arrested on suspicion of something or another and searched. In any case, a search warrant will be executed at their house sometime today and no doubt Robbo's flask will be found stashed away in a cupboard. So, you tell me, Phyllis, how can Mikey Price now account for those items of identifiable stolen property? And when Rose finds out about the severity of the crimes, she's going to drop Mikey in it big time. No way will she want to get involved in anything that heavy. The search team will also find the other items belonging to Robbo, which you have seen in the house. So, as the butcher said to the slaughter-man — he's knackered!"

The Cadet's eyes light up momentarily, but a sadness quickly returns, and they deviate away from the Detective Sergeant's. Dai senses that something is still bothering him and eases himself forward, tapping the charred contents of the Calabash into an ashtray.

"Come on then, Phyllis, what is it? What's churning the cogs around in that mass of grey matter between your ears? And by the way, they need bloody oiling: I can hear the buggers grinding away from here."

The boy forces a smile.

"I'm still worried, Sarge, you know, about what might happen to my mam and dad. What if Mikey does find out that this is all to do with me? They will no longer be safe in their own home. Mikey's an evil bastard, look what he did to Tomo! And that was in front of other police officers. God only knows what he's capable of doing when no one else is around. Or, what he could arrange from a prison cell."

A fresh bowl of tobacco is firmed into the Calabash; Dai sparks the tobacco and takes a long, satisfying drag. Smiling, he rests his elbows on the desk.
"Do you like custard, Phyllis?"
His face screws up in bewilderment.
"Yeah, I like custard, Sarge, but what's custard got to do with it?"
"Well, when they turn Mikey's house over, I have every confidence that they'll find the petrol lighter and the thermos flask. They'll probably come across property relating to crimes that the police are not even bloody aware of! And that, my friend, will be the custard on top of the cherry, on top of the icing, on top of the cake, because then he'll be, excuse my French — well and truly fucked!"
They both laugh, and as he speaks, the Detective Sergeant rummages through some sheets of A4, seeking out the Cadet's original intelligence log.
"You and your family are safe, young man. Safe and free from any possible suspicion on Mikey's side because of the shit-hot work carried out by the coppers in Pembrokeshire. They have made sure that your name is not required to be anywhere near the prosecution file: your intelligence log will no longer exist. Pat Muldoon has cremated his copy, and you can now do the honours with the original."
Dai reaches into a drawer and grabs a box of matches, pulls out a metal waste bin from beneath the desk, and holds the intelligence log above it.
"This is now surplus to requirements, because the Detectives in Pembroke Dock can say that while passing the entrance to the back lane of London Road they saw a known heroin addict coming out from a known drug dealer's house. They saw that the addict was smoking a cigarette which looked like it contained cannabis. They spoke to him, smelt the drug, seized the joint and arrested him. Upon being searched, they found powders and some identifiable stolen property. They can now go before a magistrate and, because of what THEY…"

He points the stem of the Calabash at the Cadet.

"...not YOU — have seen, found, and suspect, request two search warrants: one for Mikey's house and the other for the dealer's house.

You are one hundred percent in the clear, lad, and you've done a great job: I'm bloody proud of you — SO STOP WORRYING!

No chance! The Demon inside wouldn't allow the youngster to escape that easily, and a mocking laugh preceded words that would stay with him until Mikey Price was charged and banged up in Swansea Prison.

"Stop worrying! How can you stop worrying? What if, in return for a bit of leniency, Mikey Price tells the coppers in Pembroke Dock about the lad from Lamphey? Partial to a toke, and now a bloody Police Cadet! Who, in a past life, instigated much of the petty local criminal activity? And, what if, because he can, Mikey Price decides to arrange some heartache for his one-time buddy? Teach him a little lesson for crossing over to the other side."

Forcing a smile, the Cadet struck the match, and two pairs of eyes watched as the only document linking him to Mikey Price's prosecution case turned to ash.

CHAPTER 23

Mrs Jones was getting into a car when she spotted her lodger nearing the house,
and she waited for him, resting her arms on top of the driver's door. She seemed flustered.
"Hi, Lloyd, sorry, love, but I've got to go to our Molly's. She and Andy have had a huge row, and he's stormed out."
He recalled the bruising to Molly's wrists, and he couldn't mask the concern in his voice.
"Is there anything I can do to help?"
"No, love, thanks. One of those things, I suppose. I'll know more when I see her."
She released a huge sigh.
"I hate driving. Bernard always drove, and I was more than happy with that. But sometimes I need to use the car — especially if I have a big grocery shop."
She chuckled.
"And since you and Big Lloyd moved in, it looks like that's going to be once or twice a week."
Sad eyes picked out the tan leather steering wheel cover, and she forced a smile, pointing a finger.
"Bernard had matching gloves to go with that."
She laughed in an attempt to quell the emotion that was rapidly overwhelming her.
"And he sometimes wore an open-neck shirt with a cravat

when we went out for a Sunday afternoon drive about — very dandy, I must say. Anyway, because the car wasn't being used, I offered it to Molly on the proviso I could drive it when the need arose: it seemed such a waste to see it parked up and rusting away — no doubt she'll drop me home later."

She pointed to the house and grinned.

"Your pal couldn't wait: he's already tucking in, and yours is in the oven. Don't forget to turn it off! See you later."

Big Lloyd was licking tomato sauce from his lips and mopping the plate with a piece of bread and butter.

"All the buttered bread has gone, but Mrs Jones said there's more in the bread bin if you want some."

Phyllis shook his head in frustration — the landlady always buttered two slices each.

"Any news on the case down in Pembs? Mrs Jones just told me that Detective Sergeant Winters rang for you, and you had to rush back."

Bending to open the oven door, he started to brief his roommate a watered-down version of what had happened with Mikey Price.

"Bloody hell, Phyllis, that's one hell of a result: you couldn't wish for anything better than that. When are we going to tell Mrs Jones?"

The boy didn't answer — he couldn't concentrate. The missing money from their bedroom was weighing heavily on his mind.

"Tell me, Lloyd, and don't take this the wrong way. Have you taken any money from my stash on top of the chest of drawers?"

The larger Cadet was chewing on a mouthful, and he'd just scraped the last dregs of tomato sauce from his plate — the crust was dangling in front of his mouth.

Slowly he shook his head from side to side, and misty eyes conveyed a story: one of disbelief, hurt, and anger. He placed the bread back onto the plate, and his voice was strained as he spoke: struggling to contain his emotions.

"Unbelievable — you don't honestly think that I'd take money from you, do you? We've just joined the bloody Police Force — I want to catch the thieving crooks — not do it myself!"

Phyllis blushed and gulped — immediately wishing he hadn't asked — he could do without this extra heartache...

"N No, Lloyd, I I didn't mean it like that. I I trust you implicitly, mate. Some of my money has gone missing. It was there when I went to work this morning, a and it was gone w when I got back this afternoon. I I was hoping that you'd returned to the house and maybe borrowed some, you know, for something urgent. I I wouldn't have minded if you had — it didn't even enter my head that you would steal it. I just wanted to make sure, I I mean, to discount you from the equation."

He didn't reply, and the look in his eyes hadn't altered as he picked up the crust, popped it in his mouth, and glared at his roommate while chewing.

"Look, I I'm sorry, Lloyd. I I'm sorry if I've offended you in any way. Deep down, I I knew you wouldn't take the money without asking me, b but I I guess I didn't want to face the truth. Hell, Lloyd, someone who has got access to our bedroom has stolen money from the top of our chest of drawers. The thief wouldn't have known who the money belonged to: it could have been yours!"

Big Lloyd finished chewing and took a swig of tea.

"How much has this person taken?"

Sensing the change in his roommate's mood the boy relaxed; the nervous stutter back under control.

"At least a fiver, and the thing is maybe money has been taken before. I've never had a fiver stolen though, because I would have noticed that. But I might not have missed the odd pound coin or a 50p piece. Often I have a load of change and I don't like the feel of it in my pocket. Is it possible you've had some money taken? Money that you thought you might have lost?"

Shaking his head, he prised out a red zipped wallet from the rear pocket of his jeans.

"No, never — not a chance."

He shook it in front of the boy opposite.

"Never out of my sight, Phyllis, boy. I even sleep with it under my pillow."
Phyllis couldn't resist it.
"Yeah, but that's typical of somebody from Cardigan; you're probably dreaming about all the money you haven't spent."
He started chuckling, but that wasn't the wisest thing to say or do while bending over his plate and offering the crown of his head as a prime target for revenge. Especially as Big Lloyd was passing behind him on his way to the sink. The knuckles of his left hand rapped against the boy's skull.
"Argh, that bloody hurt."
"Serves you right — now, what are we going to do about this money?"

*

It was a couple of minutes before midnight when the lodger heard the front door closing; he had been dozing in his landlady's comfy chair. She was surprised to see him.
"Oh, hello, love, and what are you still doing up? Not like you to be awake at this time of night…"
She started to giggle.
"…Especially on a school day."
He rubbed his eyes and yawned.
"I must have dropped off. Big Lloyd went to bed, and I can remember telling him that I wouldn't be long, and well, here I am. How is Molly?"
She plugged in the kettle.
"Do you want a cuppa, Lloyd, or are you off upstairs?"
The questions were posed using a tone that willed a positive response to the first one. Precisely what he wanted to hear: part of the plan he and Big Lloyd had concocted.
"Oh, go on then, I'll join you for a quick one."
She reached for the tin of shortbread and put it on the kitchen table.
"I struggle to drink a cup of tea without something to dunk. Are you a dunker, Lloyd?"

He got up and joined her in the kitchen, reaching into the biscuit tin and grabbing a couple before sitting down.
"You know I am."
The landlady sighed and flopped onto one of the chairs.
The Cadet couldn't help but notice her unease.
"Wow, that sounded like a huge burden to be carrying around. Penny, for your thoughts?"
"Oh, it's our Molly…"
She sighed again before forcing a smile.
"… I don't want to say too much: it's a private, family matter, you know. But things aren't going too well. In fact, things seem to have got a lot worse since she dropped the car here this morning on her way to work."
He registered that response.
'Umm, Molly was here this morning. Suspect number one.'
"What do you mean? It's got a lot worse."
Yet another sigh.
"I'm sorry, Lloyd. I know you're only trying to help, but it's unfair to discuss Molly's marital problems with you, and these things will undoubtedly sort themselves out soon enough: they nearly always do.
The boy fibbed, taking advantage of his landlady's domestic problems.
"Oh, I wasn't prying. You looked so worried earlier on, and even now, you seem tense and preoccupied. I learned something the other day in Technical College. Seemingly, it's good to be able to talk to someone. That a problem shared is a problem halved. Maybe talking to April will help. Have you seen her today? Did she pop round after Molly left?"
He started chuckling.
"Wow, listen to me, so many questions. Just like a proper policeman."
Mrs Jones's face brightened a little with a smile.
"I know you're only trying to help Lloyd, and I do appreciate that, but Molly doesn't want her sister to know. I think she's ashamed of what is happening in her life at the moment,

so I haven't mentioned it to April. That makes it even more awkward for me because April did call in today, and I hid it from her when she asked me what Molly was up to. I find it all so upsetting. If April had arrived 30 minutes earlier, they would have bumped into each other, and that would have caused a massive problem. April would have seen that Molly was upset, and, well, being an overprotective sister, she would have gone straight over to Molly's house. God help Andrew if he had been at home! She has a feisty temper: quite a terrier is our April."

'Hmm, suspect number two.'

"I suppose Andrew telephoned here again this morning, and upset you like he did the other afternoon when he was looking for Molly?"

She was shaking her head as she bit into one of the shortbreads, covering her mouth as she spoke.

"No, thankfully he didn't, Lloyd."

She sipped at the tea.

"Andrew hasn't shown his face here for ages. And apart from that phone call the other day, I haven't spoken to him either. It's all very sad really. We used to be such a happy, close-knit bunch."

He could hear the emotion in her voice and spotted some tears welling in her eyes.

"Don't get upset, Mrs Jones: I'm sure things will sort themselves out. It must be horrible when matters are out of your control. Especially when it involves loved ones..."

His mind was wandering, and he was thinking about his parents: the worry and heartache that he must have caused them.

"...You probably feel helpless."

She dunked a biscuit, hovering it over the china cup as she spoke.

"Your lesson at the Technical College was a wise one, Lloyd: it is good to talk. I feel better already. Chatting with you has helped me, and I haven't said much, have I?"

Unbeknown to Mrs Jones, she'd said enough. The Police Cadet had two prime suspects and discounted a possible third.
"Yes, Mrs Jones, conversation is one of the best tonics."
Her fingers caressed her chin as she spoke.
"Now, that's an interesting surmise, Lloyd. Did they teach you that in college as well?"
His mouth was full of sodden shortbread as he replied, using the back of his hand to cover his mouth as he mumbled.
"No, those words are from my mother."
Mrs Jones started to giggle, closely followed by the Cadet.
"Mind you, she also told me that when I had whooping cough, she used to push me around in a pram following the men resurfacing the roads with fresh tar. Someone had told her that the fumes from the boiling bitumen cleared your tubes and helped you get better. It was one of the worst things she could have done: it makes the condition worse. I ended up barking like an Alsatian smoking a pipe!"
"Oh, Lloyd — now you are a tonic."
Still chuckling, he made light of the next question.
"So, nobody else popped around here this morning that you could have a stress-relieving chat with?"
She was still giggling and wiping tears from her eyes when she replied.
"Unfortunately, Lloyd, no. But I know who to come to the next time I need cheering up."

*

Restless, he lay on his back, hands behind his head, and nestled into plumped-up pillows. Less than two feet away lay Big Lloyd, and he was fast asleep. Not unusual because the alarm clock on the table between them told him it was nearly half-two. This peacefulness was unusual: there was no snoring. His roommate wasn't even breathing heavily — the Cadet could concentrate.
So much to dwell on and so much to deal with at once: perhaps he should prioritise. That's what his oversaturated brain was willing him to do. But, upon reflection, there wasn't really that

much. The only issue requiring any urgency was to seek advice regarding the missing money.

The Mikey Price scenario was in hand: no requirement for any further involvement on that matter. Most importantly, the only document linking him to the case had gone up in smoke — the same way as Mikey had dealt with Robbo's Ford Capri.

Hopefully, in the morning, Dai Insignificant will be the bearer of some good news from that Detective Inspector from Pembroke Dock.

So, who was the thief? Who would steal money from him? More pertinently — who had the opportunity?

Definitely not Big Lloyd, no way. He was way too honest, had too many principles, and even the best of actors would struggle to portray that look of hurt that he had in his eyes earlier.

Mrs Jones? Surely not, she's excellent, and she looks after him and Big Lloyd as if they were her own flesh and blood. Anyway, why would she? She doesn't need the money. Her reasons for taking in lodgers were to gain some company and have a focus in her life. Why would she jeopardise hers and Bernard's good name?

He sighed, feeling a bit uncomfortable that he'd tricked her earlier. Shocked as to how easy it was for him to conjure up such deceit. Especially when it was with somebody he cared for. He began to feel anxious about the way he'd misled her, but the more he churned it over, the more he came to realise that if she was somehow involved, then he had no other choice.

So that leaves Mrs Jones' two daughters: the lovely Molly and probably an equally gorgeous-looking April.

He'd yet to meet April, and apart from her being a nurse and working odd hours, he didn't know much about her or her husband. He knew that he also worked at the hospital, but doing what job? He didn't know, and he didn't even know his name. Mrs Jones hadn't mentioned them much. She mainly talked about Bernard: that was understandable, he was her soul mate, and now he's gone.

Molly? The gorgeous Molly. Her marriage is on the rocks, and her husband, Andy, is possibly a control freak: maybe even a bully. Perhaps Andy doesn't allow her to have any money — is she strapped for cash? Was the temptation too much? Hell, the door to his and Big Lloyd's room was probably wide open: anyone en route to the bathroom would easily see the money on top of the chest of drawers. A few seconds to stealthily creep in was all that was required. It's got to be Molly: she would know about the loose floorboard in the middle of the room, wouldn't she? It used to be her bedroom. She has taken what she thought wouldn't be missed, pocketed it, a quick visit to the bathroom, a flush of the loo, and back downstairs to her mother. As simple as that...

CHAPTER 24

Another five-pound note was added to his stash before he and Big Lloyd set off on their walk to work. They discussed the best way to deal with the missing money. What should they do?
Both were more than aware that as soon as there was any police involvement, their days with Mrs Jones would undoubtedly be numbered. They enjoyed staying with her: it was a home from home, so why jeopardise such a good thing?
Big Lloyd wanted to forget about it — write it off as one of life's experiences and don't leave any cash on view ever again. The Cadet wasn't happy with doing that, pointing out that if it had been Big Lloyd's money, would he have even suggested such an option?
Mrs Jones's house was their home, and they should be able to leave their possessions in their bedroom without the fear of someone going in there to steal.
Neither believed the thief to be Mrs Jones, and probably she didn't even have a clue that the money was being stolen, but if they approach her, will it cause friction? Yes, of course, it will — why? Because once armed with the knowledge that money is being stolen, she is going to be upset: she won't want to believe that Molly or April could be responsible. It will be made out that Phyllis is mistaken: he's either lost the money or he's spent it without realising, and the atmosphere in the house will be intolerable. Mrs Jones is bound to discuss the matter

with her daughters, and if one of them is the thief, then that will be the end of it: she will be impossible to catch.

Phyllis could sense that Big Lloyd didn't want to be involved. Hell, he'd made it quite clear that he disagreed with his roommate leaving money on display in the first place. Why didn't he keep it secure? Hidden away from temptation and gathering moths in a zipped-up purse stuck in his arse pocket like he did. So when Phyllis told him that he had added another fiver to the stash, he was pissed off and he clammed up. As far as Big Lloyd was concerned, this was not his problem.

The rest of their journey was in silence, and once more the boy was in turmoil. Yes, he had added more money to his stash, but why? Was it bait? An enticement to the thief? A, 'go on then, mate — help yourself to some more of my cash — take two if you want.' Was he luring the thief into a false sense of security? Making whoever it was feel relaxed enough to believe that he, Lloyd Hilary Davies, was so indifferent about the missing money that he couldn't be bothered to do anything about it? Did he want to flush out this vermin? Make the culprit complacent, then pounce on the thief — yes! Because he is bloody annoyed and wanted the evil bastard to be caught and strung up.

But, wasn't he being hypocritical? Isn't he just as bad as the person stealing the money from his stash? Too bloody right he is. The memories of his criminal past flooded his mind: the burglaries, the shoplifting, the drug abuse. No way should he be a copper. But having that past life has enabled him to catch Mikey Price, and isn't the cunning that he possesses going to help catch the person who is nicking his money?

A long, shrill whistle roused the Cadet from the argument with himself. Bloody hell, they were in the rear car park already. He spotted a white-sleeved arm waving from a first-floor window: the rest of the body was hidden. The voice that boomed from behind the mirrored glass was that of Detective Sergeant David Winters, and he didn't sound best pleased.

"Come up and see me now — I've got your bloody feedback!"

The arm disappeared, and the window was closed with a bang. His eyes darted towards Big Lloyd.

"I don't like the sound of that, do you? Something bad has happened. Shit, what have I done now?"

The larger cadet sighed and turned his head away: all this cloak-and-dagger stuff was getting to him. From the second his eyes read the pairings on the notice board, he knew that his allocated roommate would be trouble with a capital T, and there was nothing he could do to prevent it. Didn't he say that they were different, and that they wanted different things? Big Lloyd would be happy with regular, plod-along policing. Not dealing with drugged-up murderers and catching thieves stealing money from people's bedrooms. He needed to distance himself, but how?

Unable to look at him, his eyes were glued to the tarmac as he spoke, slowly nodding his head in agreement.

"Yeah, he sounds bloody angry. I don't know what you've done. You go see him, and I'll let Sarge know where you are."

His foot rose onto the step to the Cadet Hut, his roommate quickly on his heels. Phyllis didn't fancy facing an irate Detective Sergeant, and going by the brusque tone of his voice, Mikey had blabbed about him to the coppers in Pembrokeshire. Is this the end of the road? Is he going to be arrested and booted out? Has Mikey done a deal to save his own skin, and will it now be he that is banged up for an eternity in a prison cell and not Price?

Only a few cadets were there, and the mood was unusually sombre. The reason why hit the Cadet like a ton of concrete: Sergeant Peters had suffered a mental breakdown and was on sick leave.

'Shit — he was one of the few people to believe in him — who can he turn to now?'

He listened to the gossip, but he couldn't concentrate: his mind was on whatever Dai Insignificant wanted to see him about.

'Oh well, I'd better get it over and done with.'

He glanced over at Big Lloyd, looking for some support, but

none was forthcoming: he was refusing to make eye contact. Once again the immature façade came to the fore.
'Fuck him. Yeah, fuck 'em all — I'll sort it out myself. It's my word against Mikey's, isn't it? I'll deny everything. Yes, that's what I'll do, and let the bastards prove otherwise!'

CHAPTER 25

Meticulous as ever, Detective Sergeant David Winters was chatting on the telephone when Phyllis tapped at the open door: he acknowledged him with a wink of the eye, and a flick of the head beckoned him to enter.
"…Thanks for the heads-up, George. I dare say we'll bump into each other in the nineteenth hole on Saturday…"
He laughed and replaced the receiver.
"Come in, lad, come in. I've just heard about your sergeant. Terrible to-do that: I feel for the man. Let's hope he gets through it soon. Who's standing in for him, do you know?"
The Cadet was thrown by the Detective Sergeant's demeanour: 'Why isn't he shouting and balling?'
He had prepared himself for the worst, and a carefully rehearsed rant was on the tip of his tongue, so it was a slightly uptight voice that answered the question, which wasn't missed by the Detective Sergeant.
"I've just spoken with the others. There are a couple of names being bandied around, but I don't think they've chosen anyone yet. Sarge must have known that he might be off for a while because he's sorted out jobs for us for the rest of this week."
Phyllis didn't spot the subtle smile of amusement on the supervisor's face as he opened the desk drawer and brought out a notebook.
"Right, let's get down to why you are here. Leave the door ajar

and remain standing."

The Detective Sergeant's facial features had hardened, and gone was the concerned, caring persona. It was a solemn, stern face, and a grave tone of voice that addressed the Cadet.

"Detective Inspector Muldoon called me at home, VERY late last night..."

He paused, his eyes piercing deep into the youngster, and the boy gulped.

'Oh no, he was probably sound asleep when Pat Muldoon rang: that obviously hasn't helped his mood.'

He glanced over his shoulder, convinced that two burly uniforms would come bursting through the door at any second and take him away.

Dai continued.

"He wanted to appraise me personally with the outcome of the investigation into Mikey Price. What Mikey's explanation was and what Mikey told him about YOU..."

The Detective Sergeant pointed his left index finger at the youngster's chest.

"...and how YOUR information affected the outcome of the enquiry."

Phyllis was beside himself, his mouth as dry as sandpaper and his body quaking.

'Oh my God, Mikey HAS shopped me — the bastard! They ARE going to take me away.'

Without taking his eyes off the Cadet, the Detective Sergeant reached for his Calabash.

"I don't suppose you're aware that first thing every morning, the details of all serious incidents, important events, and such like are faxed to HQ for the information of the Chief Officers. Once the Inspector in the Operations' Room collates them, they are forwarded to all the divisions. It keeps everyone in the force up to speed with current affairs. That is why Detective Inspector Muldoon wanted to let me know first — give me the heads up before THIS news hits the proverbial fan!"

The Cadet's blank face and the shaking of his head confirmed his ignorance.

"No? I thought so — every day's a school day, eh?"

The harsh scraping sound caused by the sudden backward movement of Dai's chair as he rose to his feet startled the Cadet, causing him to flinch: the Detective Sergeant's bulk loomed in front of him.

The grave expression on Dai's face had gone, substituted by a radiant smile, and his right hand was on offer.

"I'm teasing you, Phyllis — sorry, but I couldn't resist it. Once the seed of a wind-up had been sown by Morecambe and Wise from two doors up, the joker in me took over. The whole thing went like bloody clockwork, and I want to be the first to congratulate you and to shake your hand. What you've done, considering your age and lack of experience, is quite remarkable."

A deep intake of breath masked the sigh of relief that the Cadet wanted to let rip as he took the Detective Sergeant's hand.

"Well done, young man. Well done, I'm — no — we are proud of you..."

He raised his voice.

"...Get in here, you pair of comedians."

Laughter came from the corridor, and the door barged open. In bustled Clive and Buttons: they had been eavesdropping. Both men talked over each other, giving praise, slapping the Cadet's back, shaking his hand, and playfully punching Dai on his upper arm — their faces flushed with excitement.

"You're too good an actor, Dai: your talents are wasted."

Clive joined in.

"Oh, I wouldn't say that; he's been guilty of acting all through his career. He deserves a bloody Oscar. How do you think he got to be Detective Sergeant?"

The Cadet managed a smile, overtly letting out a sigh of relief now he was aware that Mikey Price hadn't blabbed to the police about him, and dramatically, he placed a hand over his heart as he spoke.

"I thought I'd done something wrong and I was in for a bloody rollicking."

The three men burst out laughing.

The shrill ringing of Dai's phone interrupted the celebration.

"Who the bloody hell is this?"

Removing his specs and wiping the tears from his eyes, he cleared his throat as he slumped into the recliner.

"Good morning, Detective Sergeant David Winters speaking. How can I help you?"

The others could hear a male voice, but it was muffled. Dai sat up straight, glancing over to the Cadet.

"Yes, he's here with me now, Sir, and I'm just about to appraise him of the situation. Yes, I most certainly will. What time? Eleven on the dot. Okay, he'll be there."

Dai replaced the phone and sat back in the chair, his face as white as a starched sheet in the Savoy.

"That was the Chief Constable, lads."

The Detective Sergeant's eyes remained fixed on the Cadet.

"Somehow or other, and for the life of me, I don't know how, but he's aware of your exploits. He wants to see you in his office at 1100 hrs on the dot. How the hell does he know?"

He pushed up his specs, picked up the phone, unscrewed the mouthpiece, and examined it. There was nothing untoward. He checked the base — nothing. Ran his hands under his desk — nothing.

"What the hell are you looking for, Dai?"

"A bug, Buttons. My office has been bloody bugged! How else would the Chief Constable know about Phyllis' involvement?"

Clive interjected.

"Hey, hey, hey, come on, Dai, relax; let's think this through. It's got to be Pat Muldoon: guaranteed he's cracked under pressure. You know what the Detective Chief Superintendent's like at 'morning prayers'. Especially with a high-profile case like this. He'd want to know the ins and outs of a cat's backside. He hates it when the Chief Constable knows something he doesn't."

Buttons continued.

"And think about who the injured party is in this case. The

Chief Constable and the Detective Chief Superintendent are probably in the same bloody lodge as Bernard Jones. He was the Head of Planning for Carmarthenshire, don't forget."

A phone started ringing in their office, and Dai, his face more relaxed and now grinning, chipped in.

"That's probably him now. He's been earwigging what you pair have been saying. You'd better go and see what he wants."

Phyllis was laughing with the men as they slapped him on the back before returning to their office, but internally he was a total mess: anxiety had gripped him again. The truth about his relationship with Mikey Price had made him a gullible target to their wind-up, and he'd been well and truly suckered: he genuinely believed he'd been rumbled. And the conversation regarding the Chief Constable had gone completely over his head: he was clueless.

'What the hell is morning prayers? What is this lodge they mentioned? Was it something to do with golf or fishing? Scouting maybe? What's a high-profile case? And why does the Chief Constable want to see him?'

"Right, young man, it appears that you are today's centre of attention. Something I was hoping wouldn't happen, but having said that, this is an excellent opportunity for you. You're going to get the recognition you deserve from the people that matter, and they will make sure that this case will have all the T's crossed and all the i's dotted because it is personal to them. No way will anything be allowed to jeopardise the file's smooth running to and through the courts, so maybe, and this is me thinking out loud here, you'll be even safer."

Looking deflated, the Cadet sat down.

"I'm sorry, Sarge, I don't know what you're talking about: I feel inadequate — completely out of my depth."

Dai flicked the kettle on.

"To be fair, boy, that's perfectly normal. You're barely out of school. Why should you be aware of police jargon and procedures? Those things will come with experience. What has happened is highly unusual and has come to light following unprecedented circumstances. I haven't even had a chance yet to tell you what happened down in Pembrokeshire yesterday.

His eyes glanced up at the clock above the Cadet's head: it was nearing five to ten.

"Bloody hell, look at the time; I'll have to brief you later on. Do you have your tunic jacket and cap with you? The Chief will expect you to be wearing those."

"N n no — I I haven't, Sarge. They are both in my lodgings — n not far from the fire station."

"Bloody hell-fire — excuse the pun, and I've been wittering on." He reached for the telephone and dialled internally.

"Hi Alwyn, it's Dai Insignificant. I need an urgent favour..."

CHAPTER 26

Less than five minutes later, the Cadet was sitting in the back of a souped-up Patrol Car, blue lights flashing and whizzing through the town centre. He could see the people staring, gossiping, and pointing the finger. The boy smiled; how many times had he overheard adults coming to the wrong conclusions when they witnessed such a scene? He imagined what they would be saying and couldn't resist giving them a wave.

'Who is that youngster? What mischief has he been up to? Bloody tearaways. Lock them up and throw away the key. Bring back National Service, that's what I say. Never did me any harm. And where is the mother? Down the bloody bingo hall or fagging away in the pub — that's where she is.'

Dai's chat with Alwyn had been a game-changer. The Cadet was walking in through the front door within minutes, and the engine of the patrol car was purring in readiness for the return journey: poised for a quick getaway.

He kicked off his shoes and was taking the stairs two at a time. "It's only me, Mrs Jones. I'm just getting my jac—"

The appearance of Mrs Jones edging out of his room with a 'caught in the headlights' look on her face completely threw him, and he couldn't prevent the colour draining from his face. Neither could he suppress the giveaway wide-eyed look of shock and suspicion.

Mrs Jones had spotted it, and there was a brief, awkward silence before she forced a smile, pushing back the hair from her brow as she spoke.
"This is a surprise, Lloyd. I was just…"
Her hands moved to smooth the little pinafore tied around her waist.
"Umm, tidying your room. Umm, do you have time for a cuppa? Should I put the kettle on?"
Her voice was taut, lacking its usual warmth, and she couldn't maintain eye contact. On the contrary, she turned away from his gaze, mumbling incoherently about something that ended with, 'the bathroom.'
"N n no, it's okay, Mrs Jones. I I haven't got time. I I've only rushed back to collect my jacket and cap."
He recovered some composure and was dying to ask her why she was acting so suspiciously, but he didn't know what to say. She often went into their room to check it out, and that wasn't a problem. What was a problem, especially with what had happened to his money, was her look of absolute guilt.
He decided to try and act as normal as he possibly could, forcing a cheery voice.
"Hey, Mrs Jones, you'll never guess what has happened. I've got a police patrol car standing by. It's waiting for me by the front door, ready to whisk me back to Headquarters: I'd better rush."
He laughed, but it wasn't convincing.
"I feel like a VIP being chauffeured around the place."
She didn't turn around to look at him, just muttered some incomprehensible words before closing and locking the bathroom door.
'Oh my God — what just happened?'
His eyes darted towards his stash: the five-pound note hadn't been touched. He checked out the room, searching for any sign to substantiate her reason for being in there, but nothing had changed: it was still in the same dishevelled mess as earlier.
Head in hands, he sat on the bed — deep in thought.
'Why had she acted so weird?'

His thoughts were interrupted by the continuous beep of a horn, and he checked his wristwatch.

"Shit, it's 10:30."

Grabbing his tunic jacket, he rummaged in the wardrobe for his cap: it wasn't there.

"But it's always there — where the hell is it?"

A frantic search locates it beneath Big Lloyd's bed, and he rushes onto the landing. There's still no sign of Mrs Jones, and he calls out to her from the top step.

"I'm off, Mrs Jones, see you later."

No response, but he thought he could hear whimpering, and he checked his watch again.

"10:40 — shit!"

The car horn beeped again.

"O.K. I'm coming, I'm coming: I'm on my way."

He couldn't leave her. Not if she was upset, and he ran to the bathroom door.

"Are you okay, Mrs Jones?"

It was a croaky voice that responded, and it was unconvincing.

"I'm fine, Lloyd, just a bit of a headache. I'll see you later — bye."

A sharp blast from the patrol car's siren prompted another check of his watch.

"10:43 — shit, shit, shit!"

He ran down the stairs. Cleared the bottom four in one leap, picked up his shoes, and hobbled to the car in his socks.

The driver wasn't best pleased.

"For fuck's sake, boy, what have you been doing?"

"Sorry, I'm so sorry, my landlady isn't very well. Something's upset her; I tried to find out what it was, but sh—"

The siren cut him off.

"No time for that now, boy, hold on…"

He turned to his partner.

"Flick the bluey on, Tim."

CHAPTER 27

With five minutes to spare, the patrol car approached the entrance to Police Headquarters, and the unmistakable frame of Detective Sergeant David Winters was there and waiting in front of the reception door. He checked his wristwatch as he yanked open the rear door.
"What the bloody hell took you so long, Phyllis?"
He turned to the driver.
"Cheers, Greg, I owe you one."
Greg was grinning, his left hand held out towards Tim: palm up and his fingers beckoning.
"Not a problem, Dai, any time. Tim just lost the bet — reckoned we wouldn't make it back in time."
The driver was laughing as he sped around to the car park: the bacon and egg sarnies were on his partner.
Dai ushered him in through the door, quickening the pace towards the staircase.
He shouted out the question — the Cadet in his wake.
"Do you know how to salute yet? It's etiquette to salute the Chief Constable when you meet him?"
Phyllis knew how to salute: his dad had taught him, but he was a fast learner and he couldn't resist this opportunity to get one over on the Detective Sergeant. Especially after the wind-up earlier.
"No, Sarge — sorry. Sergeant Peters has taught us how to stand

to attention and stuff like that, but we didn't do any saluting."
"Well, it's good that you can stand to attention; can you march?"
"Yes, Sarge."
"Right, come on — let's get a bloody march on — give us your cap."
They took the stairs two at a time. Four flights to the second floor, then about twenty or so yards along the empty corridor to the chief constable's office.
Dai checked his watch.
"Good, we've got a couple of minutes. Right, this is the protocol: you knock on his door, and you wait until he calls you in, okay?"
Phyllis nodded, and the supervisor didn't spot the wily grin when he perched the Cadet's cap on his head.
"You march up to his desk like this."
His back was ramrod straight, his arms pumping in front of him.
"You stop and stand to attention a couple of feet from the desk, like this."
He stood like a statue, arms straight by his side and his face to the ceiling.
"Then you salute, like this."
Up went the bent right arm, his open palm to the peak of the cap.
Neither heard the door to the gents' toilet opening and closing behind them. It was the clearing of the throat, followed by a round of applause which made them turn around.
"Very fetching, Detective Sergeant Winters."
The Chief Constable's voice was deep and powerful. Befitting a man nearing six feet eight inches and weighing close to eighteen stones.
"It's been many years since you last showed me the respect of a salute. That blue band suits you, by the way. Oh, to be 16 years of age again, eh, and to know what we do now."
Dai, who had blushed the colour of a Caribbean sunset, handed

the cap to Phyllis.

"Sir, this is Police Cadet Lloyd Hilary Davies."

Dai's eyes were boring into Phyllis, and his bent right arm was going up and down. He nodded towards the cap.

The Chief Constable sussed out what was going on.

"Oh, never mind all that bullshit, come into the office, young man. You too, Detective Sergeant Winters."

The giant strode past them, grinning and winking at Dai. They held a mutual respect, one nurtured over many years of service together. The Chief Constable was not one of the new breed taking advantage of the fast-track scheme. He'd progressed through the ranks, toiling side by side with officers such as Dai. Laughing and crying with the best of them.

He covered the eight yards in the same amount of paces before booming from his office.

"Well, come on then, you two. I've got a meeting with the heads of departments scheduled for a quarter past the hour."

*

A bond was rapidly developing between Detective Sergeant David Winters and the trainee cop. Yes, Dai had his suspicions; he knew all was not as the boy would wish others to believe they were, but he genuinely believed the youngster's heart to be in the right place. What he also found reassuring was the Cadet's presence of mind not to offload any of his probable dodgy past, which would have placed the Detective Sergeant in an extremely untenable position.

Dai didn't have any children of his own: not for the want of trying, it just never happened. He and his wife, Susie, were happy with their lot. Saturdays were his, and he enjoyed a round of golf, normally finishing off at the nineteenth hole. On Sundays, they went for a tootle: generally ending up in a quaint village pub for something to eat. Not forgetting the several exotic holidays a year; lazing about and capturing the rays from dawn till dusk. But the arrival on the scene of Lloyd Hilary Davies had well and truly blown this world of contentment out of the water. The adolescent had rekindled a fire in Dai's belly which had been absent since he hung up his boots of front-line policing. And you ask any copper worth their salt — there is no substitute. A million holes-in-one cannot surpass the adrenaline rush of feeling the collar of a self-indulgent waste of space who thinks he or she is more entitled than everybody else. Detective Sergeant David Winters had been 'making do'. He knew that, but had allowed his life to drift along, and he was bored shitless with the mundane existence of pushing paper. The Cadet was a maverick — a raw talent that needed honing, guidance, and a pointer in the right direction. And he, Dai Insignificant, was just the man to do it. He couldn't be like Phyllis — Dai knew that. He was well aware that his ways were too precise, too methodical, and too safe to take the risks, but he could be there for him as a crutch. Someone to lean on and to educate him in police procedures. Dai enjoyed the boy's company, feeding off the notoriety and loving the innocence of his youth. Yes, he was a breath of fresh air.

And, if Phyllis knew of the Detective Sergeant's feelings for him and if

he had the slightest awareness of his father's love and pride, would he be so anxious? And, would he be striving so frantically to rid himself of the red rosette that was stapled to his forehead?

*

"Well, I didn't see that coming, sonny-boy. The Chief Constable has certainly taken a shine to you, and not for many years have I seen him so relaxed and informal. Going by what he said, the unlawful killing of Bernard Jones has been a right blight on the Dyfed Powys Police Force. The victim was his friend, somebody he regularly socialised with, and he'd authorised everything requested of him to further that investigation. No stone had been left unturned, yet all lines of enquiry returned diddly squat. Then, out of the blue comes a new kid in town, Detective Cadet Phyllis. He takes an interest because he can feel the pain his landlady is suffering and wham-bam-thank-you-

mam it's solved..."
The boy starts laughing.
"I was lucky, though, Sarge. I mean, come on, it's only come about because of my friendship with Mikey Price. What were the chances of him being the guy responsible for killing the husband of my new landlady? What's even more spooky is, when I was in his house, you know, that very first time, he'd already killed the guy, and I was listening to a cassette tape that Mikey had stolen from the car that he'd used to mow him down."
Instantly, Dai's demeanour changed, and he slammed his hand onto the tabletop. His voice was firm and assertive.
"Right, young man, that's the last time you mention your close friendship with Price. Do you understand?"
The Detective Sergeant was pleased with the surprised, taken-aback look on the Cadet's face: it was the effect he desired. Time for lesson number one.
"Nobody else needs to know those things, only you."
He grabbed the Calabash, relaxed in the recliner, and fired it up.
"Unfortunately, in life, you have to mix with other human beings, and in our case, deal with disgruntled members of the public. Believe me, soon enough you'll encounter someone trying to knock you off your perch. Jealousy, greed, dislike, and ambition are traits that make people do shocking things. People who you think are your close friends will stab you in the back. My old dad once said, 'David, if you only remember one thing I tell you, then remember this. If you want something to remain private, then don't tell anybody else.' I've never forgotten that. There's only one person that you can wholeheartedly trust to keep a secret, and who might that be, young man?"
"Well, going by what you're saying, Sarge, it can only be yourself."
The palm slammed onto the desk again.
"Spot on, boy, exactly right. As soon as you make your business aware to a third party, whoever it might be, then you have lost

control of it. Tell me this, who do you think makes the best police informants?"

"Oh, I don't know, Sarge…." Rubbing his chin as he thought, "…the friends of criminals maybe?"

"Excellent, yes, they're bloody good, but the top of my list every time are the girlfriends and the wives. The loved ones. The ones that the baddies are most comfortable with and trust with their secrets and plans. Everything is hunky-dory in a relationship until it goes pear-shaped, then look out! You ever heard of the saying 'hell hath no fury than a woman scorned'?"

The boy hadn't but felt that he should have — blushing as he spoke.

"I think so, Sarge, but I'm not sure."

The Sergeant noticed the boy's discomfort and could have kicked himself. He kept on forgetting just how young he was. His tone of voice mellowed.

"In a relationship, there is a trust. A bond between two people, and very often that bond is broken. The relationship ends and usually on bad terms. The love, or lust, if they haven't known each other for very long, quickly changes to a dislike. A desire for revenge germinates, then festers like a cancer. How best to get one's revenge than to blab to the police about something illicit that they'd been privy to before the rot set in? Especially if they can get some form of reward for their trouble: understand, boy?"

He nodded — intrigued.

"Picture the scene. Joe, the burglar, is alongside Tracy, the girlfriend. They're lying back and having a fag following a bout of 'how's-yr-father' — got it?"

The boy is laughing and nodding his head.

"Right, in this romantic moment of lust, he confides with Tracy, the girlfriend, and tells her all about his clandestine goings-on. But, unbeknown to Tracy, the girlfriend, Joe, the burglar, is simultaneously giving one to her best mate — Veronica, the hairdresser…"

The Cadet chuckles, taking it all in.

"...Tracy, the girlfriend, isn't best pleased when she finds out, and lust quickly turns to hate, festering into revenge. So, to whom does Tracy, the ex-girlfriend, go running? Pouring out her heart and soul. You've got it — Phyllis the Detective Cadet." More laughter as the Detective Sergeant taps the ash from the Calabash into the wastepaper bin. He was loving it — loving being this fatherly figure. Thriving on being able to pass on experiences that had taken a lifetime to accrue.

Experiences that had come from grafting in the dark, shoulder to shoulder with hard, no-nonsense miners. Breathing in dust from the depths of the Earth's core. Witnessing horrific injuries caused by archaic machinery malfunctions, and watching as many of his peers coughed their way through the shift. Spitting out the black-coloured phlegm, which in some tragic cases turned to red: silicosis having already gripped their lungs.

As a uniformed copper, having to cut the noose from around the neck of a poor soul, unable to cope with the hand that life had dealt them.

Knocking at a stranger's door on a Sunday lunchtime, the smell of roasting beef seeping out as the young mother greets you with an unsure smile. Catching her as her legs buckle, and she falls into your arms: her darling John won't be coming home today or any other.

Traumatic death is sudden, unexpected, and unprepared for. And the faceless uniform that brings sadness to their door is a buffer for grief. Absorbing their pain and suffering. Yes, the uniform walks away once the job is done, but that family's ordeal remains with the human being: sometimes for an eternity.

Many moments stay, and many do diminish with time. Fortunately, the majority of people will go from the womb to the grave without having to endure any such dire experiences.

CHAPTER 28

"You still haven't told me what happened, Sarge. You know, what happened to Mikey and Rose?"

"Bloody hell, boy, I'd completely forgotten about that and I was miles away then..."

The Detective Sergeant shivered.

"... I was back in the past and reminiscing. Old memories had crept up on me..."

He started chuckling.

"...but also we had to contend with the added distraction of an impromptu audience with the Chief Constable, didn't we? Hey, that reminds me, what took you so long in your lodgings? You only had to collect your cap and jacket, not bloody dry-clean the buggers. Did you have a shower and wash your hair?"

Dai patted his crown and sighed.

"I'm only jealous."

The Cadet started laughing, and he prolonged the laughter longer than was necessary; his brain cells churning, trying to decide what to do. Should he tell Dai about the stolen money or should he wait and see if it happens again? Which is what he and Big Lloyd had finally agreed upon earlier. He decided on the latter; after all, he'd seen that the stash hadn't been interfered with when he went back to the lodgings earlier.

"Oh, I couldn't find my cap: I'd searched everywhere and was getting all panicky, especially when the policeman kept tooting the horn, hurrying me up. And do you know where it was? Under Lloyd's bed, both our caps were there. Can you believe that?"

"Urgh, I bet it was caked in dust: you got an itchy scalp? You'll probably have bloody nits."

Quick as a flash came the response.

"So will you then, Sarge?"

"Bloody hell!"

Both hands shot to his head and started to scratch around his ears.

"I had it on as well, didn't I?"

He gave a playful wink of the eye.

"Nah, you can't get nits on a bald bonce."

Grinning, he reached into the top drawer of his desk, pulled out an A4-size hard-covered diary, and started fingering through the pages.

"These are the notes that I scribbled down when Pat rang me last night."

He reached for the Calabash.

"Right then, so you know all about the arrest of Mikey?"

The Cadet was nodding as he sat upright in the chair.

"Good, well..."

Scanning the notes, the Detective Sergeant burst out laughing...

"This is what happened..."

*

A deep growl posed the question.

"You got the W, Cadders?"

The J.P. signed document was waved in front of Bull's face.

"Got it, Sarge. Like the boss said in the briefing: the more we get on Price, the longer we keep him banged up."

"Too bloody right, Cadders. We do this for Tomo. By the time Price breathes fresh air again as a free man, he'll be too old and too bloody infirm to even think about assaulting another copper."

A square-jawed, uniformed officer carrying a heavy-duty

sledgehammer sidled up alongside the Detective Sergeant.

"We going to put the door in, Sarge?"

The bicep of the officer's right arm stretches the sleeve of his cotton shirt to the limit as he effortlessly raises the 20-pound lump of steel towards the supervisor.

"You want me to use the key?"

Bull shook his head.

"Nah, Rocky, not unless we have to. George confirms Rose to have been in the house all morning, and there haven't been any callers, so she won't know that Price has been lifted. She won't be expecting us, and if the property from the stolen car is in there, it won't even cross her mind to interfere with it."

Thick knuckles rap against the patterned glass, but there is no response, and all eyes have veered to the bedroom window, expecting the female occupant to be peeping through the gap in the curtains.

She isn't, and Bull stoops to raise the flap of the letterbox.

"Rose Price — this is Detective Sergeant Graham Williams from Pembroke Dock police station — open the door!"

There is no reply, and a few seconds pass before the command is repeated — it's an agitated voice that grates from the first floor.

"Fuck off and leave me alone. Mikey ain't here, and before you ask, I don't know where the fuck he is."

Once again, the Detective Sergeant bellows through the letterbox.

"Rose, we have a warrant to search your house for stolen property. If you don't open the door immediately, we will force entry."

The response is vicious.

"Piss off! I already told you, didn't I? Mikey ain't here, and there's sod all in this house that's been stolen. I'm in the fucking bath for Christ's sake, and I ain't moving for no fucker! Can't a lady enjoy a smoke and a soak every once in a while? Come back tomorrow!"

Sighing and shaking his head in frustration, Bull nods to the uniformed officer.

"She can't say we didn't give her a chance…"

His eyes drift to the size of the officer's bicep, then to the size of the sledgehammer, then to the frailty of the glass-panelled door, and fearing the worst, Bull grimaces and his voice lowers to a cautionary whisper.

"Just give it a gentle tap, Rocky: it's a thin piece of glass and the door's only secured by a single-lever mortice."

The officer puffs out his chest — the crisp North Wales accent differentiating him from his colleagues.

"No problem, Sarge, leave it to me — I've done the course."

He turns to the entourage, his free arm locked at a right angle to his torso, palm facing them.

"Stand back, everyone…"

The indiscriminate lump of steel at the end of a shortened shaft of solid oak smacks into the lock area, and the door springs free as if running for its life; it ricochets off the adjoining wall and judders on its hinges back into the frame. Bull's sigh of relief is short-lived: an acute, splintering, cracking sound breaks the tense silence as the glass shatters and drops into the hallway.

The grimace is prolonged as he hisses through gritted teeth.

"Bloody hell, Rocky — I said a gentle tap…"

The glare at the officer doesn't wane as the Detective Sergeant pushes the door into the hallway until it jams amidst the fragments. Muttering fucks and bastards, he sucks in his stomach and squeezes his bulk through the limited space. It was Rose's voice that severed his concentration and his eyes divert from the sharpness of the glass.

She stood with her hands on her hips at the top of the stairs and, aside from an array of pink rollers and an Aloe Vera face mask, was as naked as Lady Godiva. Her mass was plastered in soap suds, and a cigarette with a length of ash precariously hanging from the tip dangled from her bottom lip. It crumbled and fell to the gaudy, patterned carpet as she remonstrated.

"What the hell did you go and do that for, you fuckin' gorilla?

Who's going to pay for the glass? Mark my words, you plods will bankroll that repair because whatever you've been told, it is wrong. You won't find anything in here — we ain't got fuck all!"

Her right hand leaves the hip, the index finger is wagging at Bull, and her right breast is keeping time with the wag as she continues to protest.

"My solicitor will sort you out, you 'airy bastard, and I'll see you all in court."

Grinning, Bull turned to a plain-clothed female officer and winked.

"Sort her out, will you please, Cerys? There aren't many of those bloody bubbles left, and the sight of what's behind them will definitely put me off my sarnies."

Woman Detective Constable Cerys Pickters had seen it all before and thrived on these moments. Chuckling, she squeezed into the hall, leant in close to her Sergeant, and whispered.

"Think on the bright side, Bull. You don't need to fork out to see the Moulin Rouge now, do you?"

The raucous laughter fills the hallway as she climbs the stairs and ushers Rose back into the condensation. Scanning the sparse fittings, sharp eyes pick out an open packet of 20 resting on the window sill, but more important to the case and pertinent to the search warrant is a silver-coloured petrol lighter bearing the motif of an SAS cap badge. It's tucked in between the cigarettes and a steamed-up pane of frosted glass. The totally oblivious Rose curses as she forces her feet into a pair of open-toed, pink, fluffy slippers and yanks on a pink dressing gown. She stuffs the fags and lighter into one of the pockets before pausing at the top of the stairs to tie a bow in the sash and to squish the fallen ash into the carpet pile with the ball of her foot. The thin polyester garment, straining over rolls of fat, is trapped in between the cheeks of her backside and clings to the dampness of her skin as she takes the stairs two at a time; still protesting about the payment of the repair. Cerys winks at Bull and nods her head towards the bulge in the dressing gown pocket: the Detective Sergeant cottons on.

"Empty your pockets, Rose, and put the contents onto the table."

A high-alert Rose hadn't missed the officer's gesture and she turned to Cerys.

"Fuck me. You fuckers must be desperate if yr after me smokes."

Out come the packet of fags together with the lighter and a grubby handkerchief with the initials RP embroidered in one corner. It's overlapping the lighter, and Bull spots some crusted nasal secretions clinging to the needlework. Grimacing while slipping on a pair of surgical gloves, he rescues the lighter and immediately spots the eight digits engraved on the bottom. He'd scribbled Robbo's military number on the underside of his wrist before leaving the Nick, and his heart is pounding as he steals a sly glance. They are identical, and he's dying to punch the air and shout out "YES" in celebration, but that would spoil what he has in store for Rose; instead, he smiles and nods towards the watchful Cerys. She knows exactly what to do: pass on the great news to the rest of the team.

'They've got the evil bastards!'

"Well, what about this then, Rose Price? Where did you get this lighter from?"

He nonchalantly places it back on the table.

Rose stops ranting; her mind is working overtime, and Bull's attempt to play down the interest in the item hasn't worked.

'Shit, the plods are after the lighter, and I've just handed it to them on a silver fuckin' platter. Where the hell did Mikey thieve it from? He's had it since he came out of The Big House, and that was months ago.'

The face mask starts to crack as the lies spew from her lips — her voice pensive and nervous.

"I found it on the bus yonks ago: it must have slipped out of someone's pocket, and I spotted it when I sat down."

Marvelling at such a rapid, yet plausible response, she grows in confidence, and the hands return to the hips. The aggressiveness is back.

"Fuck me, man, that was yonks ago. I put it in my bag to take to the cop shop, but I completely forgot about it, and when I remembered, well, there wasn't much point then, was there?"

The finger wags at Bull again, and her voice is full of scorn.

"Go on then, King fuckin' Kong, tell me, one's been reported as stolen, hasn't it?"

Bull sat down and openly sighed.

"Rose, Rose, Rose…"

His right hand scratches at the stubble covering his neck — a lull before the kill. He was going to enjoy what was coming next: savour the moment. He'd reached the point where everything had clicked into place. They had found the equivalent of the link piece to an impossible-to-do jigsaw, and Detective Sergeant Graham Williams could now relax and play a little game with one of the most infamous of undesirables on his patch. As he'd done countless times with all those other self-indulgent dregs of society who had unleashed unwarranted misery on the nicer persons in life. Those normally innocent members of his community who, unfortunately, he only ever got to meet because they were the victims of crime.

"Let me tell you a little story, Rose Price — do sit down."

A sardonic smile added to the confidence in his voice as he dragged out a chair from beneath the table and gestured with the palm of his hand.

"Come on, join me. Make yourself at home. Whoops, I completely forgot, you are at home. Here, have a fag and relax."

He chose one from the packet, handed it to her, picked up the lighter and sparked it into life.

Fidgeting with her gown, Rose edges closer to Bull, sucking on the filter as the tip enters the flame.

"There you are, Rose, sit back and enjoy."

A grinning Cadders appeared at the doorway, holding up a brown-coloured cushion with a gold fleck. Smiling at the find, the Detective Sergeant gestures to him.

"Come in, Detective Constable Caddering. Rose might want to sit on that plushness while she enjoys her fag and listens to the true story that I'm about to tell her."
Brushing away the offer of the cushion, Rose takes a long drag and stalls for time. Her brain is hurting: too much to think about. Too many things to try and recall, and this beast of a copper is too bloody smug.
'Where the hell did Mikey get that fuckin' lighter from? And that cushion? Why did the copper bring that in here? There must be a connection, and what about the other cushion in the living room? And the matching bloody blanket. I'm sure they all turned up at the same time. What the hell has Mikey done?'
Her ears strain to pick up any clues from the excitable chit-chat filtering through from the rest of the house, and it's the brisk tapping of the lighter on the tabletop that summons her from her thoughts: her eyes deviate towards those of the Detective Sergeant's.
"Now that you're sitting comfortably, Rose, I will begin. Once upon a time, in a town far away from here, there was a man who owned a petrol lighter, and just like this one, it had eight numerals engraved on the bottom."
Bull shows it to Rose before continuing.
"This is a military registration number and it is unique to an individual. When the man in the story retired from the army, he was presented with the petrol lighter together with a couple of other commemorative items, and each one had his military number engraved on it. Exclusive presents for him to cherish forever."
Rose takes an extra long drag, the face mask hiding the annoyance on her face: she is seething.
'For fuck's sake, Mikey, you idiot. Why didn't you scrape away those numbers? How many times have you been told to get rid of any identifiable shit? Hell, Mikey, that's fuckin' basics.'
Bull can smell her discomfort and smiles as he moves in for the arrest.
"Can you read out the number to me, Rose? I want to entertain

you with a magic trick. A trick that you would never have believed to be possible."

Her returning smile is forced and laced with venom.

'The smug bastard — what's he going to do now?'

She swallows several times, her eyes squinting to make out the numbers.

"Well, it looks to me like 04680431."

The underside of his wrist is shoved in front of her face.

"Snap! Now that's what you call magic!"

She can feel her anxiety churning, and the hatred for this pig of a man is growing by the second, but showing no emotion, Rose decides on another ploy. The only one she knows: all-out attack.

Exposing the left thigh as she crosses her legs, she takes a long drag on the cigarette and rests her elbow on the table. Her chin is cupped in the palm of her hand, and her eyes delve into Bull's as she seductively blows the smoke into his face while speaking. Her voice is sensual and sultry.

"I already told you, big boy: I found the lighter on a bus, so it makes no difference to me what numbers are on the fuckin' thing. Do you think I would have left them there if I thought it was stolen property? I'm pleased that the man will get his precious lighter back, but let's be honest, he has caused me a load of aggro, hasn't he? Perhaps you should give him some advice from me."

The voice changes, and the aggression is back.

"Tell him to be more fuckin' careful with his stuff when he's travelling on a fuckin' bus!"

Blinking away the smoke, Bull smiles, his eyes not deviating from hers.

"The person who stole this lighter also stole the man's car, and there is no happy ending to this story, Rose. Unfortunately for you, a beautiful damsel in distress and a handsome prince do not exist. In this TRUE story, the thief drove the car into a busy town centre where it bulldozed into a pedestrian who was in the middle of the road, and within the safe confines of a zebra crossing. And do you know what happened then? The thief left him dying in the roadway."

Rose shot up from the chair, and a breast escaped as she wagged her finger in Bull's face.

"Well, that's got fuck all to do with me. I just told you, didn't I? I found the lighter on the bus!"

Cerys pops her head around the door.

"Sarge, there's another cushion and a blanket in the living room together with a Sanyo cassette player and some tapes. They all match the property reported as stolen from the Ford Capri at the same time as the lighter."

The chair scraped across the floor as the Detective Sergeant sprang to his feet.

"Cover yourself up, Rose, and listen carefully to what I have to say. I am arresting you on suspicion of the murder of Mr Bernard Jones. Do you wish to say…"

A chilling scream spewed from her lips, and the other breast flopped into view as her nails lunged at the officer's eyes.

"I haven't killed no one — you smug fuckin' arsehole — it's got fuck all to do with me."

*

Protesting, the Cadet stood up.

"But she didn't kill Bernie Jones Sarge — it was Mikey: Mikey must have done it. Rose probably took a liking to the lighter, and Mikey wouldn't have had any option but to let her have it."

The Detective Sergeant sat back, grinning; his hand rising up and down at the wrist. It was deja vu.

"Hey, hey, calm down. Let me finish, young man, let me finish. I told you, if you remember, that sometimes we need a little bargaining chip: something to loosen the tongue. The thought of being charged and put behind bars for the rest of your natural life certainly encourages the tighter-lipped amongst us to suddenly find their tongues. Even more so when they haven't got a bloody clue as to why they are being interviewed. Phyllis did remember, and he was annoyed with himself: how could he have forgotten that? Reddening, he flashed a tight-lipped smile, nodded, and sat down again.

The Detective Sergeant's grin had turned to a supportive smile.

"Right, good, let's move on then, shall we? They keep Rose waiting in the panda car at the back of the police station until Mikey is brought from his cell to be given his prescription of methadone. Bull's plan is to bring Rose into the holding area at the same time, and it works a treat.

Seeing Mikey is like a red rag to a bull…"

The Detective Sergeant laughs.

"…No pun intended, and Rose flies at him, screaming for him to come clean, that it's got fuck all to do with her. She hasn't murdered any fucker, but if she did cop the blame, then he'd be her first fucking victim!

They dragged her off him and bang them up in separate cells, far enough away from each other so they couldn't talk and get their stories to match."

The Cadet is wide-eyed.

"Wow, Sarge, those tactics were brilliant."

Dai taps his nose and winks.

"Ways and means, boy — ways and means. Now brace yourself because this is excellent news. They've got the tobacco tin, yeah? That was on Mikey when they tugged him. They've got the petrol lighter, yeah? That was next to Rose's bath. Guess what, Phyllis?"

They said it in unison.

"They've only gone and got the thermos flask as well."

"Ha ha, you can't get a much better result than that, young man. It looks like you've got your full house.

The flask was found at the back of a cabinet under the kitchen sink — wedged between a nest of silverfish basking in a rotting dishcloth and some discarded Brillo pads. The search team nearly missed it: purely because of the filth — the grime and dust had made it virtually unrecognisable. Seemingly, when the stopper was unscrewed, the stench was overpowering, and sprouting from the remnants of forgotten coffee was enough fungi and mould to manufacture a batch of bloody penicillin!

But that mattered not. Engraved on the bottom, for the eyes of all and sundry to witness, particularly those of Your Honour, the Judge, was Taff Robbo's unique military number.

The adolescent rose from the chair and wandered aimlessly around the office; his breathing was deep, his hands were pushing through his hair, and his body was trembling. That terrifying memory of seconds away from being discovered when he was hiding in Mikey's wardrobe still haunted him. All the what-ifs and could-have-beens were a plague on his thoughts. He shuddered — there would have been two certain outcomes if he had been captured:

1. His disappearance without a trace from the face of the planet.
2. Mikey Price not being locked up in a police cell at this present moment in time.

The Detective Sergeant could see that the Cadet was in turmoil, but what could he do? He had immersed himself in this plight by choosing a path that only leads to sleepless nights. An inability to off-load worries and not being able to talk to those closest to you can weigh down heavily on even the strongest of minds. The Detective Sergeant had seen it many times before but never in someone so young. Phyllis was holding back — he'd been economical with the truth. Dai knew that, hell, he'd been a Detective for too long not to know. But he also knew it was impossible, without implications, for him to divulge the truth now, even if he wanted to. The consequences of his choices would be a burden that he would have to bear alone. A burden that would increase in weight with every future dodgy turn he decided upon. And danger is this boy's food and drink: he courts it. Unable to look the other way or to take an easier option because if he does, he ends up fighting with himself. It is much simpler for the boy to front up and tackle what is before him rather than spend hours upon hours of turmoil battling with the Demon within him if he doesn't. Dai also knew that eventually the Cadet's past would catch up with and consume him: it always does.

"You must be wondering what the outcome is?"
He stopped pacing around the office, sat down, and sighed; his right foot constantly tapping the floor.
"This is all fantastic, Sarge. I've been very lucky, and going by the praise from the Chief Constable, what you're about to tell me now must be pretty good too."
Dai sat back in the recliner.
"You make your own luck, sonny boy, and you're absolutely right about the praise, but this outcome is a bit more than merely pretty good. Not only did they recover the three identifiable items, but they also recovered everything else that was recorded on the crime report, apart from, that is, the A.A. road atlas of Great Britain."
Phyllis shrugged.
"Well, I suppose that went up in flames. Mikey might not have seen it."
"You're partly correct when you suppose it went up in flames, sonny, because it did. But you're wrong when you surmise that Mikey might not have seen it — he's only gone and coughed to using the atlas to start the bloody fire."
The Cadet shook his head.
"Unbelievable, Sarge. So what's happened to him, and what about Rose?"
Dai smiled — picturing in his mind what she might look like.
"Rose? Oh, she'll be released on police bail pending further enquiries. I doubt whether she'll ever be charged with anything. Another bargaining chip for the detectives to use.
'Play ball, Mikey, and we'll keep your mother out of it.'
And as for Mikey? Well, enquiries are still ongoing. South Wales Police have been contacted regarding the robbery in Neath, and they are sending a couple of detectives to liaise with Pat Muldoon and his team in Pembroke Dock. Mikey is denying all knowledge of that crime at the moment, and they don't have any evidence to put him at the scene. None of the stolen jewellery, or the iron bar used on Mr Moore was found during the search of Price's home address, so unless they get a

confession, it sounds like the only chance of potting him will be if the witness picks him out on an identification parade. A long shot, but you never know.
What has been established is that Price was released from Borstal on the morning of the crimes, and he'd been issued with a rail ticket to Pembroke Dock. So it looks like the robbery in Neath had been planned, and if it hadn't gone pear-shaped, Robbo's Ford Capri would no doubt have been found burnt out somewhere a bit closer to home, and more significantly, Bernard Jones would still be alive..."
The shaking of the head, and the glare in the Detective Sergeant's eyes said it all.
"...It didn't take long for the scumbag to re-offend, eh? Bloody waste of time locking up little shits like Price! Anyway, he'll be charged later on today with something to keep him in custody, and he'll go before the magistrates in Haverfordwest tomorrow morning. The prosecution will ask the bench for a remand at the police station for two or three days. Why? Well, not only do they have the horrific robbery in Neath to sort out, but also another serious crime has come to light, and Price is the prime suspect.
Did he ever mention a bloke from Liverpool? Name of..."
The Detective Sergeant glanced at his notes before edging forward on the recliner and resting his arms on the desk; his eyes locking onto those of the Cadet.
"...Barry Murphy?"
Phyllis sat up in the chair, shaking his head, and he couldn't prevent the nervous swallow before replying: he'd sensed a sudden change in the Detective Sergeant's demeanour.
"N No, Sarge, t to be honest, M Mikey never really said a great deal..."
His mouth was suddenly very dry.
"... Why? W what's this Barry bloke got to do with it?"
The Detective Sergeant wasn't convinced with the response: he didn't know whether to believe the Cadet or not. Was Phyllis telling the truth? He hoped he was, but he couldn't be sure. It

bugged him that he still suspected the Cadet to be holding back on the full extent of his involvement with Price, and rightly or wrongly, Dai had turned a blind eye. But the ball game had changed: the enquiry was shifting to a much higher level — the most serious of all crimes had come into play. And as a result of the information he'd received from Pat Muldoon, he suspected Phyllis to be selective with the truth again. Was the boy trying to ascertain how much the police knew about Price's involvement with Barry Murphy before deciding whether to comment or not?

"Barry Murphy is missing. There has been no trace of him since his release day from prison, back in late November of last year…"

Dai shook his head as he spoke.

"…no sightings at all in his home city of Liverpool. The only certain fact is he was last seen getting into a maroon-coloured Austin 1800 outside the prison gates. And guess what, young Phyllis? That car had been reported as being stolen from and returned to Pembroke Dock. It had been driven in excess of 650 miles. That fact could be determined, but no other evidence was found. Do you know why?"

He didn't have a clue, but for some reason or other, he was feeling very guilty, and the more he tried to relax, the more the anxiety gripped him.

He shook his head as he replied — his face flushing, and the sweat from his armpits was clearly dampening his shirt.

"I I d don't know, Sarge. W w why should I know?"

The supervisor ignored the question.

"The reason why no evidence was found is quite simple: it had been set on bloody fire! Coincidence or what?"

The boy didn't respond: he couldn't because he genuinely knew nothing about what the Detective Sergeant was on about. Dai's attitude had changed towards him. His tone was now challenging, accusing even, and his eyes were boring into him. 'Bloody hell, Dai thinks I know something and I'm holding back.'

"You'll never guess who shared a cell with this Barry Murphy?" Phyllis took a deep breath. Obviously, it was Mikey Price.
'Bloody hell, Mikey, what the hell have you done?'
"I I don't know, S Sarge, but going by what you're telling me, I I guess it was Mikey."
"Too bloody right it was. And what do you think the detectives found in Mikey's wardrobe at the foot of his bed: hidden underneath a pile of stinking laundry?"
Dai's eyes remained fixed on the Cadet's, who was shaking his head again — his heart racing.
'That must have been the same wardrobe where he had hidden from that fat, smelly bloke; all he could remember seeing in there was dirty underwear and socks.'
His reply was unconvincing, beads of sweat breaking out on his forehead. Answering a question with a question, which came across to the suspicious Dai Insignificant that the boy was fishing for information before committing himself to a response.
"I I d don't know, Sarge…"
He couldn't maintain eye contact.
"…W w what was there?"
That was one question too many, and the Detective Sergeant couldn't restrain himself any longer. He rose from the recliner, his bulk towering over the Cadet, and he pointed a wagging finger.
"You tell me, young man. You're the one who was in the bloody wardrobe. Are you taking me for some kind of fool? Look at you, you're sweating like Billy Bunter in a steam room and stuttering more than Porky bloody Pig. Why are you so nervous? What the hell are you keeping from me? This is not some playground game. Mikey Price is suspected of murdering Barry Murphy! We already know he's capable of that, don't we? For Christ's sake, he mowed down an innocent man on a pedestrian crossing and left the poor bugger for dead! What the hell do you know, Phyllis?" You've been bosom buddies with Price for months!"

The tears spilled out. It was all too much — the adolescent was worn out and way out of his depth.

"I I d don't know anything about B Barry Murphy, Sarge. I promise. I I'd never heard that name until now. The only thing I saw and smelt in that wardrobe was dirty socks and skid-marked Y fronts. I I'm nervous because I'm scared stiff that you think I'm somehow more involved, and that something terrible is going to happen to me and my parents. An an and I'm terrified I might lose my job because of my friendship with Mikey Price."

The Detective Sergeant reached for his Calabash, turned away, and flicked on the kettle. He could feel the heat blistering on the back of his neck, and he sucked in the calming effect of the tobacco, telling himself to cool down as he poured the boiling water onto the instant granules. Dai was well aware that he'd committed a cardinal sin by becoming too attached to the boy. He'd allowed himself to be carried away on the euphoria; the exhilaration that Phyllis had brought into his life had liberated him from a mundane existence, and he didn't want to spoil it. But had he dropped his guard? Not scrutinised the facts as he should have done because of not wanting to jeopardise what was developing? More importantly, had he made a huge error of judgement? And if he had, could he still rescue the situation?

He rewound the last few minutes: relived every sentence and, on reflection, realised that the boy hadn't done or said anything to make him have a go at him with such venom. It was all the years of deceit and dealing with lying shits: mistrust and suspicion were deeply ingrained in his thought process. As far as Dai was concerned, every suspect was lying until he could prove otherwise, and that mindset had led to the doubt in the Cadet's account. The reality hit him, and he sighed. How could he have got it so wrong? He believed the boy to be telling the truth, particularly in relation to Barry Murphy. No doubt he's been holding back, lying even, about his involvement in drugs and petty crime, but there is nothing,

as yet, to confirm those suspicions. And those life experiences and his association with adolescent criminals are moulding him into what he is now. Yes, I don't think he has a clue about who Barry Murphy is. No way could he muster up so much emotion. But he had to be sure, and perhaps this outburst was the only surefire way of finding out.
He turned back to face the Cadet.
"I'm sorry, Phyllis, if I came across a bit heavy: I had to be sure. Sure that I trust you implicitly and believe that what I report back to Pat Muldoon will be the truth.
Hell boy, you've unearthed not a can of worms but a tank full of bloody rattlesnakes! This enquiry is huge: a possible murder in Liverpool, an horrific armed robbery and theft in Neath, the death of a prominent local council official in Carmarthen, drugs offences, a failed attempt at a robbery, and an assault on a police officer in Pembroke Dock. What else is going to come to light?"
He pushed the mug across the tabletop.
"Here, have a bloody coffee."
The Cadet wiped a tear away, and took a long, satisfying swig; enjoying the comforting warmth of the hot ceramic against his skin. It was sodden eyes that were fixed on the huge man in front of him as he continued to relay the sequence of events.
"When they searched the house, the officers found a black-coloured hold-all in the bottom of the wardrobe in Mikey's bedroom, and in the hold-all were possessions belonging to Barry Murphy: they included his prison release papers. That must have been the wardrobe where you were hiding — could the hold-all have been in the wardrobe at that time?"
'That's the reason for Dai's outburst. It was only a matter of days ago: the bag must have been in there. Probably underneath Mikey's stinking Y-fronts. No wonder he thought I was holding back.'
He took a sip of the coffee — thinking before he spoke.
"I I don't know, Sarge. It might very well have been, but if it was, it must have been covered by the underwear because

otherwise I'm sure I would have felt it beneath me: I was kneeling on something soft — not hard. It was cramped and dark. All I saw and smelt was dirty underwear, and I was terrified. As soon as I could, I just legged it."

He sipped at the coffee again, his mind troubled by something else that the Detective Sergeant had said.

"You mentioned an attempted robbery in Pembroke Dock: who was robbed, Sarge?"

A preoccupied Dai looked up from the diary.

"What? Oh, that's something and nothing compared to the possible murder of Barry Murphy. But it's yet another bargaining chip. The detectives in Pembroke Dock lost sight of Price for a few minutes when they were surveilling him, and during that time it looks like he tried to rob an elderly lady: it was witnessed by the victim's neighbour. There are ongoing enquiries about that incident, and we'll get an update on that later on. As I said, it's a possible bargaining chip: it can be swept under the carpet if Price plays ball and makes admissions in relation to the more serious crimes.

Phyllis was chewing on a nail, his face streaked with tear tracks, and it was a broken voice that asked the questions.

"Is the lady okay, Sarge? Was she injured?"

Inwardly, Dai sighed, deeply regretting the earlier outburst. The boy had been dragged through the mill, and yet all he was thinking about was the welfare of a complete stranger.

He cleared the emotions from the back of his throat before speaking.

"She's fine, Phyllis. Seemingly, she wasn't even aware that it had happened."

He checked the walk clock, wanting to move on.

"As I said, we'll be updated later on. Price was interviewed months ago in relation to the taking of the Austin 1800 and its possible use in Murphy's disappearance. He denied all knowledge, and there wasn't enough evidence to arrest him. Now it is completely different. The discovery of Murphy's holdall in Price's wardrobe refutes his negative explanations, making Price the prime suspect to his probable murder. Mark my words, Phyllis: Price is in deep shit.

He's made an admission to stealing Robbo's Ford Capri, but he hasn't commented as to why he was in Neath. And as I mentioned, he's denying anything to do with Michael Moore's robbery; they'll probably struggle to prove that without a positive I.D. Even if he agrees to a lineup!

He's admitted to stealing Robbo's SAS memorabilia and the other items from the car before razing it to the ground, but he's denied using the car to murder Bernard Jones. That was a non-starter anyway, just a spot of scaremongering, you know, getting his and Rose's backsides twitching so they'd admit to the lesser offences. Nobody actually believed a charge of murder was ever on the cards."

Phyllis jumped out of his seat again.

"But Mikey killed him, didn't he? He ran the car straight into Bernie Jones, knocked him for six and left him on the roadway to die. We know that he was driving the car, he's admitted that. So how come it's not murder? It doesn't seem right to me."

The Detective Sergeant held out an upturned palm.

"Okay, okay, calm down and I'll explain. I didn't particularly want to go down this route because it's complicated, but I suppose you need to understand the basics. At least then you'll have some knowledge when you speak with Mrs Jones later on..."

Inwardly, the Cadet sighed. 'Shit — I didn't tell Mrs Jones about Mikey's arrest: I was so wrapped up last night with trying to find out who might have stolen my fiver that I completely forgot. I'll have to tell her later.'

"...Murder is one of a select few offences where, unless the defendant has admitted guilt or there is strong evidence to prove otherwise, the prosecution has to establish a certain state of mind. In simple terms, did Mikey Price intend to kill Bernard Jones?

In order to prove his intention, he needs to make an admission that he did so. Something like: 'I saw the guy on the crossing, so I floored the accelerator because I wanted to kill him.' That proves a state of mind — an intent.

Evidence to counteract a denial of any intent could come from an eyewitness. Something along the lines of: 'I saw the driver of the car change its course and aim the vehicle at Bernard Jones.' Or: 'The driver increased the car's speed when he saw the pedestrian on the crossing.'

Mikey has said that he didn't do any of those things. He said that he didn't even see Bernard Jones on the crossing. That it was dark, pouring with rain, and Bernard Jones must have been wearing dark-coloured clothing. Unfortunately, the police cannot disprove that explanation.

Eyewitnesses do say that the car was driving way too fast for the road conditions, and Mikey has admitted that to be the case. Many years ago, in their wisdom, the law lords came up with a specific offence which caters for such an eventuality, and when they consider all the evidence, the police will probably charge Mikey Price with that offence: 'Causing the death of Mr Bernard Jones by dangerous driving.'

More facts will come to light overnight and during the next couple of days; no doubt there will be more charges — I should have an update by midday tomorrow, so pop in and see me.

Trust me, Phyllis, Mikey Price won't be a free man for a very long time to come. This news will spread like wildfire, and there'll be reporters buzzing around Carmarthen and Pembroke Dock like bloody bees around their Queen. But Mrs Jones will have to be informed first, and no doubt a senior officer will visit her this morning."

He checked the clock again.

"In fact, I'd be astonished if one hasn't already done so. They won't be able to keep the lid on this story for much longer: once the press officer releases a statement, it will be on every Welsh news bulletin and the national news channels. TV cameras will be everywhere."

The Detective Sergeant shakes his head and grimaces.

"You might even spot Rose Price — just hope and pray that

JON H. DAVIES

she's got some bloody clothes on."

CHAPTER 29

They chatted on the way to the lodgings. Well, Phyllis did the talking, and Big Lloyd did the listening. He filled him in about most of the events, including the bizarre behaviour of Mrs Jones earlier on in the day. That startled expression, which changed to very sheepish, was most peculiar and suspicious. Completely out of character, considering she had been made aware that a double-crewed police patrol car was hanging around with its engine ticking over right outside her front door. Normally, he would have been bombarded with a plethora of searching questions, and they would have been attached at the hip before she waved him off, straining to catch a glimpse of the patrol car driver and raising her hand to any inquisitive neighbours on the other side of net curtains.

On the contrary, there was nothing. She couldn't wait to get out of his way and escape into the bathroom from where he heard her crying: yet she insisted that nothing was wrong.

"You say that the money was still there and Mrs Jones hadn't done any tidying up?"

"That's right, Lloyd. Maybe I disturbed her. Maybe she'd only just gone in there. I don't know. All I know is, I surprised her by coming back at that time of the day. She wouldn't have expected anyone to come into the house then, would she? What do you think?"

A mischievous grin lit up his face.

"I think that hopefully when you left, she went straight back in there and tidied our bloody mess up — save us having to do it."
He sped away laughing, Phyllis's punch to the bicep connecting with nothing but fresh air.
Big Lloyd burst in through the front door, kicking off his shoes while shouting.
"We're back, Mrs Jones — what's for grub?"
Phyllis was right behind him and panting.
"Is that all you think about?"
The scowl on the larger Cadet's face was a clear indication of his increasing lack of patience with his roommate.
"Ugh, you're a bright bugger talking. Normally you'd be shouting out the same bloody question."
"Now, now you two, less of the squabbling and less of the swearing. Big Lloyd, I'm surprised at you!"
Her voice was uplifting and her demeanour affable yet assertive; completely opposite to how she was earlier. She was back to her usual, confident self.
"Come in here, boys, I've got something important to tell you. I'll put the kettle on."
Phyllis frowned, perplexed, shaking his head as he sat down at the table.
'What the hell is going on with her?'
Big Lloyd's nose was twitching like a hamster's.
"Do I detect steak and kidney pie, Mrs Jones? I love steak and kidney pie."
Phyllis was pissed off with the disinterest in the missing money.
"You love any pie: wrap a bit of puff pastry around a bloody slug, and you'd shove it in your gob!"
The larger cadet was at the end of his tether: fed up with sharing a room with someone who was a magnet for trouble.
"And you'll be eating those bloody words now as I ram them down your throat!"
He shot up quickly, but Phyllis was much faster and had darted from the table with the larger cadet in close pursuit. Mrs

Jones's rebukes falling on deaf ears...

He took the stairs two at a time, laughing hysterically, nearly tripping in his haste, and got into the bathroom just in time to lock the door. He could hear the chaser breathing heavily on the other side: panting.

"Oh well..."

He gasped.

"...that bit of exercise has made more room for the steak and kidney pie. You stay in there all night long, good boy, and don't you worry about your portion going to waste. It won't — I'm going to enjoy the bloody lot!"

He strode away, his footsteps heavy on the stairs, followed closely by the angry voice of Mrs Jones.

Listening out for his roommate, Phyllis edged from the bathroom and crept across the landing. Silently, he pushed open the bedroom door.

'Shit, the five-pound note has gone! Maybe I knocked it off the cupboard when searching for my cap earlier?'

He dived into a push-up position between the two beds, peering into the semi-darkness. There was nothing apart from the other dust-covered cap. He knew that he was clutching at straws: he'd purposely weighted down the five-pound note with some loose change.

He sat at the foot of the bed with his head in his hands, staring towards the heavens and begging: "Give me a bloody break!"

The door burst open, and the roommate screamed as he dived at Phyllis.

"Got you! Nowhere for you to run and hide now, is there, Phyllis Doris?"

He pinned him to the mattress and wriggled up onto his chest.

"Get out of this then, you fuc—"

He stopped in mid-sentence. Tears were rolling down his roommate's cheeks, spilling onto the quilted bed cover. Too embarrassed to maintain eye contact, Phyllis freed his arms and turned away — rubbing at the tears as he spoke.

"The five-pound note has gone!"

"Shit!"
The news had hit Big Lloyd with the force of a raging rhino, and he clambered off. Exhaling loudly, he lay down on his own bed with his arms resting on the pillow behind his head — staring up at the ceiling. He didn't need or want this hassle.
"Shit, shit, shit," he spurted out the words. "Are you sure?"
Phyllis propped himself up onto his elbow.
"It's not here, Lloyd. I've checked everywhere, and it was definitely on the chest of drawers when I came back at about 10:30."
"Come on, you two. I'm dishing out…"

*

"Okay, now I've got you here, and it's nice and peaceful because you're eating. Do you want to hear my news?"
Phyllis guessed what she was going to announce — bloody hell, he'd completely forgotten about Mikey Price…
"I had a visit today from a senior police officer: a Chief Inspector no less. Alun Williams was his name. Do you know him? Very young for a Chief Inspector: tall, dark and very handsome…"
She had propped up the family photograph on a worktop and winked at her Bernie.
"Not a patch on you, my darling."
Laughing and with her eyes sparkling, she smiled at the two boys.
"Do you want to know why he came? I'll tell you."
Fearing the worst, Big Lloyd's heart sank and his face dropped; he put his fork down onto the plate — 'what trouble were they in now?'
"They've found the man who killed my Bernie."
Her smile started to quiver: the recent revelation was all too much for her, and tears freely escaped. Her voice was strained, and she trembled with emotion as she nodded towards Phyllis.
"Seemingly Lloyd, he's from your end of the world, and only a young man too. I couldn't believe it when the Chief Inspector told me. After all this time, then out of the blue, they catch

him."

She glanced at the photo again, wiped a tear away with the back of her hand and smiled at her husband.

"We'd given up any hope of ever finding out what truly happened, hadn't we, my precious?"

She turned back to her lodgers.

"So when the Chief Inspector came here this morning, not long before you did love."

She nodded at Phyllis.

"You can only imagine how I felt."

She gripped the table edge as her legs buckled, and all the grief, sorrow, and anger that had built up inside her since her husband's death was released in one almighty wail.

Both boys rushed to console her. Helped her into a chair, and held her while she sobbed. Their eyes locked onto each other's, neither having to say a thing. Both knew what the other was thinking: 'That's why she was acting so strangely this morning.'

Mrs Jones suddenly stopped crying, shrugged the boys away, and stood up.

"That beast of a man is not going to influence my thoughts for another second. I refuse point-blank to allow it. Now, your meal is going cold, and I need to blow my nose."

"Can I tell her, Phyllis?"

She heard the question, caught Phyllis nodding, and her hands strayed to her hips.

"Can I tell her what?"

Big Lloyd pointed at the boy opposite.

"The reason why it's suddenly come out of the blue, Mrs Jones, is down to Sherlock Holmes here ..."

CHAPTER 30

The Cadet's mind was awash with thoughts: what to do, how to do it, and most importantly — when?
Lying in bed and staring at nothing but darkness, he sighed in frustration. What a futile waste of time that brainstorming chat with his roommate had been. He wasn't the slightest bit interested, and why was that the case? The answer is simple: he didn't want to rock the boat and jeopardise what they had here with Mrs Jones.
"It's your fault, Phyllis, you should keep your money locked away like me. Why did you have to leave more on display again? That was irresponsible, madness. An invitation for it to happen again."
The comfort of their home life here with Mrs Jones was clouding his judgement, influencing his thought process. Would he be thinking along the same lines if the thief was targeting his cash or, God forbid, his food stash!
Phyllis couldn't get his head around why Lloyd wasn't curious as to who was coming into their bedroom while they were at work? As a trainee police officer, why didn't he want to catch the thief?
They should be able to leave out on show whatever they wanted: it was their room — their space. Why should they have to worry about some trespasser rummaging through their stuff?

You guessed it — no ideas had come from his roommate's lips, and his response to Phyllis's suggestions, before he started snoring, was noncommittal.

"Sort it out yourself, Phyllis: it's your problem, but I'd prefer things to be left as they are. We have a great home from home here, and I don't want you to put it at risk."

But it wasn't home, was it? At home, your parents or your siblings wouldn't steal money from you, would they? And at this moment in this home, the parent and the two siblings are the prime and only suspects.

Earlier, Mrs Jones had fired off a load of searching questions about Mikey Price. He couldn't respond to many of them because he genuinely didn't know the answers, but the ones that he did know, well, let's just say that he had to be very selective with the truth. And even the censored answers hadn't managed to remedy the slump in her shoulders; neither did they stop her chewing at her fingernails, but she did seem a little brighter and was more accepting of how the police had dealt with Mikey Price by the time she had sloped off to bed.

He'd also explained the reason why he returned to the house earlier on in the day, and she became upset: tears once more overspilling.

"I'm so sorry, love. The Chief Inspector hadn't long left, and I was, well, I suppose I was stunned. I must have wandered upstairs, and I found myself in your room just staring out of the window. George, that's next door's moggie by the way, was precariously balancing on the high wall separating our two houses, and he was spraying everywhere, you know, marking his territory."

She paused for a few seconds, looking right through her lodger, then she smiled, shaking her head.

"Who in their right mind calls a cat George?"

Phyllis could see more tears tinkling on the edge, and he reached over and grabbed

some tissues from the box on the worktop; he handed them to her across the table, and caught hold of her hand. Comforting it in his.

"George knew precisely when my Bernie was eating kippers for breakfast..."

She sniffed and shook her head again, lost in the moment.

"...How did he know that? It wasn't as if it was a regular occurrence: maybe once a fortnight, if that. But he would suddenly appear on the window sill, pawing at the glass, meowing to be let in."

The tears rolled freely down her cheeks, some missing the tissues and dripping onto the tablecloth. She was smiling and giggling simultaneously, the tears soaking her lips — her eyes wide and glistening with the moisture.

"Bernie would pretend that he couldn't see him, you know, teasing him by turning his head away and winking at me."

She laughed, dabbing at her cheek with the tissue.

"And George would tap all the more. I knew Bernie would eventually relent: he always did. He would open the window and share his kippers with a cat. Such a kind, loving man. And do you know, Lloyd? George hasn't been back since that evil Mikey 'what's-his-name' took Bernie away fro—"

She broke down...

Phyllis moved to comfort her, but she waved him away, continuing to talk: her voice weakened and croaked.

"I'm fine, love, I'm fine. I was thinking about it right at the moment you came back for your cap. What if George fell off that wall and died? Well, it wouldn't really matter, would it? He's got another eight lives..."

She paused — sniffing loudly — repeatedly swallowing: struggling to compose herself as sopping wet fingers failed to fend away the torrent of tears — resorting to dabbing at them with a sodden Kleenex as she blinked through a fine film of moisture to focus on the watery eyes that were gazing back at her.

"Why couldn't my Bernie have nine lives, Lloyd? It doesn't seem right that God should gift nine lives to cats, does it? My darling husband would be here right now if that were the case,

with his arms wrapped tightly around me and telling me, as he always did: 'Everything will be alright, my love — everything will be fine.'
Oh, Lloyd — I miss him so much…"
And that was the moment — as he held a sobbing and bereft Mrs Edith Jones in his young arms. The moment that Phyllis knew she was incapable of stealing anything from him, Big Lloyd, or indeed from anybody else. And that was what was plaguing him and preventing him from drifting off to sleep.
He needed to rest his brain: the adolescent was desperate for sleep, and in the morning he would confide in Dai Insignificant. Yes, he had made up his mind — this couldn't go on any longer. It needed sorting out, and Dai would know what to do. He'll know how to catch Molly or April — maybe even both of them — who knows.

CHAPTER 31

The usual aroma greeted Phyllis into the Detective Sergeant's office, and there behind the desk sat the big man himself. Immaculately attired as always, specs balancing on the tip of his nose and cursing as he pushed them back to the bridge in order to lift his head to greet the visitor. Checking his wristwatch, his voice sounded puzzled.
"Oh, alright, lad? You're a bit early. I doubt whether we'll hear anything until midday at the very earliest, and that's if they remember to keep us in the loop."
Phyllis didn't have a clue what the Detective Sergeant was talking about: the only thing on his mind was catching whoever was nicking the fivers from his stash. Dai spotted the vacant look and outstretched his arms in a questioning gesture.
"Mikey Price? The killing of Bernard Jones? Court appearance this morning?"
He tapped on the desk top.
"Hello, is there anybody there?"
Phyllis slapped his forehead.
"Shit! Sorry, Sarge, I'd completely forgotten about that."
It was a puzzled Detective Sergeant who removed the Calabash, and cleared his throat.
"You've completely forgotten about THAT? How the bloody hell can something as big and as important as THAT

completely slip your mind? Dozens of trained detectives spent weeks whittling away at a budget the size of the Civil List and didn't find a bloody iota of evidence. Yet you come along. Dip into your Levi's for a couple of quid. Spend it on a bottle of Jack Daniel's, and hey bloody presto, it's all done and dusted in a day on the piss in Pembroke Dock!"

He shoved the Calabash back between his lips and sucked on it like Geronimo.

"It was only yesterday that we were dealing with THAT! Excuse my French, Phyllis, but for fuck's sake, boy, what the hell can be more pressing in your life right now than Mikey bloody Price? By the sound of things, you've already relegated him to the second division. Hell, man, I'd have milked that result for bloody years!"

It all came blurting out, and the Detective Sergeant shook his head in astonishment.

'Yes, this boy was indeed a maverick: a walking bloody time bomb.'

It was unbelievable that so much drama could happen to one person in such a brief period of time. Hell, he needed a drink, and he licked his lips as he reached for the bottle of Bells tucked away in the bottom drawer of the desk. For special occasions only, he would reassure anyone who was brave enough to ask, and this was one of them. Sometimes a wee dram in a hot cup of tea provided the necessary inspiration. It always hit the required spot, lubricated the old grey matter, and it didn't expand the waistline to the same extent as a bourbon biscuit.

He briefly paused the sucking on the Calabash at the point where the Cadet related the true facts about why it took him an age to collect his cap and jacket from his lodgings. The youngster failed to pick up on it, and Dai didn't press the matter any further. There was nothing to be gained by mentioning that slight evasion of the truth now: he would store away that minor misdemeanour for another more appropriate time.

"Right, Phyllis, there will be no happy ending here, and I can only promise you one thing: it's all going to end in tears."

The Cadet gulped, crossed his arms, and rested them on the desk. The heebie-jeebies were back in residence — they'd invited their mates around and were causing bloody havoc.

"We can set a trap, for want of a better phrase, and going by what you've told me, we will without doubt catch the person responsible. But this is a no-win situation. Whatever the outcome, Mrs Jones might still want you to leave her home. She will see it as a lack of trust. So, young man, what do you want me to do?"

He didn't have to think about the answer: every possible scenario and all the ifs and buts had been churning around in his head all night.

"I want to catch whoever is stealing my money, Sarge, and no matter how much I like Mrs Jones, under the present circumstances, I can't stay there: the not knowing is driving me mad."

"Okay, boy — a wise choice."

He picked up the phone and dialled internally: it only rang twice.

"Hi Stu, it's Dai Insignificant. Can you pop up and see me? Got a bit of a sensitive problem."

Phyllis couldn't hear the response, but going by Dai's reply, he got the gist of it, and started to laugh.

"No, Stuart, I haven't got to visit the bloody clinic again!"

He slammed down the handset.

"Cheeky bugger — no respect whatsoever..."

*

Detective Constable Stuart Edwards worked in the Scenes of Crime Department. Unusually young in service to hold the post of S.O.C.O., but he just had it. It, being the nose, the gift, the desire, and the knowing where to look, what to do, and the best way of doing it. If there were fingerprints at the point of entry to a burglary, he'd spot them and sticky-tape them away. If there were clothing fibres snagged on a jagged piece of glass, he'd pluck them into a sample bag. He knew where evidence should be, and if it was there, he'd find it. Nothing was too much trouble: he would always go that extra mile. The words no and cannot did not exist in his vocabulary.

"Stuart, meet Lloyd — Lloyd, meet Stuart."

They shook hands as Dai continued the introduction.

"Lloyd is better known as Phyllis, Stu, and being that there's another Lloyd in this equation, it'll be less confusing if we refer to him by that name."

The geeky detective with the John Lennon-type spectacles held out his right hand.

"Argh, so you're Phyllis."

Bushy sideburns running to his jaw widened with the smile.

"How come you've been lumbered with that name then?"

Dai intervened.

"Bloody hell, Stu, we haven't got time for all that: this is the situation —"

*

"It's pretty simple, Sarge. I dealt with a similar case only a couple of months ago at the Athletic Ground. Someone was nicking money from clothing hanging in the changing rooms during the game. To cut a long story short, I treated a five-pound note with a special compound, only visible under ultraviolet light. When the thief handles the note, the compound transfers and leaves a residue with whatever it comes into contact. As I said, the thief can't see it under normal lighting, but he can't wash it away by accident either. We've got about 24 hours tops before it naturally fades away, but the sooner it's tested under an ultraviolet lamp, the better. In this particular case, the thief was one of the ground staff: a bloody idiot. He had access to the changing rooms when the players were on the pitch, and the silly bugger helped himself. Cheeky so-and-so went into the clubhouse after the game and was knocking 'em back. The treated fiver was safely in the till, and the thief's fingers, together with the arse pocket of his jeans, had blue dye all over them.

Surprisingly, the club never took the matter any further, and though there was a bit of argy-bargy regarding the wasting of police time, their decision was respected. Perhaps it was too much of a coincidence, mind you, that a few days following the thief's exposure, he was spotted limping through town. Not a pretty sight by all accounts: two black eyes, a broken nose, and a thick lip. Funnily enough, no complaint was ever made to the police: he insisted that he'd crashed into a door while sleepwalking…"

No comments were necessary from the two listeners: the smiles said it all, and Phyllis was well and truly hooked. He could listen to Stuart and Dai discussing past cases all day long. Detective work and undercover policing. That's what he wanted, and as soon as he was experienced enough, that was what he would do.

"So how do we play this then, Stuart?"

"Simple, Dai, we get someone like, say, Bella from Training. You know her, quite tall, slim, blonde, a fine —"

Dai raised his arm.

"Yes, yes, thank you, Stu. I can picture her quite clearly now. And what part is Bella going to play?"

"Well, what I suggest is this —"

CHAPTER 32

The skeletal frame sitting upright in the wheelchair was unrecognisable in comparison to how he would have been described less than twelve months ago. Gone were the puffed-out ruby-coloured cheeks and gone was the Mexican-style moustache. His face, now gaunt and grey, was unable to smile and his eyes no longer sparkled with devilment. His recollection of the incident, however, was as vivid as the day it happened. Locked away in a time capsule and preserved in his memory bank for this very occasion.

This was Mr Michael Moore's day of reckoning. Shortly, he would come face to face with the Thug who put an end to normality as he remembered normality to be. Once again, he would look into eyes that were lifeless, but on this occasion, he would have no fear: he, Michael Moore, had the upper hand. The jeweller was in control of the Thug's destiny, and he intended to cherish the moment: nothing else mattered.

Mikey Price had agreed to the line-up, confident in the notion that the witness would be unable to pick him out.

"Fuck me, Mary, he only saw my bloody eyes before I battered him, and I don't have to speak so he won't recognise my voice. The fat bastard has got no chance!"

His solicitor, Mary Jenkins, from Jenkins, Williams, and Evans, had advised against it.

"You don't have to do it, Mikey. They've got nothing on you

apart from your presence in Neath that day and cannot put you anywhere near that jewellery shop."

Mikey had sold the gold cufflinks and the heavy bracelet to a local fence many months ago. He got a good price for them too. Some unsuspecting member of the community would no doubt be more than happy with their cut-price merchandise. He chuckled as he reminisced and looked around him.

'Could very well be one of these fucking coppers.'

He'd had a good gander at the others, and the laughter increased as he chose a spot in the line-up: third from the end.

'Bloody hell, all these stooges look like me. I'd have a job to pick my fucking self out!'

Inspector Kay Colley was the presiding officer, and she briefed the witness.

"Mr Moore, if you identify a suspect, there is no requirement for confrontation. Indicate your choice to me, and I will terminate the proceedings immediately. Your safety is paramount."

He nodded an acknowledgment, fully aware that he had already planned and practised a more dramatic revelation — one much better suited to this momentous occasion.

Chaperoned by two burly officers, Mr Moore was pushed into the sparsely furnished room: an irritating squeak with every revolution of the right wheel a blight on the tense silence. Black-out curtains had been drawn, and powerful strip lamps spotlighted the occupants.

A gap of roughly three feet, about the same width as Mr Moore's granite counter, was between him and the lineup: all similarly aged males of similar stature, and wearing identical clothing — green-coloured Parkas over black-coloured roll-neck sweaters. The fur-edged hoods were pulled over their heads, and the roll necks covered their noses. Only the eyes and brows of each man were visible to the witness.

The wheelchair was positioned square-on to each individual, and the witness gazed into their eyes. No other part of their body was relevant, and each man stared straight ahead: they had no desire to make eye contact. The severity of the occasion had got to them, and many were taut— consumed by anxiety and overwhelmed with pangs of guilt. Yet only Price was a suspect. The others had been rounded up from the streets and factories that morning. Volunteers, each provided with the necessary clothing and rewarded with a token remuneration.

Michael Moore was calm, controlled, and fixated. He afforded each of the participants the respect they deserved because he knew that without them, this procedure would not be possible. He had scanned the line-up as soon as the wheels rolled onto the parquet flooring and had spotted Price immediately, but he wasn't going to make this easy for him. Oh no, he wanted to make him sweat. There was no rush: his mind had been occupied with nothing else since that life-changing day — a few more minutes would not hurt. And, never once had he lost faith that God would provide him with this opportunity to seek retribution.

The assumed lack of certainty had the opposite effect: one which Mr Moore hadn't anticipated. One which would raise his attacker's spirits, then ultimately destroy him: the longer he dawdled, the more confident Price became.

'Mr Skin and Bones hasn't got a fucking clue…'

He'd obviously noticed the drastic change in his victim's appearance, but Price felt no remorse: Michael Moore had deserved his plight, and any anxiety that might have been festering inside the suspect was no more.

'You're fucked, you freak. Now fuck off back to Neath and oil your fucking carriage.'

The closer he got to Price, the more difficult it was for Michael Moore to control his heart rate: something he hadn't planned for. Why should he be so apprehensive? This is what he had yearned for, wasn't it? He recalled the advice of his highly recommended therapist.

"Deep breaths, Mr Moore. In through the nose, hold it for the count of six, then out through the mouth. Expel the trauma to the atmosphere and rid it from your body forever."

He practised that strategy — it didn't work — Price was next.
He could feel his grip tighten on the armrests.
'Breathe, Michael, breathe...'
Tears were welling in his eyes.
'No, no, no — don't cry — you must not cry — breathe, breathe, breathe...'
Mr Moore's attendee, Sam, had been there for him since day one. He was his nephew, his sister's eldest: tall, strong, and devoted. Together with his mother and under the guidance of Mr Moore, they had taken over the day-to-day running of the shop: it helped finance their family arrangement.
Michael and Sam had a carefully thought-out plan, but would it work? Would the wheelchair-bound witness be strong enough? They would soon find out.
Sam already knew that his uncle had spotted his attacker and he was aware of his position in the line-up. The tapping of Michael's knuckles on the right armrest confirmed the initial information, and the three digits spread out on the same section of the wheelchair clarified his spot.
Sam was as anxious as the men in the line-up: it was unbearable. Not allowing any outside assistance, Sam had lived his uncle's trauma during every conscious hour of every single day. So how would he react to being face-to-face with that monster? Would he be able to restrain his emotions? Did he have the strength of character to prevent him from grabbing the beast by the throat and squeezing the life out of him. As the life had surely been cruelly robbed from his beloved uncle? His palms were moist with sweat as they tightened on the wheelchair's handgrips.
'Breathe, Sam, breathe...'
Detective Inspector Patrick Muldoon hovered — unseen and tucked behind the one-way, mirrored screen. He too had been hoodwinked.
"Bloody hell, Bull, it's not looking too good, is it?"
Bull chewed on his fingernail, willing the witness to point the finger at Price.

"He's got to pick him out, Pat, we've got nothing else. Look at the state of the poor man — Price has a lot to answer for."
Mikey Price felt no emotion when once again he came face to face with his victim: there was no sympathy, no remorse, and no regret that he had ruined the man's life. Eyes devoid of expression ignored him and, as if he wasn't even there, they focused on the backdrop of the magnolia-painted woodchip wall paper.
The jeweller sighed in defiance.
"Pull me back a little, please, Sam."
His nephew knew the drill: they had rehearsed it repeatedly since receiving the call from Detective Sergeant Tony Beech.
The change in position unnerved the suspect, and his eyes deviated towards the wheelchair.
'What the fuck's going on?'
Michael Moore had spotted the movement and could sense Price's fear: it made him stronger, and gnarled fingers uncurled from the armrest to rest clammy palms on the padded leather. Muldoon elbowed his Detective Sergeant, a smile breaking out — softening the worry lines.
"Look at this, Bull, he knows it's him — he only knows it's him!"
Sam stooped to lift his uncle's feet from the supports and place the polished, soft-leather brogues onto the wooden floor. Their eyes briefly met, and the nephew smiled through the tears — they were nearing the end of an epic and traumatic journey.
Michael Moore blinked his away and paused to allow fresh blood to circulate into soles that could no longer be relied upon to support his body weight.
'Don't you show the pain, Michael, you can do this. God will give you the strength.'
His wrists, calves, and thighs quivered as they strained within the cashmere of the Italian-tailored suit, and every ounce of grit was summoned to propel him from his forced mode of mobility. He confronted his attacker, and their eyes locked until Price, totally defeated and deflated, turned away. What else could he do? He had seen the venom in the eyes of the

youngster pushing the wheelchair, and he'd be no match for the two burly coppers.

Michael Moore, unable to smile, rejoiced internally as he followed those lifeless eyes that had been forever present in his memory and pointed an index finger. It was a hoarse and tired voice that addressed the presiding officer.

"Inspector Colley — this is the animal that attacked me..."

*

"Good afternoon, Criminal Statistics, Detective Ser..."
"Dai, it's Pat in Pembroke Dock. Got an update for you: bloody great news — the witness from Neath has picked out Price on the line-up."
Dai punched the air.
"That's shit-hot news, Pat: congratulations. Looks like he's going down for a very long stretch. Anything on the Liverpool enquiry?"
"Nah, nothing, Dai. Disappointing, and we threw everything at him! Even threatened to set loose Rose on him, but he just clammed up. He's terrified of something or someone. Bull and Cadders could sense it — he wouldn't even acknowledge his friendship with Murphy."
"What about the detectives from Liverpool? Did they provide anything extra to help push the enquiry on?"
"Nothing. Well, nothing of any evidential value anyway. Murphy's mother reported him as a missing person when he didn't show up. But not a lot was done for a couple of weeks. You know the score: he's not what you'd call one of their favourites. Very much like Mikey Price to us. A few statements were taken months ago from Murphy's prison mates, but they just confirmed his eagerness to get back out onto the streets. They didn't have a clue what could have happened to him. Price was briefly spoken to around the same time as you're aware, but that was before Murphy's hold-all was found. Anything extra from the Cadet?"

"No, nothing, Pat. And to be perfectly honest, I don't think he knows anything about Barry Murphy, and he couldn't confirm whether the hold-all was in Price's wardrobe or not. I tend to believe him: he must have been shitting himself at that point. He's bloody lucky not to have been rumbled."

"Too bloody right he is. We could be investigating the sudden disappearance of a Police Cadet, and with even less to go on than the Murphy enquiry. I doubt whether Rose and Mikey Price would have left any trace of the Cadet's visit to their flea pit."

Pat took a gulp of black coffee.

"Price is back before the court tomorrow morning: it's pointless keeping him in the cell any longer. He's coughed to everything bar the suspected murder of Murphy. Merseyside Police are continuing that investigation and are seeking advice from the powers that be before deciding whether to charge him or not. At least that ongoing enquiry adds more weight to our request for Price's remand in custody pending trial. The last thing we want is for that evil bastard to be back out on the streets again."

CHAPTER 33

"Bring up Michael Cornelius Price."
The courtroom was packed: mainly the press jostling for a prime spot, together with inquisitive locals and those in the community with an axe to grind. The defence and prosecution teams filled the front rows: reams of papers perched precariously on the shelf by their knees, and high above in front of them for all to see was the bench. The stern face of Agnes Charlotte Freeman, the presiding Justice, was flanked by two other distinguished magistrates and just below them, within earshot, was their adviser: the Clerk to the Court — Mr Rupert Foster-Lee.
An insipid-looking man, wearing a dark, woollen suit, white shirt and black tie, was peering over reading glasses perched precariously on the tip of a hooked nose as the defendant's head came into view.
The voice was firm but shrill.
"Remain standing and give your full name to the court."
Price did as ordered. Those lifeless eyes, ignoring the clerk, fervently scanned the faces in the public gallery until he picked her out and acknowledged her with a wink and a nod of his head.
His mother's smile was forced, strained even, as she sat uncomfortably in the shadows of the mezzanine. A crammed criminal courtroom was not her first choice of a place to visit

on a Friday morning, but no matter what he had done, Mikey was her flesh and blood. And he was all she had — Rose would never turn her back on him. The smile dwindled as she offered a limp wave of her hand and gulped: the mother was not looking forward to doing what Mikey had demanded of her when she briefly visited him in the cells earlier.

Searching for the witnesses, Price turned to check the rows of seats behind him, and a taunting grin of recognition stretched his gaunt face. He raised a mocking hand to them.

'Welcome to my sordid world, Mr Jeweller and Co. All dolled up in your finery. You must have received a fucking good payout...'

The grin dissipated and the eyes narrowed.

'Odds on, you added a few diamond rings to that insurance claim, didn't you? Same old story — money goes to fucking money!'

His glare drifted and picked out three elderly women: one wearing a mulberry-coloured duffle coat. Their eyes were glued to him and an undeniable, unwavering look of contempt pierced deep into his soul. He gulped, his eyes swiftly moving on to the row behind and there he was. A beast of a man, towering head and shoulders above the others; sitting directly behind Michael Moore and his family.

'That's got to be Mr SAS, and I'm well impressed. Fuck me, he's built like a brick shit house. I knew you couldn't stay away, Mr SAS: I've got what you want, haven't I? But you can't be sure that I've got it, can you?'

The grin returned, and he winked at him.

'If my gut feeling is spot on, Mr SAS, you're going to be my little fucking lap dog over the next couple of days. You'll do exactly what I want you to do: if you want your key back — you have no choice...'

Taff Robbo's eyes bored into Price. Disdain had distorted a normally handsome face, and only years of self-discipline thwarted the desire to yank the arsehole from that wooden pulpit and rip his fucking head off.

Price held the grin and the taunting gaze until, from the corner of his left eye, he spotted him. Him, being somebody he never dreamed would be there. Somebody who he knew could be easily manipulated. Somebody who could assist with and carry out the plan that he'd recently entrusted to his mother. All his Christmases had come at once, and with excitement overwhelming him, he spun back to face her. His eyes pierced into her, willing her to look behind him and to notice who was sitting there. He tossed his head to the left in an over-demonstrative attempt to attract her attention as to who was behind him. Finally, Rose spotted him, and a conniving smile lessened the worry lines that had been meandering around her eyes like the contours on an O.S. map.

"Yes — a go-between. Mr Grammar School boy is going to be my fuckin' go-between."

*

The Cadet couldn't stay away. How could he? As soon as he became aware of Price's court hearing, he knew he would have to make an appearance. How else was he supposed to put his mind at rest? How else could he protect his mam and dad? He needed to speak with Mikey: try and convince him that he had nothing to do with his arrest. But how was he going to get near him in this packed-out courtroom?

He'd got there early and chosen the seat, close to the back and within easy access of the exit. From there, in the shadows, he felt safe and he could monitor what was going on.

Dai Insignificant had wanted to carry out the big 'sting' today. Plant the treated five-pound note in his bedroom and entice the thief to steal it. But Phyllis couldn't cope with that. It would be impossible for him to deal with such an important event while another equally important one was happening at the same time. Fortunately, the cadets had been granted an extra day off. Normally, on a Friday, they attended the local technical college, but something had gone wrong with the sewage system, and luckily for him, the college had been forced to close. He'd lied to the Detective Sergeant: made up a cock and bull story that a fence had blown down at home during a recent storm, and his dad had injured his back while struggling by himself with the repair. The boy wanted to take advantage of this unexpected, longer weekend break and help his father with the concreting in of some new posts. Dai had fallen for it.

"No problem, sonny, we'll arrange it on Monday. Hope your dad feels better soon."

Shit, in three or four days' time, he would discover the identity of the thief. But, and this was a big but, there was a major downside: he might never see Mrs Jones again.

She hadn't wanted to attend the court hearing, shaking her head in defiance as she explained.

"What's the point? I don't want to allow myself to become emotionally involved and I fear that by seeing his face and listening to his voice I won't be able to forget about him. I don't care what awaits him in the future: it's not going to bring my Bernard back. Is it?"

He'd got up early to catch the train into Haverfordwest, and Mrs Jones, as usual, was fussing over breakfast.

"You be careful handling those heavy concrete posts, Lloyd. That's all your mother needs right now is you getting a bad back as well as your father..."

She tapped him on the shoulder, dislodging a spoonful of cereal back into the bowl.

"...And don't forget to give them my regards."

He'd entered the courtroom quietly confident that nobody would know who he was. Why would they know? None of the detectives in Pembrokeshire had ever met him, and he certainly didn't know any court officials.

How wrong he was. Sat directly behind the prosecuting solicitor, his chin cupped in the palm of his hand, was Detective Inspector Pat Muldoon. Questioning eyes narrowed to a frown as his fingers absentmindedly caressed sporadic patches of stubble he'd missed with the razor earlier.

"Who is that youngster? I don't know him. What's his reason

for being here?"

A couple of seconds later, realisation hit Muldoon with a ten-pound lump of lead. The hand slapped against his forehead, and the fingers pushed through his hair.

"Oh no, no, no. I'll bet my bloody pension that he is the informant. What the hell are you playing at? You stupid idiot!"

The clerk of the court was still reading out the list of charges when Rose Price placed her ample backside on the pew alongside Phyllis. She was between him and the exit, and the clerk's shrill tone was vibrating in the background when he turned to face her.

"...belonging to Gareth Bryan Roberts. Contrary to Sections 1-7 of the Theft Act, 1968. Charge number 3. That you, in Neath, in the County of..."

He forced a weak smile and Rose's face lit up, exposing a missing row of teeth. Her voice was a whisper but assertive.

"There's a cafe across the road, Brucie. Meet me there, now!"

She stood up and furtively glanced across the courtroom before heading for the exit. All eyes, as far as she thought, were on the clerk.

'Thank fuck for that. The least people here that know my business the fuckin' better."

*

The window seat in Barristers' Beans overlooked the impressive recessed entrance to the Court House, and sat there nursing his second cup of percolated coffee was a forlorn Phyllis: alone and replaying in his head what had just happened.

Rose Price had stayed with him for as long as it took to brief and threaten him. The plaque between the canine and the lateral incisor on the left side of her top row had bulbed. It glistened under the diffused lighting, and the youngster had fought the urge to recoil from the stench of her hot and rancid breath.

"Don't fuck this up, Brucie. Mikey's depending on you. You told him you were forced into joining the Filth and that you were going to suss things out so you two could get up to some really hardcore business. You reckoned that you and Mikey would never get nicked. Well, Mikey's been fuckin' nicked, ain't he? You seen him yourself: stood in that brown wooden box across the road and he's going down for a long stretch unless you can get that oversized gorilla in the blue suit to do what he needs to fuckin' do. If Mikey goes down for killing Barry Murphy, he's taking you with him!"

The Police Cadet was monitoring the comings and goings across the road, sipping on cold coffee as the thoughts churned around inside his head.

'One consolation to be thankful for: Mikey doesn't think it was me who grassed him up. At least my parents are safe — for now. But unless I can get Taff Robbo to play along, I'm in deep shit. Mikey will do anything to get a reduced sentence: I'm finished if I can't get Robbo onside.'

"Shit — there he is."

Taff Robbo's bulk filled the entrance to the courthouse as he paused under the decorative overhang to pull up the collar on his jacket: it had started to drizzle. Trained eyes instantly picked out the youngster in the coffee shop, and then the obese pantomime dame sheltering next door in the entrance to 'Tantalising Secrets.' He shuddered as he pictured her in a Basque and Fishnets, his mind briefly wandering back to the aftermath of a binge-drinking session in Bangkok…

Smiling, he stepped into the dampness and turned right towards the River Cleddau. The massive shop window of the Gent's Outfitters directly in his path acted like a mirror, and the smile widened. As anticipated, the youngster was on his tail. He'd almost fallen out of the cafe; struggling to put on his coat while being berated by the pantomime dame. Turning right into Quay Street, Robbo lost sight of his follower, but that mattered not: he knew of the ideal spot for their little pow-wow. His van was in the car park of The Bristol Trader Public House, some hundred and fifty yards or so up that one-way street, and on his way to the court earlier, he'd noticed a quiet

service area: it would be on his left, just after the General Post Office. He quickened the pace.
Phyllis had sprinted to the junction but couldn't see him.
"Where the hell is he? He's vanished. He must be in one of the shops."
Pulling at the hood on his anorak, he jogged along, checking out each premises until he reached the General Post Office: the windows had frosted glass.
"Shit! He could be in there."
He slinked up to the entrance and paused until a customer came out. It was an elderly lady, and he held the door for her, giving him a chance to check out the inside.
"No, he's not in there. Where the bloody hell is—"
Strong arms grabbed the Cadet and dragged him into the shadows. His scream, muted by the mass of a cologne-scented hand, had fallen on deaf ears as his feet dangled in mid-air.
The Valley's accent sang at him: Robbo's breath freshened with the fragrance of extra strong mints.
"What's your fucking game then, Sonny-Jim?"
Wide eyes pleaded with the ex-military man; indecipherable speech trapped by fingers the girth of a baby's wrist.
"Listen to me, lovely boy. I'm going to slightly release the grip on your tonsils, but if you scream — I'll yank the fuckers out. Do you understand me?"
The fear in the boy's eyes and the erratic nodding of his head were enough confirmation for Mr Gareth Bryan Roberts. He lowered him to the ground and removed his hand.
"Right, I'll ask you again, what's your ga—"
"He's got your key, Mr Roberts. Mikey's got your key!"

CHAPTER 34

It's dusk and the souped-up engine in the Ford Transit Van purrs as it cruises north along the M6. Gone are the smart navy blue suit and fashionable soft-leather brogues. The highly trained ex-military man is all in black, and a specially adapted accessory waistcoat hangs on a hook behind him. Soft-soled leather boots are his choice of footwear, and goat-hide gloves are his go-to hand covering.
As usual on the brink of a mission, his heartbeat is raised, but that wasn't a cause for concern: he performed better under duress.
"Fail to plan — plan to fail."
He whispered it to himself repeatedly: an idiom hammered into him throughout his time in the special forces, and he laughed.
"Bloody hell, matey, that's well and truly gone by the board with this little job."
His left hand adjusts the de-mister towards the condensation gathering by the vents, and he moves in closer to the screen. Hunching over the steering wheel, he stretches his back and ribs, opens another pack of extra strong mints and pops one in. "What a time to have given up the fags! No need for any anxiety, Taff, sometimes you can overcomplicate matters. Hell, it's not as if you're up against the bloody bandits in the jungle, is it, matey? Just a few shits pumped up on speed and barely

out of nappies. And, they won't be expecting you."

A murmur from the passenger seat interrupts his thoughts, and his eyes drift from the screen and come to rest on the youngster curled up and sleeping. Robbo tugs at the blanket that has slipped towards the boy's knees.

"No wonder he's out of it, bloody hell, he's been dealt his fair share of drama lately. If it weren't for him, they wouldn't have nabbed that piece of shit, and I wouldn't have this chance to get back the key to my safety deposit box. I thought that had long gone: melted in the inferno of the blaze."

He sighs and continues talking to himself.

"Our Tommy would have been close to this lad's age, wouldn't he, love? Hell, Debs, Tommy might have turned out to be a fine lad like this one. What do you think? Full of grit, and balls like a fucking stallion, eh?"

A weak smile adds a sparkle to the watery eyes. He could picture the look of disapproval on his wife's face: she hated his use of coarse language. Debs was from posh stock and lured unwittingly into a romance by a confident, handsome, swashbuckling free spirit. His hand sweeps away a solitary tear: it still got to him, even after all these years. His wife and son had been snatched away from him at childbirth, and he wasn't even in the fucking country: where was he? You got it — fighting some other fucker's battle on the other side of the bloody globe.

He reaches for the comfort of the hip flask nestling in the gaiter cover of the gear stick, and takes a long swig, smacking his lips together as the brandy hits the spot before sliding down his gullet. A deeper sigh escapes, and the sad eyes return to the monotony of the road ahead. In less than one hour, they'd be in Liverpool...

*

The sign is momentarily trapped in the full beam, and the white lettering stands out against its blue background — Services 1m.

"Perfect — local to their destination, and the Cadet is dead to the world. The least the boy has to witness, the better."

Robbo's eyes scan everywhere as the Ford Transit Van prowls the rows of parked vehicles. What he's searching for has to be spot on, and there she is, the same make, colour, and year as his. He drives into the darkness of a space three or four vehicles away, kills the lights, switches off the engine, and breathes.

The cockpit of the target vehicle is empty, there are no pedestrians in the vicinity, and it's parked in a quiet area of the services. Well away from the continuous hustle and bustle of the main drag. The heavy breathing alongside him confirms what he was hoping for, and he reaches for the waistcoat, immobilises the interior light, then slips out onto terra firma.

Pausing briefly to listen, Robbo is confident that there is nothing of concern, and he eases the door onto the first catch. Seconds later, he's crouching by the registration plate at the rear of the target vehicle; a flat-head screwdriver in hand and unscrewing the first fixing. Out of the blue, there's movement in the cargo area.

"Shit, some fucker is in there!"

The handle squeaks as it turns; the door pushes out and up, and light floods everything immediately below it.

By the time brown leather slip-ons and thick shins in blue jeans enter his arc of vision, Robbo is prone by the rear end of a Morris Minor Traveller. The wearer groans as he stretches, squeezes out a fart, and pisses onto the roadway. Pushing the door closed, he locks it and ambles away towards the facilities.

"Bloody hell, Taff — that was close."

Six minutes later, the ghost plates are fitted, and Robbo is back in the driver's seat. For all intents and purposes, he is driving a white-coloured Ford Transit Van registered on the Police National Computer database as belonging to a Norman Harold Braithwaite from Preston in Lancashire.

Pulling off the black, close-fitting woollen hat and tucking it into his waistcoat, he senses the youngster watching him: their eyes meet and Robbo winks. His face is caught in the headlights of oncoming vehicles, and there is a warmth to it.

A feeling totally alien to him has gripped him, and he can't get his head around it. Why does he have an overwhelming urge to protect and cherish this stranger? Hell, he's only known the boy for a few hours: is it because he's the same age as the son he never had the opportunity to hold close to his heart? Is it guilt? Does he blame himself for what happened? Is the debilitating emotional grief that consumes him every day affecting his judgement? He doesn't know.

'And I don't bloody care! If my baby boy had lived and was in a similar predicament as this youngster, then I would expect someone like me to look out for him. This chance meeting has injected you with a feel-good factor, Mr Roberts, so embrace the moment — bottle the fucker and preserve it forever like an elixir you can dab against your skin. Feed off the comforting fragrance for an eternity because you never know. You might never have to feel like shit again.'

"Are you hungry, boy?"

Phyllis straightened, recovered the blanket from the footwell, and circled his head to stretch out the stiffness in his neck. Familiar squelching, cracking sounds filled his inner ear and brought back the recent, haunting memory of the precarious situation in which he found himself when he last experienced similar noises.

'How the hell has he got himself involved in such perilous circumstances yet again, and in less than a bloody week?'

He was anxious about the task ahead, but at the same time, he felt confident and safe in the company of the man alongside him. He'd already witnessed Robbo in action and wouldn't want to be on the receiving end of that strength again.

He delved into his pocket.

"Yeah, I am, Mr Roberts. I haven't eaten since breakfast. I've got some mone…"

Robbo had reached into a built-in storage compartment, and an unlabelled ration pack landed on the Cadet's lap.

"Tear the corner off and suck on the contents. It'll keep you going for a while. We can eat in style once the job's done. Oh, and call me Robbo. Mr Roberts makes me sound like a bloody tax inspector."

Phyllis laughed: the man's warmth and generosity had relaxed him.

"What flavour is it?"

Robbo shrugged, flicking a mint around his mouth with his tongue.

"I don't know, I never asked. They're all full of good stuff, though. And, before you ask, no, I haven't had them since I was de-mobbed, and yes, they are legit."

He grinned and winked.

"Ask no questions — get no lies."

Like a calf attacking an udder, the Cadet's mouth circled the packaging.

"Wow, Robbo, this is bloody gorgeous…"

Licking his lips.

"…Banana and raspberry and Ummm…"

Robbo helped him out.

"Noooo — not banana, raspberry and blackcurrant. That's my favourite."

He winked again.

"Give it back."

CHAPTER 35

Only a handful of flats in the two high-risers were conspicuous by their darkness as Robbo drove from the access road and into the residents' parking area. He tucked the van under the canopy of a mature sycamore, wound down the window, and killed the lights.
They had a clear view of both foyers, and two skinheads in their late teens were sitting on the flight of steps leading up to one of the blocks; there was no activity outside the other. Cigarettes dangled from their lips, and going by the pungent smell filtering across to Robbo's nostrils, it wasn't just tobacco they were taking on board.
"I reckon those two are waiting for someone, don't you? It's bloody freezing out there — not the weather to be hanging around in without purpose."
He pointed a finger.
"Look, the taller one's checking his watch again. Second time in as many minutes."
As if on cue, a beat-up Vauxhall Viva with a dodgy exhaust turns up, and the two skinheads stand up.
"What did I tell you, youngster? I've wasted my life — should've been in the bloody Flying Squad!"
It pulls up alongside them, and there is chit-chat, which, frustratingly for the two watchers, can't be overheard. But what they do witness is an exchange. A large bar-of-chocolate-

size rectangular package from the hand of the driver and some bank notes from the hand of the taller skinhead.

There is a shout of, 'See you next week, Beef' before the two skinheads stroll away.

"Well, going by the size of that package, youngster, what do you think? Enough grass to satisfy their cravings for a while or maybe even a nine-ounce bar of resin? Are they dealing a bit of a blow to finance their habits? Who knows, but they definitely weren't hanging around on those steps, freezing their bollocks off, waiting for a box of bloody Milk Tray, were they?"

Phyllis laughed at Robbo's humour; his eyes wide with excitement as he recalled his conversation with Rose Price in Barristers' Beans, just a few hours earlier.

"Mikey found a weird-looking key in the car belonging to that SAS gorilla. You know, the monster in the blue suit who was sitting in front of us in the court. Don't ask me why, because I don't fuckin' know why, but Mikey took it and kept it. He has it tucked away somewhere and it's hidden. The key wasn't even mentioned when The Filth interviewed Mikey. Yet, they asked him about everything else. Even wanted to know about a poxy road map. So why not ask about the key? It must have been important to Mr SAS for it to be locked away in the glove compartment together with my lighter and Mikey's tobacco tin. Why, if he didn't give a flying fuck for it, would it be there with his precious SAS shite? And why didn't he report its disappearance to the cops?

Mikey reckons it's the key to a safe or something like that, and whatever Mr SAS man is storing in it is as dodgy as fuck. On the other hand, it's so valuable that he will do anything to get it back.

Well, Mikey doesn't need big bucks right now, does he? What he needs is a fuckin' miracle. So listen, and listen good, Brucie-boy, because one way or another you are going to pay if Mikey gets life for something he ain't done!

The cops think Mikey has something to do with the killing of a mate of his: a bloke from Liverpool, name of Barry Murphy.

Mikey didn't kill him, but he saw who did. And he can't tell the cops, can he? If he does, he's a dead man. Mikey is going down no matter what happens, and if he grasses up the killers of Barry Murphy, those bastards will get to him inside.

Murphy's body has never been found, and until it turns up, my Mikey is the prime and only suspect. Murphy was battered to death with bloody baseball bats by a gang of blokes, so when the cop doctor examines the body and sees that more than one person was involved, it will take all the heat off Mikey. If he goes no comment, then they won't be able to prove that he was the killer.

Now, this is what happened ..."

The Cadet's hand is trembling as he points towards the driver of the car.

"Robbo, do you remember what I told you? Beef is the name of the first guy to whack Barry Murphy over the head with the baseball bat before all the others piled in. If that driver has got a spider web tattooed on the back of his neck, then he is the Beef we are looking for."

Strong hands tighten around the steering wheel.

"Well, he's in no hurry to drive away, is he? He's hanging around here waiting for someone to turn up. And we ain't going nowhere until we find out who that someone is."

*

Edwin Clarence Baptiste hadn't spotted the white-coloured Ford Transit Van pulling into the car park: he'd been sprawled out on a faux leather lounge chair with one leg dangling over the side and a telephone handset glued to his right ear. Deep in conversation with Jim the Dealer, the gang despot took a long toke on a reefer the size of a Cuban cigar and released the residue through his nostrils as he spoke — his voice deep and confident.

"You're spot on, Jim. I have got the means at my disposal, but what you also know is this: reliable and trustworthy staff don't come fucking cheap. And, for what you're proposing, we're going to need a fair few of 'em..."

Wincing, he raised his head off a cushion and bloodshot eyes peer through the window and out onto the car park.

"I gotta go, Jim: Beef's turned up in a fucking tractor. Meet me as planned in the Dog and Duck in…"

He checked his Rolex.

"…say, an hour? I've got a bit of business to see to first."

He rolls off the chair and crawls the couple of feet to the corner of the room where he tugs away the carpet from the grips alongside the skirting board. Pushing dreads away from his eyes, he lifts a section of loose floorboard and his heart rate races when a package wrapped in an oily rag comes into view. Thin lips curl into a menacing sneer as long, slender digits unwrap a well-lubricated and pristine-conditioned semi-automatic pistol.

Dark brown eyes roll as he coos.

"There you are, my beautiful baby — the time is now right for us to go out and play."

*

The Cadet rises off the seat in excitement: his voice raising by a few decibels as a wavering finger points towards the West Indian.

"That's got to be him, Robbo — yes — it is him: look at the scar running down his left cheek — that's the leader of the gang — the one they call John!"

The experienced ex-soldier takes a hand from the wheel, and the palm slowly moves up and down at the wrist; his voice is quiet but forceful.

"That's good, youngster — well done. But for this to work — you've got to stay calm…"

His eyes are glued to the two targets as he winds up the driver's window.

"It looks like we'll be on the move in the not-too-distant, and no doubt things will happen very quickly. Whatever I tell you to do, just do it — do you understand? No questions — we haven't got time for any of those: you've got to trust my judgement and react quickly to everything I say."

JON H. DAVIES

A heavy sigh and a long, deep breath follow the Cadet's nod of the head: the heebie-jeebies are back in play.
'What the hell is this man going to do?'

CHAPTER 36

Edwin Clarence Baptiste scans the car park, and suspicious eyes delve through the darkness into the cab of the white-coloured Ford Transit Van. He'd never noticed a van parked there before, and his head juts forward, eyes straining to check for any occupants.

Robbo reacts.

"Bloody Hell, kiddo, he's eyeballing us! Get your head down and keep it down."

Baptiste can't make out anybody in the shadows and stoops to speak through the driver's window. His head nodding over towards Robbo's van.

"I thought the Tranny under that tree might be a bit dodgy, but it looks empty, and thinking about it logically, it's no different to any of the others dotted around the car park."

As if searching for reassurance, he turns to check it out again.

"Yeah, it's probably some bloody builder getting his leg over in one of the flats."

He steps back from Beef's motor, grimacing as he gives it the once-over.

"Bin this fucking tractor, mate: the last thing we want is the Bizzies pulling us over for driving a Massey Ferguson down Sefton Street."

He tosses a set of keys into the lap of his right-hand man.

"We'll take the Cortina: they don't know I've got that yet, and

while you're at it, point the full beam on that van and give the front seats a once-over: it'll put my mind at rest."
Frustration is slipping into the voice of the ex-military man.
"What the hell is he saying? I haven't been able to make out a bloody thing since I wound up the window."
The Vauxhall Viva rattles into life, and seconds later, the cab of the van is flooded with light as the loud engine noise nears.
The whisper is tinged with urgency.
"Bloody hell, sonny — keep shtum and don't you bloody move — it looks like he's on his way over to us!"
Baptiste's thoughts return to the business ahead, and he strikes a match, sucks on the skunk-laden reefer, and chats to himself.
"Nothing personal, Jim, it just so happens that you've outgrown your usefulness, and now it is my time. In less than one hour, this end of Liverpool will belong to the Rasta from Bridgetown, and no one, I repeat, no one will have the nerve to ever shit on me again."
Feeling the biting chill attacking the back of his neck, he shivers and tugs at the collar of the full-length black leather coat, draping to the top of his boots. His hand delves into the deep side pocket, and fingers search for and find the firearm. They curl around the grip, and energised by the power surging through his body, he stands tall, inflates his chest, and shuts his eyes — his voice heavy with emotion.
"All those years of pain, hardship, and racist discrimination will be no more: nobody will have the balls to disrespect me again. Barry Murphy is gone, and soon to be followed by Jim Mackenzie. Those that matter will know who is responsible — they will know that I am now the main man, and will have to give me the respect I am due."
Raising both his arms to the blackness of the skies, he shouts out like a manic Gospel preacher.
"Ladies and gentlemen of Merseyside. May I introduce to you the one and only — Edwin Clarence Baptiste."
Darkness returns to the cab of the Ford Transit, and the loud

engine noise ceases; a door is opened, then slammed shut, and heavy footsteps approach the two occupants. The urgency is back in the whisper.

"Listen, kid, when our door opens, we pretend to be asleep, okay? Leave all the talking to me."

The Cadet can feel the full force of Robbo's heart against his back. The thuds are slow, and the breathing is deep, controlled, and solely through the nose. Contrarily, his breathing is erratic, and his heart is beating like a pair of maracas.

'Are we going to die?'

He shuts his eyes and finds himself in the front row of the cinema. The image projected onto the silver screen is vivid: Barry George Murphy being whacked to death with a multitude of baseball bats. He gulps: 'Shit — does the same fate await us?'

Hinges creak as the door is yanked open, and anticipating pain, his body tenses. A chill of dread shoots down his spine, but where is the sudden ingress of freezing cold air? And where is the accusing shout from a Scouse accent before the door is slammed shut? The breath that he'd been holding in gushes out, and his eyes fully open when he realises that it was the door to a car parked alongside them.

"Don't you move..." whispers Robbo, "...I'll check it out."

Before the ex-military man's head reaches dashboard height, another engine roars into life.

"Right — they've swapped cars — stay down for a sec while I have a quick peep."

He sees a light-coloured Ford Cortina pulling alongside the West Indian.

"Sit up, youngster — that John guy is getting into the front passenger seat of the new vehicle, and they're soon to be on the move. Memorise the shape of the tail lights: you'll need to be able to spot them at a distance. There's a fine line between those two jokers cottoning on to being followed and us having a total loss — we'll stay put until they're out of sight. One wrong move, and believe me, they'll suss us out — we'll have to give them space until we have the safety of cover from other vehicles."

He turns to face the Cadet; intense eyes unable to conceal the gravity of the situation.

"But, if we give them too much space — well, need I say anymore?"

The youngster swallows: his forehead furrowed with concentration as he monitors the Ford Cortina exiting the car park. It joins the access road and his eyes are straining to pick out the dimensions of the rear lights before it goes out of view. It makes no difference when he pushes further forward on his seat and the anxiety intensifies.

'We can't lose them — we can't lose them...'

Robbo fires the Transit into life and edges in pursuit; monitoring the Cortina as it approaches a T junction. The indicator flashes for a right turn and it's gone: out of their sight and in the general direction of the Mersey.

Robbo floors the accelerator and eases off just prior to the junction. In the distance, headlights illuminate chevrons on the offside of the road.

A finger points, and the voice is raised but controlled.

"That's it, Robbo — approaching that left-hand bend."

"Spot on, kiddo — you're getting the hang of it. Once it's out of sight, I'll be able to switch on our headlights."

His laugh eases the tension.

"At least then we'll be able to see where we're bloody going."

The Transit eats up the distance to the bend, and at the apex, they catch sight of the Cortina: it's held at a T junction with a major thoroughfare, and its left indicator is flashing...

There are no vehicles for cover, and the approach is dark and deserted. Conscious of being stuck directly behind it, Robbo relaxes the pressure on the accelerator, shouting out in frustration.

"Go on — go on — turn you fucker! Turn, turn, turn..."

It turns and joins the heavy stream of traffic.

"Right — now we've got our work cut out! You're going to need eyes like a bloody raptor to keep tabs on its position. Just remember the shape of the tail lights."

The van is held at the junction, and several vehicles have already driven past. Robbo's eyes strain to look for a natural break in the traffic — there isn't one, and his heart rate quickens.

"We're going to lose them if we don't join this stream of traffic right now. We can't afford any more cars between us, and there's one hell of a line approaching."

Phyllis is beside himself: Robbo is nudging the van onto the main thoroughfare into a gap that isn't there, and the vapid, male driver of the approaching car is eyeballing the huge man behind the wheel — no way is he going to slow down and allow that 'giant' out.

The boy's left hand finds the grab handle above the door.

"It's impossible, Robbo — we've got no chance — maybe the next car will let us out…"

"Fuck it — shit or bust — hold on, son."

The other hand grips the seat as the man alongside him stamps on the accelerator, and tyres screech as they propel the Transit Van towards the middle of the carriageway. Dipping the clutch, spinning the steering wheel, and momentarily yanking the handbrake causes it to slide into the gap with only inches to spare. The screeching of brakes, the long blast on the horn, and being drowned by the light of a constant full beam tell the story.

Flashing a grin, the Transit wheel spins in pursuit of the Cortina, and Robbo winks at the Cadet.

"Well, I can tick that off my bucket list — never had the opportunity to try it out before."

His eyes are dazzled by the light locked onto the driver's wing mirror, and he smiles, blocking the irritation with his hand.

"That was a close one — you got the target car, kid?"

Wiping the beads of sweat from his brow, the Cadet loosens his grip on the grab handle.

"I've got it, Robbo: there are seven vehicles between us. It's in front of that dark-coloured pick-up truck."

"Good — well done. You monitor your side, and I'll look after mine. That way, we won't miss any sudden deviation."
Phyllis nods — the adrenaline pumping.
'We can't lose it — we can't lose it.'

CHAPTER 37

Twenty-three-year-old Charlie-boy Lee is Toxteth-born and bred. His mother, Cherie, gave birth to him when she was barely 15 and went on to drop another three in as many years. Needless to say, the child was on the books of the Liverpool City Council Social Services Department from the moment he took his first breath, and the early years of life on the sprawling estate were tough: the abuse and bullying were relentless until puberty. Then he grew, and the bullying ceased. Eighteen inches in three years saw him shoot up to 6 feet 7 inches, and with shoulders and a neck like a brown bear, he was formidable.

Five years of joy-riding, playing catch-me-if-you-can with the bizzies; his addiction to the martial arts, together with his sheer size, had earned him a reputation and a street cred sought after solely by a certain clientele.

Yes — the Driver was in demand.

Dressed in a black pinstripe suit, white shirt, and black tie, the two-hundred-and-fifty-pound hunk of muscle was sitting behind the wheel of the gleaming, black-coloured Mercedes-Benz S Class cruising Park Road, and he was carrying! His client, enjoying the comfort and safety of the back seat, had requested that extra protection, and he was paying for it — big time.

Jim 'The Dealer' Mackenzie wasn't taking any chances. Dragged

up on the council estates of Greenock, the illegitimate son of a hard-drinking and abusive docker was as streetwise as they come. He'd been steadily drip-feeding titbits of dodgy info to test the allegiance of a possible business partner: could the person be trusted with a bigger slice of the pie? The answer was no, and the grating Glaswegian accent rumbled within the confines of the soundproofed interior.
"Does that fuckin' Rasta, John the fuckin' Baptist, think I just come off a fuckin' banana boat like he fuckin' did? Dictating to me when and where we fuckin' meet. What a fuckin' liberty!"
You guessed it — Jim was pissed off.
Since the sudden demise of Barry Murphy, his enterprise had ballooned: jettisoning the intermediate dealings of the one-time heroin addict into the Mr Big of the Westside of Liverpool, and word on the street had reached his ears.
"Watch your back, Jim. Baptiste wants what you have, and he's planning to take you out."
The hip flask kissed his lips, and a long swig of a single malt filled his mouth: he gargled in a failed attempt to dilute the thick mucus that always seemed to line the back of his throat nowadays. The raspiness was still in his voice...
"If that fuckin' gangly, Rasta wants a war, he can have a fucker. But it ends tonight in The Dog and Duck."
His eyes veer from the street to the bulk of Charlie-boy Lee.
"To get to me, John, you're going to have to go through the Driver."

*

Phil Doran, the licensee of The Dog and Duck, has a reputation for serving a good pint, good grub, and turning a blind eye. Unlike most of the other licensees in the area, what Phil sees stays inside his head. In other words, as far as The Bizzies are concerned, Mr Doran never sees a bloody thing.
The Olde Worlde Pub is within walking distance of the main road, and access to the oak-pillared front door is via a leafy avenue of immaculately presented, semi-detached houses. Car parking is limited: restricted to maybe half a dozen pull-ins

across the pavement in front of the lounge bar windows. Any spare slots on the avenue are like rocking horse shit. To the rear is a large car park which, conversely, backs onto a dark and drab industrial estate.

Baptiste was early.

"Drive down Oak Leaf Avenue, Beef, we'll check out the front first, then the back. Jim's infatuation with perfection has brought about his downfall: he's been banging on about this job for weeks, and every time we meet, he lets slip more and more information. Now I have enough, and Mackenzie is surplus to requirements: his rule ends tonight."

He sweeps the dreads away from his face and laughs.

"He doesn't have a Scooby-Doo what I'm planning — like a lamb to the fucking slaughter."

*

"The Cortina is flashing to turn left, Robbo, and so is the car directly behind the pick-up truck."

"Well done, son, and it's good that they're both turning: it provides us with a bit of cover."

"It's turned and is out of my sight, closely followed by the other car."

The boy turns towards the experienced man.

"Do you think they are together?"

Robbo shrugs his shoulders.

"Not sure, son. Probably a coincidence, but who knows? I dare say we're going to find out sooner rather than later, though."

He eases off the accelerator, switches to side lights, and makes the turn into Oak Leaf Avenue. The two vehicles are forty-odd yards ahead of them and moving too slowly for comfort: if the Transit continues at its current speed, it will catch up with them and have nowhere to go.

"Hold on!"

He spins the steering wheel and swerves to the left side of the road, mounting the pavement and coming to a halt on the double yellow lines running back to the junction. Killing the side lights, he keeps the engine ticking over.

"You okay, youngster? I know your view is a bit limited because of the parked cars, but I couldn't risk following them along this street. Oh, hello, our friends are indicating to pull into the left, and they've slowed right down and, bloody hell, they've stopped and double-parked. The following vehicle is having to squeeze past, and, wait for it — it's carried on going: that answers your question... Bloody good job we were able to grab this spot...
Would you believe it, our lot are off again: very slowly — nigh on crawling past the boozer on our right. Can you see it?"
Phyllis nodded, his neck straining to get a better view: his whole body tingling.
Robbo continues.
"Yes, it's definitely the pub that they're interested in — the Cortina has gone past and has stopped in the middle of the road again. The West Indian is out and is walking over towards it. And he's out of my sight."
Tension is slipping back into the Cadet's voice.
"What are you going to do, Robbo? What if he's meeting someone in there?"
Once more, a calming hand of experience moves up and down at the wrist, and Robbo smiles.
"You're doing well, sonny. There's not a lot we can do at the moment, and the positioning of the Cortina tells me he's got no intention of staying where he is for long. Maybe for now he's just checking out who is inside the pub. We don't know, but the good thing in our favour is we're in the best place. From here, we're under no pressure to do anything: we just watch and wait."

*

Baptiste returns to the Cortina.
"Just as I thought, Jim's not 'ere yet. The lounge bars are bloody heaving, but we usually get a quiet table overlooking the car park at the rear. It's bloody chockers on this street, so he's gonna have to drive through the industrial estate and park out the back."

A prestigious-looking estate car is indicating to pull out from a parking space in front of one of the semis, and Baptiste gestures with his left hand.

"Pull into that spot, Beef; unless Jim drives halfway around the town, he's gotta come the way we just did. He won't recognise this motor, so we can sit here and bide our time.

(Simultaneously)

"Stand by, youngster, the West Indian is back and into the Cortina."

Robbo releases the handbrake, selects first gear, and pauses, his foot hovering over the accelerator.

"We'll give him a bit more space, then I'll pull out, but I won't put on any lights. It's so bloody gloomy they won't even notice us."

Frustrated that he can't see, the Cadet edges forward on his seat as Robbo curses, yanks up the handbrake, and knocks the gear lever back into neutral.

"They've parked up again and turned the bloody lights off. What the hell is going on?"

He pops in another extra strong mint…

*

The Scouse accent is strong.

"Which way do you want me to get you to the boozer, Mr Mackenzie? Through the industrial area and park out the back? Or down that street full of trees and posh 'ouses?"

Jim laughed.

"The posh 'ouses, Charlie, and do yr best to park in the front: that manky industrial site gives me the bloody creeps."

The black Mercedes makes a right turn and the powerful full beam floods Oak Leaf Avenue; Charlie-boy Lee pays no attention to the white Ford Transit van pulled in at the junction, his focus is on the road ahead.

"All looks good 'ere, Mr Mackenzie, but the parkin' outside the pub is full…"

He flicks on the windscreen wipers.

"...and it's started to bloody piss down. Wot do you want me to do?"

Jim curses, the accent now more exaggerated as it always becomes when his mental capacity is challenged.

"Shite bloody weather! Drive around the back and get the motor as close as you can to the pub door. You got the umbrella? This mohair coat of mine doesn't like getting wet and it cost me a bastard fortune."

The Driver curses under his breath.

'Fuckin' ponce!'

His face in the rearview shows no emotion.

"No problem, Mr Mackenzie — all part of the service."

The S Class slows down as it passes The Dog and Duck, and the two occupants check the vicinity for any sign of Baptiste's car; eyes also strain to get a view of the pub's interior through the steamed-up windows.

Jim checks his Rolex.

"There's no sign of Baptiste: we might be a wee bit early, Charlie. Carry on around the back and see if his motor's parked up. If it's not, you'll have to go in and check it out: see if he's in there."

"No problem, Mr Mackenzie — I know just the spot."

*

Slouching in their seats, the Despot and his right-hand man are unnoticeable to the Driver and his client as they glide past. But Baptiste recognises the black Mercedes.

"Shit! — Jim's doing better than I thought. He's only gone and hired the fucking Driver."

Feeling for the reassurance of the shooter, he shouts out the thought that is now monopolising his mind: his skunk-sodden brain warped with paranoia.

"Why the fuck did he go to the expense of bringing that fucking ape along?"

He turns to confront his right-hand man; piercing eyes boring into him, and his tone is questioning — accusing.

"Some fucker's tipped him off!"
Wide and offended eyes glare back at Baptiste. Born in a terraced house within a stone's throw of Stanley Park, Beef's accent is as pure Scouse as the Driver's, and the tone is defensive.
"'Old on, John, erm, erm, it's not fuckin' me, I'd never fuckin' shit on you. Erm, erm, it's gotta be one of the others."
A seething Baptiste has turned away: wild eyes now monitoring the Mercedes, and they see it take a right at the T junction.
"No time for this now, Beef: we'll come back to it later. Follow the fuckers, but give them a minute or so."
(Simultaneously)
"There's a lot of interest in that boozer, youngster. That chauffeur-driven Merc that just passed us has slowed right down, had a good gander, and now it's on the move again. I'd bet my house on it that the two jokers in the Cortina are waiting for the occupants. It's driven slowly past them and now it's heading towards the end of this road. There are brake lights, a right indication, and it's turned out of my view..."
He rubs his hands together in front of him.
"...Let's see what the Cortina does..."
The voice is heavy with disappointment.
"...Bloody hell — it hasn't even budged! That's well and truly smacked my hunch on the arse. Good job I'm not a betting man — I'd be bloody homeless. See, youngster, there are never any certainties in life. I would have sworn that those two cars were connected in some way — would you bloody believe it, the Cortina is on the move again, and it hasn't put any lights on: now, what does that tell you?"
The Cadet is learning quickly and gives a chuckle.
"I think that you won't be needing a 'For Sale' sign outside your house, Robbo..."
The man's left hand slaps the youngster on the thigh.
"Ha ha — spot on, kiddo."
His nail slices through the wrapping of another pack of extra

strong mints while speaking.

"Just like I initially thought — this is it. Something is about to happen and fingers crossed we'll get an opportunity to grab hold of that West Indian. Here, suck on one of these…"

CHAPTER 38

The night is dismal: dark, drab, and wet. Potholes overflowing with grime litter the access through the industrial site, and sporadic H.G.V. trailers doze in their temporary resting spots on both sides of the road. A shaft of light from the only non-vandalised lamp standard emphasises the constant torrent of water gushing from the heavens, and Charlie-boy Lee, striving to avoid the craters, curses under his breath.
"Fuckin' weather! The Merc will be bastard filthy! Be nice if this job runs smoothly and I can get back 'ome in time for a couple of wets down The Fox and 'ounds."
Turning into the parking area at the rear of The Dog and Duck, he tucks it underneath a mock, Victorian-style gas lamp; switches off the engine and turns to face his client. Eerily, Jim's face is lit up by a flash of lightning, and Charlie boy winces, instinctively ducking as the thunder cracks directly overhead.
"What's the plan, Mr Mackenzie?"
Pulling up the collar of the mohair coat, Jim shivers.
"I'll stay put for now, Charlie. You check out the boozer and see if John's in there."
The Driver scans the car park before stepping into the downpour. Popping the boot, he grabs a large golfing-type umbrella, and with hunched-up shoulders, scurries towards the entrance.
The elements are Baptiste's ally. Charlie-boy Lee is too busy

avoiding puddles and the drenching rain to notice the unlit Ford Cortina sliding in between the trailers. Its engine is ticking over, and Beef has a perfect view of the Mercedes.
"The Driver's gone into the pub, and Jim's in the motor by 'imself . Now's yr chance, John. Go on, mate — fuckin' do 'im!"
Baptiste takes a long toke on another skunk-filled reefer, and a head already saturated with thoughts of betrayal can no longer rationalise: deranged and accusing eyes bore into his main man.
"No, Beef, don't you tell me when or what to do. Just remember that I'm the fucking Daddy around here: I'm the brains in this outfit and you work for me — you got that? Now prove your loyalty and YOU fucking do him!"
He held out the Smith and Wesson, and Beef instinctively took hold of the grip, his hand trembling as thoughts raced through his mind. All the times that, without question, he has done what's been asked. He's always been loyal, always been there at the drop of a hat.
Baptiste's Barbadian twang roused him from the moment — yelling!
"Go on you fucker, shoot him — shoot him!"
Sad eyes glanced at the firearm, then back to his boss, and the Liverpudlian's lips quivered as the words softly passed his lips.
"Ow many times do I 'ave to prove my loyalty to you, John? I do everythin' you ask. Yet you just accused me of blabbin' about you to Jim Mackenzie. Well, Jim's alright — I could work with Jim, but your 'ed is fucked up, and to be 'onest , I've 'ad a fuckin' guts full of the constant criticism, and so 'ave the lads. They're as pissed off as I am, and no doubt will follow me."
He pointed the gun at Baptiste's chest and the index finger of his right hand caressed the trigger.
"No, John, at this moment in time — I'm the fuckin' Daddy!"
A flash of lightning lit up the horrifying scene, and the gunshot was masked by the crack of thunder. Torrential rain that had been battering against the Ford Cortina gained entry by gushing through the shattered window and hammering

against the corpse of Edwin Clarence Baptiste. It was slumped against the door: eyes wide, dreads flapping in the wind, and with a hole in the chest the size of one of Robbo's mints — the bullet had passed straight through the heart.

Beef's eyes dart across to the Black Mercedes — no change there: Jim is totally oblivious, and there was still no sign of Charlie-boy Lee. Suddenly, he's drenched in a cold sweat and engulfed by an overwhelming desire to puke. An innate sense of self-preservation kicks in, and swallowing repeatedly to stem the eruption of vomit, he quickly wipes over any surfaces where his fingerprints might be. Switching off the engine, he takes the keys and while holding onto the murder weapon, mutters to himself as he steps into the deluge.

"Nobody else knows about this motor, and nobody knows that I was 'ere — I'm in the clear."

The noise from the rain splattering against the roof of the Ford Cortina masks the close proximity of Robbo's Ford Transit Van, and Beef, startled by the sudden presence of a vehicle, keeps his head low and tucks the firearm into his body. Turning his face away, he strides back to the entrance of the industrial estate.

"Whoever is driving that motor can't 'ave seen wot 'appened. It's too dark, and it's too fuckin' wet."

*

"Bloody hell, youngster, did you see that? Beef's just taken out the West Indian!"

"W w what are we going to do, Robbo?"

The Cadet was shaking uncontrollably.

"W w we can't just do nothing."

The Transit hadn't slowed, and Robbo had turned his face away from the murder scene.

"Don't you eyeball him — keep your eyes to the front. Make him think we haven't noticed. This is our chance to nab him — get our job done — and go on home."

Wide eyes bore into the ex-military man.

"W w what do you mean, n nab him, Robbo? He, he's got a bloody gun!"

A calm, reassuring voice responds.

"That's my problem, kiddo: nothing for you to worry about. Did you see the state of that John bloke? He's definitely a goner, so HE's no bloody use to us anymore. And, most importantly, there's nothing we can do for him, so don't you go fretting over that: the bullet went straight through him, and the bloody window."

Robbo clocks the Mercedes parked beneath the mock gas lamp standard and nods towards it.

"I doubt we'll ever find out if that was anything to do with the Cortina, but for what it's worth, my money is on it being some sort of drug deal that has gone horribly tits-up."

Checking the wing mirror, he sees Beef make a left turn.

"Right, the killer has walked out of this shithole and is heading back the way we came. He's going to be in one hell of a state, and the last thing he'll be expecting is someone like me to pluck him out of thin air."

He three-point turns the Transit.

"Just do as I say, sonny — you'll be fine."

CHAPTER 39

Beef is drenched; his eyes have sunk into their sockets, his face is as white as the wings on a mute swan, and he's gnawing at the fingernails on his right hand. The left arm is dangling alongside the left leg, the hand is by the knee, and it's gripping hold of the Smith and Wesson like a mother would her toddler's hand on the verge of a busy highway. He's blabbering to himself as he strides through the rain: repeating the same words over and over.

"Nobody else knows about this motor and nobody knows I was 'ere — I'm in the clear.

Nobody else knows about this motor and nobody knows I was 'ere — I'm in the clear."

He pays no notice to the white-coloured Ford Transit van that is driven past him and makes a left turn into Oak Leaf Avenue, some thirty or forty yards further on. Robbo pulls it onto the double yellows at the junction, kills the lights, kills the engine, grabs the waistcoat, and opens the door.

"Listen, kid, I haven't got much time before he reaches us. Whatever you might see or hear, don't move a bloody muscle. Do you understand? This won't take long."

He closes the door and is gone.

Phyllis's eyes immediately locate the passenger wing mirror, and his body contorts to get a rear view. There is no sign of Robbo, but he sees the murderer turn onto the tree-lined

Avenue.

"Oh my fucking God, he's got the gun in his hand — bloody hell, Robbo!"

He leans across the driver's seat — straining to get a view from that wing mirror: there is nothing but darkness and endless rain.

"Robbo, where the hell are you?"

The ex-SAS operative is crouching at the front of the Transit Van. Black goat-hide gloves cover his hands, and a black ski mask covers his head and face. It is imperative that the target doesn't catch a glimpse of him…Focussed and with a concentration level of one hundred per cent, he listens for the target's footsteps: the timing has to be spot on.

'Go!'

He sprints around the blind side of the van, the soft-soled leather boots soundless on the tarmacadam surface.

'By now the target should be approaching the passenger door — he is.'

Less than three seconds later, Beef is unconscious and has crumpled like a sack of excrement into Robbo's arms: the lightning-quick karate chop to the carotid sinus was all that was necessary.

He gives a little shake of his head, allowing a contented smile to momentarily break the determination etched on his face.

"You've still got it, Taff…"

His eyes are everywhere as he gathers the Smith and Wesson from the pavement and drags his captive through the rear doors of the Transit Van. Closing them, he flicks on a strip lamp, flooding the cargo area and spotlighting the tattoo on the back of his captive's neck.

"There it is — a spider web — bingo!"

Mindful that he doesn't have much time before the man regains consciousness, he props the body upright against the wood-panelled side and reaches for his preferred means to incapacitate — Gaffer Tape. Wrapping it around the torso enough times to pin in the arms, he bites it off and concentrates on the eyes and mouth.

"We don't want him seeing anything or disturbing the neighbours, do we, Taff? Just leave enough of a gap for this vermin to breathe through his nose and be able to listen to what I have to tell him."

Taking a step back, he admires his work before reaching for a water bottle and takes a long, thirst-quenching swig; he chucks the rest at the captive's face.

"Wake up, you murdering bastard!"

*

The thick-set male with the spider web tattoo on the back of his neck, the one they call Beef, sits and struggles in the dark. He can't move his arms, he can't move his eyelids, and he can't open his mouth. His breathing, solely through congested nostrils, is erratic, and he can hear thuds of heavy rain pounding against a metal surface directly above him.

'Is he in some kind of storage container? Who was it that plucked him from the street and why?'

Fear grips him.

'What are they going to do to him?'

A petrol engine comes to life, and the container vibrates.

"Shit — I'm in a fuckin' van."

He topples over as the van speeds away, and struggling to right himself, he crashes into the plywood-cladding on the other side — muffled screams fall on deaf ears.

*

(Simultaneously)

Wide, terrified eyes greeted the man in black as he yanked open the driver's door, jumped in, and accelerated away. They had just witnessed how effortlessly a known killer, still in possession of the murder weapon, had been rendered powerless with one simple blow to the side of the neck.

Robbo tears off the ski mask.

"We need to get far away from here and fast. Ideally, somewhere deserted: this area is going to be crawling with cops once the body of that West Indian is discovered."

"W what are you going to do, Robbo?"
The driver's eyes don't divert from the road.
"What we came all this bloody way to do. Find out where the body of Barry Murphy is stashed and get the message to the cops. I get my key back and you can live your life without the fear of your parents being hurt. I don't think anyone is going to meddle with us once word filters through the jungle drums of the prison system to your mate Price — do you?"
"B but h how are you going to get Beef to tell you?"
Robbo laughed.
"Listen, kid — he's trussed up like a turkey on Christmas Day. He can't see, he can't speak, and he's shitting himself. He's just murdered his best mate, and he knows that I know that he's done it. I've got the killer, I've got the murder weapon, and I know where it happened. That's better than Colonel Mustard with the candlestick in the bloody dining room. Stop worrying, kiddo. As far as he's aware, I'm working by myself, so you are well and truly out of the equation. And trust me — he will tell me — and he ain't going to lie."
They enter the docks and multi-storey brick warehouses on either side of the road, closed for the night, rise from empty pavements. The only source of light comes from a telephone kiosk which is at the crossroads of two normally very busy throughways. Robbo clocks the perfect spot: a space in between two other Transit Vans on an off-road parking lot. He sneaks into it and kills the engine.
"Do not get out of the van, and if a vehicle or a pedestrian comes into your view, do not let them see you. I won't be long."
Robbo's teeth are gleaming in the darkness, and a hand reaches out — gives a reassuring squeeze to the boy's thigh.
"Oh, and by the way, sonny..."
He winks.
"...Give us a smile."

*

The door opens, and a sharp, salty breeze hits the captive side on. He flinches and murmurs — the murmurs turn to high-pitched and muffled squeals.

Recalling the selection course to the Regiment, Robbo smiles: over those several long and arduous days, he went to hell and back — the waste of space in front of him wouldn't have lasted two minutes.

'This is going to be a stroll in the park.'

He slams the door behind him, and the captive struggles to free his arms. Fear of the unknown has gripped him, and his muffled screams are deadened by the gaffer tape, as his head shakes erratically from side to side.

Robbo sits opposite him, waiting for him to calm down, and apart from the clattering of rain, there is silence. Beef is in deep shock: soaked to the skin, shivering, dishevelled, thirsty as hell, and the incessant thuds on the metal roof are driving him stir-crazy...

The struggling ceases, and Robbo leans in; blows into his captive's right ear, and recoils with the speed of a viper — deftly avoiding the violent flick of the head towards the spurt of breath.

He sits back — watching.

'Ten seconds should do it, Taff... Eight, nine, ten.'

He blows into the left — that action achieving the same response.

"Feisty fucker, aren't you? What's your name again? Oh yes, I remember: it's Beef, isn't it? Perhaps I should leave you alone for a few days to reflect, Mr Beef..."

Robbo releases the door handle, and the captive squeals. Struggling to stand, he fails miserably, and the shrill cries intensify.

"Oh, don't you want to be left alone, Mr Beef? Here, in the dark?"

Robbo's tone of voice changes to a ghostly, slow whisper.

"Are you scared of the dark, Mr Beef? Is the bogeyman coming to get you?"

Tugging the door firmly closed, Robbo rises to his feet and, while stooping in the limited space, kicks out at the captive's chest, causing him to topple over.

He shouts at the top of his voice.

"I am the Bogeyman, you piece of shit — I am your worst fucking nightmare!"

Whimpering, the captive strives to sit up, and Robbo kneels on his left thigh, pinning him to the floor — the barrel of the firearm pushed into the soft flesh below the chin. The tone of voice is calm, assertive — in control.

"You don't know where you are, do you? And, apart from me, no other fucker does either. Which way do you want to die, Mr Beef?"

More pressure is applied to the Smith and Wesson.

"The same way you murdered your Rastafarian buddy?"

There is a momentary pause.

"Or maybe the way you murdered Barry Murphy? Remember him?"

Another pause.

"Should I whack you over the head with a lump of timber? Or are those deaths too quick? Should I just leave you here to rot?"

The forceful shaking of the head and the muffled yelps are a clear indication that none of the options are agreeable.

"Okay, I get it, Mr Beef: you don't want to die. But maybe your squeals are more to do with frustration — possibly even thoughts of betrayal? Who amongst your cowardly gathering of little shits has been blabbing? How come I know so much about your sickening history?"

The pressure of the firearm is released.

"I have total control over your destiny, Mr Beef. You have just murdered your buddy, and I would imagine that within the next half hour or so, every available copper on Merseyside will be searching for his killer and the weapon that was used to extinguish his miserable life."

He sniffed.

"What a coincidence — I have them both. And now you also know that I am fully aware that you have killed before. How do I know that? That's what you are thinking at this precise

moment. How does this man who has just plucked me out of thin air know so much?"
Beef forces his head from the floor and strains to turn it towards the voice; there are more murmurs.
"I know that you murdered Barry Murphy: that you were the one who struck the fatal blow. Hell, you were so close to him at the time, you probably heard his skull shattering…"
The sound caused by Robbo placing an index finger inside his mouth and dragging it against a puffed-out cheek echoed within the confined cargo area.
"…popping like a coconut."
The murmuring ceases, there is silence, and Robbo knew that he had him. It was just a matter of time…
He rips away the tape covering the captive's mouth and pulls him into a seated position. There are traces of spittle caked across the man's lips, and Robbo chooses another water bottle.
"Do you want a drink of water, Mr Beef?"
The captive nods his head — his voice is hoarse.
"'Ave you got any fuckin' Strongbow?"
Robbo puts the bottle to Beef's lips.
"No Strongbow, Mr Beef. You are stuck with Adam's ale."
He tilts his head, gulps until the water trickles down his chin, and turns his face away.
"Get rid of the mista, will ya? Beef will do. Wot do you fuckin' want from me? What do I 'ave to do? Erm, you seem to be 'olding all the fuckin' cards."
"I'm pleased that you see it that way, Beef. You are absolutely correct, and it's all very simple. All I want you to do is tell me where you have hidden Murphy's body, and then I will let you go."
Shaking his head in bewilderment, he starts to laugh.
"Why the fuck are you interested in that piece of shit? You givin' his mam one or wot?"
Robbo kicks out, catching Beef full in the ribs, winding him — forcing him back to the floor. He kneels on him again, and the assertiveness is back in the voice — threatening.

"No fucking questions! And quit the laughter. This is no joke. Listen carefully to what I am going to tell you because I will not repeat myself.

I don't give a toss for you, Barry Murphy, or his mother. Now, you tell me where the body is, or I will dump you outside the nearest police station with a note glued to your forehead saying, 'I dun it!' And the Smith and Wesson that has been rammed into your neck over the past few minutes will be tucked into the waistband of your jeans like Billy the Fucking Kid!"

The captive twists his head, struggling to breathe: the pain in his chest is excruciating, and his speech is laboured.

"I could tell you any ol' shite, 'ow are you goin' to know if it's kosher or not?"

"Because, Mr Beef, I am going to drag you across the road to a telephone kiosk, and I'm going to dial 999. You will ask for the police, and you will tell them the exact location of Murphy's body. And, just to speed things up a little, you will tell them that the body is being moved within the next two hours."

CHAPTER 40

For those in mourning, filled with grief, and who wish to visit loved ones when they have passed away, a cemetery can be a welcome place of tranquillity and solace. Especially when the sun is shining, flowers are in bloom, and shade can be sought under the canopy of the ever-present yew tree.
On an eerie, wet, and windy night in autumn, however, it can be the bleakest place in town: a haunt for the souls who are not at rest. An unforgiving nightmare where the darkness plays tricks with your eyes, and apparitions are everywhere.
Robbo had driven to such a place following Beef's surprise revelation to the bizzies. The transit is parked far enough away and under the watchful eyes of the Police Cadet with Beef securely gagged and tethered in the cargo area. The ex-SAS operative, however, is concealed in the undergrowth with an eyeball on the gravestone of Dorothy Edwina Callaghan.
Resting in peace below Mrs Callaghan is her loving husband, Liam, and trespassing above her, allegedly wrapped in a moth-eaten Persian rug, is Barry George Murphy.
Robbo sees the approaching headlights and can hear engines, but it's not, as normally would be the case, a hearse leading an entourage of mourners. No, it's a panda car leading a Liverpool City Council utility van.
Two Bobbies alight from the front seats, put on their helmets, pull up their collars, and look for shelter: there isn't any. An

official-looking male in a black-coloured gabardine raincoat gets out of the back, struggles against the hurricane to lift the hood over his ears, shields a clipboard from the elements, and points a torch into the darkness.

"This way, officers, the grave is just over here."

Robbo is near enough to satisfy his curiosity and confident enough in his expertise in camouflage and concealment to not be discovered. To the untrained eye and mindset of those unable to comprehend an individual's skill, courage, and audacity to be in such close proximity, there was nobody there. But Robbo's thought process when choosing his observation post had taken into consideration the human factor. People are not fond of a north-easterly bone-biting gale, and they don't like getting wet. Guaranteed, upon arrival, the coppers will shiver before taking a cursory glance around. Then they'll complain and moan about being singled out for this god-forsaken task. Do the bare minimum, leave whoever draws the short straw to guard the scene overnight, and come back in the morning when hopefully there'll be somebody around who can give them a hot brew and a ginger biscuit. As usual, Robbo was spot on.

The Council Official organised the grave digger, and the Bobbies held the torches.

"I know you have a job to do, officers, but this is highly controversial and very disrespectful to the deceased."

He pointed at the memorial flower vases by the headstone and instructed the man with the spade.

"Leave those where they are for now, Joe: just lift the turf at the foot of the grave."

He turned to the officers.

"If the young man is buried here, he will be very close to the surface: it's a two-casket grave, so there wouldn't have been much room on top of the second coffin."

Two pieces of turf, each measuring approximately nine by nine inches, were removed and put to one side, but when the spade dug into and disturbed the compacted soil beneath, the stench that had been trapped for months hit the grave digger full on. He recoiled, tripped over the pieces of turf, fell into his boss, and vomited over the gabardine raincoat.

Wincing, the larger of the two Coppers covered his nose.

"It looks like we've found Murphy then, Bill: the stinking, filthy bastard!"

*

"There is a corpse in a carpet on top of your grandmother's neighbour, and it's in one hell of a state."

Robbo presses the Smith and Wesson into the flesh below the captive's chin and rips away the gag.

"If it's not Murphy, I will come for you, and I will nab you: you'll be cut, tethered, gagged, blindfolded, and left bleeding in the wilds for the carrion to savour."

The cold steel is rammed further into the soft tissue, causing the bottom row of teeth to grind against the top.

"Savvy?"

Beef nodded, and the pressure on the Smith and Wesson eased.

"Mista, I don' know who the fuck you are, but I do know you can take me out anytime you want. On me mother's life — the body in that grave is Barry Murphy."

That was good enough for Robbo. It was time to dump this oxygen thief and head on home. A job well done.

'He's cacking his pants, Taff — no way is he lying.'

He dragged the captive out of the cargo area, sat him against a tree, sliced through most of the gaffer tape, and whispered some final words of wisdom into his left ear.

"If you hear this voice again, Beef, it means that you have lied to me. An action that you will deeply regret for however long you have left on this planet. Don't you ever forget our little get-together this evening and how easy it was for me to make your acquaintance. And you'd better remember this — I don't make idle threats."

*

The 16-year-old's eyes were weary, and his voice croaky as he gazed across at the man driving the van.

"What next, Robbo?"

A warm smile softens the battle-hardened face.

"I'll tell you what's next, youngster: we get well away from this city and we pull into the first services on the M6 where we celebrate a cracking result by treating ourselves to a slap-up meal. Then we find a quiet spot and get our heads down: sound good to you, kiddo?"

Phyllis nodded, returning the smile.

"Sounds good to me, Robbo."

CHAPTER 41

The man couldn't sleep, which wasn't unusual for him following a successful mission. It always took an age for the adrenaline to return to wherever it came from. He checked on the youngster, and a warmth came over him: the boy was out of it. He'd done well, and Robbo had taken to him, but in the morning, that would be it. They'd say their goodbyes and wouldn't see each other again. Well — not for a while anyway — too risky.

As it stood, there was nothing to link any contact between them and nothing to put Robbo's Ford Transit Van in Liverpool. The ghost plates had served their purpose and were now in one of the many litter bins dotted around the car park. Only the guy with the spider web tattoo on the back of his neck knew of Robbo's existence, and the recall of his many squeals and screams brought a smile to his lips.

"Beef won't be blabbing to anyone about how he was taken off the street like a mere child, and trussed up ready to serve on a platter."

On their way home, Robbo would sling the Smith and Wesson into the depths of the River Neath at Briton Ferry: lay it to rest forever in its grave of sinking mud.

And the key? Well, by Monday afternoon, the identity of the body in the carpet will be confirmed as being that of Barry George Murphy, and the manner in which he'd been murdered will be known. Mikey Price will be off the hook, and Robbo can pay a surprise visit to the Pantomime Dame in Pembroke Dock. He grinned again, recalling her in Haverfordwest, lingering in the doorway of 'Tantalising Secrets,' and shuddered as he pictured her in all her glory.

It grated on him that he had helped Mikey Price, but, and he sniggered.

"The sooner that lowlife is out of clink, the sooner I can get my hands on the evil bastard!"

And it will be a relief to get his key back. Robbo had resigned himself to it being astray forever.

He'd lost count of the times he'd lain awake during the witching hours, mentally torturing himself with what-ifs and maybes? What if it wasn't in the car when it was stolen? What if he'd put it somewhere safe? What if he'd inadvertently left it in the lock of the safety deposit box, and somebody had helped themselves to the contents? It was torturous that he couldn't make a tentative enquiry to discount that scenario: no doubt it would highlight his predicament, and the bank security might suggest a forced entry. Bloody hell, if the contents were still intact, that's the last thing he needed.

He'd turned his modest terraced house upside down and searched every nook and cranny. Then his shed, and then the house again. At least now he knows who's got it, and he'll have some fun getting it back…

It was the key to a bit of luxury when the moment was right: his retirement pension pot. Legally and morally, though, Robbo knew it was a pot he shouldn't have, and that's the reason why he was unable to report the missing key to the police or to the bank. But, didn't they just do what any other men would have done in their situation? In those circumstances, what else could they do?

Alright, they had been found in the pockets of dead men. Men whose lives had been brought to a premature and horrific end. But hell, they were at war, weren't they? And where did the raiding Indonesian guerrillas get them from in the first place?

Probably robbed them from a swamp mine that they'd stumbled across: massacred the workers and shared them out. Robbo's eyelids grew heavy, and the weight eventually forced them to close. He drifted into a slumber that was restless and, as was the case most nights, filled with haunting memories, flailing arms, and deathly screams. Vivid recollections of life-threatening patrols across the Sarawak border into Kalimantan. Hiding and sleeping in damp, reptile and insect-infested makeshift camps for months on end. Mapping the terrain, setting booby traps, seeking out the enemy, and radioing in their pinpoint locations: the air strikes would do the rest.

Much of the inner jungle in Borneo was treacherous, and visibility was poor. To avoid detection, the use of hand signals was paramount; whispering was the norm, and the mental stress was debilitating — relieved only by a spirited camaraderie.

Robbo's dreams always concluded with that life-changing day: the day when the contents of the safety deposit box were discovered.

*

Sergeant Joey Smith was leading the patrol, and as usual, the going was arduous and slow: pausing and listening for minutes on end. No progress could be made until they were absolutely positive that an ambush was not lurking on the other side of the dense mass of greenery in front of them.

Corporal Bill 'DJ' Griffiths was the radio operative, Taff Robbo the sniper, and Timmy 'Bang Bang' Filey — explosives. A band of brothers, woven together as tight as a Scotsman's kilt. A bond as impenetrable as many of the acres of jungle they temporarily called home.

It was the overwhelming stench of death that stopped the patrol in its tracks on that particular day. Instinctively, they fully widened their mouths to listen, then gagged as the stink hit the back of their throats.

"Fucking hell," whispered Bang Bang, his hand covering his mouth. "That ain't no animal."

DJ raised a thumb of agreement, choking to stem the cough that was battling to escape and give away their presence. Smithy raised the palm of his hand and beckoned for Robbo to venture forward. His index finger pointed to his eyes, then to the dense mass of greenery blocking their view. No words were necessary: Robbo knew what he had to do — it was his expertise.

The barrel of the AR-15 poked through the foliage, and the high-powered sights revealed the extent of the carnage — it was sickening.

Ten victims were strewn across the clearing: each one a goner. Each one caught in the blast of a trip-wired booby trap. One of several strategically placed and mapped by the band of brothers several days earlier. Mutilated beyond recognition, their bodies had been ravaged: no chance of survival — an instant death.

The sniper, his face streaked with camouflage cream, and his body streaked with sweat, scanned the clearing with the powerful lens, then further into the undergrowth on the other side. Was there an ambush in waiting? Satisfied that the latter was a negative, he turned away from the feasting carnivores and signalled to his mates with a thumbs-up.

They'd witnessed that look of horror on Robbo's face many times before, and Bang Bang was the first to whisper.

"One of the Claymores, Taff?"

Robbo gulped and nodded.

"Yeah, and they must have been bloody close. It's a ten-man raiding party, and they're in a bit of a mess — no survivors."

Smithy chipped in, sensing the need to boost morale.

"The mine did its job then: good work, Bang bang. It could so easily have been us in their position. DJ, you radio it in, and we'll have a quick gander. I don't want us to hang around here for too long. Taff — you cover us."

That was when they found the raw diamonds — fifty-two of

the soon-to-be-sparkling, little treasures. And that's when the pact was made: share them out and never speak of it again.

CHAPTER 42

"What the hell were you thinking, Phyllis? Turning up at the Magistrates Court like you did? We've been pulling out all the stops to keep your name out of the prosecution file. Doing our damndest to protect you as the informant, and you turn up at the hearing like Miss bloody Marple!"
The tired smile that had briefly brightened the Cadet's face when he saw the Detective Sergeant waned, and he couldn't stem the giveaway reddening of his complexion. His eyes shifted away from the glare as he sat down: his mind once more in turmoil.
'How the hell does Dai know I was at the court? I didn't recognise anybody, so who saw me that knew me? Did they see me with Rose? Did they see me go off with Robbo? What else does Dai know? Are they going to find out that we witnessed a murder, kidnapped the murderer, and disposed of the bloody murder weapon?"
He tried to disguise the deep breath that he needed to take, but he couldn't.
'Sod it, I'll be truthful. Well — to a point.'
Tired eyes fixed on the man across the desk.
"I am so sorry, Sarge, I couldn't stay away. I needed to find out if Mikey suspected me of being the informant."
The eyes drifted back to the floor, stalling for time: conjuring up a response that could tug on any possible paternal strings

the Detective Sergeant might have.

Tears would definitely help and they were easy to generate: the boy was shattered — already overwhelmed by the incidents over the weekend, and now this revelation. He let them run down his cheeks, raised his head, and as the distressing response blurted from his lips, his voice broke with the emotion.

"I am beside myself with worry that my parents will be targeted, Sarge. What if he gets to them and kills them? It will be all my fault."

The Detective Sergeant rose from the recliner, and the prepared rollicking that had been festering in his mind since Pat Muldoon had telephoned him on Friday lunchtime was discarded to the graveyard of unused speeches. Tugging open the top drawer in the tall filing cabinet, Dai grabbed a roll of toilet paper from his emergency stash, chucked it into the Cadet's lap, stretched over the desk, and patted him on the shoulder.

"Dry your eyes, sonny, and tell me exactly what happened. Things might not be so bad after all."

The Detective Sergeant's demeanour had softened, and the terse tones had been replaced by a warmth of compassion. The Cadet breathed a sigh of relief. He hadn't completely escaped unscathed from the boiling hot water, but he was a lot closer to the cooler fringes. In order to get out and towel himself dry, his story had to be convincing, appeasing, and contain some element of truth. He just wished he knew what the hell Dai's informant had seen and where he or she was when they saw him. If it was all contained inside the courtroom and he hadn't been seen driving away with Robbo, then a diluted version of events should get him back in Dai's good books.

He slightly bowed his head and dabbed at the tears with the toilet tissue, a seemingly innocent enough action but one that gave him some respite from the Detective Sergeant's probing eyes. He retained the emotion in his voice.

"Like I explained last week. My dad isn't very well, and he

needed my help. That's why I couldn't get involved in the planting of the treated five-pound note in my lodgings. I had to see Mikey before he went to prison on remand. I had to find out what he knew, Sarge. I needed to find a way to protect my parents."

Phyllis sniffed, tore off more tissue, and blew his nose. He desperately wanted to bow his head to the floor and get some respite from Dai's glare, but he daren't. This had to be convincing — there couldn't be any furtive glances away from the supervisor's scrutiny. He slumped in the chair, dabbed at his eyes again, forced a sigh, and swallowed before feigning a weak smile.

"I was sat in the back of the court, and Mikey spotted me. He smiled, genuinely appearing pleased that I was there, and that took away some of the anxiety. Then Rose came over to sit by me, and she told me that Mikey would probably be going straight to prison following the hearing and that I wouldn't get a chance to speak with him. She felt uncomfortable sitting in the courtroom and asked me if I fancied a coffee in the cafe across the road. As soon as we got in there, she tried pumping me for information about the prosecution case, but I lied, Sarge. I told her that I didn't know anything."

The Detective Sergeant was nodding his head.

"Good, that's good, Phyllis. Very good — what happened next?"

"Well, I told her that it was only by accident that I found out about Mikey's court appearance, and being that I had a day off, I came to give him my support. Thankfully, I think she believed me. Rose and Mikey are convinced it was pure chance and bad luck that he got arrested. That the police were probably watching Lugsey's house and Mikey just happened to be in the wrong place at the wrong time."

He sighed again, blew his nose, and sensing that Dai didn't have the ammunition to challenge his version of events, he relaxed somewhat, feigned another weak smile, and looked him directly in the eye.

"After talking with Rose and seeing Mikey, it felt like a huge weight had been lifted from my shoulders. I went home, helped my dad all weekend, and he dropped me off here, at the front entrance, about 20 minutes ago."

Processing the information, the Detective Sergeant leant back on the recliner, flicked on the kettle, reached for the Calabash, and firmed fresh tobacco into the bowl.

"That all seems plausible enough to me, son. I'll phone Pat Muldoon and brief him later on."

He lit the pipe, made two mugs of black coffee, and put one in front of the Cadet.

"By the look of you, I think you're in need of one of these and a couple of matchsticks: help to prop your bloody eyes open! You look shattered — this case is taking its toll on you. Okay, Phyllis, it's time to move on. Time to draw a line under Mikey bloody Price. He's gone to the big house on the hill pending trial and will likely be banged up there for a long time. Especially if they can pin the murder of that bloke from Liverpool on him. That, what's his name, again? Barry Murphy. You say your dad dropped you off here this morning? So you haven't been back to your lodgings yet? You don't know if any more money has gone missing?"

The mention of Barry Murphy sent a time bomb ticking that had been lying dormant in the Cadet's thoughts for the briefest of moments. The boy had hardly slept — all he could see whenever he shut his eyes was the murder that he and Robbo had witnessed. A murder they had failed to act upon — one they had agreed should be forgotten about and never mentioned again. But he was struggling. Yes, as Robbo had quite rightly pointed out, it had nothing to do with them. It would have happened whether they were there or not. He recalled Robbo's words:

"We were gifted with a present from the gods, son. We had something to use to blackmail Beef, and to save his skin, he had no option but to talk."

No doubt it would have been more difficult to extract the whereabouts of Murphy's body from Beef without that bit of leverage, but Robbo was quietly confident that it wouldn't have been a problem. It was his tone that had unnerved the Cadet: cold, calculating and chilling.

"Ways and means would have found a way in the end. In my experience, it always does. A bit of pain and fear of the unknown always loosens a stubborn tongue. And that's all you need to know. In fact, the less you know, the better."

That titbit of information just made things worse: he'd overheard the shouting and the squeals coming from the back of Robbo's van, and all Phyllis could picture in his mind if Robbo didn't have that leverage were graphic scenes of extreme torture. It was a blessing that their road trip to Liverpool had been successful: they had achieved what they had set out to do. Phyllis no longer had the worry hanging over him of injury to his parents, and Robbo would get his key returned. But what about the murders of that tall Rastafarian guy and Barry Murphy? What about those?

The clicking of the Detective Sergeant's fingers in front of the Cadet's face startled him — bringing him back to the moment.

"Bloody hell, Phyllis, where the hell were you?"

"S sorry, Sarge. I I was miles away. The whole thing with Mikey Price has got to me."

Nodding his head to the previous questions.

"Yes, that's right. I don't know if any more money has been stolen, and I won't see Mrs Jones until later on today."

Dai sucked on the Calabash as he thought.

'The boy looks worn out — too much happening to him at too young an age.'

Inwardly he laughed.

'Reminds me of how I used to be all those years ago.'

Blowing out the smoke, he took a gulp of coffee and sighed as his eyes wandered around his tiny, drab office without a view.

'And look where I've bloody ended up.'

"Your eyes are like piss holes in the snow, son: you need to go back to bed and have a bloody good kip. Are you up for putting the wheels in motion today, or do you want to leave it for a

while? See how things pan out?"
The response was immediate — blurted out.
"N no, Sarge, don't cancel today. I need to get it sorted. That's why I look so tired: the not knowing is keeping me awake. I have constant thoughts swirling around inside my head. Who can it be? Surely not Mrs Jones? She is like a mother to me: it can't possibly be her. I would be devastated. And Molly? Well, I don't know. I've only met her the one time, and like her mother, she was lovely. It's got to be the other daughter — hasn't it? April's her name. I haven't met her yet, so I don't know what she's like, but who else can it be, Sarge?" According to Mrs Jones, they were the only visitors to the house when the first fiver was stolen. And thinking about it, Mrs Jones is not going to allow any old, random person to wander upstairs in her house. It's got to be someone she trusts: someone she cares about.
The supervisor held out his hand.
"Bloody hell, boy, take a breath — you'll have a bloody heart attack."
He winked, and there was a warmth in his smile as he spoke.
"Or more likely — give me one!"
The Cadet burst out crying and laughing — the tears flowing freely down his face before finding his mouth. His body was overheating: burning up with anxiety and he wanted to scream out, 'leave me alone — leave me alone.' But he couldn't; he deep-sighed, ripped off more of the toilet tissue, blew his nose and lied.
"I'm sorry, Sarge, it's been one hell of a couple of weeks or so, but I'm okay now…"
Fidgeting with the soggy tissue, he forced a tired smile, which didn't get anywhere close to adding a sparkle to red, puffy eyes underscored by dark circles — he lied again.
"That bit of laughter did me the world of good."
The man sucked on the Calabash, savouring the taste as he paused to think.
'It's a damn shame Evan Peters isn't around. The boy gets on

well with him, and that's what he needs right now: somebody he trusts. Somebody he can open up to and offload some of the shite that is massing inside his head. Yes, it's a damn bloody shame.'

He blew out the residue and took another gulp of coffee.

"Urgh, this is bloody freezing! Put the kettle on, youngster."

He winked again and flashed the gold-veneered incisor, trying his best to put the boy at ease.

"It's your bloody fault. Kept us gassing like a couple of old-timers playing bloody dominoes."

Rising from the recliner, the Detective Sergeant took hold of the mugs.

"I'll go and swill these two out."

Dai needed the time out of the office: his mind was saturated with what to do. He wasn't used to dealing with someone so young: his experience was with hairy-arsed coppers. Men he could kick up the backside and tell them to get a bloody grip. But this situation was more delicate: he was supervising a 16-year-old bloody child for Christ's sake. He had more of a duty of care towards him and needed to be more compassionate. But wasn't he dealing with a child who, not realising the consequences of his actions, had got himself entangled in a sordid and violent adult world? It wasn't a game of cops and bloody robbers that he was playing. One where he could chuck his teddy out of the pram and stomp off because things aren't going the way he wants them to. Yes, he's a maverick who has solved a cold case and will no doubt go on and become a bloody good copper, but at this moment in time, he needs to step away from everything and leave it to the grown-ups. He rinsed the mugs and spoke to the reflection looking back at him from the mirror above the aluminium sink.

"That's what you're going to have to do, Mr Winters — try and distance the boy away from the enquiry into the money being stolen from his bedroom."

Phyllis was also glad of the time alone: he'd got up, flicked on the kettle, opened the window, and mumbled as he took on board gulps of cold, fresh air.

"Bloody hell, that was a close shave: I thought for a moment that Robbo and I had been rumbled."

He gazed up at the looming dark clouds, put his hands together, and prayed.

"I haven't asked you for much lately, have I? If you are listening, please let there be some good news today. Please let that body that is buried in Liverpool be identified as Barry Murphy. And, just one more thing, please don't let it be Mrs Jones who is stealing my money — let it be somebody else — anybody but Mrs Jones."

The kettle clicked, and the steam was disappearing through the open window as the Detective Sergeant re-entered the room and shivered.

"Bloody hell, Phyllis, put the wood in that hole. It's like flipping Siberia in here!"

He put the mugs down on the table.

"Fill those buggers up again — I've got a phone call to make."

*

"Right, I've arranged for you to be here with me for the rest of the day: you can get on with filing those reports on top of that cabinet. I've been meaning to do that for the past few days, but..."

He winked again.

"...some deranged youth has had me rushing around like a blue-arsed fly. I'm popping down to see Stuart."

He laughed, sucked on the Calabash, took a magnifying glass from the top drawer of the desk, and held it out in front of him; stooping and speaking through the side of his mouth, as he disappeared into the corridor.

"We need a good plan of attack, Doctor: help us to detect the mysterious case of the Police Cadet's missing five-pound notes."

CHAPTER 43

The house was in darkness aside from a faint shaft of light creeping into the passageway from the slightly ajar kitchen door, suggesting to the Cadet that his landlady was in the conservatory. It was her favourite room. A room where happy memories flooded her mind, and if she closed her eyes and concentrated, she could hear Bernard's soft and soothing voice. He used to read to her extracts from classics such as Forster's 'A Room With A View', and she would swoon in the romance of Italian culture.

The boy was going to miss her. He was going to miss her laughter, the warmth of this house, and the welcoming smells of her cooking. He was under no illusion that tonight would probably be his last, and as he sat on the bottom step of the stairs taking off his shoes, a troubled-looking Mrs Jones came from the light to greet him.

"Don't know if you've heard? Big-Lloyd's had to rush home! Poor boy, his father has been taken seriously ill. Oh, and I've had a phone call from the police station. Some girl called Bella? They've got to come out and check your room, make sure that it's all in order. Seemingly it's protocol because I'm a new landlady."

She shrugged.

"Matters not to me, so I said it was okay. One of the training staff, someone called Stuart, is coming here at nine tomorrow morning. She said he could come later if nine was too early, but I'd rather get it out of the way. At least I won't have to hang around waiting: I can pop out after if needs be."

The sparkle was back in her eyes and she wagged a finger at the Cadet.

"So you make sure that room's tidy before you go off to work in the morning. Oh, and do Big Lloyd's half as well. Otherwise, they'll be getting Pickfords in to ship you out — no more Eve's pudding for you then, young man."

She chuckled as she strode back into the kitchen, knowing full well that she'd end up doing it. She wanted to anyway — it had to be right. Those two lads were a breath of fresh air: she couldn't imagine her life without them.

The boy felt sick — what had he done? She's such a lovely person. She treated him and Lloyd like she would her own family, and look what he's gone and done to repay her kindness. No wonder Lloyd's gone home. Something wrong with his dad? Yeah, right, he's making sure he's not around when the proverbial shit hits the fan. He rested his head in the palms of his hands, muttering to himself.

"I can't say that I blame him though. He didn't sign up for any of this crap, did he? It's my call, and it's my problem to sort out."

He was chewing on his nails when he joined Mrs Jones in the heat of the kitchen. No more money had gone missing from his room, and he was concerned that maybe he'd rushed into confiding with Dai Insignificant — should he have left it a while longer?

The telephone rang and Mrs Jones slipped off one of the oven gloves.

"Who can this be at this time of night? Aren't families sitting down and enjoying a meal? I was just about to dish out."

Eyeing the clock again, she tutted, and her tone of voice was sharp.

"Good evening, Carmarthen 2149, Mrs Edith Jones speaking. How can I..."

A warmth replaced the sharpness.

"...Oh, hello, Detective Sergeant."

She glanced in the oval-shaped mirror, tidying her hair with her free hand.

"Yes, Lloyd is here, and he's just about to tuck into homemade steak pie and mashed potatoes. I'll get him for you now."

Grinning mischievously, she held out the telephone, raised her voice, and spoke like the Queen of England.

"Lloyd, dear, it's Detective Sergeant Winters."

Mixed emotions swept through the Cadet as he took hold of the receiver. Joy that his landlady was back to her playful best, sadness that it would definitely be short-lived, and an overwhelming feeling of dread.

'What the hell is so important that Dai feels it necessary to be phoning him at this time of the evening? The sting is all planned and ready to go. Surely it's not being cancelled?'

"Hi Sarge — it's Phyllis."

"Alright, Lloyd Dear..." he chuckled, "...sorry to delay your feast on homemade pie and mash, but I've just come off the phone to Detective Inspector Pat Muldoon. I thought you'd want to know why he rang — maybe the news will cheer you up a bit. The police in Liverpool have found the body, well what's left of it, of a Mr Barry George Murphy."

The boy, struggling to curtail an almighty sigh of relief, looked up and mouthed towards the ceiling — 'Thank you, Lord.'

"W wow, w what happened, Sarge?"

"I don't know all the facts, only what Pat has been told, which isn't a lot. Seemingly, they received a tip-off as to the location of the body, and this afternoon it has been identified as the missing person. Unfortunately, this is good news for Price but not for you. The pathologist's examination of the remains suggests he was badly beaten about the head and torso with quite a few blunt instruments. Indicating that there were several attackers. If Price stays schtum, like he has been to date, there's no way the prosecution will be able to pin a murder charge on him. This means he won't get such a long sentence.

How do you feel about that?"

The Cadet was ecstatic, fantastic news, and no mention of the shooting of the Rastafarian either. That suggests the police in Liverpool haven't linked his death with Beef's tip-off. He took a deep breath before speaking, using the pause to rid any joyful emotion that might be in his voice.

"Never mind, Sarge. It's good news for Murphy's family. At least they can stop fretting now and be able to start grieving. Not so good for me though…"

He sighed and lowered his voice, conscious that Mrs Jones would be ear-wigging.

"…but, as I mentioned earlier, I don't think there is a problem anymore between Mikey and me."

The Detective Sergeant was shaking his head in bewilderment. 'That boy will never cease to amaze me — always thinking of others.'

"Well, that's very admirable of you — I'm impressed. Enjoy your pie and mash, Lloyd Dear, and I'll see you tomorrow morning."

CHAPTER 44

Tomorrow morning couldn't come soon enough; the Cadet had opened the curtains, made his bed, and tidied the room. Everything was in its place, so there was no reason for Mrs Jones to fuss around. Hopefully, all she'd do is have a cursory glance to check that it would pass the 'police inspection.'
He'd been going over the plan as he readied himself for work.
Dai Insignificant had cleared the sting with the Detective Chief Superintendent, who had authorised the signing out of four five-pound notes from petty cash.
Phyllis had two of them and had already placed them in position on top of the small chest of drawers — weighted down by spare change. Stuart had the others, and they had been dipped in the invisible compound and were hanging in his dark room, drying out.
Part one of Stuart's plan, the duping of Mrs Jones by Bella, had worked, and Stuart was confident that part two would be just as successful.
Stuart and Dai had decided to plant not one but two treated five-pound notes, and the reasoning for that course of action was that the bigger the temptation, the more likelihood of a result. Also, they were mindful that if two notes were put on display but only one had been treated with the compound, there was a distinct possibility that the thief could choose the untreated one.

Prior to the treatment, Stuart had recorded the serial numbers and cleansed both notes, thereby removing all historical fingerprints. The next person to handle them with gloveless fingers should be the thief, and from that moment on, they would have a window of several hours to identify and apprehend the culprit.

Guilt was eating away at him, and he was struggling to chat like usual with Mrs Jones over breakfast. She was banging on about how pale and shattered he looked. And how he'd done too much over the weekend: mixing concrete with his dad and erecting a new fence when he should have been resting on his days off. The lies were spewing out of his mouth in response to her innocent yet probing questions, and he was fearful that she might cotton on that something else was untoward if the questions continued.

He breathed a sigh of relief when he escaped from the house unscathed, and it was only when he was nearing the town centre that his mind started working overtime.

'What if the thief takes the fiver or both of the fivers before Stuart gets there and does the exchange?'

"Shit, they hadn't thought of that, had they?"

Mrs Jones had commented earlier about how pale and tired he looked, so should he go back and feign illness? Once Stuart arrived, he could have a remarkable recovery and head off to work? Great idea — he'll do that.

He started jogging back to his lodgings but stopped abruptly.

"Hang on a sec — Mrs Jones will telephone work to tell them that I'm ill, and Stuart won't bother coming. There would be no point, would there? Yeah, this is a bad idea — it could spoil everything, and exactly the same problem would exist on the next occasion."

He turned around but only got to roughly the same point when another thought stopped him in his tracks.

'What if Mrs Jones notices the money and moves it somewhere safe? She might think that it's too much of a temptation for the copper who was coming to inspect the room? Hell, what if she

is the thief and takes one or both of the fivers before Stuart gets there? She could deny being the thief and blame the theft on Stuart. Especially if she'd left him in the room on his own.'
He clasped his head in his hands.
"Stop thinking all this stuff!"

*

It's 09:45 — the Cadet is sat in the canteen, and he has a bird's-eye view of the entrance. Stuart shouldn't be long; he's bound to call in for a cuppa, and the boy can find out if everything went according to plan?
He'd spent the last hour or so helping out Clive: updating criminal record cards, and while pulling a face like he'd just bitten into a sour grape, the Detective Constable had mouthed to him the reason for his twin brother's absence.
"Buttons has got a dose of the shits! Poor bugger was stuck to the bog all night long."
Grimacing while leaning back in his chair to monitor the comings and goings along the busy corridor, a concerned Clive slowly shook his head, sighed through pursed lips, and lowered his voice to a whisper.
"Best you stay at home with your arse next to the pan!"
He tapped the tip of his nose and winked.
"That's what I advised this morning."
He paused to stand up and poke his head into the corridor before pushing the door into the frame. Still whispering, he placed a hand on his abdomen, gave it a rub, and shook his head.
"You never know, Phyllis, it could be a contagious stomach bug. And the last thing anyone needed in this bloody place was an epidemic like that running, excuse the pun, through the office staff."
Phyllis had slipped away. The enticing aroma of freshly grilled bacon was wafting up to the offices, and Clive had given him the green light, handing him some change.
"Bring me back some of that pig. White bread, not that shite with seeds, and make sure it's smothered in brown sauce."

He grinned.

"And grab one for yourself."

The canteen was filling up, and Phyllis checked his watch again. It was nearing 10.

"Where the hell is Stuart? Has something gone wrong?"

A long queue had formed, and it was nearly out into the corridor when the scenes-of-crime officer tagged onto the end. He was deep in conversation with another man, someone who Phyllis had never set eyes on before, and the presence of the stranger stopped the Cadet from rushing straight over. He chose instead to raise his hand and wave: it worked. Stuart's nod of the head, a reassuring smile, and a thumbs-up relieved the boy's anxiety. He could relax — the trap was set.

Suddenly, he was ravenous and he joined the queue for the hot bacon sarnies. Laughing, joking, and flirting with the canteen staff; fooling around with the girls from the offices as if he didn't have a care in the world. And at that precise moment in the youngster's life, he didn't. A heavy weight had just been lifted from his shoulders.

Less than one hour had passed, though, before the demons returned and his mind was plagued with questions. What, if anything, was happening to the two dodgy fivers?

Subconsciously, he was tapping a record card against his puffed-out cheek, and each time it connected, a gust of air spurted from his lips. This, in tandem with his fingers strumming against the desktop, was driving the man alongside him nuts.

Clive was striving to compile an urgent statistical update for the Detective Chief Superintendent: one which should have been in his in-tray by close of play yesterday, and the frustration was building to a crescendo. Buttons, the master of report writing, was halfway through it yesterday afternoon when the sudden rumblings and gripes in his stomach made him writhe around in agony. The outcome was him waddling to the gents like Donald Duck with his hand clutching at the seat of his pants.

"Those bloody field-picked mushrooms, Clive. Gone right through me, and my guts feel like they're being stabbed by a thousand needles. I can't risk it anymore: one absent-minded fart, and I'll no doubt follow through... I'm going to have to go home."

The formulation of intricate reports was not one of the elder twin's
attributes: especially one that was already late and would be meticulously scrutinised by Mr Scrupulous himself. He had read the same sentence over and over again, and the constant tapping, and blowing like a blue whale, was interfering with his concentration. The outburst through gritted teeth was inevitable.

"For Christ's sake, Phyllis, if you don't file that f...ing card — I'll ram it up your f...ing arse!"

It brought the Cadet to his senses.

"S s s sorry, Clive. I I I've got something on my mind. Is it okay if I take an early lunch?"

Clive sprang from his seat, opened the door, and dramatically gestured to the corridor.

"Be my guest — best idea you've had all bloody morning — bugger off to wherever youngsters go and give me a chance to finish writing this bleedin' report!"

CHAPTER 45

He didn't need to be told twice: the Cadet was out through the office door and gone. In less than thirty minutes, he would be able to find out if any or both of the five-
pound notes had been interfered with.
He had to check it out — didn't he? Yes, it would put his mind at rest. But what if it ruined the plan?
The torment commenced.
'No point in going there yet, boy: it's much too early. Wait till at least mid-afternoon. If they are going to be nicked today, then they'd definitely be gone by then.'
'Maybe it's not too early though. Maybe they've gone already, and the only way to know for sure is to see for yourself. And, if there has been a theft, it will give Dai more time to arrange the troops.'
'But what if you spook the thief by coming back in the middle of the day? Hell, the thief could be there now. You'll be in deep shit with Dai and Stuart for wasting their time. You'll have ruined the whole plan.'
'Yes, but what if a fiver has gone? What if they've both gone? Better to act sooner rather than later — isn't it?'
Phyllis had to take the chance: his armpits were sodden and exuding that stale, pungent odour of nervous energy. The not knowing was driving him loopy, and his ability to rationally process information was rapidly diminishing.

Still battling the demon, he reached the steps leading up to his lodgings, and it was then that he spotted a familiar-looking car parked on the opposite side of the road.
"Hang on a sec — that's Molly's car."
His head pushed forward.
"I'm sure that's the car that Mrs Jones was driving the other night. It is — it's Molly's car. What the hell is one of the prime suspects doing here? More importantly — what the hell should I do now?"
Having a battle with one's inner self is exhausting, and there is no winner. Only extreme mental torture for the individual. Hence, the trauma resulting from a person's inability to rationally regulate their thoughts can sometimes lead to that person making a rash decision. The Cadet made one.
Overheating, he unclipped his tie, undid the top button on his shirt, and took the flight of concrete steps two at a time.
A paving stone path, bordering a lawn, led to the front door, and it branched off to the right where it met the house, running beneath the large window of the 'L'-shaped lounge/dining room towards the boundary of the premises next door.
Stooping to get out of the line of sight of any 'suspects,' he scurried like an orangutan across the damp grass before dropping to his hands and knees to shuffle beneath the sill of the picture window. He cursed as tiny shards of stone bit into his skin, and only at that point did he realise that his haste had led him to a predicament. How was he going to raise his head above the sill? He needed to know what they were doing inside — that was paramount, but before he could set eyes on them, they would see the top of his head. Unless that is, nobody in the room was looking towards the window. Could he take that chance?
He sat cross-legged, panting and with sweat trickling down his spine. Closing his eyes to calm his breathing, he pictured Robbo and Dai Insignificant; they were laughing at him — shaking their heads in disbelief.
What the hell was he doing? More to the point, what did he

expect to see Molly and Mrs Jones doing? Did he think that they'd be waving five-pound notes above their heads while hopping up and down on the Axminster? Doing an Irish jig and belting out: 'We're in the money.'

An attention-seeking clearing of the throat startled him: disrupting his thought cycle, and his head spun towards the sound. Frantically, his eyes strained through the patchy beech hedge separating next door's garden, but there was no sign of anybody, and he was just about to carry on with the planning of his next move when an older male voice came from above.

"Morning, nice day for it?"

A hand shot to cover his mouth, but it was way too slow to stifle the shocked exclamation: "Shit — who the hell is that?"

His head bent backwards to an impossible angle before searching eyes could focus on their neighbour who was leering down at him from the penultimate rung of an extended ladder, clasping a paintbrush in his free hand and clinging on with the other. Why had he not spotted it up against the roof guttering when he arrived? He knew why — too preoccupied with what one of the prime suspects was doing at the scene of the crimes. He gathered some composure, forced a grin, waved a pathetic, limp-wristed hand of acknowledgement, and whispered.

"Yes indeed, Mr. Swisson, a perfect day for painting."

It was the look of bafflement on his neighbour's face, together with the awkwardness created by an overlong silence, that spurred the boy into speaking again and accounting for his bizarre behaviour.

"We are playing a game of hide-and-seek, and Mrs Jones doesn't know that I'm here. I'd better get on."

Mr Swisson felt the need to reciprocate the whisper.

"Oh, right — Lloyd, isn't it?"

Phyllis nodded.

"Well, Lloyd, I'm sorry if I startled you and maybe gave the game away. Brilliant fun, eh? Takes me back to playing with my own children…"

He paused to think.

"...but they were only seven or eight back then."
Waving the paintbrush at him and chuckling.
"Hey, but you're never too old, are you? Good on you, Lloyd, and good luck. Oh, and pass on my regards to Edith, won't you? Lovely lady."
The boy gestured a thumbs-up, turned away, and, sensing the neighbour's eyes boring into him, decided that he'd better do something.
Swivelling back onto his knees to face the window, he slowly inched his scalp to sill level, then stopped in his tracks.
"You can't do it this way — it's ridiculous. Imagine what it must look like to those on the inside of the house."
He pictured the scene. A head slowly appearing into view, like Punch sneaking up on Judy, and all that would be missing was a bunch of 5-year-olds, pointing and screaming out.
"He's behind you. Look — he's behind you."
He checked out Mr Swisson, and the neighbour's eyes were concentrating on the painting job. Good — the boy could relax and crawl back towards the front door. Once past the window, he'd be able to stand up and sneak a peek without it appearing so suspicious if spotted by anyone inside.
The stealth wasn't required, and what he saw kick-started the rest of the day's events. Not only were Molly and her mother sitting around the dining table and engrossed in conversation; they were in company with a doppelgänger for Molly — it had to be April. Molly was crying, and Mrs Jones was comforting her. April was sitting opposite Molly, her arm outstretched and holding onto her sister's hand. Amidst them were two white sheets of A4 and on top of those were two blue-coloured pieces of paper: the same size and shape as five-pound notes.
With his heart beating like a rock breaker, he forgot where he was, edged to the centre of the window, and pressed his nose up against the glass.
"Shit, are they my five-pound notes? They look like five-pound notes. Bloody hell — they've got my five-pound notes!"
At that precise moment, an old banger of a car rattled past

the house and backfired. The Cadet didn't react as fast as the women did, and his nose was still squashed up against the window pane when their heads spun around. Three pairs of eyes glared at him as if he were some kind of perverted voyeur, and two seconds too late, he ducked out of their view.

"Shit! Why did I just do that? Why didn't I do something normal like smile and wave? What was the point in ducking out of sight when they had clearly seen me?"

Thinking of an excuse, he crawled towards the door.

"Got it, I'll pretend it was all going to be one big prank. I'll tell them I was going to bang on the window to startle them, but the backfire of that bloody banger spoilt it."

Belly laughing, he opened the door into the warmth of the house and shouted out.

"I was going to knock on the window to surprise you, but that backfire spoilt it. I'm bursting for the loo. I'll join you for a cuppa when I come down."

Kicking off his shoes, he took the stairs two at a time and paused on the landing — chewing at his fingernails.

'Molly is here and so is April. Together with Mrs Jones, they are the prime suspects: the three people who had access to the bedroom when the money was stolen on the first occasion. If those two pieces of blue paper on that dining table are the treated five-pound notes, then they must be in it together.'

Heightened senses pick out the swishing sounds from the door skimming across raised carpet fibres as it glided into the bedroom, and chancing his luck for a second time in as many days, he closed his eyes and prayed.

"Please, God, help us catch the thief, but let it be somebody else. Not Mrs Jones or her daughters."

He opened his eyes and they were gone — both of them — the sting had worked!

Mixed thoughts whirled around inside his head: should he be elated or devastated? Whatever the outcome of the next few hours, he knew that there would only be one certainty: he and Lloyd would not be sleeping in this room ever again. Watery eyes looked down onto Lloyd's empty bed, then over to his own, and happy memories flooded his head. He bit at his bottom lip.

"Don't you cry, Phyllis — don't you bloody cry."

He slapped his cheeks.

"Come on — snap out of it. You've got to be strong: the person who has been stealing your money is probably sitting downstairs laughing at you. Get a bloody grip."

Mrs Jones shouted from the kitchen.

"Come on, Lloyd, your coffee is going cold. April is here and she's dying to meet you. And she's brought some carrot cake."

'What should he do?'

"Shit, shit, shit. They've probably moved the five-pound notes out of sight. I can't go in there: my body language will give me away."

He glanced at his roommate's bed again, and a brief smile battered through.

"Flippin' hell — if Lloyd was here now, he'd want to eat the bloody carrot cake first! I know what I'll do."

He grabbed the leftover change, ran down the stairs, picked up his shoes, and shouted out while opening the door.

"I've forgotten something really important at work, Mrs Jones — I won't be long."

Muting the probable reply by slamming the door behind him, he jogged down the steps, sat out of sight on the pavement, and forced on his shoes.

"There's a kiosk at the bottom of the hill — I'll phone Dai from there."

CHAPTER 46

"Criminal statistics, De—"
"They've gone, Sarge, b both of them, and the thief is in the house now; d drinking coffee and eating b bloody carrot cake. I I didn't know what to do."
The Detective Sergeant didn't have to draw on his many years of experience to deduce the identity of the excitable caller.
"Woah, slow down, Phyllis, and take a deep breath, or we'll both end up in bloody casualty clutching our chests. Now, start again and speak slower this time."
The urgency was still in the voice.
"I I haven't got any more ch change Sarge, s so the p p pips are going to go soon."
There's a noticeable frustration in the Detective's voice.
"Where are you? Y y — bloody hell you've got me at it now! You say that both five-pound notes are gone, and the suspects are in the house now?"
"Y Yes Sarge, M M Molly, her sister April, and Mrs Jones. I I think they are all involved"
Peep peep peep—
"W Water street — I I'm in W Water Street, S S—"
Peeeeeep.
The Detective Sergeant replaced the handset and immediately picked it up again. His finger dialled 324. The phone was ringing, but no one was answering.

"Come on — come on — pick up the bloody phone."
"Sergeant's office, Sergeant Lew—"
"Henry — it's Dai Insignificant. Can you get a panda to meet me at the side entrance ASAP? Got a bit of a delicate incident going down just off Water Street, and the Bobby might have to make an arrest. Oh shit, we're going to need a female as well. Not urgent at the minute, but can you get a PW on standby?"
The old head of a beat sergeant knew better than to ask any questions.
"Consider it done, Dai."
The Detective Sergeant dialled another extension.
"Scenes of Crime, Stu —"
"Stuart — we're on. The two fivers have been lifted, and young Phyllis is waiting for us in Water Street; the suspects are in the house now. Meet me by the side entrance: I've got a panda on standby."
"Blood hell, Dai — that was quick: they've barely had time to dry!"
He was chuckling.
"I'll grab my kit — see you downstairs."
The Panda was ticking over as the Detective Sergeant and Stuart jumped in.
The probationary constable could sense the urgency in the supervisor's voice.
"Right, son — hit the blue lights and use that bloody horn. We need to be in Water Street and in double quick time."
The little Morris 1100 wheel spun away from the kerb towards a sharp bend at the crest of a steep hill which led down to the main A40. The sudden acceleration forced the Detective Sergeant back into his seat and instinctively he grabbed hold of the seat belt.
"Bloody Hell, Stirling Moss — watch this blind bend — it's a bastard."
Stuart was laughing in the back, and the Detective Sergeant spotted the smirk on the young driver's face.
"Go on then, what's so bloody hilarious? What's tickled you

pair?"
It was the scenes of crime officer that answered.
"I would imagine Chris has driven at speed down this hill a few times, Sarge."
Dai hadn't taken his eyes off him.
"Oh well, no disrespect, sonny boy, but you only look about 15."
The constable was laughing.
"No problem, Sarge, you've got to wind these buggers up, or you won't get anywhere fast. What part of Water Street are we heading for?"
The Detective Sergeant shook his head and shrugged.
"Damned if I know yet, why? Does it make a difference?"
"It's a one-way street, Sarge. Starting from Lammas Street by the Monument, until it reaches Saint Catherine Street. From that junction, it's two way. To avoid the heavy traffic in the town centre, it's easier to join it at the Saint Catherine Street junction, but at that point, it's No Entry to all vehicles wanting to go towards Lammas Street."
Dai sucked on the Calabash.
"Shit — do you know of a telephone box around there?"
The uniformed copper changed down as the Panda approached the major road.
"Yes, Sarge, there's one on that very junction."
He tapped the windscreen with the stem.
"Go for that, son — go for that."
The main road was busier than usual, and Pandas don't have sirens: that luxury was reserved solely for the souped-up patrol cars driven by specially trained Traffic Officers. Yes, the blue light was flashing, the horn was blasting and the headlights were on full beam, but the motorists didn't notice.
Dai was losing patience.
"Typical — we're going to be stuck here until next bloody week!"
The young driver intervened.
"Would you mind if I do a little risky manoeuvre, Sarge? It's the only way we're going to get anywhere fast."

The grip was tightened on the seatbelt.

"Go for it, sonny — do what you have to do."

He increased the revs on the engine.

"Put your hand on the horn, Sarge, and close your eyes."

Chris floored the accelerator, handbrake turned onto the filter, and the little car hurtled against the oncoming traffic towards the junction where they needed to turn right.

The older officer clasped his hands together in prayer.

"Oh my God, we're all going to die — where the hell did you learn to drive like this?"

The youngster didn't take his eyes from the road.

"Back roads of Carmarthen, Sarge. I've got a 1964 Mini Cooper S with HS2 carbs, roll cage — the works. It's a brilliant rally car — you'll have to come with me for a spin sometime."

Dai bit onto the stem of the Calabash as he shouted.

"Listen, sonny, the only carbs I know anything about come in a hefty dollop of mashed potatoes. I'll stick with my Volvo Estate, thank you very much."

Less than a minute later, they were nearing the telephone kiosk and couldn't miss the animated Police Cadet waving his arms around and jumping up and down like a shipwrecked survivor on a desert island.

Dai was quick to take the mickey.

"Pull up there, Chris — alongside Robinson bloody Crusoe."

The sarcasm flew over the young officer's head, but Stuart was cracking up in the back and enjoying the moment.

Dai Insignificant was on top form. Loving every precious second of his time with these much younger officers, and the feelings were mutual. They cherished every possibility to feed off his experience. The Detective Sergeant was as important to them as they were to him. They wanted to be in his company and they thrived off his confidence, his know-how, and his maturity. Aspiring to one day be something like him.

The Police Service has a conveyor belt of characters, finely honed from years of working with officers such as Dai Insignificant. Picking up the differing traits and mannerisms of many as they progress their careers to a point when they are ready to tread in the footsteps of the ones they once revered.

Stuart opened the rear door for the Cadet to squeeze in, and the Detective Sergeant spun around to speak with him.

"Right, young Phyllis, what's happened? Fill us in."

The Cadet was unsure about the driver: he'd never seen him before, and Dai could sense his reluctance to speak.

"Come on, lad, spit it out. Chris needs to be made aware of what's been happening: he might have to arrest someone as a result of the information you tell him."

He spurted out everything, and the supervisor took control.

"Okay, this is what we'll do. Stirling Moss here will taxi us up to the house, and we'll park, if we can, directly outside."

Dai turned to Phyllis, aware of his decision to protect the adolescent, but already guessing what the boy's response will be.

"You don't have to come in with us if you don't want to. You do not have to face these people, but it's your call — I'm giving you the choice."

The Cadet was nodding as the words were coming out of the Detective Sergeant's mouth; sheer determination etched into the youngster's brow.

"I want to, Sarge. It's something I need to do."

"Okay, I thought you'd say that. Chris, get on the blower, find out from your Sergeant if he's managed to organise a WPC."

"Stuart, you got everything you need in that briefcase?"

"Yes, I'm good to go. You'd be surprised what I can fit inside this little beauty."

The radio had been crackling in the meantime and Chris briefed the Detective Sergeant.

"Jos Protheroe is on standby in the Nick Sarge; just give the nod, and someone can get her up to us."

Dai was already opening the door.

"Right — we're all set to go. Gentlemen — follow me."

CHAPTER 47

Edith Jones had watched the police car arrive: her neck straining to see it squeeze into a parking space directly behind the car she'd given to Molly.

She hadn't moved from the window since her lodger ran away from the house earlier. His bizarre behaviour had been totally out of character, especially the shenanigans at the lounge window. Did he think her that gullible to believe his cock-and-bull story? And his over-the-top laughing police man stunt? Dearie, dearie me, I wasn't born yesterday? No, there was something afoot. Something he couldn't tell her, and that grated on her more than anything. Yes, she hardly knew him, barely a few weeks, but during that short time, a loving relationship had blossomed. They had laughed together, cried together, and the fact that she could open up to someone so young spoke volumes of the warmth and compassion the boy possessed.

Lloyd was the son she'd never had: a boy she was proud of. Hadn't he caught the man who prematurely ended the life of her greatest love? She knew that he had a crush on Molly: no way would he miss out on the chance to flash a smile and show off in front of her. So why did he scurry away?

April was equally as gorgeous, and he had yet to meet her, but he would have noticed her beauty earlier. Again, why not pop in to say hello before rushing back to work?

Spotting the passenger door opening, Mrs Jones stepped back into the room. A very handsome, well-dressed man, in his early fifties, was getting out.

He pushed the door closed and hugged the side of the Panda car, making it easier for a van to pass him by safely. The rear door opened, and she recognised the young man getting out.

"Hey, it was he who came to inspect the boys' room this morning. That's odd — why is he coming back again? Maybe he's forgotten something."

Suddenly the nerves kicked in.

"Oh no, there's probably something wrong with the room. Maybe the handsome man is his boss, and he's come to inspect it as well."

Then she saw Phyllis getting out of the back: his face looking anxious and pale. She clasped her hand to her mouth — butterflies tearing around inside her tummy.

"I'm right — there is something wrong with the room. It's not suitable, probably too small. I knew I should have given them April's room. Lloyd is here to say goodbye, and he will take Big Lloyd's stuff away with him as well."

She didn't want them to go: she loved their company and she loved being their weekday mum.

"Oh please God, let everything be okay. Please don't take my boys away, like you took my Bernie."

Mrs Jones hadn't noticed the presence of the young uniformed officer: she'd rushed from the window, and while checking her appearance in the hall mirror, the shrill tone of the doorbell startled her. The shiver was still pulsing through her core as she took a deep, composing breath, smoothed a stray hair into place, and forced a smile as she opened the door.

The supervisory officer was first to speak.

"Mrs Edith Jones? I am Detective Sergeant Winters. This gentleman is Detective Constable Edwards, and this one is Police Constable Grey."

He nodded towards Phyllis.

"You know Cadet Davies. Is it possible that we can come in for a little chat?"

The welcoming smile had taken a downward tilt once she'd spotted the uniformed officer bringing up the rear, and in need of reassurance, her eyes sought out her lodger's. He couldn't return his landlady's gaze: the adolescent was too embarrassed, and his face was tilted towards the carpet.

'Oh my God, Lloyd can't even look at me. What on earth have I done?'

Her insides were churning, and trembling hands gripped the sides of her dress. She swallowed, trying hard to control the emotion in her voice, but her mouth was suddenly very dry. The clearing of the throat to generate some moisture failed, and the hoarseness remained.

"Yes, yes, by all means, do come in. Are you here in relation to the boys' bedroom? I know it's a little bit on the cramped side, but it's clean, comfortable, and always heated."

Moist eyes sought out the Cadet's — desperate for any sign of solace.

"You've never complained, have you, Lloyd? And neither has Big Lloyd. And both boys love my cooking."

She was twittering on, her brain becoming suddenly very fuzzy as she struggled to stem the tears.

'Oh, Bernie, where are you, my precious love?'

Phyllis couldn't look at her: desperately wishing that this wasn't happening. She obviously didn't have a clue about the stolen money, and if Molly or April had taken it, then why the hell are they still here?

Mrs Jones led them through the kitchen and into the dining area; her face drawn, the lines under her eyes accentuated, and tears spilling onto her cheeks.

She tried to smile.

"These are my two daughters, Molly and April. You haven't met April, Lloyd. You keep on missing each other."

Both were standing with hands on hips; their eyes glaring at the police officers. They'd managed to pick out titbits of the conversation and were alarmed to see the tears rolling towards their mother's mouth.

It was Molly who posed the questions; her voice teeming with anger.

"What the hell's going on? Why are you here? Lloyd, what have you done?"

Placing a protective hand on the Cadet's shoulder, the Detective Sergeant ignored the daughter.

"Mrs Jones, there is nothing wrong with the size of the boys' bedroom: that's not why we are here. We are here because somebody has been stealing money from their bedroom."

She shouted out in surprise.

"What! Money is being stolen from his room? Ridiculous! Lloyd, you haven't said anything about this to me. Why haven't you come to me? Why won't you even look at me?"

Realising that he'd made a huge mistake by bringing the youngster into the house, the Detective Sergeant raised an upturned palm before answering.

"Mrs Jones, this has been very awkward for him — he's been in turmoil: not knowing what to do or whom he could trust."

Both hands rose to rest on her heart, tears flowing freely.

"But Lloyd, surely you can trust me? You don't think I would steal money from you, do you? I've welcomed you into my home with open arms. Why would I do such a thing? Why would I jeopardise this arrangement? I've never stolen anything in my life..."

The hands moved to cover her face.

"...this is all so upsetting."

Once again it was the Detective Sergeant who replied.

"Mrs Jones, we are not saying that it's you. It could be anyone who visits your house and has access to Lloyd's bedroom."

The Cadet's eyes hadn't strayed from the carpet, and in his arc of vision were the dining table legs, a black-coloured leather shoulder bag, and a pair of navy-blue suede boots. The wearer of those boots was surreptitiously kicking the shoulder bag further underneath the table.

Furtively, he raised his head to check out the tabletop and steal

a glance at the two sisters standing on the other side.
Mrs Jones didn't miss this eye deviation.
"Molly? You think Molly would steal from you? Oh, Lloyd, I'm very disappointed in you, and I'm surprised that you couldn't tell me first before blabbing to your Detective Sergeant Winters."
She turned towards Dai.
"We spoke the other afternoon, Sergeant, if you recall. You telephoned to speak with Lloyd: you wanted him to return to work..."
She splayed her arms out in front of her.
"... was this the reason for his urgent summons to Police Headquarters? So you could plan this — what do you people call it — RAID on my house?"
Dai Insignificant sensed a situation arising that required nipping in the bud, and once more an upturned palm was held out.
"Woah, this has gone far enough. The boy is only 16 years old — let's not forget that. And over the past week or so, someone has stolen four five-pound notes from his bedroom. He was unable to tell you about it, Mrs Jones, because he didn't want to spoil the special relationship that you have. He didn't even tell me about it until a few days ago. So the answer to your question is no. That's not why I phoned here the other afternoon. The reason for that call was to discuss the apprehension of a certain Mikey Price: a person you are now well aware of. It is impossible for both Lloyds to continue living here in these circumstances: not knowing who is stealing the money. Lloyd had been placed in a very awkward position, and quite rightly, he came to me."
Molly removed a hand from her hip and wagged an accusing finger towards the Detective Sergeant.
"Well, it could be Big Lloyd, couldn't it? It seems strange that he's suddenly not here. Father seriously ill? Yeah, like that is true. He's done a runner, hasn't he? It's obviously him!"
The Detective Sergeant was calm, collected, and in control. He

flourished on confrontation, and shooting down theories was bread and butter to him. The three suspects didn't stand a chance.

"Young lady, before you cast any more wicked aspersions on the character of somebody who is not here to defend themselves, perhaps you should listen to what I have to tell you. Big Lloyd, as you refer to him, is at home in Cardigan, and he is doing some work for me. I arranged for him to go home yesterday. I wanted him to be well away from this toxic environment. He needed my protection from malicious and unfounded accusations such as you are implying.

Mrs Jones, you have given them a comfortable home away from their families, but they are not safe here: someone is stealing from their room. It is our job to catch the person responsible, and I have protected Big Lloyd by taking him completely out of the equation. Money has been stolen from the room this morning, and Big Lloyd couldn't have committed that crime, could he? He was safely at home with his parents — well away from the extreme sadness that this awful situation is creating."

Impressed and unable to hide the look of surprise on his face, Phyllis glanced up at his supervisor.

'Wow, Dai, you kept that one close to your chest: you didn't even tell me. What a genius move to make.'

He recalled the supervisor's words of advice and his own response during the pep talk just a matter of days ago.

'If you want something to remain private, then don't tell anybody else.

I've never forgotten that. There's only one person that you can wholeheartedly trust to keep your secret, and who might that be, young man?'

'Well, going by what you're saying, Sarge, it can only be yourself.'

CHAPTER 48

That peep across the table had told the Cadet all he needed to know.

The wearer of the navy-blue-coloured suede boots was April, and the two white sheets of A4 paper were an official letter from a local firm of solicitors. The smaller, blue-coloured pieces of paper were no longer visible, but the boy had a pretty good idea as to their current whereabouts...

Mrs Jones couldn't prevent the flow of tears from eyes that conveyed nothing but affection as she reached out a trembling hand.

"Lloyd, I don't know what has happened. My world has been turned upside down again, and I can't understand it. I trust every person I invite into my home, especially one who might go upstairs to use the bathroom. Why would they steal from your room? They may as well be stealing from me. Why would any guest of mine do that?"

Eager to set the wheels in motion; to move the enquiry on, and to protect the boy from being made to feel guilty about reporting the thefts, the Detective Sergeant butted in. Unfortunately, his word selection upset the landlady.

"Mrs Jones, we decided that the only sure way to successfully solve this conundrum and discover the identity of the thief was to set a trap."

The distraught widow was unable to cope with such a startling revelation and, sensing her legs buckling, slumped onto one of the kitchen chairs. Burying her face in the palms of her hands, she started to sob, and Molly rushed to console her. Everyone's eyes were on them — everyone, that is, except for Phyllis and April.

April had taken advantage of the distraction, and the Cadet's eyes were glued to the elder sister's outstretched leg: watching it kick the shoulder bag further out of sight. It was now impossible to spot unless someone bent down to search underneath the table.

Dai continued.

"Mrs Jones, this detective is a highly trained scenes of crime officer."

The widow parted her hands, revealing eyes that were black from smudged mascara, but also a deeply furrowed brow, and she pointed a finger at Stuart.

"Hang on a second, that man was here this morning — inspecting the boys' room. I was led to believe that he was a member of the training department — here to check out the new lodgings. That's what the girl told me on the telephone yesterday."

She shook her head in disappointment.

"Was wanton deceit so necessary for your trap, Detective Sergeant?"

Sighing heavily, it was a blushing Stuart who raised a hand in apology.

"Sorry about that, Mrs Jones: I needed access to the boys' room without arousing any suspicion. I came here to plant two five pound notes that had been treated with special chemicals. When someone comes into contact with them, they transfer onto the skin and leave a blue-coloured dye."

The landlady stood up and folded her arms.

"But I've been duped, surely that can't be ri—"

Seeing an awkward confrontation arising, Dai spoke over her: instantly quelling any distraction away from the material facts.

"And those two five-pound notes have already been interfered with, Mrs Jones. They are missing from the boys' bedroom — where are they — who is the thief? You have been here the whole time: you must know."

She sat down again — deflated — pleading her ignorance. Tear-sodden eyes deviating away from the Detective Sergeant's.

"I don't know. I've already told you that, Detective Sergeant Winters."

In an act of sheer contempt, Molly stepped forward; shoved her hands out in front of her and twisted them — palms up, then palms down.

"Well, where are your special chemicals, Detective? I can't see anything."

April did the same.

"And neither can I. Unless I'm going blind."

Back on track, and having no desire to have to explain how the procedure worked at this point in time, the Detective Sergeant ignored them.

"Mrs Jones, this is very important. After Stuart left your house this morning, and before Lloyd came back to check his room, has anybody else, apart from your two daughters, visited you?"

Molly answered for her mother, her arms folded high on her chest, tutting in frustration, and nodding towards Stuart.

"I was here not long after that policeman: Mum told me that he'd been here checking the room and that I'd just missed him. Nobody else could have been here: there just wasn't time. I don't understand how anyone could have taken the money."

Her gaze shifted to Phyllis, mistrust written all over her face. Lowering her voice, the tone was laced with condescension.

"Are you sure the money has gone, Lloyd? Have you checked everywhere? Are you absolutely sure that you haven't spent it?"

Dai raised his arm, indicating for the Cadet to remain silent.

"Mrs Jones, have you stolen two five-pound notes this morning from Lloyd's bedroom?"

Her eyes were closed — her mind churning over what

had happened earlier: Lloyd's irrational behaviour now made complete sense.

'The poor boy couldn't confide in me, could he? He knew that I'd have to protect Molly and April if they were involved.'

She slowly shook her head as reality hit home: there wasn't going to be a happy ending — her boys would never sleep in this house again.

Another tear escaped as she opened her eyes, faced the detectives, and held her hands out; twisting them in the same fashion as her daughters. They were moist and saddened eyes that appealed to her lodger.

"I have never and would never steal anything from anybody, let alone from you, Lloyd. You have a special place in my heart."

The adolescent managed a weak smile, fighting to stay composed. He wanted desperately to believe her, but didn't he see the two five-pound notes on the table earlier? Now surely in April's bag, which she has suspiciously kicked out of sight.

Dai intervened.

"Molly, have you been into the boy's bedroom this morning and stolen money?"

She placed an arm around her mother, resting her head on her shoulder.

"Certainly not. It would never cross my mind to steal from anybody. To be perfectly honest, I have noticed money on top of the chest of drawers a few times. You can't miss it when you're walking back along the landing from the bathroom. But even if I was that way inclined, it would be a bit of a stupid thing for me to do — don't you think?"

"April, the same question to you?"

"And the same answer to you, Sergeant — NO! This whole affair is simply ludicrous!"

"Okay ladies, we have come to the moment of truth. Have you handled the money or haven't you? One very simple test will determine whether or not you have recently been in touch with the treated money and will help to prove your innocence. Stuart informed you earlier that when the chemicals come

into contact with the skin, they leave a residue. You've shown me your hands, and to all intents and purposes, there are no signs of any contamination. Do you agree?"
Not one of them spoke, only a slight nod of the head.
"Have any of you touched the two five-pound notes that Stuart placed in Lloyd's room this morning?"
They shook their heads.
"You cannot see this residue with the naked eye. It would be a pointless exercise if you could. No doubt you'd attempt to wipe it away. But it is visible when exposed to ultraviolet light."
Three puzzled faces glanced at each other before turning to watch Stuart: monitoring his every move as he unclipped the briefcase, removed a spotlight and attached a large battery. He looked up and forced a smile.
"Any volunteers? And, before you answer, I can assure you that nobody will feel anything: exposure to the beam of light is not detrimental to your well-being."
"I'll go, first, Mum."
Molly removed her arm from around her mother and, with a petulant glare of defiance, prodded out both her hands: the palms facing up.
Phyllis's heart was hammering against his rib cage as he chewed on a thumbnail: unsure as to what outcome he wanted.
'Hell, she seems so confident.'
Stuart clicked on the light and hovered it over her outstretched hands.
There was no sign of any blue dye.
"Can you turn them over, please?"
She did as he asked, and there was nothing.
She huffed, repeatedly slapping her palms together in front of her as she turned towards her mother.
"Go on, Mum, this is a joke. A complete and utter waste of time."
April barged forward.
"I'd like to go next, Mum, if you don't mind? This whole

situation is ridiculous. Heck, I haven't even been upstairs this morning…"

She shook her body.

"…but I'm desperate for the loo now: those two mugs of coffee have gone right through me."

Phyllis's eyes widened to the size of dinner plates.

'What! No way! You're bluffing! It's you, April! You're the one who has been acting suspiciously: trying to hide your bag. The five-pound notes have got to be in there.'

Much to Molly's amusement, April dramatically flicked back her hair, tutted, and checked her wristwatch as she held out her hands — palms up.

"Please be quick, Detective, I need to visit the little girl's room."

Stuart ignored the remark — he knew that one of the three would test positive. They had to — the notes were missing, and there hadn't been any other visitors to the house. One of them was either guilty or lying.

He hovered the light, clicked it on, and there was nothing.

Glaring into Detective Sergeant Winters' eyes, April exposed the backs of her hands to the beam of light, and it was the same outcome.

As she was grinning and hoisting her right hand above her shoulder, the Cadet was shaking his head in disbelief and disappointment: why had she been acting so suspiciously? Surely, it can't be Mrs Jones?

April posed the question to the Detective Sergeant.

"Please, Sir, may I be excused?"

Dai humphed and cleared his throat.

'No doubt somebody here is lying. That smirk will soon be gone from your face, young lady.'

His response was courteous, playing along for the time being.

"Yes, madam, do as you please. And thank you for your co-operation."

Molly was chuckling, her hands gripping and massaging her mother's shoulders.

"Come on then, Mum, let's put an end to this stupid fiasco."

Giggling nervously and unable to stop her hands from trembling, Mrs Jones stood up and offered them out for the test. Her eyes heavy and her voice tired.

"They appear to have a mind of their own, don't they? Isn't it weird how one can feel so anxious, even though they know perfectly well that they are innocent?"

Stuart clicked the light back into action and hovered it over the upturned palms.

There was a definite blue hue present on the right hand — the test was positive.

Molly gasped.

"Oh my God! How can that be?"

April, yet to leave the room, had crossed her legs and was swaying from side to side when she screamed out...

"No, no, there must be a mistake: our mother wouldn't steal."

Edith Jones was shaking her head in denial: sobbing uncontrollably — her eyes transfixed on the blue dye.

"I haven't touched the money — this can't be happening."

The Cadet chewed at his bottom lip, his right hand vigorously rubbing at his chin. Desperate to rush to her and put his arm around her. Tell her that everything will be okay — that maybe her hand accidentally brushed up against the notes when she checked the room earlier?

The room went deathly quiet, and all eyes were focused on the shade of blue spotlighted by the ultraviolet beam. Shocked faces masked differing thoughts and opinions.

During the commotion, Stuart's experience had been screaming at him that something was untoward. The blue was confined solely to the edge of the palm connecting the wrist to the little finger, and that shouldn't be the case.

He kept his suspicions to himself.

"Turn your hands over, Mrs Jones. Let's check the other side."

She did so, and once more the test was positive.

More gasps and murmurings from the watchers. They could clearly see bright traces of the blue dye concentrated between the thumb and index finger of the same right hand.

She protested, her head shaking from side to side.

"I don't believe it: it's impossible — I haven't touched that money — I haven't touched it. I wouldn't steal."

Tears were bursting out from red, sodden eyes which were frantically scouring the room in desperation. Appealing for someone to believe and help her. Finally, she slumped back onto the chair.

"Please, please — will someone believe me?"

Noticing the Cadet's upset a few seconds earlier, the Detective Sergeant had been monitoring him, and spotting the movement towards his landlady, he placed a preventative hand on his shoulder. They locked eyes, and all that was necessary for the Cadet to realise that it was important for him to hold back and wait was the slightest of a negative shake of the head and the briefest of smiles.

It didn't make sense to Stuart. Yes, the blue dye confirmed contact with the chemicals, but the position of the markings was all wrong. They shouldn't be there — unless? He winked at Dai.

"Give me a minute, please, Sarge. Mrs Jones, have you changed your clothes since I was here earlier? Something about you is different."

She'd had enough, and nonchalantly pushed her open arms out towards him. Her demeanour was calm and lethargic: resigned to her fate.

"Stuart, these are the same clothes that I was wearing earlier."

Standing up, she stood with her feet apart and theatrically raised her hands above her head.

"Go on then, frisk me if you want: you won't find anything."

Wanting to reassure her daughters, she turned away from Stuart to face them, and that's when she saw it and remembered. Her finger pointed and wagged at a floral-coloured pinafore strewn behind the kettle on the kitchen worktop.

"Yes, you are right, Stuart. There was something different about me earlier. I was wearing that. I took it off as soon as you went back to the Police Headquarters."

All eyes zoomed in on the pinafore, intrigued. What was its relevance?

"Do you mind if I shine the light around the pockets in your skirt, Mrs Jones? And is there a pocket in the pinafore?"

She nodded as she spoke.

"Stuart, you can shine your light wherever you please if it helps to prove my innocence. And yes, there is a pocket in the pinafore. It's in the front.

Her hand caressed the side of her cheek, and her eyes narrowed as she glanced inquisitively down at her skirt, then over to the pinafore.

'What is he up to?'

Stuart knew something was amiss and was trying a different tack.

"Phyllis, can you grab the pinafore and put it flat out on the table so I can check around the pocket?"

The Cadet was as flabbergasted as everyone else in the room as he collected the pinafore — it should be April with stains on her hand — not Mrs Jones.

'What the hell was going on? And why did he need this bloody pinafore?'

The Detective Sergeant could see where this was leading. He'd also realised the significance of the positioning of the blue dye on her hands and had cottoned on to Stuart's thought process. These tactics were a masterpiece of kidology, and very soon, as long as the Detective Sergeant played his part, and kept a lid on the Cadet's emotions, the identity of the thief would have to be revealed.

Stuart pointed the light beam at the pockets in her skirt. There was no blue dye.

"Using your left hand, can you please empty the pockets, Mrs Jones?"

"There's nothing in them — I'll show you."

She put her hand in and pulled out the linings.

"See, they're empty."

Stuart hovered the light over the pinafore. Same result — nothing.

"Can you check the pocket, please, Phyllis?"

It was empty, and Stuart shrugged — he knew that was going to be the case.

"I thought as much, over to you, Sarge."

Dai loved it when a crime was on the verge of being detected, and credit where credit was due — Stuart had played a bloody binder.

"Edith Jones, I will ask you one more time. Did you steal the money from Lloyd's bedroom this morning?"

He held up an open palm.

"And, before you answer, I now have sufficient suspicion to believe that you are involved in the commission of an arrestable offence, so I must caution you."

Her hands came up in front of her face — her fingers covering her eyes.

'If she couldn't see him — he wasn't there.'

The Detective Sergeant's words were succinct and clear, but to the suspect, they were muffled and distant. Not even in the same room as her.

"You are not obliged to say anything unless you wish to do so, but what you say may be put into writing and given in evidence. Do you understand, Mrs Jones?"

She, Molly, and April had been reminiscing that morning, as they often did. And as always when the three of them got together, the family photograph was never too far away. Today was no exception, and there it was, taking pride of place on top of the kitchen worktop, next to the kettle. Her husband's velvet-brown eyes were alive again and smiling at her, comforting as he whispered.

'It's all going to be okay, my precious darling — I promise you.'

He gave her strength as he always did, and she smiled back at him before answering.

"I saw that there was some money on top of the chest of drawers in their room when I made sure it was clean and tidy before your detective came this morning. I don't know how much money was there because I never touched it, and I haven't been in their room since. So no, I haven't stolen any money."

The Detective Sergeant delved into the internal breast pocket of his three-piece suit — intending to add more pressure to the tense situation.

"Mrs Jones, I have a warrant here to search your house for stolen property, namely two chemically treated five-pound notes. It would save a lot of time, intrusion on your privacy, and be advantageous to you if you show me where they are."

She sighed.

"The money is not here, Detective Sergeant — how many times do I have to tell you? I never touched it."

He nodded at Stuart to take over.

"Mrs Jones, if you haven't touched those treated five-pound notes, then the only way the chemicals can be on your hands, in the position that they are, is if you were in contact with the thief immediately after the crime was committed. There is no other explanation: the blue colouring is too vivid. You haven't got any marks on your fingers, so how did you pick them up?"

She sat in silence, deep in thought — shaking her head in denial.

"There are no stains on your skirt or your pinafore. If you did manage to pick them up without the use of your fingers, then where did you put them? The first and most obvious place would be that big pocket running the entire width of your pinafore."

She looked up at him.

"How many times, Stuart, I have not touched the money? That's why there is no blue on my fingers or on my clothing."

"Then how can you account for the chemical stains on the edge of your palm and the back of your hand? Most peculiar, don't you think?

His eyes picked out Molly and April — appealing for their help.

"But not if my theory is correct. Between me leaving the house this morning and Molly's arrival, another person other than April must have visited you. Somebody you trust implicitly — somebody you hold in high esteem, a family friend maybe — somebody who, in your eyes, couldn't possibly be guilty of committing this crime. And, Mrs Jones, unbeknown to you, that person has stolen the money. You know who it is, don't you? You also know that they held your hand while saying goodbye: a farewell that passed the chemical residue from their fingers onto the bottom and back of your palm. Who are you protecting, Mrs Jones? Who is the thief? Who visits you and, while here, uses the bathroom? Used it this very morning — it is the same person who has stolen all the money."

She bowed her head, unable to continue looking at him. Her eyes once more pooled, some tears escaping and dripping to the tiled floor.

"Who is it, Mum? Tell the officer what you know."

"Yes, Mum, listen to Molly, please. If what the detective is saying is true, then you've got no option but to say. You could be arrested if you don't! Is this person worth it? No! Look at all the upset that it has caused."

Her eyes locked onto the family photograph, and she gave the most fleetest of smiles. How indebted was she to her friend for not throwing it away. What a treasure — bringing so much joy and comfort. Being able to smile at it and talk to her beloved whenever the need arose. To have Bernard among them while they chat and reminisce was a godsend, and what strength it is bringing to her now, during such traumatic circumstances.

'Charlie,' she thought, as she brushed a tear away. 'I will always be in your debt.'

She faced her daughters, embarrassed that they were looking at her in this state. A normally attractive, proud, and strong mother was now a traumatised and dishevelled mess. A faint, barely audible whisper rasped from deep within.

"I have lost my beloved husband, your father; I am going to lose both Lloyds and now it would appear I will also lose someone I believed to be a very dear friend. Somebody who, considering what he has done for me, I genuinely believed couldn't possibly steal from me."

You could hear a grain of sugar land in a ball of cotton wool. Everyone was holding their breath in anticipation of a revelation: too scared to breathe in case they missed her muted speech.

Sheepishly, her eyes sought out Dai Insignificant — his handsome face softened by a warm, compassionate smile, and she so wished that those soulful, empathetic eyes were not focusing on her in this sorrowful state.

Slightly tilting her head to one side, a coy smile broke out as she spoke.

"I've been a very silly woman, haven't I, Detective Sergeant Winters? A very blinkered, vulnerable, and most certainly naïve woman."

She paused, took a deep breath, and sighed. The emotion increasing in her voice as the words passed her lips.

"He's not my friend though, is he? Of course, he's not — he can't be, can he? Nobody would do such a wicked act to a friend, and the sad thing is, I trusted him implicitly."

Reaching for the tissues, she dabbed away the tears from her cheeks, and the attractive, young widow's eyes glistened as she reminisced.

"Thinking back, there was always a threat, but the threat was made with humour so it didn't actually seem like a threat. This morning, for example, just before he left, there was a threat.

'Don't tell anyone that I come here, Mrs Jones. I don't want my Alice finding out that I'm guzzling bacon sarnies in your house when I'm supposed to be on a diet.'

But at the same time, he puffed out his cheeks, pursed his lips and blew out a load of air. Then he forced his tummy out: making it look huge which made me giggle.

Gradually the threats increased, you know, became more serious: more consequential.

'If my Sergeant ever found out that I come here, he would put his foot down and stop me calling. I'd never be able to see you

again, Mrs Jones.'
As he was speaking, he was performing a stamping action with his right foot and limping around the kitchen with a funny grimace on his face. It was hysterical..."
She laughed through the tears — chewing on a nail.
"So, I never did tell anyone about my funny and caring visitor.
Traumatised eyes picked out her two daughters.
"Not even you, my beauties. I'm so sorry — I've been ever so lonely since your father was taken from us. Tony was like a breath of fresh air. We'd become such close friends, and I didn't want to lose his company. I didn't want to believe it was him. Up until the very last moment, I wanted to protect him; hoping that Lloyd would suddenly realise where the two five-pound notes were, and then everything could return to normal."
She gently shook her head, those pitiful eyes now appealing to Dai Insignificant.
"And policemen don't steal, do they, Detective Sergeant Winters?"

CHAPTER 49

It was Chris who broke the silence.
"She's on about Carrots, Sarge. Carrots has a wife called Alice, and he's working a day shift today. Are you on about Tony O'Sullivan, Mrs Jones? Was he here, in your house this morning?"
She gazed at the much younger officer and suddenly felt very old.
'Why do all police officers look like they should still be at school nowadays?'
Her response was laboured, her words slurred — her voice broken.
"Yes, officer. He comes here most mornings when he's on an early turn. I get him the best back bacon from the indoor market, and he loves it: thickly sliced with a smattering of English mustard. Reckons it slides down into his tummy without touching the sides."
The chuckle was short-lived as she recalled the scenes of crime officer's words, and a scowl momentarily blighted her beauty.
"And yes, Stuart, you are right. He always visits the bathroom before he goes: reckons he's got a weak bladder, and the tea runs right through him. He said that he should cut out the middleman and just pour the full mug straight down the loo."
The scowl melted away, and she chuckled.
"I was always a happier person following his visit. No matter

how depressed I had been feeling, he was able to raise my spirits with a joke, a funny story, or sometimes just acting the fool."

The chuckle shifted to a cynical laugh.

"He's played me for an OLD fool, though, hasn't he? A lonely woman whom he could charm with his gift of the gab and his ginger curls: strikingly handsome, hiding behind that smart police uniform of his. And yes, Stuart, he always holds my hand before he leaves, and he kisses me on the cheek. I will miss him."

"Chris, pass me that bloody radio! ....Detective Sergeant Winters to control, over."

He was answered immediately.

"Go ahead, Dai."

"Remind me of the phone number here, Phyllis?"

"2149, Sarge."

"Henry, can you please telephone me on 2149?"

"Will do, Dai."

The phone started to ring.

"Do you mind Mrs Jones?"

Past caring, she shook her head and the Detective Sergeant went into the passageway, pulled the door ajar and picked up the telephone.

"Henry — that job I was telling you about. The one involving the Cadet. We have a suspect, but you're not going to like who it is — he's one of yours."

The reply could be heard in the kitchen.

"ONE OF MINE?"

"Yes, Henry, he's one of yours — it's Tony O'Sullivan."

Dai lowered his voice, but it was a pointless exercise: anything above mute would have sounded like he was speaking through a megaphone.

"Bloody arsewipe has gone rogue, Henry. Can you give him a shout and find out where he is? I'll hang on."

Chris's walkie-talkie crackled into life.

"989 — 989 from Control — over."

There was no reply, and the police sergeant tried again.

"989 from control — come in, Carrots."

The tension among the listeners was tangible; they were willing the policeman to answer his radio. They wanted to hear his voice, find out where he was, desperate for him to be apprehended.

Again, there was no reply from the suspect, and it was another officer's voice who broke the silence.

"Control from 609, over."

"Go ahead to control, Arthur."

"I saw Carrots about five minutes ago, Sarge. He was entering the bookies on the Main Street. The new one, you know, next to Pack and Go Travel Agents."

"Okay, Arthur, thanks for that. Nothing important — I'll try him again later on."

The beat sergeant was back on the telephone.

"You got that, Dai? It would appear our boy has got a bit of a problem."

"Thanks, Henry, grand job, mate. Carrots better hope he's backed a winner: he's going to need every bloody penny. Do you mind if we hang on to Chris for a bit longer? We'll be contactable via the pocket-set if you get an update. And can you ask Jos to stand down, please? Thankfully, we won't be requiring her assistance."

"No problem, Dai, consider it done. And by the way, I know Edith Jones and her late husband, Bernard. We were in school together. A lovely family who don't deserve all this grief. Tell her how sorry I am."

"Will do, Henry."

Mrs Jones didn't need telling. She'd overheard the conversation, and the weak smile and nod of the head said it all.

Dai took her hands in his.

"Someone will keep you updated, Mrs Jones, and I'm sorry about all the upset you have had to endure..."

A long sigh escaped as he shook his head.

"...This could have been a lot less painful..."

CHAPTER 50

"Good day, Mrs Lewis, and what a beautiful one it is too. A bit nippy in the shade, but I like that — blows the cobwebs away, doesn't it? And how's your Dylan? I heard he's been picked for The Quins on Saturday. Tell him well done from me, will you? It'll be the Scarlets next and then Wales, eh?"

The smile and laughter soon dissipated, and Mrs Lewis's response was lost in the breeze as he strode confidently along the Main Street.

Police Constable 989 Anthony O'Sullivan didn't give a toss for the woman or her son. He had one thing on his mind and one thing only: the 3-30 at Cheltenham — a sure thing over the sticks that afternoon. The gelding was a long shot, but the Constable had been tipped the wink that he'd have a 'go-faster' jab just before the off. The horse was a certainty to pass the post ahead of the field, and Mr Carrots was about to clean up. Oh yes, things were looking good and finally, he'd be able to afford that brand-new twin tub his Alice had been nagging him about.

He was at one with the world: two of what looked to him like brand-spanking-new five-pound notes were tucked safely away in his breast pocket. Courtesy of that pair of dozy wannabes.

"I mean, who in their right mind leaves money hanging around on show like that? They don't deserve to have it, and they obviously don't miss it. That gullible Edith Jones would have enlightened me by now if something had been mentioned. She doesn't miss a chance to gossip, that one — silly old bag. Doesn't half make a mean bacon sarnie though — thickly sliced, with a smattering of English mustard. Just how I like it. And that younger daughter of hers, that Molly, well, she's a bit of alright, but something's not quite right at home. I mean, she was there again this morning. Saw her parking up as I left, didn't I? Don't miss much, me, you know. I'm as sharp as a bloody tack, I am."

Sharp Carrots might be, but he hadn't been sharp enough to spot the panda car turning onto the Main Street, and he didn't notice Arthur 609 clock him entering the bookies either.

CHAPTER 51

Chris tucked the Panda car behind a blue-coloured Bedford C F Van, parked about twenty-five yards away from the bookmakers, on the opposite side of the road. From the driver's seat, he could covertly see any comings and goings, and provide a running commentary to the others.
Detective Sergeant David Winters twisted in the passenger seat and winked at the Cadet.
"Right, sonny, you say you've never met Carrots before?"
A nod of the head was the response.
"Good — in that case, it'll be better if you are the one to have a sneaky-beaky look inside. You don't need to have any contact with him, just a quick glance into the bookmakers as you casually stroll by. Chris will be monitoring your every move from here, so stay on the same side of the road and once you've walked past, tuck yourself out of sight into a shop doorway. And don't forget, it's a thumbs up for yes and a thumbs down for no. Are you up for it?"
Phyllis was biting at his lower lip as he gave another nod.
"Of course, I am, Sarge. I want him caught more than anyone."
"Good — I guessed you'd say that. Right, if it's a thumbs up, stay where you are, and we'll go in and nab the waste of space. If it's a thumbs down, then we'll pick you up and revert to plan B."
"What is plan B, Sarge?"
Dai turned to the driver and shook his head.

"Don't know yet, Chris!"

The explosion of laughter relieved the tension as the Cadet slipped out onto the pavement, his movement masked by the Bedford van.

The wind howling through the confines and shade of the busy street lined with shops and cafes was biting, and the boy shivered, hunching his shoulders and tugging at the collar of his donkey jacket. He recalled the chat he'd had with Robbo on their way back from Liverpool. The ex-SAS operative had told him about the time he'd become detached from his mates while on the tail of a surveillance-conscious and armed extremist in Malaysia. The team had spread out to look for him following a total loss in a busy city centre department store, and Robbo had spotted him. Unable to covertly communicate, he had to monitor him through several other stores until the others caught up and the threat was taken out.

"Always use natural cover, kiddo, and blend into what is around you. Look through it and not around it."

The Cadet flushed when he recalled what had happened in Mrs Jones's garden earlier and decided on a plan.

'I won't walk in front of the van: that bent copper might be looking out onto the street and spot me. You never know, he might have noticed me around the offices or in the canteen at Police Headquarters. I'll use it as cover.'

He'd noticed a Buckley's Brewery dray parked a few vehicles behind the Panda car. Its engine was ticking over, and the driver was offloading firkins and lugging them over to an already busy public house.

'If I cross the road from the rear of that truck, I'll only have about a car's width of open road to worry about.'

Guessing what the boy was thinking, Detective Sergeant Winters watched his protégé with the aid of the Panda's wing mirror.

'Bloody Hell, if he's acting like this now, God help the baddies when he's let loose on them in a couple of years' time.'

Chris couldn't understand what was going on.

"Where the hell is he going, Sarge? Doesn't he realise the bookies are in the other bloody direction?"

Dai grabbed the uniform copper's arm.

"Stop! You might blow our cover if you open that door. Monitor him in the rearview — you might pick up a few pointers. Just remember how important it is for us to secure evidence. It's imperative that we recover those treated five-pound notes in O'Sullivan's possession."

"But he's gone, Sarge, behind that beer lorry: I can't even see him now."

He let go of the arm, sucked on the Calabash, and tapped the steering wheel with the stem.

"Think about it, Chris. If you can't see him, then neither can bloody Carrots — can he?"

Stuart was taking it all in and could sense Dai's pride. Over the past few days, the scenes of crime officer had noticed a resurgence in the Detective Sergeant's enthusiasm for the job: he was getting back to how he used to be, and a firing on all cylinders Dai Insignificant was a mean man to cross. The passion was back and soon to erupt all over that bent copper in the betting shop, skiving and gambling away somebody else's money.

Stuart was glad it wasn't he who was in PC Anthony O'Sullivan's shoes right now. No way were they anywhere near fast enough to outrun the molten heat that was about to devour them, and it was a seething Detective Constable who was nodding his head to his thoughts.

'Yes, Carrots deserves all that's coming his way.'

Phyllis was parallel with the Panda car on the opposite side of the road, resisting the urge to glance over and give a cheeky wave. He was quietly confident that his colleagues wouldn't have seen him crossing the open stretch and had been chuckling as he matched the step and stoop of the drayman who provided the mobile natural cover...

The Detective Sergeant had spotted him, but only because he'd been watching for it, and he shook his head in bewilderment...

'Who the hell has been giving you lessons, sonny-boy? Absolutely spot on...'

The Cadet hugged the facades of the tall buildings, taking advantage of the dark shadows being cast by the overhanging roofs — sucking in a deep breath as he passed the Travel Agents — the Bookies was next.

A slight deviation of his eyes was all that was necessary to spot the uniformed police officer perched on a stool in the corner. A mug of something was on the counter in front of him; his helmet was to the right of that, and apart from the female assistant, the shop was empty.

He backed into a doorway two doors up, and from that vantage point, he could remain concealed and just make out the wing mirror of the Panda car.

Chris had been commentating on his movements.

"He's going past now and, hang on, what the hell, he's gone into a shop a few doors up. I can't see him at all now, Sarge! He's — woah — cancel that — I can see his arm and it's a thumbs up, Sarge. It's definitely a thumbs up."

Dai had already opened the door.

"Come on then, let's nab the thieving bastard. No need for the briefcase, Stuart: we've got enough suspicion. We can put him under the spotlight, excuse the pun, later on. Back in the warmth and comfort of the bloody police station."

The Cadet saw Chris getting out of the Panda car and raise his arm to the oncoming stream of traffic — bringing it to a standstill. Stuart scrambled out of the same side and made a beeline for the bookies, but there was no sign of the Detective Sergeant.

"Where the hell's Dai Insignificant? I can't see Dai?"

He started laughing when the Detective Sergeant appeared from in front of the Bedford van. The Calabash was gripped between his teeth, and his left hand was supporting the small of his back as he hobbled awkwardly across the road.

In his eagerness, Stuart had tripped over the kerb and landed heavily on the pavement. Dai stooped to help him but was ushered away.

"I'm fine, Sarge — you carry on. Go and grab that worthless shit!"

A limping Detective Sergeant was the first into the betting shop, and he pushed open the door with such venom that it clattered against the interior wall.

Removing the Calabash, he pointed it at Carrots.

"Come here, you bent, thieving rat."

The beat officer recognised the Detective Sergeant immediately, and he also clocked the uniform in close pursuit. Springing from the stool, he grabbed his helmet and aimed it at the immaculately attired man, catching him full on in the face. Chris blocked the exit, but the sheer bulk of Carrots, using a forearm to the neck, effortlessly barged the shorter officer out of the way. Spotting the S.O.C.O. picking himself up from the pavement, Carrots ran in the other direction and fled towards the concealed Police Cadet.

The youngster saw him coming.

"Shit — he's bloody huge. A much bigger bloke than I thought he'd be. Wait, wait, wait — now!"

He dived from the doorway, rugby tackled the uniformed officer around the legs and knocked him to the flagstones. The Constable screamed out in shock and frustration, struggling violently in an attempt to escape.

"Hey — I'm a police officer — you are in big trouble. Get off me and let me go!"

Stuart dropped onto him, smothering any chance of a getaway; his elbow accidentally colliding with Carrots's mouth, and he whispered through gritted teeth.

"Shut the fuck up — you sickening, sack of manure! The only place you'll be going to and staying there for a very long time is Swansea Prison!"

Blood was seeping from a cut to the bridge of Dai's nose as he staggered out of the betting shop and loomed above the disgraced police officer. He uttered the dreaded words that nobody ever wants to hear.

"I am Detective Sergeant David Winters of the Dyfed Powys Police Force, and I am arresting you, Anthony O'Sullivan, on suspicion of theft of monies from Police Cadet Lloyd HILARY Davies."

There was an exaggerated, over-emphasis on Hilary, and Phyllis grinned when Dai glanced over and winked. Mouthing the words to his mentor: "You bastard, Sarge."

CHAPTER 52

"Lloyd, I'm so sorry about all that has happened and I fully understand why you couldn't confide in me."
Phyllis cuddled his landlady.
"And I'm sorry that you had to endure all that heartache, Mrs Jones. It must have been horrific, especially as you didn't have a clue."
She held out a hand to Big Lloyd.
"We must put it all behind us. One bad man has already taken away a huge slice of my life and I'm not going to waste a second more on another."
"Does that mean that we can sleep here tonight then, Mrs Jones?"
"Listen, you two: wild horses and the whole of the Chinese Empire couldn't drag you away from us."
The two cadets looked at each other.
"Us, Mrs Jones? You said us."
She laughed.
"Yes — us means Molly and me. I'm pleased but also sad to say that Molly has moved back home to her mum: I need help to keep an eye on you two. She'll keep on top of you!"
Picturing the scene, the smaller cadet grinned, but Big Lloyd was troubled.
'Now that there is another mouth to feed, will he get as much to eat?'

Mrs Jones beamed at Phyllis.

"April thought you might be wondering why she was so engrossed in
hiding her black shoulder bag beneath the table. She knew that you'd spotted her and she was praying that you wouldn't say anything."

His eyes lit up.

"Wow, I'd forgotten about that — I was convinced it was April: what was all that skullduggery about?"

She sat down.

"Well — this is my second bit of fantastic news. Your landlady is going to be a grandmother. April was about to tell me when it all kicked off. The positive pregnancy test was in her bag, and you police would have spoilt my surprise if you searched in there for the five-pound notes. April's at the hospital now — getting checked over."

"That's great news, Mrs Jones…"

He turned to his roommate and winked.

"…Big Lloyd will make the best of babysitters. Just don't leave any rusks close to hand: he'll be dipping them in his coffee and we'll soon be calling him, Bigger Lloyd!"

Laughing, he deftly avoided the punch to the bicep and grinned at Molly.

"When you caught me looking at you through the window earlier, I noticed two pieces of blue paper. They were on top of a solicitor's letter. I thought they were the treated five-pound notes."

Mrs Jones's eyebrows met as she frowned.

"I haven't a clue what you're on about: do you know, Molly?"

Molly started giggling.

"They were Co-op coupons, Mum. I'd grabbed my mail when I was
rushing from the house this morning and opened it here. I put them back in my handbag just before the police arrived.

She turned back to Phyllis.

"And the letter? Well, sadly, that's to do with my impending

JON H. DAVIES

divorce."

CHAPTER 53

"Charged, bailed, and suspended. Not a bad end to a horrible and embarrassing episode. Nothing worse than a bent copper: unfortunately, it casts a dark shadow over us all."
"What will happen to him, Sarge?"
The Cadet shuddered.
"I'd hate to be banged up with the likes of Mikey Price."
Dai blew out a mouthful of smoke and re-adjusted the position of his ill-fitting specs to rest above the dressing on his nose. He sat back in the recliner and relaxed.
"Well, youngster, he'll definitely lose his job and be very fortunate to avoid a prison sentence. God only knows what he's been up to: he refused to answer any questions during the interview. Stayed shtum and used no comment all the way. Wouldn't even acknowledge his bloody name! The evidence against him is overwhelming, though. Stuart's magic lamp highlighted traces of blue dye on the fingers of his right hand; one of the five-pound notes was still in his tunic pocket, and the other was in the till at the bookmakers. Both matched the serial numbers recorded in Stuart's little book. And, to top it all, Victoria Charles, she's the branch manager, has made a witness statement. Seemingly, he's a regular punter, and yesterday was the third occasion in a week or so that he's been in there on duty. Each time he has gambled away a five-pound note."

Phyllis squirmed around on the chair, his mind picturing Carrots and Mikey Price scrapping over the top bunk in a prison cell.

"So, do you think it was all down to the gambling and his greed for easy money then, Sarge?"

"I don't know, lad, who does? He's well-liked by his colleagues and renowned for being a smooth talker — one hell of a charmer by all accounts…"

He sucked on the Calabash, pointing the bowl at the Cadet before setting it to rest in an ashtray.

"…but thankfully, that's not an offence, is it? Otherwise, a few well known characters would be joining Carrots and Mikey Price in the big house!"

Grinning and adjusting the knot on his tie.

"Me included… Apparently, his wife is a bit demanding, so that could have been a contributing factor. You might have heard of the type? Not happy with keeping up with the Joneses, she wanted to better the buggers.

Seemingly, when they searched their house, it was like an Aladdin's cave of gadgets. But there was one item out of place: a rusty old twin tub — odd that. Maybe he was struggling on a copper's wage and couldn't cope with her cravings…"

Shrugging his shoulders.

"…Or maybe he was just a bad 'un!"

"It's all so sad, and such a waste, Sarge. Even Mrs Jones, after what he had put her through, couldn't find a bad word to say about him. To her, he was a breath of fresh air. Charming, as you said, with the gift of the gab and a great listener. Carrots made her laugh and he made her happy when she was deep in the doldrums. He was the one who got her interested in taking in lodgers, so I suppose I should be grateful to him, shouldn't I?"

He sniffed, scratching the back of his neck as he posed the question.

"But what makes any policeman, let alone someone as amiable as Carrots, turn to crime, Sarge?"

The supervisor's eyes fixed on the Cadet's, and he cleared his throat — pausing for effect. This was his chance to sow a very important seed: one which would hopefully germinate deep in the adolescent's soul, branch out, and remain with him for an eternity. A necessary message conveying a hard-hitting warning that would manifest in the forefront of his brain every time he neared the crossroads of temptation.

"I don't know, is my honest answer to that question, but what I can promise you is this. When a cop starts to go rogue, it doesn't matter if he or she is the nicest person in the world. It is not acceptable, and that rogue cop won't be able to prevent the long fall from grace. There is no going back, young man. It is a continual slide, further and further down the slippery path to Satan's hell. And trust me, Phyllis, once you're in the company of that evil bastard, well — there ain't no way back from there…"

THE SLIPPERY PATH

A moving fictitious account of an adolescent's start to life in the Dyfed Powys Police.

Jon H Davies has made his home in Pembrokeshire, South West Wales.

He was encouraged to write this book following the successful publication of a short story in the men's health magazine, Movember — widely distributed throughout North America and the United Kingdom.

The interesting characters he has had the pleasure to meet during his thirty two years service with the Dyfed Powys Police have generated enough funny, sad and deeply emotional moments to fill a plethora of novels — this is the first one.

I hope you enjoy the read — Kind Regards, Jon.

ACKNOWLEDGEMENTS

Many thanks to my extremely patient and beautiful wife, Alison — how you put up with me, I will never know.

I sincerely thank Dylan Davies for his excellent design and production of the cover for THE SLIPPERY PATH.

Fond memories of the late Mr Thomas Robert KING. (13/06/1956 - 29/04/2025)
So sadly missed — 'I told you I'd do it, Rob!'

Printed in Dunstable, United Kingdom